A FAMILY CLAIMS ITS BIRTHRIGHT

PROVIDENCE GREENHILL—The unshakeable will of this beautiful, young widow anchored her family against the lust of dangerous men and the cruel turns of fate . . . but who would shelter her own shattered heart?

SARAH—Her luminous blue eyes and stunning beauty attracted the best and worst of men, but a strange destiny awaited her among a savage tribe where she would be held captive as a cherished goddess.

WINSOME—As ambitious as she was lovely, her passion was ignited by a strong embrace that stole her innocence forever . . . and suddenly her fortunes could become a family's ruin.

FELICITY—Inheritor of her mother's indomitable courage, a free-spirited and breathtaking woman, she carried in her heart a shame that only a stunning quest into the wilderness could erase . . . that only an unexpected love could absolve forever.

Destiny's Daughters

Destiny's Daughters

EDITH PIÑERO GREEN

BANTAM BOOKS
TORONTO · NEW YORK · LONDON · SYDNEY · AUCKLAND

DESTINY'S DAUGHTERS
A Bantam Book / February 1986

ISBN 0-553-25167-8

Published simultaneously in the United States and Canada

Bantam Books are published by Bantam Books, Inc. Its trademark, consisting of the
words "Bantam Books" and the portrayal of a rooster, is Registered in U.S. Patent and
Trademark Office and in other countries. Marca Registrada. Bantam Books, Inc., 666
Fifth Avenue, New York, New York 10103.

PRINTED IN THE UNITED STATES OF AMERICA

H   0 9 8 7 6 5 4 3 2

Destiny's
Daughters

Philadelphia 1731

. . . .

Gather not my soul with sinners,
nor my life with bloody men.

Psalm 26:9
A Psalm of David

"The man's dying, Viddy. Dud's dying."

"It seems wrong, Jonas; a good man like that being taken before his time."

Jonas Greenhill sat on the bed watching Providence as she stripped herself of her undergarments. She was luscious to behold, with her black hair, high cheekbones, and rich, full mouth, her sleek, golden body so unselfconsciously naked. When, as a boy, Jonas had collected horse chestnuts, breaking open the prickly pods to extract the smooth, sensually shaped chestnuts in all shades from pale honey to mahogany, the most prized had been the golden tan chestnuts that he would polish to a high gloss and set in rows on the shelf beside his bed. Providence was to him another object of perfection. Her graceful body, her skin glowing with golden light, reminded him of that early passion.

Jonas was himself a handsome man with fine, straight features and dark, expressive eyes, but without the perfection of body that he so admired in Providence. His strong, well-proportioned upper body was supported by spindly legs, a malformation with which he'd been born, although one that seemed insignificant to those who knew him well and nonexistent to the beautiful woman commanding his attention. His eyes caressed Providence's breasts and roseate nipples, the subtle curve of hip and thigh that, at thirty-nine, had lost none of its enticement. "You're even more beautiful now than when we married," he was roused to say.

"And your sight is a good deal dimmer than it was eighteen years ago."

"Isn't it you who are always telling me how this tradesman tucks an extra apple into your basket or that tradesman gives you a tuppence of starch for a ha'penny?"

"We were talking about Dudley Hull," Providence

reminded Jonas. She slipped the white cotton nightdress over her head and began to remove the pins from her hair. "Will you see him tomorrow?"

"You know I make time to see him every day. It's not easy, Viddy. He's resigned to dying, but Elisha's fate is constantly on his mind, and I find it hard to offer him comfort."

"No wonder. Elisha won't be able to run the tavern after his father dies. He's too far gone into drink. Lord knows it's a waste to leave the place to him. I shiver with dread every time I think of having Elisha for a next-door neighbor."

Jonas was distracted again watching Providence pull her combs loose. Her hair cascaded over her shoulders like glistening black satin. "A few days ago Owen asked me how I'd kept you all these years."

"Owen Hatch, the weaver? What a rude thing to say, but then he's not the most tactful of men. Nor the brightest either. What did you tell him?"

"That I keep you in camphor."

Providence laughed, but refused to be diverted from the subject at hand. "Lord knows what will happen once Elisha takes over the tavern. It will probably collapse for lack of care."

"You thrive on worry, Viddy. Tonight it's Elisha Hull. Last night you were upset because Berry told us he wishes to be a printer."

"He's our eldest. I expected him to be a baker like you."

"Still, his ambition's an honorable one. To listen to you one would think he craves to be a burglar."

"He's been working in the bakery for a year now."

"He's seventeen and old enough to know his own mind. He went to see Ben Franklin on his own, and Franklin thought enough of him to consider taking him on as an apprentice. How can we stop him from doing what he's set on doing? It wouldn't be right. Now, stop brooding over trivialities and come to bed."

"In a minute." Providence commenced combing out her hair.

Jonas fell silent, then said again, "Come to bed, Viddy. I want to get some sleep."

Providence smiled. "I know what you're after, and it isn't sleep."

Jonas saw the sparkle in the quick glance she threw him. "I can see through those eyes right into your thoughts, Viddy."

"Oh? And what am I thinking?"

"That you'd not be averse to some rough-and-tumble to shorten the night."

"I'm thinking that in the morning I shall make a bowl of custard for you to carry to Dud."

"Come closer. Are you sure you're telling me the truth?"

When Providence put down the comb and bent her head over him, Jonas raised the hem of her nightdress and slipped his hand between her thighs. "Liar," he murmured. "You're as moist and swollen as a bitch in heat."

"Ssh. The children may hear you."

"No they won't," Jonas whispered as he coaxed her onto the bed and into his arms. "They've been asleep for hours."

Spring had come late, and the room was cool. May sunshine filtered through the front window, spangling Dudley Hull's head and shoulders but providing him no warmth. His mane of white hair was spread over the pillow, and he plucked aimlessly at the hem of the sheet. Next to him the bowl of custard lay untouched. "I'll be dead soon, Jonas," he said with an effort.

Jonas met his friend's gaze steadily, but made no attempt to deny what was apparent to them both.

"Jonas," Hull went on, "I knew we'd be friends the first time I saw you."

"I knew it, too. You helped me and Viddy when we moved to Philadelphia . . . how long ago was it? Eighteen

years? You rented me your stable for pennies and later you
sold it to me for a fair price so I could turn it into a proper
bakery. Since then you've listened to my troubles and
joined my celebrations. There's no friend in the world I
cherish more than you."

"I'm glad you feel that way. It makes me less reluctant to
ask a favor of you."

"What is it, Dud?"

"It has to do with Elisha. Elisha was only nine when his
ma took ill and eleven when she died. That was the year
you come to Philadelphia in 1713. So you seen how he grew
up wild and turned hisself into a drunkard. Still, he's my
son, Jonas. He's all the family I got left. Now I'm dying,
I'm afraid what will become of him."

Jonas reached out to press Hull's shoulder. He knew how
much Elisha had disappointed his father and how Hull
went on loving his son despite the disappointment. "He'll
have the tavern, Dud. That'll keep him."

"You're wrong. That's part of what I want to tell you.
He'll not have the tavern. He's fixed to sell the tavern to
Albert Cottle, who owns the sundries shop across from
you."

"Cottle? I didn't know he made profit enough selling
thread and candlesticks to buy himself a tavern. Anyway,
the tavern's not Elisha's to sell, is it?"

"Not yet, but it will be when I die, and the bargain
Cottle struck with Elisha won't empty his purse neither."

"Selling the tavern, that might not be unwise, Dud."

"Selling it to Cottle will be. Maggie, the barmaid, she
told me about it last night. She heard Elisha and Cottle
talking yesterday. She come on them in the taproom, and
when she heard what it was they was saying, she come to
tell me about it. Elisha signed a paper saying that when I
die, Cottle's to get the tavern for room and board and a
lifetime of liquor."

Jonas shook his head in disbelief. "That makes no sense.

The tavern's valuable. Elisha could sell it for a handsome profit."

"Somebody could, but not Elisha. I should have realized it long ago."

"Have you spoken with him? Did you tell him you know what he means to do?"

"I spoke with him. He told me that what he does once I'm gone is his business; that he'll be glad to be done with me preaching at him." Dud's voice cracked and he paused before going on. "Listen, Jonas, Elisha would of give up the tavern for the promise of the liquor alone. I know that now. He's too besotted to know what he's doing. If it wasn't Cottle cheating him, it'd be someone else."

"What does Cottle want with the tavern? He has a business of his own."

"Men with money are buying more and more property down here near the docks. He'll hold the tavern for a while, then when the time's right, he'll sell it for five times what he paid for it, Elisha be damned."

"Talk to Cottle if you can't talk to Elisha. Tell him you'll not permit it."

"I sent Maggie to ask him to come here, but he said no. Why should he come? He don't want to deal with me now that he's made such a sweet deal with Elisha. Don't you see? Once he gets hold of the place he'll no more care what becomes of Elisha than he cares what becomes of me."

Jonas stroked Hull's shoulder, trying to calm him. His efforts to speak were robbing him of strength. "I'll help you sell the place, Dud, if that's what you want of me."

"No. There's no time, Jonas. But there's something you can do." He reached up to grasp Jonas's sleeve. "Reach under the mattress. Poke your hand under, way under."

Jonas did as he was asked, feeling the hard edges of a leather case jammed between the rope springs and the mattress.

"Pull it out and open it," Hull instructed.

It turned out to be a writing case. When Jonas lifted the

lid he saw that the case contained a folded sheet of paper sealed with wax. "It's my will," Hull explained. "Maggie helped me write it. I want you to take it to the courthouse and put it in the safekeeping of the bailiff. But first I want to tell you what's in it. I'm leaving the tavern to you, Jonas."

Jonas gave a surprised grunt and started to object, but Hull silenced him by shaking his head. "I've writ in there that the tavern's yours so long as you look after Elisha. He's to be kept comfortable and all his needs seen to. Those are the stipulations. Once he's gone the tavern's yours to keep or sell or pass down to your sons. He'll not live forever, Jonas. He's a sick man with no future in front of him. I just want to know that he'll live out whatever time he has in comfort and dignity."

"If you want me to sell the tavern for you, I'll be glad to oblige, not for my profit but for yours. You can hire a lawyer to hold the money and dole it out to Elisha whatever way you think best."

"I told you there's no time. Anyway, he'd spend the dole the first day he got it, and not on keeping hisself alive neither. He'd drink it up, then sleep in the streets till the next dole was due. Jonas, with nobody to watch out for him, Elisha'll be dead inside a year. It'll be an act of mercy to him and to me if you'll say yes. And it's not like you'll go unrewarded. Like you yourself said, the tavern's valuable and sure to be even more valuable in a few years."

"I don't want any rewards, Dud. Our friendship means more to me than that."

"I know. But I couldn't ask you to help me if I didn't have some way of repaying you."

"I have a bakery to run. I'm a baker, not a tavernkeeper. How can I manage both?"

"You can hire someone to run the tavern."

"I have my family to take care of, Dud, Viddy and my five children."

"I'd not refuse if you was in my place and asked me to look out for your children." Hull's curled fingers clutched at the sheet and sweat beaded his forehead. "It's a lot to ask, Jonas. I know it is, but if I can't ask it of you, then I can't ask it of anyone." Hull had exhausted himself. He lay back breathing heavily, unable to go on talking.

Jonas walked to the window and looked through the wavery glass at the distorted images in the street below. He wasn't looking for a way to say no, but preparing himself to say yes. He realized he had no other choice. He and Dud had been friends too long to permit Jonas the luxury of refusing. He closed his eyes for a moment to compose himself, then turned, walked back to the bed, and held out his hand.

· · 2 · ·

Only four of the Greenhills went walking on Sunday. Despite the balmy weather and Jonas's tempting promise to buy her coconut meats, eleven-year-old Sarah had elected to return home after church service, while Beriah had volunteered to watch Felicity, not yet two and still too young for a Sunday's stroll.

Providence, in yellow poplin, her gleaming black hair coiled under a muskmelon bonnet, and Jonas, in cocked hat and silk camlet coat, strolled toward the waterfront with the thirteen-year-old twins, Mordecai and Aaron. Providence had been upset the night before when she learned of Jonas's commitment to Elisha Hull. She could foresee nothing but trouble in trying to help someone who wanted no help, even though she understood why Dudley had asked the extraordinary favor and why Jonas had accepted the responsibility. It remained that this disruption in their lives was a cause for worry, coming as it did right after Berry's decision to abandon the bakery. "How will you manage, Jonas?" she asked now. "I can't help you, not with Felicity to look after."

"I'll find myself someone newly arrived from England or Germany who wishes to earn a few pounds before moving on. That will give me time to arrange for an indenture."

"You can't trust the bakery to someone inexperienced, especially if you must divide your time between the bakery and the tavern."

"I'll manage. I always do, don't I?"

They walked on. The shops and offices along the waterfront were closed, the commercial bustle replaced by indolent Sunday strollers. Enterprising men, mostly West Indian, hawked their wares on the wharves to customers seeking bargains in fruits and exotic souvenirs. Providence and Jonas shooed the boys in front of them, crossed King Street, and walked out onto the central dock where they found a bandannaed Carib selling coconuts and raw sugar. While Jonas dickered over the price of the nine-pound loaf of muscovado, the twins joined a crowd watching a tall, broad-shouldered young man sitting on a barrel near the water's edge playing a dilapidated set of bagpipes.

"He'd better watch out the constable doesn't catch him playing his pipes on the Sabbath, or he'll finish his day playing on the bars of the workhouse," Providence commented.

"Perhaps I should rescue him by offering him the job," Jonas suggested.

"Good heavens, he hardly looks like a baker's apprentice."

"Judging by those tattered clothes, I'd guess he'd be grateful for any kind of work."

"Well, I'd not be grateful to have the sound of those bagpipes in my ears day and night."

The piper was dressed in shabby petticoat breeches, wide in the legs and cinched in at the waist with a frayed leather belt. His sleeveless shirt was a multicolored patchwork of fabrics, and he wore a broad-brimmed green felt hat. The little that showed of his face was heavily freckled, weathered, and fierce looking. He was keeping time to the music by energetically banging the heels of his scarred boots against the side of the empty barrel, and Providence thought it remarkable, given his muscular attack, that he didn't break a hole in the side. When he'd finished playing he stood up and they saw that he was very tall and broad-shouldered, and when he swept off his hat it was to reveal a bristly shock of red hair that increased his look of ferocity.

Mordecia and Aaron stared up at him in fascination, Aaron finally venturing a timid "Good day, sir."

"And a good day to you," the piper returned in an accent that fell somewhere between a burr and a brogue.

Providence thought she'd never seen anyone quite so formidable, but he was friendly enough, grinning and leaning down to ruffle Aaron's hair.

"Will you play again?" Mordecai asked. "You play fearful well."

"Nothing would please me more," he agreed cheerfully.

Jonas walked over, dug into his trousers pocket to extract a coin that he handed the piper, and the piper returned to his perch to oblige with another tune. When he'd finished Jonas asked his name. "Davey Macneill," he replied.

"Mine's Greenhill. Jonas Greenhill. Tell me, when did you land?"

"I come off the *Raven Maid* yesterday. She's a brigantine out of Dublin. I'm one of your Scotch-Irish, a farmer from Ulster."

"Judging by the fact that you're piping for your bread, I'd guess you're hard put for cash."

"I traded off my belongings, except for my pipes, for food and water on the ship. But as soon as I earn enough for it, I'm moving west."

"It'll take you some time to earn enough for that," Jonas observed.

The piper smiled engagingly. "I figure to hire out to load and unload cargo or to haul in fish from the Delaware. They say there's a decent market in rock and perch, and I've done a lot of fishing in Donegal Bay."

Providence, suddenly alert to Jonas's intention, poked

him with her elbow, but he ignored her and asked the piper if he knew anything about baking.

"No more than what goes into the making of soda bread," he admitted.

"Would you be interested in learning?"

"If there's pay attached to it, I'd be interested."

"I'm a baker in Bull Dog Alley," Jonas went on. "That's not far from here. I'm looking for help."

"I've earned nine pence today. If you can match it, I'll take the job."

"I'll up that one and give you room and board as well."

"Jonas," Providence cautioned in a low voice, "we've no room for a boarder. We're squeezed too tight as it is."

"He can sleep in the shop and take his meals with us."

"My mother's a fine cook," Mordecai interrupted to suggest.

Both boys were glowing with anticipation. It was obvious that they shared none of Providence's trepidation.

"And you can teach us the bagpipes," Aaron suggested enthusiastically, which caused Providence to shudder inwardly.

"What do you say, Mister Macneill?" Jonas asked.

"It would only be temporary. I'd be on my way soon as I'd earned enough."

"Understood."

Providence sighed. Another unlooked-for turn of events.

The piper took Jonas's hand and pumped it. Then he offered Providence his huge paw, and she took it gingerly before signaling to the twins and walking away to leave Jonas to settle the details. When he caught up with her back on King Street she said shortly, "Jonas, I cannot believe you actually hired that man."

"Why not? He seems a bright fellow. He doesn't look like a drinker and the children took to him right off."

"We've no room for him, and we can no more afford to feed him than we can afford to feed an elephant. And those bagpipes! We won't have a neighbor talking to us."

"Don't be uncharitable, Viddy. It's not like you."

Providence had just promised herself to remain conscientiously opposed to the piper, but she couldn't resist Jonas's affable assumption that she'd come around in the end.

"Well," she added resignedly, "he's not much to look at, but I suppose he'll be just the thing to scare off burglars."

Bull Dog Alley, a narrow commercial street near the docks, was, like most of the streets in Philadelphia, unpaved and treeless. The Bull Dog Tavern and the Greenhill house (once the tavern's stable) had been built almost fifty years earlier, before the local artisans had begun to make extensive use of the plentiful clay in the region, and they were the only two buildings in the alley built of wood instead of brick.

On Monday morning Beriah went to call on Ben Franklin, and soon after he left Davey Macneill arrived, sauntering into the shop and dumping his bagpipes onto the floor. "Well, I'm here," he announced genially, "delivered just like promised."

"Come in, Mister Macneill," Jonas greeted him. "I've been waiting for you."

"I'll be glad if you was to call me Davey. I scarce know who you're talking to when you call me mister."

"Davey then. Come in. I'll show you the shop. I've cleared a spot in back and put in a cot for you."

The shop was small and the tour brief. Afterward Jonas handed Davey a leather apron that he put on while Jonas checked on the oven that he had fired hours earlier. Finding it ready, he swept off the linen cover protecting the loaves of risen but unbaked bread on the trestle table. Then he stacked some loaves on a long-handled bake paddle and showed Davey how to slide the loaves into the oven and how to arrange them with space between to insure even baking.

Beriah was back by nine, carrying an issue of Ben Franklin's *Pennsylvania Gazette* and brimming over with joy.

He was introduced to Davey, and after a surprised but tolerant appraisal of the red-haired giant, he said happily, "Mister Franklin told me I'm to start next Monday, Pa. He thinks I'll do well."

"Don't tell that to your ma," Jonas suggested. "She'll say he should *know* you'll do well."

The pealing doorbell marked the arrival of the first customer, and for the next few hours the three men worked side by side to serve them.

It wasn't until a lull near noon that Jonas found time for his visit to Dudley Hull. As he stepped into the street he heard a voice call out and looked up to see Albert Cottle waving at him from an upstairs window above his sundries shop. Cottle's rasping voice was as much a part of him as his pink-veined cheeks and flabby jowls, and Jonas cringed as the ugly voice assaulted him with the news. "Have you heard? Hull's dead."

Jonas stared up at Cottle without acknowledging what he'd heard, feeling suddenly that time had jolted to a halt. It had come then. For all his preparedness it had come and caught him off guard.

"Died during the night," Cottle went on. "The burial's tomorrow in the Presbyterian burying grounds."

Jonas despised Cottle for the relish with which he imparted the news, but took some inner satisfaction from knowing that Cottle had an unpleasant shock in store for him as well.

A sign tacked on the tavern door announced that the tavern would be closed that day and the next, and Jonas entered to find the tavern deserted. The doors to the dining room were shut, but he opened them and went in. The area in front of the fireplace had been cleared to make room for Dudley Hull's coffin, which rested on two linen-draped crates. His body was clothed in black except for a white cravat at his neck, and his hands were clasped over a Bible on his chest. Jonas thought, looking at him, that Dud had never in life been a somber man and that it was wrong to make him appear somber in death. Had it been up to Jonas he'd have laid out his friend in scarlet britches and vest.

Jonas bowed his head in prayer, reached out to lay his hand on Dudley's shoulder one last time, then went to look for Elisha. He found him alone in the tap room, sprawled at a trestle table with a tankard of ale set before him. He was a travesty of his father, tall and gaunt, with the same long nose and wide mouth, but with a blotched face and eyes rheumy with drink. He greeted Jonas blearily. "Ah, it's Jonas Greenhill, ain't it? I guess you've come to pay your respects on this sad day."

Jonas wondered what Elisha knew of sadness, or of any other human emotion for that matter. "I've come to pay my respects, and I've come to talk to you about the tavern."

"About the tavern? What about the tavern? What business have you with the tavern?"

"I know about your arrangement with Albert Cottle."

Elisha stared up at Jonas with a baleful expression. "Then talk to Albert Cottle about it." He lifted the tankard of ale and tipped back his head to drain it dry.

"There's no need. Cottle has no claim on the tavern. Before your father died he took steps to see that Cottle would be prevented from buying it."

"The tavern's mine now."

"It isn't, Elisha. It doesn't belong to you and it's not going to belong to Albert Cottle."

"The will's in the hands of the bailiff," Elisha declared thickly. "It's all arranged."

"The will may be in the hands of the bailiff, but when it's read you'll find out that your father didn't leave the tavern to you. He left it to me."

Elisha's hand tightened around the handle of his tankard. "What?" he blurted out hoarsely. "You bastard! You're lying!"

"It's true, Elisha."

"I'm his son," Elisha bawled, struggling to comprehend. "You've been trying to work your way in for years, hoping to make him like you better than me, but I'm his son, not you! He wouldn't do that to me."

"Not *to* you," Jonas returned, softening his tone a little. "He did it *for* you. I promised to see that you're taken care of."

"I'm twenty-nine years old, and you're not ten years older than that. I don't need taking care of, not by the likes of you. And don't pretend you care what happens to me. You want it all for yourself."

"I want nothing for myself beyond the satisfaction of keeping my promise to your father."

"You think I believe that?" Elisha returned angrily. "You tricked him into it."

"You know better. I respected your father. I would never have done anything to harm him, and I'll do nothing to harm you. You'll have a home here, food, clothing, whatever you wish. There's only one thing I mean to deprive you of, and that's the opportunity to drink your life away."

Elisha was livid. "Cottle and me struck a bargain," he maintained desperately. "I'll go to the law."

"If you're wise, you'll not fight it, Elisha. Instead, you'll realize how fortunate you are to have had a father who thought more of you than you deserve and a protector willing to do more for you than you deserve. There are better things than drink, Elisha. If you give me the chance, I'll prove it to you."

Elisha raised his tankard to his lips, realized it was empty, and with an hysterical cry flung it at Jonas. It missed its mark and hit the door jam, then clattered hollowly to the floor.

3

Dudley Hull was dead. Providence heard about it from Jonas at the midday meal, but it wasn't until he came into the house again before supper that he told her he'd spoken with Elisha.

"Of course he took it badly," Providence said matter-of-factly.

"He'll become accustomed to it."

"No he won't. He'll do his best to make your life miserable, to say nothing of what Albert Cottle will do when he hears about it."

"I'm not easily intimidated."

"No, nor reasoned with either," Providence concluded, dropping her voice as Beriah, with Davey Macneill in tow, followed his father in from the bakery.

Davey was the center of attention even before he unloaded a pocketful of mementos for the children: a pair of lacquered chopsticks from Japan for the twins to share, a ha'penny rag doll for Felicity, and a piece of brittle yellow brimstone hung from a ribbon for Sarah. All but Sarah fell on the gifts with eager squeals of delight. Sarah, eyes apprehensive, refused to accept the bauble, not even when Davey explained that he'd chipped it from a volcanic mountain called Vesuvius on the east shore of the Bay of Naples. "I don't want it," Sarah muttered. "It's the devil's stone."

Sarah at eleven was a pretty girl with deep-set blue eyes, a pale complexion, and blond hair that was unique in this family of brunettes. She was unique in other ways, too; overly imaginative, with what Providence characterized as "morbid leanings," and a constant worry to her parents, who felt helpless to cope with her fragility. Now she hung back, unwilling even to touch the piece of sulpher Davey held out to her.

17

Not so the twins. "If you've no use for the brimstone," Aaron ventured, "I'll take it."

And so, while Providence apologized for Sarah's rudeness, Davey unperturbedly slipped the shard of sulpher into Aaron's hand.

Despite Sarah's rejection Davey was made much of by Beriah and the twins, who peppered him with questions. "If you're a Scotsman," Beriah asked once they were seated at the table, "why do you sound so much like an Irishman? Where exactly do you come from?"

"I'm as much a patchwork as my shirt, lad; a Scotsman born but an Irishman raised. My ma and pa, my brothers and sisters, they live in the southern uplands near Dumfries. The last I seen of them was in 1723 when I was a lad of twelve, for I was taken to Ireland by my uncle, I was, on account of he saw the virtue in a helper as big and strong as me. I lived in Ireland with Uncle Robert and the wife he took him, Mary Delany of Larne. Stayed till she died and he remarried. Then I decided to strike out on me own. Been a lot of places since I was fifteen: Japan, Portugal, and the Canaries, France, even to Norway. Been through a lot, too, I have."

"Still, it was worth it to see the world," Aaron gushed admiringly.

"That's right, Aaron. I feel that way myself. I always say Satan has his uses."

Davey continued to regale them with stories while he downed a second, then a third, helping of stew, followed by three bowls of milk pudding swimming in sweet cream and nutmeg, and a mug of hot pokeberry tea. When he'd finished he thanked Providence, then excused himself to return to the shop carrying a pile of bedclothes Providence had given him to make up his pallet.

"He finished the curds and whey," Mordecai said wonderingly after he'd left, "three portions, each one big enough for two."

"No more than I expected," Providence remarked. "He has the appetite of a goat."

Sarah, who hadn't spoken all during supper, and who had only picked at her food, got up suddenly and went to lean against her father's shoulder. "Papa," she said anxiously, "his hair's red as fire."

Jonas drew her close. "You've seen redheads aplenty, Saree."

"Not like him. Not so large nor so fierce nor with a voice so loud. Remember how you read me from *Macbeth*? 'The instruments of darkness tell us truths, win us with honest trifles, to betray's in deepest consequence.'"

"You've a good memory, but surely you don't think that poor Davey Macneill is the devil, Saree."

"He spoke of Satan, Papa. He told Aaron that Satan has his uses. He tried to give me the devil's stone."

"I've never heard tell that the devil's a Scotsman by the name of Macneill. Now, let's have no more talk about devils."

On the day following, Jonas returned to the tavern for a second visit with Elisha. The inertia of the previous day had turned into activity. The doors to the tavern stood open and people paraded in and out while the tavern drudge, a half-wit named Needle, polished the wooden finial on the bottom stair post and hummed happily as if he were participating in some joyous ceremony. Jonas climbed the stairs to the second floor and saw that the parlor door to Dud's—now Elisha's—rooms was partially ajar. It was impossible not to hear Elisha talking inside, his thick drawl suddenly interrupted by a sharp blast from Albert Cottle. "It's your duty to inform the sheriff that Greenhill forced your father to put his name to that document."

Jonas shoved open the door and saw Cottle hovering like a bird of prey over Elisha, who lay slumped in a chair near the window. "I knew nothing about that will until I visited Dud just before he died," Jonas announced grimly.

Cottle straightened up with surprise and turned to face

him. "Of all Hull's visitors you were the most regular, coming every day and sometimes twice a day. I heard it from everybody. I don't believe you came out of kindness."

"I don't care what you think. Dud was a friend, and what I did, I did out of friendship."

"You don't own the tavern yet," Cottle returned harshly. "There was a contract between me and Elisha, a contract that's legal and binding."

"Neither legal nor binding," Jonas returned shortly, "and least of all ethical."

"I want something to drink," Elisha interjected. His vest was unbuttoned and his hair uncombed. There was no question but that he had already been drinking, even without the empty pitcher that lay on its side at his feet.

Cottle strode past Jonas out into the hall and called down the stairs to Needle to bring up a fresh pitcher of ale. In the meantime Elisha reached out for his pipe on the table next to him, then fumbled around on the tabletop for his tinderbox. He finally managed to pick it up, but his hands were shaking and he was unable to strike a light. Cottle reentered the room and crossed over to help him, striking the light and igniting the spunk, which he held to Elisha's pipe as Jonas watched in disgust. Elisha was as helpless as he was useless, no more able to resist Cottle's plotting than he was able to resist his help.

"You're a fine one to speak of ethics," Cottle picked up after he'd ministered to Elisha. "You used trickery to get the tavern, and no doubt you'll try trickery to keep it. But you're not the only one who knows ways to get what he wants. You'd best keep that in mind."

"Dud would have burned the place down rather than let you have it," Jonas returned, "and I'll not let you have it either."

"We'll see about that, won't we?"

Realizing that further talk was pointless, Jonas turned to leave, jamming his hat onto his head and skirting around Needle, who stood just outside the door in the hall holding a fresh pitcher of ale. "We'll see, all right, you sneaking bastard," Jonas mumbled to himself as he headed back down the stairs.

By the beginning of the following week, with the disposition of Dudley Hull's will and the commencement of Beriah's apprenticeship, it began to look as if life were resuming a more normal routine, with only Sarah's unreasonable mistrust of Davey Macneill to cause concern. She wouldn't speak to him and refused to enter the bakery. She had also begun delaying her arrival at the table until Davey finished eating, a tactic not lost on Davey, who took to excusing himself whenever she entered the kitchen. This caused the twins to complain that Sarah was making Davey feel unwelcome, and they, in turn, began warning her of the consequences she faced by setting herself against him.

On Tuesday morning Sarah's appearance at the table chased Davey off in the midst of a story about Caribbean pirates, and before Providence could intervene, Mordecai retaliated by warning Sarah that Davey was as likely as not to snatch her soul one night while she was sleeping, a likelihood that Aaron was quick to second.

"Mordie, leave the table," Providence commanded. "You too, Aaron. Both of you should know better than to tease your sister with such nonsense."

The boys obeyed, but not before Aaron, with a conspiratorial wink toward his brother, surreptitiously dropped the piece of brimstone Davey had given him into Sarah's pocket.

Providence saw the chidren off to school, then, leaving Felicity with Jonas in the bakery, went to market. Returning an hour later she was brought to an abrupt halt three blocks west of the alley by the sound of the fire bell. Shortly afterward she saw a horse gallop around the corner pulling one of the three new fire wagons that had recently been put into service. At first she couldn't see any sign of fire, but as

she continued to walk toward home she spotted a wisp of
smoke drifting over the rooftops from the direction of the
bakery. She picked up her skirts and ran, finding herself in
company with others responding to the alarm. By the time
she reached the northern end of the alley, a crowd had
gathered, and the tendril of smoke had turned into a
choking black cloud. She rushed forward, but someone
shouted, "Stand back!" and blocked her path with a
roughly out-thrust arm.

"What is it? What's burning?"

A woman standing nearby turned, and Providence recognized Mistress Willock, the silversmith's wife. "It's the
tavern," Mistress Willock informed her. "The men are
already fighting it. I seen your husband amongst them."

"Good Lord, I left the baby with him."

"She's all right," Mistress Willock assured her. "I seen
Jonas hand her over to Alina Pettigrew for safekeeping."

Unable to make any headway, Providence backtracked,
running around the corner to High Street where Claypool
Court bisected High and Bull Dog Alley north of the
bakery, then cut through the court to emerge back of the
currier's shop. She circled the shop and came out into the
middle of the alley where once again she was impeded by
the crowd. She could see flames billowing out of the third-
floor windows of the tavern now, and a group of men
supporting a hose on their shoulders while one of them
aimed the stream of water.

The fire wagon was positioned nearby and two men were
manning the pump for those who held the hose. Usually
the wagons were pulled by hand, but this one was a
lumbering affair built by a Philadelphia wagon maker, with
wood fittings instead of brass. It required the strength of a
horse to pull it, but the alley was narrow, a close fit for horse
and wagon, and the horse pawed the ground nervously.
Providence spotted Jonas working alongside of Davey
Macneill on the bucket brigade, then saw Alina Pettigrew,
the shoemaker's daughter, standing a few yards from the

fire wagon and holding Felicity in her arms. Thank God, Providence thought. At least her family was safe from harm.

There was a ladder propped against the side of the tavern and Providence's attention was caught by the sight of Henry Johnson, the glazier, scrambling up to the topmost rung to hack away at the wooden rain gutter, which was ablaze. Suddenly there was a loud crash as a portion of the rain gutter parted from the roof and swung down like a pendulum to strike the side of the fire wagon. The horse reared and someone shouted an order to remove it from between the wagon shafts before it bolted. Alina Pettigrew and a number of the spectators moved back to a more secure spot as Davey slipped out of line, leaped forward, and began fumbling with the horse's buckles. The horse shied, and Davey grabbed his mane and with one powerful hand held him still as he worked to release the wet leather straps with his free hand. Barnaby Pettigrew, the shoemaker, almost as tall as Davey and equally strong, rushed in to help. Between them they succeeded in detaching the horse from the wagon, and Davey led the horse away.

Providence thought at first that the subsequent shout was meant for Davey and Barnaby, but then she saw members of the crowd staring upward. There was someone leaning out a second-story window amid swirls of flame and thick smoke. "It's Hull! someone shouted. "It's Elisha Hull!"

The men fighting the fire had caught sight of him. Henry Johnson and Barnaby Pettigrew rushed to move the ladder to the front of the building while the men holding the leather hose turned its long nozzle upward. There was another cry as Hull scrambled out onto the windowsill and began flailing his arms weakly. It was obvious that he was barely conscious. Not even his terror could overcome the dazed, drunken condition he was in.

"He's afire!" someone screamed, and Providence saw the flames licking at his jacket and trousers.

Davey darted forward and swung himself onto the ladder, but Hull was beyond knowing that help was on the way. He teetered precariously on the windowsill for another horrible moment, then suddenly lost his balance and tumbled from the window ledge, bouncing off Davey's shoulder and plummeting to the ground.

There was a terrible moment of silence, and in that moment Providence's eyes dropped to the fire wagon and to the movement of something or someone underneath. She craned her neck to see, then felt her knees go weak. It was Sarah. Providence had no idea what she was doing there when she should have been in school, but there she was, tugging at her skirts in a desperate attempt to free herself from something that was holding her in check. "Saree!" Providence cried, her voice thin with fear.

Sarah's skirts were pinned under the wagon wheel, and there were flames licking at the wheel axle inches from her head. Miraculously, Providence's cry was heard by Alina Pettigrew, who stood halfway between Providence and the wagon. She turned, and seeing Providence wave frantically toward the wagon, followed her gaze, then in a voice stronger than Providence's shouted for Jonas.

Jonas looked up, heard what it was she shouted to him, and rushed to the wagon. He threw himself down and crawled underneath, ripped at Sarah's skirts until he'd freed her, and then pushed her out into the open. For a brief instant Providence saw Jonas framed by an aureole of flames before the rear axle of the wagon snapped, sending one of the rear wheels spinning out like a top. With a sickening thud the chassis fell, pinning Jonas underneath. Again Providence screamed. Then suddenly Barnaby Pettigrew was there, leaping to one of the wagon shafts and raising it sufficiently for Jonas to drag himself free. Providence started to push her way forward, but quite unexpectedly her knees buckled under her and she crumpled to the ground in a faint.

4

"I can't believe Elisha's dead," Jonas said weakly. "Just before the alarm sounded I went next door to try to talk to him again. Maggie said he was drunk and not to bother."

"Ssh," Providence soothed. "Be quiet now. Just try to rest, Jonas."

"I shouldn't have listened to her. I should have gone upstairs. I might have saved him."

"Don't blame yourself. What happened wasn't your fault."

They were interrupted when someone rapped on the front door, and Providence went to admit Barnaby Pettigrew. "How's Jonas?" he asked wearily.

"Come see for yourself," she invited, leading him back into the parlor. "I sent Davey for the doctor. It looks like he opened his leg, knee to ankle, and maybe broke a bone as well."

Pettigrew lumbered over to the settle and patted Jonas on the shoulder. "I once seen a man pressed flat as a well cover when a wagon turned over on him. Be thankful it ain't worse."

Jonas accepted the lugubrious comfort with a feeble smile, then asked, "Where did they take Elisha's body?"

"They took him to Robert Jacoby's carpentry. It was the hitching stone killed him. He split his skull on it. They'll fit him out for his coffin and bury him tomorrow."

"The fire?"

"The fire's out. The second floor's burnt to a cinder, but the rest of the building's got mostly smoke and water damage. Albert Cottle and me was inside. It looks like the fire started in Elisha's parlor. At least it was his parlor got the worst of it. I figure he must have been drunk and set hisself afire. We found this in the room." Pettigrew reached into his jacket to pull out a blackened tinderbox. "Albert says it's yours."

25

Jonas looked at it and shook his head. "It's not mine. It's Elisha's. I saw him with it last week."

"He says he sold it to your wife. He says he remembers it because it was the only one amongst a shipment that had sprigs of wheat etched on the cover."

"Let me see." Providence took the tinderbox out of Pettigrew's hand. "I did buy a tinderbox from him a few months back, but this isn't it."

"Maybe you forgot what it looks like. Anyway, it don't matter. Elisha ain't got no use for it anymore so you might as well keep it." Pettigrew put the tinderbox on the table next to the settle. "Well, I'm going home to wash the soot off me now that I seen Jonas is all of a piece. Don't come to the door. I'll see myself out."

Beriah came home moments after Pettigrew left, word of the fire having reached the printing office, and a few minutes after that Davey came in with Dr. Littlebank, who lived in Hearthside Court, only half a dozen blocks from the alley. Littlebank had been the Greenhills' physician for years, but now he had reached the age where both memory and eyesight were something less than keen. However, he was still capable enough to diagnose what Providence had by then surmised for herself. Jonas's leg had been gashed by the wheel axle and his shinbone cracked by the weight of the wagon falling on him. Beriah went next door to Stedman Talbot's cooperage for wood staves, and the elderly doctor dressed Jonas's wound, then bound up his leg using the staves as splints before collecting his fee and leaving.

Afterward Providence went to look for Sarah. She found her upstairs in her bedroom, sitting at the window and staring out at the damaged tavern next door. "Saree, I want to talk with you."

Sarah turned and met her mother's eyes defiantly.

"How did it happen? What were you doing next door when you should have been in school?"

"It wasn't my fault that Papa got hurt," Sarah declared.

"I didn't say it was. I simply asked you what you were doing there."

"It was the devil's stone," Sarah explained. "I wanted to make *the davey* take it back. That's what killed Elisha and nearly killed Papa and me."

"What are you talking about? Are you talking about the brimstone of Davey Macneill? Where is it, Saree? Do you have it?"

Sarah dug into her pocket and fished out the small, brittle piece of sulphur. Providence, unnerved by the events of the past few hours, grabbed it from her, threw it to the floor, and ground it to powder under her heel. "There," she declared energetically, "it's gone, Saree. It can't do anyone harm anymore. Now let's hear no more about devils and devil's stones. Suppose you tell me how you persuaded Dame Gubbins to let you leave school."

But Sarah had said all she intended to say, and no amount of scolding elicited anything further. Later Providence learned from the twins that all three children had arrived at school as usual that morning. It hadn't been until Dame Gubbins, the schoolteacher, had sent the twins into the back garden to apply themselves to learning their sums that they had lost sight of their sister. When they had been called indoors half an hour later, Dame Gubbins had told them that Sarah had complained of a stomach ache and had been sent home. But when Providence asked Sarah about it she would neither confirm the story nor offer an alternative explanation.

Providence was more disturbed by Sarah's strange behavior than she cared to admit, and on the following morning during breakfast she made known her intention to accompany Sarah and the twins to school. They were the first to arrive and were met on the doorstep by Dame Gubbins herself, a large-featured woman with wide-spaced teeth, close-set eyes, and an officious manner. Dame Gubbins shooed the children inside with a flap of her apron before closing the door behind them and saying coolly, "I assume you have come because of Sarah?"

Providence nodded. "The twins tell me that Sarah came home yesterday because she was feeling ill."

"What did Sarah tell you?"

Providence had anticipated the question. She was certainly of no mind to mention Sarah's obsession with the piece of brimstone and said merely, "She came home soon after the tavern fire broke out. You know about the fire, of course."

"The stench of it drove us out of the garden and into the house," Dame Gubbins admitted.

"There was so much confusion," Providence went on, "that I scarcely had time to ask. She was excited, too, and I could make no sense of what she told me. She didn't appear to be ill."

"Sarah did not leave school because of an upset stomach, Mistress Greenhill. That was merely the excuse I gave your sons. She misbehaved. She was supposed to be doing her sums, but she was preoccupied, and when I told her to remove herself to the garden, she simply rose and left altogether."

Providence started to speak, but Dame Gubbins held up her hand for silence. "There's more to it than simple disobedience, however. The girl is an unhappy influence on my other pupils. Sometimes she frightens them with her strange talk, and at other times she encourages them to mimic her behavior. I had already made up my mind to speak to you about her."

"Saree is a sensitive child," Providence began. "We—."

"She is more than sensitive," Dame Gubbins interrupted. "She is obsessed by a discontentment that manifests itself in disruptive ways, Mistress Greenhill. If you had not visited me this morning, I should soon have visited you. I have come to the decision that I will not accept Sarah as a pupil next year."

"Surely her behavior doesn't warrant such an extreme measure?" Providence returned in a startled voice.

"School will end in five weeks," Dame Gubbins went on, as if Providence hadn't spoken. "I shall not ask you to remove Sarah before then, but I shall not permit her to return in the fall. This is not a decision I have come to lightly, nor is it one I shall be persuaded to alter."

"Suppose there were to be no further incident?"

"There will be further incident. The girl cannot be controlled. She is unpredictable. Sometimes she speaks out of turn, and sometimes she refuses to speak at all, even when called upon to recite. There are times when she seems possessed by the notion that someone or something intends her harm, speaking of devils and demons in much the same manner as the misguided girls of Salem once spoke of witches. Sarah has always been quieter than most, and always less responsive to instruction, but lately her conduct has become increasingly unmanageable. Frankly, I think she will be better off at home where she can be supervised and, if need be, protected."

It was a shock to hear spoken aloud, and from an outsider, the suspicion that had begun to haunt Providence of late. It was true. Sarah wasn't like other children. As time went on she seemed to dwell more and more in a world of imagination and unreal fears. But to accede to Dame Gubbins the possibility that Sarah might be afflicted by some sickness of the mind was unthinkable. Providence recovered her poise sufficiently to say, "I accept your decision. I request only that you tell her nothing about our talk. I prefer to speak to her myself after school has ended."

On the way home, however, Providence was less composed. There was a history of dementia in her family. Her father as well as one of her cousins had each manifested a morbidity that ruined their lives and hastened their deaths. Now something was wrong, something was frighteningly wrong, with Sarah. Her terror of Davey Macneill—had she not spoke of him as *the davey*, as if he were less than human?—was, indeed, unnatural, as was her belief that there might be some mystical power in a bit of brimstone? Providence dared not speak to Jonas about Sarah, she decided, not now while he was unwell. Yet the truth must be faced sooner or later, and the thought of it filled her with foreboding.

It was ironic that the laws enacted by a pacific Quaker government should rest in the hands of a tyrannical police force. Gerard Howell, the sheriff, was a short, burly man whom no one liked, but who inspired respect because of his bad temper and bullying manner. Three days after the fire, Howell, accompanied by a constable, descended from a two-wheel dump cart in front of the Greenhill house and knocked on the door. When Providence opened it he demanded admittance, saying that he had come for the tinderbox found after the fire in Elisha Hull's rooms.

Providence, bemused into compliance by his aggressive conduct, said, "I'll be pleased to fetch it. Will you tell me what you want with it?"

"I'll tell you that after you fetch it."

However, Howell didn't wait for her to fetch it. When she walked into the parlor he signaled to his constable to follow and marched into the parlor behind her.

Jonas looked up in surprise, as Providence picked up the tinderbox from the table next to the settle and handed it to Howell. "What is it, Sheriff?" Jonas asked. "What do want with that?"

Howell pocketed the tinderbox, then said matter-of-factly, "There is reason to suspect that you may have deliberately set fire to the Bull Dog Tavern in order to bring about the death of Elisha Hull."

Jonas, momentarily forgetting his helpless condition, struggled to get up. Failing that he said in a shocked voice, "I? Set fire to the tavern? Are you mad? Who accuses me?"

"Albert Cottle has given me certain information."

Jonas glanced quickly at Providence, then said, "What information does he claim to have?"

"He told me that he found this tinderbox at the site of the fire, in Elisha Hull's parlor to be exact. He tells me that the tinderbox is one he sold your wife some time back."

"That's not true. It doesn't belong to me."

"Then what are you doing with it?"

"Barnaby Pettigrew gave it to me after the fire."

"Gave it to you?" Howell asked pointedly, "or returned it to you?"

"I tell you it isn't mine. And even if it were—"

"You were seen in the tavern a few minutes before the fire started," Howell pointed out.

"But I never saw Elisha."

"You and Elisha Hull quarreled about the disposition of Dudley Hull's will. Is that not so?"

"No, it isn't so. Elisha was unhappy about the will, but there was nothing to quarrel about."

"He was unhappy because his father, for reasons not fully determined, left the tavern to you instead of to his son."

"His father left me the tavern because he knew that Elisha was incapable of running it, or, for that matter, disposing of it to his benefit."

Howell's smug expression made it clear that he gave no credence to anything Jonas was telling him. "I've come to deliver you to the workhouse, Mister Greenhill."

"You intend to arrest my husband?" Providence inquired in total disbelief. "Where is your warrant?"

"I merely intend to bring him to the workhouse to question him further."

"You cannot take him without a warrant."

"I am taking him," Howell assured her calmly, "and unless you want it noted that he defied the law, you'd best let him go."

"I won't let him go."

"Will you come willingly?" Howell asked Jonas.

"My wife is right," Jonas said in a stunned voice. "You have no right to remove me forcibly."

"I mean to take you one way or the other."

"No!" Providence declared. "Don't you see he's in no condition to go with you?"

But Howell was determined, and it soon became clear that Jonas would only do himself harm by resisting. Providence watched in horror as he was hoisted onto his good leg, then half-dragged, half-carried, out to the cart.

A few minutes later Providence stormed into Albert Cottle's shop where she found him unpacking thread, his bristly head bent over an assortment of wooden spools, his coarse red cheeks puffed out in concentration. He looked up as she entered and returned her fierce stare calmly. "What can I do for you, Mistress Greenhill?"

"How dare you ask me that?" she returned in an enraged voice. "You accused Jonas of setting that fire. Why did you do that?"

"Why, that's not what I done at all. I only pointed out that the tinderbox we found belongs to him."

"But it doesn't. That isn't true." Providence strode across the room and planted herself directly in front of him. "You know it isn't true. You've accused Jonas of a crime he didn't commit. How could you do anything so vicious? Are you so lacking in conscience that you'd ruin an innocent man merely to get revenge?"

"Your husband cheated Elisha Hull out of his rightful inheritance, and when he cheated Elisha, he cheated me. Whatever it is that leads to his conviction is justified, because he's guilty. That's the way I see it."

"I don't understand. What do you hope to gain by hurting Jonas?"

"I hope to get what's due me. Elisha and me had an agreement."

"What good is that now? The tavern didn't belong to Elisha. It belongs to Jonas."

"It won't belong to him if he hangs for murder. It'll be like the will never existed. But my agreement with Elisha, that's down in black and white, and it will stand whether Elisha's alive or dead."

"So that's it. That's what you have in mind. Well, you'll not get away with it."

"You've got it wrong, Mistress Greenhill. It's your husband who'll not get away with it. Now, if you don't mind leaving, I've got my work to do."

Providence couldn't contain her rage. She picked up the nearest object to hand, a wooden quilling wheel that sat on the floor near her feet, and heaved it at the window next to the door, taking some satisfaction from the deafening noise it made as it shattered the glass.

· · 5 · ·

It began to rain that night, and Providence lay awake until dawn listening to the hollow thunder roll in across the water as she struggled to deal with the problems she and her family faced. Most immediate, of course, was the need to help Jonas. The house had erupted in chaos when she announced that Jonas had been arrested. The twins had clung to one another like frightened fox cubs, and Berry had to be restrained from rushing out to the sundries shop to confront Albert Cottle. Davey, of necessity included in the family conference, had assured her that he would give whatever support he could to the cause of clearing his employer's good name, while Sarah hysterically insisted that it was Davey who lay at the core of their trouble and fled the parlor to hide in her room.

Providence had taken charge as best she could, but her composure had been a sham to cover her panic. She didn't know how she would cope, but finally resolved to visit Jonas in the morning, give him whatever comfort she could, then go directly to the courthouse and lodge a complaint that he had been taken without warrant. Surely petitioning the court was the logical first step to obtaining Jonas's release and showing up Albert Cottle as the fraud he was.

After breakfast the following morning Providence put on her rain cape, an oiled rose-colored wrap called a ro- quelaure, told Davey she would return as soon as she could, and leaving Felicity in his charge, set out to visit Jonas. The prison was in the center of town and consisted of two stone houses with sharp-pitched roofs; one the debtor's prison, the other the workhouse reserved for criminals. Providence was admitted by the gatekeeper and directed upstairs to the second floor where Jonas was being held. She found him lying on a sagging cot in his cell with his splinted leg stretched out stiffly in front of him. His face was pale, and he had dark pouches under his eyes. When he saw her he tried to sit up, then winced and lay down again.

Providence hurried over and kissed him, then dropped to her knees next to the cot and began rearranging his clothes and smoothing his hair. "They hurt you bringing you here," she said angrily.

"No, I'm all right. Don't fuss so."

"Don't lie to me, Jonas. I can see that you're in pain. What can I do to help you?"

"Nothing now. You might bring me a flask of brandy when you come next time."

"Jonas, don't talk about next time. I'm not going to let them keep you here. I intend to inform the court that Howell took you without warrant. They'll have to release you."

Jonas reached for her restless hands and held them to quiet her. "Howell brought me news this morning, Viddy. Last night the chief justice of the court signed the warrant, and this morning it was registered with the court clerk."

"Oh no."

"I'm to be formally charged with arson and murder."

"They can't do that to you. Jonas, I thought about it all night. Even if Cottle goes on claiming that the tinderbox is yours, they could never prove that you used it to set the fire."

"There's more to it than that, Viddy. Howell says that

Maggie and Needle were both witness to the fact that Elisha couldn't have set the fire himself."

"Maggie? Surely Maggie wouldn't speak against you?"

"No, but she wouldn't lie either. The reason I didn't go upstairs to see Elisha the day of the fire was because Maggie told me he had drunk himself into a stupor."

"What does it matter?"

Jonas said impatiently, "Presumably Elisha was unconscious when the fire started."

"No one would take Needle seriously, Jonas, and Maggie will explain that you didn't go upstairs."

"She doesn't know that I didn't. She couldn't swear that I didn't. All she can say is that she didn't see me go upstairs. And remember that dozens of people saw Elisha fall from his window. His clothes were ablaze and yet he was in no condition to help himself, scarcely aware of what was happening to him. No one will believe he was capable of igniting a fire with that tinderbox. I saw him try to use it once before when he was drunk. He couldn't do it. No, Viddy, everyone knows that someone else was responsible for setting the fire, and only you and I know it wasn't I."

Providence gazed into Jonas's eyes for a long moment before she silently mouthed the name of Albert Cottle.

Jonas shook his head. "We have no more right to accuse him than he had to accuse me."

"But he told me that if you're convicted, he'll claim ownership of the tavern. He had motive for killing Elisha and for accusing you."

"We'll never know what actually happened, Viddy."

"Well then, even if we can't accuse Albert Cottle of murder, we must still find a way to discredit him. I'm going to speak to Ben Franklin. He knows Andrew Hamilton, and I'm sure he will introduce me to him. If anyone can help us, Hamilton can."

"He's the most illustrious lawyer in the colonies, Viddy. Why should he agree to take my case?"

"Why should he not? You're innocent, and the law is just.

I believe in it as firmly as I believe in God's mercy. I'll persuade Hamilton to help you, I promise you."

Jonas heard the catch in her voice and realized suddenly that she was as much in need of reassurance as he. "I have no doubt that Hamilton will take one look at you and say yes to whatever you ask. Now, tell me. How are the children? How did they take the news?"

"I had everything I could do to prevent Berry from choking the truth out of Albert Cottle. The twins were upset, but they're your sons and brave boys. They'll be fine."

"Saree? Is she all right?"

"It's more difficult for her. She's so emotional and so easily frightened. She wishes to see you. They all wish to see you."

"Not here. Not in this tomb of a cell. I should hate to have them see me weak and ill."

"You'll be stronger soon."

Jonas lifted one of her hands to his lips, then said ruefully, "Sometimes I wonder why you chose a poor cripple like me, Viddy. It's damnable to be entrapped in a body that creaks and cries and betrays me at every turn. Do you remember that day in Salem when we were in the woods, and suddenly you commanded me to strip naked so you could examine my poor body?"

Providence smiled at the memory. "You were ten and I was a grown lady of thirteen. Sara Whithedd doubted you had a male organ, and though I told her you did, I wasn't quite certain. I wanted to see for myself. You were so indignant with me. You kept threatening to leave, but I knew you would finally do as I commanded."

"I was humiliated, but I would have done anything for you." Jonas reached up and drew her face down to his, then kissed her. "It's still true, Viddy. I'd still do anything for you."

"Then rest, stop brooding, and get well."

The determinedly light admonition invited a light response, and Providence was surprised when Jonas said quietly, "Berry's already a man, but I shouldn't like to die before I see all my children safely grown."

"Die? You're not going to die. I shan't permit it. You have too many responsibilities to fulfill."

At last she elicited a fleeting grin. "Five mouths to feed, five bodies to clothe, and five minds to shape. Yes, I'd say that's reason enough to stay alive."

He was wrong about the number, but Providence didn't correct him. There would be time enough after his release to tell him what she'd known for some weeks now. The five Greenhill children would soon be six.

Hamilton sat on a chair that the warden had brought into the cell. His cane lay across his knees and his swollen legs were stretched out in front of him. He didn't give an impression of great physical vigor, perhaps because he was portly, or perhaps because the gout from which he suffered was reflected in the pain-etched lines of his face. He did, however, exude an almost initimidating air of authority. "Innocent you may be," he was saying, "and in my opinion innocent you are. But one fact is irrefutable. You did have something to gain from Elisha Hull's death."

"It's also irrefutable," Providence interjected, "that Albert Cottle had something to gain by accusing Jonas of Hull's death."

"That is something we shall ask the court to consider," Hamilton conceded.

"Let them also consider the fact that I was arrested without warrant," Jonas added bitterly.

"There's no question that you were capriciously arrested, Mister Greenhill. However, by accepting the warrant post facto, the court has reduced any protest we might make to a question of principle only. Even if we were to argue and prove the original illegality, it would only delay your prosecution, not prevent it. Therefore we shall protest the incident as outrageous but forgo the opportunity to contest it. It's certain, on the other hand, that although you were arrested and charged in the wrong order, you shan't be tried and hung in the wrong order."

Providence glared at the lawyer, and he quickly amended the blunder. "Or hung at all, for that matter."

He went on to discuss procedure, the necessity for an affadivit stating Jonas's financial means, the request for setting bail, the determination of the trial date, a dozen details that compounded the bewilderment Providence and Jonas were already experiencing. Later, after Hamilton left, Jonas said in a troubled voice, "I wonder how far the news about me has traveled. I suppose it's all over town by now."

"Gossip is capable of rendering good as well as evil," Providence reminded him. "After Mister Hamilton presents your case in court everyone will know you were wronged. Then let's see how successful Albert Cottle will be at finding someone to defend *his* reputation."

"He'll have to defend more than that once I get out of here."

"You'll not be much use until your leg heals. Here, let me look at it before I go." She loosened the splints and unwound the bandages. The wound was seeping pinkish blood, and the flesh around it was swollen and discolored. "I'm going to ask Doctor Littlebank to see you," Providence said worriedly.

"It's the dark and damp in here that keeps me from healing," Jonas said. Then he added with grim humor, "I'm surprised there's not mushrooms sprouting under my cot."

But Providence found no humor, grim or otherwise, in the situation. She brought Littlebank the following morning. After making his examination, the doctor offered the opinion that Jonas's recovery was indeed progressing more slowly than expected but that Jonas would heal with time. This vague prognosis was welcome without being entirely convincing, especially to Providence, who was beginning to be alarmed about Jonas's lingering malady.

A few days after the doctor's visit Hamilton informed Jonas that the court's quarter session would end in a week and that the bail hearing had been arranged for the following Monday. At that time the trial date would also be set. The days between seemed interminable, with no breaks in the waiting except for the few hours spent assessing Jonas's monetary worth and preparing an affadavit to be presented to the court. Then the fateful hour arrived, and with it a setback that no one had foreseen. The court, in the person of a judge named Gilbert Beadleson, scheduled the trial for the first of August, about a month and a half away, and had set bail at eight hundred pounds, in two separate sureties of four hundred pounds each.

"Why?" Providence demanded helplessly. "Why such an outrageous sum?"

"Beadleson says he deems the double crime of arson and murder deserving of extreme assurances." Hamilton answered.

"That's not why," Jonas said dully. "I criticized him once for favoring his friends in court, one in particular who is a Quaker and a member of the assembly. You remember it, Viddy."

"I can't believe he'd be so unscrupulous," Providence asserted.

Jonas turned to Hamilton. "I was angry because Beadleson excused Richard Strong from a fine for neglecting to clear the tree stumps from his property, after fining the Widow Clay two pounds for the same offense."

"And so you spoke out against him?" Hamilton asked.

"I spoke directly to him. I stopped him in the street and accused him of being unethical."

Hamilton nodded but said soberly, "I'll appeal the decision. However, I must be frank. If there is prejudice of the sort you suspect, then it's doubtful that the appeal will succeed."

Hamilton's pessimistic assessment proved correct. Jonas's appeal was rejected, and he faced the prospect of spending the rest of June and all of July in prison.

It was only a day later that he fell. It happened after a sleepless night wondering how he was to endure another six or seven weeks of solitude and inactivity. It seemed to him that his sanity depended on his physical recovery, and that his physical recovery could be achieved through self-discipline. Just after dawn he put his will to the test by trying to stand. But he overestimated his strength, and with nothing to grab onto, he lost his balance and fell. One of the splints broke, and he screamed as a sharp sliver of wood pierced the flesh of his calf and lodged in the still suppurating wound. The warden heard his cry and came to his aid. He wrestled Jonas back onto his cot and pulled the splints free from his leg. However, the warden didn't count ministering to the sick among his duties, and by the time Providence arrived an hour later she found Jonas lying exhausted and weak in a puddle of blood.

She immediately went to fetch Dr. Littlebank, who probed and poked and announced finally that there had been no futher damage to the bone and that, if anything, Jonas had merely delayed the knitting by another few days. As for the wound, Littleback decided that it might respond to a poultice soaked in alcohol and tobacco juice, which he thereupon applied with assurances that nothing was better for preventing infection.

Just before he left he said solicitously, "Mistress Greenhill, I do not . . . quite comprehend . . . the circumstances of your husband's . . . predicament. However," —Littlebank rocked back and forth on his heels while Providence waited impatiently for him to finish—"in my opinion he is a man above . . ."

Providence never heard what it was he considered Jonas

to be above, because the word continued to elude him as he left with a vague smile and a faltering step.

The rest of the week passed uneventfully. Providence helped Davey in the bakery early each morning, firing the oven and shaping the loaves, and worked with him again whenever possible during the afternoon. The rest of the time she spent with Jonas, whose condition continued to fluctuate, better one day and worse the next. Providence treated the wound as Dr. Littlebank instructed, but each time she unwrapped his leg she found fresh blood seepage. Then one morning Jonas developed a fever, and when Providence looked at his wound she found pus mixed with the blood.

It was then that she decided to call on the services of another doctor. Having heard that Jeremiah Bandy was physician to Thomas Penn, proprietor of the colony, she went to his house near the Market Street Wharf and persuaded him to accompany her back to the prison. Bandy turned out to be a supercilious gentleman who had trained at Edinburgh University and was, according to his own estimation, an expert in diagnosis and *materia medica*. He examined Jonas, listened to his feeble explanation of the treatment he'd so far undergone, then said, "Well, sir, tobacco is not indigenous to this colony and therefore ineffective as a remedy. White poplar gum is what should have been prescribed since poplar is native to the cooler northern climate. It's a simple matter of *similia similibus curantur*, or treatment of like with like. Littlebank should have known that. However, there's no use discussing what should have been done. Before applying the poplar I must cleanse the wound and give you a bleeding."

"It seems to me I've bled enough already," Jonas said weakly.

"Your wound is rank with decay. It is necessary to encourage the flow of blood in order to carry off the corruption."

"He's feverish," Providence protested. "I'm afraid that it will debilitate him still further."

"Fever opens the pores and helps purge the infection." Bandy demonstrated his sufferance of ignorant women by drawing in a deep breath, then continued patiently, "Your husband must be kept well-covered in order to retain his body's heat. Tomorrow morning you will again cleanse the wound and reapply the poplar gum and change the dressing. I shall administer a dose of Jamestown Weed, which should help cool the offending humors. Now you must let me go. I have other patients to attend."

After he'd gone Providence said that she had given Felicity over to Davey Macneill's care that morning and would remain with Jonas. Jonas was dubious of Davey's capability as nursemaid, but Providence reassured him, explaining that since Jonas' arrest Davey had appointed himself second in command, making himself indispensible to the household and reciprocating the children's adoration with blustering affection and good humor. "He's an intelligent man, Jonas, and he has turned out to be a good one despite his ferocious appearance. Lissy plays with him as if he were some large, engaging toy. Berry treats him as if he were an older brother, and the twins emulate him in everything. It is only Saree who refuses to fall under his spell."

"Then keep him, Viddy," Jonas murmured. "Persuade him to stay. No matter how Saree feels, keep him. You'll need a man to help you."

Providence didn't pretend to misunderstand. "Don't talk as if you're dying. You're going to get well, Jonas, and you're going to get out of here and come home."

"Yes, of course. But if anything should go wrong . . ."

"Jonas, Berry is coming to see you this evening, and if you will only change your mind about the others, I'll bring them tomorrow."

"No. Don't bring the others. I don't want them to see me like this." Jonas passed a hand across his forehead, then closed his eyes. "I'm tired, Viddy. I'm so tired."

After a moment Providence leaned down to touch his cheek. He had fallen into a fatigued and stuporous sleep. He slept throughout the afternoon and into the evening. When Beriah arrived Providence attempted to wake him, but although he opened his eyes briefly, he seemed unaware of his surroundings and soon lapsed back into unconsciousness. It was apparent that instead of improving, he was getting worse, and for the rest of that night Providence and Beriah took turns sitting with him, occasionally wiping the perspiration from his forehead and wetting his lips with a damp handkerchief, but helpless to rouse him into wakefulness.

At dawn Providence sent Beriah to fetch Dr. Bandy who came, reluctantly and irritably, but resigned to humoring the demands of unreasonable wives.

"My husband is delirious," Providence said anxiously. "I can barely touch him, he's so hot. Surely it's not wise to let him go on burning up this way."

"I told you yesterday that the fever controls the bodily fluxes," Bandy informed her shortly.

"I've seen people die from too high a fever."

"I'll stay, Ma," Beriah proposed. "You need to rest."

"No. I'll be all right. You can do no good here, Berry, and Mister Franklin will expect you this morning."

So Beriah went to the printing office while Providence waited with Bandy. At midmorning Jonas's incoherent mumbling ceased and his breathing seemed to become less labored. Bandy said finally, "It is time to dose him with the Jamestown weed and repeat the bleeding."

Since Jonas was no longer conscious, it was necessary for the doctor to combine the Jamestown weed powder with water and feed it to him through a thin leather tube that he forced down Jonas's throat. Providence watched apprehensively, but said nothing for fear she might interfere with the success of the delicate procedure. The leeches were next, not only placed on Jonas's chest but at the site of the seepage to draw out the noxious fluids. The treatment took forty minutes, and when it was over Bandy left again, but not before saying reprovingly, "I should, of course, have been sent for weeks ago, before Littlebank was permitted to work his outmoded remedies on the patient. However, I have managed to reverse the spread of the infection, and there's nothing more to be done except hope that he is strong enough to make a recovery."

· · 7 · ·

Davey was talking with the ebullient wife of Barnaby Pettigrew. Mistress Pettigrew had her plump bosom, as well as her elbows, planted on the counter as she confided, "Barney told me that Jonas denied it was his tinderbox, and Barney believes him, but what good will it do what Barney says? It still comes down to Albert Cottle's word against Jonas's."

"It appears to me people would sooner believe Mister Greenhill than that conniving rascal," Davey commented.

"Jonas is settin' in the jailhouse with no chance to defend hisself until he comes to trial. Meantime Cottle's signed a statement as to what he claims to know against Jonas. Besides which, he's been arguin' his case to everybody who sets foot in his shop, tellin' how Maggie the barmaid seen Jonas in the tavern just afore the fire broke out. And how Needle heared Jonas say old Dudley would have burnt down the place to keep Cottle from gettin' it, and how Jonas said he'd do likewise."

"Sure and nobody would take that brainless one's word for it?"

"Needle ain't got the wit to lie no more than he's got the wit to know he's damning an innocent man. No doubt he didn't hear it right, but he heard something like it if he said so. I guess in the end it won't be what *did* happen but what *seems* to have happened that'll count against Jonas. The fire started in Elisha's parlor, where Elisha was sleepin' off his drunk. There was no candle burnin' in broad daylight and no fire burnin' in midsummer. Elisha couldn't of ignited the spunk from his tinderbox, not in the condition he was in, so it stands to reason somebody else must of done it. And Cottle claims it was Jonas's tinderbox. It was the only one he had that was etched out with sprigs of wheat, and he got it recorded in his ledger that he sold it to Providence Greenhill. I seen the entry myself. He parades it out to every customer who goes into his shop. Barney says Viddy told him she did buy a tinderbox in May, so I guess that's true enough. Still, it don't say nothing about sprigs of wheat, so I'm sure he's lyin' about that. Well, I says it's unjust and there's no one more deserving to be caught out than Albert Cottle, but there don't seem to be no way to show him up to the law."

Mistress Pettigrew sighed and launched her bosom from the counter. "Tell Viddy that Barney and me is thinkin' on her, and that Barney means to speak up for Jonas in court—whatever good it'll do."

Davey watched her leave the shop, then turned his head to regard Felicity, who was napping on Davey's pallet, her face flushed from the warmth of the bakery, her small pouting mouth slightly open and her protective arms entwined around the rag doll Davey had given her. Davey frowned, thinking about what Mistress Pettigrew had said about the tinderbox and the sprigs of wheat. Suddenly he dashed around the corner of the counter, threw open the front door, and called to Mistress Pettigrew, who glanced around and then walked back to confront him. "Did I leave something?" she asked curiously, beginning to count her packages.

"No. Mistress Pettigrew, will you do me the favor of watching the shop for a few minutes? Little Lissy's lying there asleep, so she'll not be a bother to you."

Mistress Pettigrew said dubiously, "You'll not be long? I've a busy afternoon ahead of me."

Davey gave her his assurances that he'd return within ten or fifteen minutes. Then once she reentered the bakery he strode across the street and pushed open the door to Albert Cottle's sundries shop. The interior was cool and dim. There were no customers strolling among the jumbled piles of merchandise, and Davey didn't see Cottle until the jangling door bell brought him out from the back store-room. When he recognized Davey he said unpleasantly, "You're not welcome here. I don't sell to the Greenhills nor to nobody who works for the Greenhills."

"That's your right, Mister Cottle," Davey returned pleasantly. "Only I didn't come to buy. I come to look at your ledger."

"My ledger's my business," Cottle returned.

"I hear you been showing it to all the neighbors. I just wanted to see for myself where it says that Mistress Greenhill bought a tinderbox from you in May."

Cottle positioned himself between Davey and the counter but changed his mind about stopping Davey as Davey advanced on him. "Get out," he demanded angrily, but with a tinge of panic edging his voice.

"I'm not planning to do damage to it," Davey said amiably. "I just want to see it."

The ledger lay open on the counter, and Davey turned it toward him. Just then the shop bell pealed again and he glanced toward the door to see Needle enter. Cottle shouted out, "Needle, listen to me. You go get the constable."

Needle grinned at him vacantly, and Cottle said more imperatively, "You heard me. Go get the constable. Hurry up now. Go do as I say."

The door slammed and once again the bells clamored, in the wake of Needle's departure.

By then Davey had found the entry he sought, on a page inscribed "*May 12, 1731. Tndrbx, Prv. Greenhill, 1s.*" "It says nothing here about sprigs of wheat," Davey pointed out to Cottle.

"I know what I sold her. It was the only one I had with a wheat design etched in it."

"You'd be a liar if it wasn't the only one, wouldn't you?

The law might begin to ask you questions if they found out you was lying. They might turn the tables on you if they found out you was lying, begin to ask you why you'd lie, what you'd gain by lying, maybe even what you'd gain if Elisha Hull was to die?"

"Get out of my shop!"

"And did you not sell any other tinderboxes during the months of May and June?" Davey asked. He ran his finger down that page and the next and the one after that. "Here's the name Hull, Mister Cottle. It seems you sold one of the Hulls a tinderbox on May nineteenth."

"So what. It didn't have no wheat design on it."

"So you say, Mister Cottle. But suppose one of them other boxes you sold had sprigs of wheat on the cover? Look here. There's two more entries here for tinderboxes with the names Scoggin and Hatch next to them."

Cottle's normally florid face turned a deep shade of crimson. He reached out and shut the ledger. "They was immigrants headin' north. You ain't goin' to find them customers."

"Still, let's suppose you were lyin' now, about there only being one tinderbox with sprigs of wheat. Suppose there were four?"

"Get out."

"And if there were four, why not six or eight or a dozen?"

"I told you to get out. If you don't get out, I'll have you arrested."

Davey began to stroll around the shop surveying the merchandise. As he brushed past Cottle, Cottle backed up a step, then quickly turned and darted for the door to the storeroom. He had one foot in the room when he felt Davey take hold of his coattails. "Mister Cottle," Davey said politely, "I'd like to see what's in there."

Cottle jerked loose, leaped into the room, and tried to shut the door, but Davey placed one large boot in the aperture and slammed the door back into Cottle's face, sending him reeling into the room. Davey had to stoop to get through the door himself, and once inside he threw the bolt, locking himself and Cottle inside. The room was filled with crates and barrels, far too many to permit an orderly or methodical search. "Would you be of a mind to help me look?" Davey inquired genially. "It'll be less wearing on the merchandise."

"You'll hang for this," Cottle proclaimed.

"I'd not count on it, Mister Cottle. I think you place too much faith in hanging."

Davey noticed that some of the crates and barrels were nailed shut, but others had been opened, and he decided to start with those. He picked up the nearest barrel, upended it, and watched as an avalanche of shuttlecocks piled up at his feet. The crate next to it contained clay porringers that shattered as Davey emptied them out onto the floor. Forgetting his terror of Davey, Cottle ran forward to intervene. Davey wound his arms around Cottle, pinning his arms to his sides, and lifted him off the floor. He squeezed Cottle until Cottle's neck cords stood out, then released him. Cottle staggered back and sat down among the shards of clay. "My ribs," he said groaningly.

"Just a friendly hug to show I've no hard feelings, Mister Cottle."

Davey snapped the lid off a nearby barrel and peered inside. It was half full of candleholders. He pushed it over, then picked up the barrel and tossed it away from him. The clatter it made hitting the wall was compounded by a sudden pounding on the door and shouts from someone who claimed to be the constable. Davey ignored the commands to open up or pay the consequences. He finished prying open the lid of a shallow crate holding some beaded purses, then overturned a box filled with spectacles, spilling them out onto the floor. The commotion in the shop grew in volume, and the door groaned as a shoulder was applied to it. Cottle interspersed threats against Davey with desperate cries for help, the cries rising to a crescendo as Davey kicked over a barrel of inkpots, adding a viscous black puddle to the mess already on the floor, then followed by dumping half a dozen bolts of imported silk onto the inkpots.

Davey was getting discouraged. There were more supplies than he could investigate in the time he had left. He leaned down and picked up Cottle by the fabric of his vest, holding him aloft so that Cottle's face was level with his own. "As you can see," Davey said conversationally, "I'm not a violent man. Still, now and then I've been known to lose me temper. It would save us both a lot of trouble if you'll tell me the whereabouts of your tinderboxes."

"There ain't none in this room, I tell you."

"It was you tried to stop me coming in here, and I don't know why you'd bother, less there was something in here you didn't want me to find."

"Help!" Cottle screeched as the attack on the door became more vigorous. "Help! He's trying to kill me!"

Davey opened his hands and Cottle plummeted to the floor, then crawled rapidly away from Davey and collapsed onto the crate containing the beaded purses.

Davey's eyes narrowed. He dove for Cottle again and Cottle covered his head with his arms as Davey swooped down on him. Davey slid the crate loose from under Cottle's head and pulled out the purses. There were only eight of them. Underneath, snugly packed side by side, were a dozen or more tinderboxes, and as Davey removed them from the crate he saw that each one had a sprig of wheat etched into the cover.

Cottle looked up at him fearfully, but Davey had no more interest in Cottle now that he'd found what he'd come for. As another thud shimmied the door on its hinges, Davey walked over, unbolted the door, and emerged into the shop. A constable stood facing him, backed up by Needle and a handful of neighborhood people who had converged into the shop behind them. Among them Davey saw Barnaby Pettigrew, and he waved to Pettigrew to move in closer as he warned the constable away with an upraised hand. "You're all friends to Jonas Greenhill," Davey announced to the onlookers, "and I know how you feel about Albert Cottle. So I know you're going to be glad to hear what I'm about to tell you."

Providence had stayed by Jonas's side all the previous day waiting for some change, but she wasn't rewarded by so much as a flutter of his eyelids. She had been exhausted but afraid to nap for fear he'd call out to her and she wouldn't hear. Countless times during the afternoon and evening she had leaned over him watching for some indication that he had begun to improve. His face was white and his breathing shallow, but when she placed her hand on his forehead and felt that it was cooler, she had begun to believe the worst was over.

Beriah came and left again, leaving a supper basket and urging her to eat, but she wasn't hungry. Near midnight she touched Jonas's cheek, and smoothed back his hair for the hundredth time. Then, satisfied that he was comfortable, she stretched her cramped muscles by pacing the cell, before returning to check on Jonas again and to renew the vigil, which lasted throughout the night and most of the following morning.

Finally, near midday, slumped at the foot of Jonas's cot with her head resting against the wall, she fell asleep. It was a restless, semi-conscious state in which bewildering images of Jonas and the children drifted through her mind. She was bothered by her inability to tell which were recollections and which were imaginative creations. Was Berry still an infant? Was the baby she nurtured within her body already born? She struggled to wake up but couldn't.

It was Beriah who finally woke her, joyfully bursting into the cell to shout, "It's over, Ma! They're going to set Pa free!"

Providence sat up. "What did you say?"

"It's true. It was Davey did it. He proved Mister Cottle was lying about the tinderbox!"

Providence stared up at her son as if she thought he'd gone mad.

"It's true," Beriah repeated elatedly. "Cottle admitted he lied."

"I can scarce believe it." Providence turned her head to look at Jonas, then slid off the cot and dropped to her knees beside him. "Jonas," she whispered. "Jonas, wake up. Berry is here. He has wonderful news."

She took hold of Jonas's hands, then felt the coldness in them. "Jonas?" Clutched by fear, she slipped her hand inside his shirt. For an instant she was deceived into thinking she felt the beat of his heart, then realized that it was her own pulse she felt.

"Ma?" Beriah asked in a frightened voice.

"He's dead," Providence answered.

New Castle 1744

. . . .

Thou shalt make them as a fiery
oven in the time of thine anger:
the Lord shall swallow them up in his wrath,
and the fire shall devour them.

Psalm 21:9
A *Psalm of David*

Today her mother and *the davey* had gone to town, and she was locked in her room. This wasn't unusual. She was locked in her room whenever there was no one in the house to watch her, just as she was locked in her room every night. She had prepared for today's imprisonment by lugging in a log from the woodshed. It was almost three feet long, a thick log of white ash still covered with bark. She set to work stripping it, deciding which creature it contained and how the creature could best be released. It came to her finally: a hawk, strong and swift, with needle-sharp claws, a creature fierce enough to hold even *the davey* at bay.

How clever he was, Sarah thought. As clever as he was dangerous. She had been eleven when he went to work in her father's bakery in Philadelphia, but she had known from the first that he wasn't who he pretended. She'd learned about the devil and how he sent his emissaries to insinuate themselves among ordinary mortals. Hadn't her teacher, Dame Gubbins, told her time and again that evil wore many disguises? Then *the davey* had appeared, unnaturally tall and loud, with a shock of the devil's red hair and with calculating, all-seeing eyes that belied his friendly manner. She had recognized him at once, and her perception of his wickedness had been confirmed when he brought with him a series of afflictions to plague the righteous. Old Mister Hull had died. Then the tavern next door to the bakery had caught fire, killing Mister Hull's son. Right after that Sarah's father had been arrested and sent to prison, and he'd died there. In the thirteen years since, *the davey* had established himself as part of the Greenhill family, accompanying them to New Castle, acting the part of a benevolent uncle to the twins, sharing their mother's confidences, ingratiating himself with Sarah's sisters. But not with Sarah. She was on to him and he knew it. It was her knowledge of him that kept him in check, and he would destroy her if he could for possessing that knowledge.

It was necessary to be constantly alert to *the davey*'s strategies to destroy her, but she wasn't a fool, nor was she helpless. She looked around her, taking comfort from the variety and number of guardians. There were dozens of them: the rearing bear on the shelf, the fox, the ferret, and, in the corner, the statuette of an Indian in loincloth and feathered headdress. The Indians, Sarah knew, were children of nature; fleet, fearless fighters and believers in the spirit gods who protected them from demons of the underworld. *The davey* could neither harm an Indian nor disguise himself as an Indian. Therefore her Indian was her most powerful guardian. In her room she was totally safe from *the davey* and his strategies.

And *the davey* wasn't the only one capable of strategy. She spoke when it pleased her, rejected *the davey*'s overtures, and went on protecting her family by keeping his identity to herself. Then, too, whenever she found the opportunity she ran away. So far she had always been caught and brought back. (How could they be expected to know why she was running, or from whom?) But she would run again. She had a pound note hidden behind a loose baseboard under her window, and she had her knife and her guardians. There was reason to hope.

The Greenhill property consisted of fifteen acres, most of it in uncultivated meadow and woodland at the base of a broken ridge of hills. The buildings were clustered in a meadow about a quarter of a mile from the public road, the mill separated from the house and barn by a creek that supplied power for the mill as well as water for the household and barnyard necessities.

Providence had bought the property from the widowed sister of Barnaby Pettigrew, a Philadelphia neighbor, and the mill had provided her with a comfortable livelihood since her arrival in Delaware in 1731. Not all of her children had come with her. She had left one, seventeen-year-old Beriah, behind to finish up his printing apprenticeship under the master printer Ben Franklin. Since then Franklin had staked Berry to the equipment necessary to open a print shop of his own in Williamsburg, Virginia, and that was where Berry had been living for the past six years.

At first it had been only Davey Macneill who helped Providence in her initial struggles to run the mill and provide for the family with their single cow, their two horses, and the small patch of tillable kitchen garden that kept them in potatoes and beans. Then when the twins were grown they joined Davey in the mill, while Providence kept the house and the mill's ledger books.

Now she left Davey out back unloading the supplies as she entered the house through the back door and went down the hall to hang her bonnet on a peg near the front door. She could see two of her daughters through the hall window. They were striding out of the woods, Felicity in front with her bonnet flapping loose on her back and Winsome hurrying to catch up. What now? Providence asked herself. Was it the usual set-to; elder against younger, obdurate against willful? They fought so often, and Providence could never decide if the antagonism was superficial or lay deeper. She sighed and untied her bonnet.

She had shopped for provisions, haggled with Moses Fairbank over the price of an iron winch, and picked up the burlap Eb Bordman had been holding for her. Now she was tired. Visiting Eb's general store was always trying because it meant dealing with Eb as well as the shopping. And there was no effective way to deal with a man as persistent as Eb. To say nothing of his cats. "What's a woman like you to do without a man to take care of you?" he'd boom. "How can a female run a business without a man to advise her? Tell me it ain't true that children need a man to hold them in line."

"The twins are twenty-six years old, Eb."

"But what about your gels? Two gels just short of

marrying age and an addlepate like Sarah. And what about the heavy work a female's got to do round the house?"

The last question had been squelched by the appearance of Davey emerging from the brewer's toting a keg of cider that Eb couldn't have rolled much less lifted. But had Eb been chastened? Not for a moment. He'd merely pulled out Beriah's letter and said, "What's a boy to think, him a long ways off from his ma, knowing she's got no one to look after her proper."

There was a dull thud overhead, and Providence raised her eyes ceilingward. Poor Sarah, locked in her room like some wild animal. Providence hated to do it to her, but at twenty-four Sarah's behavior remained unpredictable. She had been a good part of the reason why, thirteen years earlier, Providence had moved the family from Philadelphia to New Castle, hoping the move might have a stabilizing influence on Sarah. But New Castle hadn't cured Sarah, and Providence knew now that nothing would ever make her whole and well.

She went upstairs to unbolt Sarah's door and found Sarah sitting cross-legged on the floor carving on a piece of wood that was taking sharp form under her knife. Sarah had become a carver in wood these last six years, a pastime Providence encouraged because it seemed to help hold Sarah's furies at bay. But the pastime had become itself a consuming obsession. The room spilled over with Sarah's handiwork, renderings of creatures animal and human, fanciful pieces that reflected her developing skill, from the first primitive stick dolls to the intricately carved bear that she kept on the window ledge. "We're back, Saree," Providence said quietly. "Is everything all right?"

"Yes, Mama."

"Come downstairs. Davey brought in the new keg of cider. We're going to have some."

"No, thank you."

"You should have come with us today. We stopped at the Rouse farm, and Mister Rouse showed us the sow's four new piglets. Then we stopped at the Websters'. Mistress Webster reminded us about their picnic next Sunday. I said we wouldn't miss it. Oh, and, Saree, I brought home a watermelon. Come downstairs. I'm going to slice it up."

"I'm busy, Mama."

"The carving will wait." Providence turned her head toward the door as Felicity called up the stairs, then said to Sarah, "I want you to come down. Do you hear?"

"Yes, Mama."

Providence shook her head, then clattered back down the stairs to find Felicity standing in the hall with her hands on her hips. Behind her Winsome staggered through the open door. "You're red as a beet, Winnie. Lissy, why aren't you wearing your bonnet?"

"Mama," Felicity exclaimed, "do you know what Joss Wrentham called me?"

"I have no idea."

"Only a female."

"You are a female."

"But not 'only' a female."

"Lissy challenged him to a swimming race across Horseshoe Cove even though she can't swim," Winsome said, out of breath.

"I'll learn to swim," Felicity declared.

"We were watching the boys swim," Winsome explained importantly, "and later we watched them pitch chuckers. They wouldn't let Lissy join in, but then they changed their minds and she did and she won over Asa and Sam, but not over Joss. So Joss said that no girl could do better than him at anything, and Lissy said she can ride a horse better. And you know she can, so Joss right away said, 'At swimming,' then laughed at her and called her only a female. And so she challenged him to a swimming race."

"That was rather reckless, Lissy," Providence said calmly. "Now come help me in the kitchen. I've brought a watermelon."

"Mama," Felicity burst out exasperatedly, "please don't change the subject."

"I've had quite enough of the subject."

"Who's going to teach her?" Winsome demanded. "There's nobody who can. You can't swim and I can't swim, and Mordie and Aaron can barely swim. There just isn't anybody."

"I don't know about that."

They all turned to face Davey as he ducked his head through the doorway leading into the hall from the kitchen. He had put on weight over the years, and he wore side-whiskers now, but his hair was as red as ever and his brogue was as broad. "There might be someone."

"Davey," Providence said firmly, "take the wagon over to the mill and dump the burlap. The girls and I will slice up the watermelon and bring it over with a pitcher of cider."

"Wait, Mama," Felicity cut in. "Davey, can you swim?"

"I never would have trusted myself to the briny if I couldn't."

"Could you teach me how?"

"Why not?"

"Well, but I mean, will you?"

"Sure I will. Nothing to it."

Felicity rushed over to throw ecstatic arms around his waist. "I knew it. I knew I'd find someone."

"Oh, for pity's sake," Providence declared. "It's not enough I've got a carver. Now I've got a swimmer as well."

In the end, just as Providence feared, Sarah couldn't be persuaded to leave her room. Providence, Felicity and Winsome carried the cider and watermelon down to the mill, and the twins and Davey joined them outside to sit on the grass on the mill side of the creek, just over the wagon-wide wooden bridge.

"Hiram Sheffield is thinking of switching his business to our mill," Mordecai announced as he accepted the piece of watermelon his mother handed him.

"When did that come about?" Providence asked curiously. "Was Mister Sheffield here today?"

"No. I heard it from Barbara."

"I doubt that his daughter's word can be trusted, Mordie."

"I know it's not anything definite, but she told me her father's been quarreling with Gans Ober and that she heard him say he was thinking of switching mills. So she suggested he switch to us, and he said he'd think it over."

"I'm not sure I'd agree to it in any event," Providence reflected. "It's wrong to use one's friendships to advance one's fortune."

"I don't see why."

"Besides," Felicity butted in, "everybody knows that Klaus Ober is sweet on Barbara, and it would be like spitting in Klaus's face to take his business as well as his girl."

"We can do without talk of spitting," Providence remonstrated.

"We can charge less, Ma," Aaron put forward. "We're also better liked."

"And no wonder," Mordecai joined in. "Ober lowers his prices to get new customers and charges the difference to his older customers. Everybody knows that."

"Ober has been here twenty-five years to our thirteen," Providence returned. "His mill is the largest around and he has six sons to help him. I can't believe Mister Sheffield would simply quit him to switch to us."

"We've nothing to complain about," Davey interjected. "We have enough customers to keep us comfortable. Sheffield's business might not be worth the trouble."

"We'll never get rich on our customers," Mordecai argued. "They're good for a few acres of corn, just enough to store in their own bins with nothing left over to sell. They don't earn anything from their planting, and that means we don't earn anything from them. Sheffield farms two hundred acres and sells more than half of his crops. If he earns, we earn."

"There are three of us," Aaron added. "We can do a good job for him, a lot better than we're doing now if we put our minds to it. Not all the crops come in at the same time. We can handle it."

"There could be trouble," Davey suggested. "The Obers are hard men, and as Lissy just now put it, Klaus would probably think he'd been spit on."

"I wouldn't waste my spit on him," Mordecai said in a disgruntled voice.

"We're exciting ourselves over something that hasn't yet happened," Providence offered sensibly. "Let's give it time. That way we won't feel foolish if nothing comes of it. Anyway, there's something else to talk about. There's news from Berry. Mister Bordman gave me a letter from him that came by post rider yesterday." Providence set down her cup and rummaged for the letter in her pocket.

"Go on and read it, Mama," Felicity said impatiently. "What's the news? Has Berry finished paying Mister Franklin for the printing press?"

"Better than that," Aaron interjected. "He's getting married. Am I right, Ma?"

Providence asked in astonishment, "How did you know?"

"Berry told me and Mordie about Nedda when he was here last December. After all, he's thirty now. It's about time he got married."

"Her name's Nedda?" Felicity asked.

"Nedda Byrd," Mordecai supplied. "Read it, Ma."

"That's what I'm about to do. *Dear Mama and family,*" Providence began. *It is Sunday afternoon and I have just now come home from performing an important errand, so important that I hasten to report its consequences before I eat my supper.*

Providence raised her eyes briefly, then went on. *I cannot recall whether or not I have ever mentioned the name Byrd to you.*

James Byrd is a glazier here in Virginia. His family was one of the first to settle here and he is someone it has pleased me to know for two years. His wife's name is Mary, and they have one child, a daughter named Nedda.

Again Providence glanced up at the expectant faces before continuing. *For the last ten months I have been calling on Nedda Byrd, Mama, but I did not wish to speak to you about my intentions toward her until I was persuaded that Nedda's affections were as firmly fixed as my own. Yesterday I dared to declare myself, and she responded favorably. Today I approached her father to request her hand, and he and Mistress Byrd gave us their blessing.*

Providence waited out the volley of exclamations, then went on. *We have not as yet set a date for the wedding, but I have explained to the Byrds that early winter would most suit your convenience since the work at the mill will have ceased, and there will not yet be such inclemencies of weather as to make travel difficult.*

"Can we go, Mama?" Winsome exclaimed.

"I don't know how safe the waters are," Providence answered, "what with the Spanish hanging about looking for any opportunity to harass English vessels. Then, too, passage would be expensive."

"If Sheffield hires us, we'll be able to afford it, Ma," Mordecai suggested.

"He's right, Ma," Aaron seconded.

"We'll see. But come now, don't you wish to hear the rest? He goes on to describe Miss Byrd in most glowing terms."

"Do go on, Mama," Winsome said encouragingly. "Is she pretty?"

"I'm sure she's not as pretty as you," Davey teased, "so you'll have no cause to be jealous of her."

"Stop making fun, Davey."

Davey laughed. "I'm not making fun. I'm just pointing

out that Miss Byrd will have to go some to match the Greenhill girls for looks."

"Davey," Providence said with mock severity. "Winnie's head is turned enough without you turning it further. Now pour me some cider and let me get on with the letter."

·· *9* ··

The news of Beriah's betrothal remained the chief topic of conversation until another occurence supplanted it. Providence heard the news on the following Friday morning from Esther Webster, her nearest neighbor to the north. Mistress Webster came by to remind Providence about the picnic on Sunday that would celebrate Paul Webster's departure for Yale College, and told her, at the same time, that Indians had been sighted on a road twenty miles northwest of the Greenhill property, only ten miles west of the town of New Castle.

"They were a band of Iroquois, maybe ten or twelve in all," Mistress Webster declared, "brazenly camping on the edge of Ned Slater's land."

"That's all? Just camping?"

"They had no reason to be there unless they were planning trouble. The next thing we know they'll be stealing people's livestock and waylaying white women."

"They're probably just out on a hunting expedition. There's no reason to suppose they're anything but peaceable."

"There's no such thing as a peaceable Indian," Mistress Webster scoffed. "The Indians hate us as much for being white as the Spanish and French hate us for being English. If I were you, I'd keep an eye on the family for the time being."

"I mean to."

Later Providence told Davey and the others about the

Indians. It was agreed among them that if there actually were trouble, Davey would move into the house from the mill, where he normally slept, and they would set up a system of watches. For the time being, the girls would stick close to home and the twins and Davey would carry guns whenever they drove the wagon or the horses off the property. Outlaw Indians were infrequent, but it was best to be cautious.

There were three Websters, Esther and her husband Lyman, and their grandson, eighteen-year-old Paul. The Websters were sheep farmers, and Providence maintained a barter relationship with them as she did with a number of her neighbors. With the Sibbes it was so many bushels of corn in exchange for its milling. With the Waddingtons it was apples and with the Websters it was sheep, enough out of the fall slaughter to see them through winter. The arrangement worked to everyone's benefit, and the cooperation between close neighbors had expanded to include one another's troubles and celebrations as well as the products of one another's labors.

It was a beautiful day for a party, and the guests, forty-odd of them, arrived promptly, carrying their contributions to the picnic along with their own plates and utensils. The Greenhills were prominent among them. Providence, soon to celebrate her fifty-second birthday, was tall and slender, the lines in her face still too fine to be defined as wrinkles and her violet-blue eyes still capable of drawing admiring glances. The twins were not only good-looking men, brown-eyed and brown-haired, tanned and strong, but were mirror images of one another, so well matched that it required a second careful look to tell them apart. Felicity and Winsome, on the other hand were nothing alike. Winsome was light-complexioned with luminous brown eyes and thick chestnut hair which, contrary to fashion, she wore loose down her back. At thirteen her figure was already rounded and feminine, and she utilized it to pleasing and provocative effect, basking in the frank praise she elicited from men and boys alike. Felicity, at fifteen, was truly beautiful, with a willowy figure, delicate features, and her mother's astonishing blue eyes. Spunky, boisterous, and utterly unselfconscious, Felicity was nonetheless set apart by an innate reserve that made her less vulnerable to the kind of lascivious admiration accorded Winsome.

Providence had promised Mistress Webster three rhubarb pies, and she placed them on one of the half-dozen long boards set up between trestles on the lawn, before going to seek out their host and hostess. Mordecai and Aaron drifted off on pleasures of their own, Mordecai to look for Barbara Sheffield and Aaron to join the clanging camaraderie at the horseshoe pitch. Davey's chief interest at these affairs was the food, not surprising considering the variety and goodness of the offerings. Knowing he'd be asked to play the bagpipes sooner or later, he settled himself between the platter of crabs and the cold roast chickens, with his bagpipes across his knees.

Winsome and Felicity found the guest of honor in company with Alice Sibbes and Nancy Rhodes. Paul Webster was going to Yale to study for the ministry, but with his sharp profile, satiny black hair, and seductive manner, he more nearly resembled an Arab sultan than a Delaware minister, and there were those who would have said that for him the ministry was sailing against the wind. His mother, the Webster's only child, had fallen prey to temptation and Paul was the product of her misconduct, born minutes before she died. It was commonly held that Paul's religious ambitions resulted from his grandparents' eagerness to dilute the taint of bad blood, for certainly he displayed no evidence of any spiritual conviction of his own. "Make room for the Greenhill sisters," he commanded playfully when he spotted Felicity and Winsome walking toward him.

Felicity smiled briefly, and Winsome dipped her knees in mock curtsy.

"I've been wondering when you'd get here." Paul spoke to them both, but it was plain that his attention was given to Winsome.

"It doesn't look like you've been waiting very anxiously," Winsome said poutingly. "You seem quite happily occupied."

"I'm always anxious when it comes to you, Winnie," Paul teased.

Winsome tossed her curls saucily, and Felicity gave her a little pinch to remind her to behave.

"When do you leave, Paul?" Alice Sibbes inquired.

"Tomorrow." He cocked his head, still looking at Winsome. "Will you write to me?"

"Are you soliciting letters from all four of us?" Winsome asked coquettishly, "or are you asking me alone?"

"I think you know the answer to that," Paul returned with a lazy smile.

Alice and Nancy exchanged annoyed glances, then Alice said shortly, "I'm going to watch them pitch horseshoes. Want to come, Nancy?"

Nancy nodded and the two girls stalked off.

"That wasn't very nice," Felicity said sharply. "You snubbed them, Paul. As for you, Winnie, thirteen years old and flirting as if you're grown. I should tell Mama on you. It's disgusting."

"You're jealous," Winsome accused.

"I most certainly am not."

"I might consider letting you write me too, Lissy," Paul offered magnanimously.

"Oh, for heaven's sake, I'm going to look for Mama."

Felicity left them and marched across the lawn. She spotted Davey talking to the Widow Temple, or rather, being talked to by the Widow Temple. Davey, unlike Paul Webster, found his popularity with women somewhat dismaying, especially at gatherings such as this where he was forced to juggle them like tenpins to keep them all content. Felicity didn't stop but waggled her head sym-

pathetically as she passed by. She found her mother
conversing with Mary Chiltern and joined them. Miss
Chiltern was Esther Webster's spinster sister who eked out
a living as the local schoolmistress and held a bleak, if
resigned, view of the world. "We all have our troubles to
bear," she was saying as Felicity walked up. "Esther and I
had a brother named Albert who wasn't right either.
Fortunately he passed on when he was nineteen."

Providence slipped her arm around her daughter's waist.
"We were talking about Saree," she murmured.

"I felt badly leaving her behind this morning, Mama."

"So did I. Lord knows I tried to persuade her to come. I
did everything short of dumping her headfirst into the
wagon. But if we'd forced her to attend she'd have tried to
run off, and I don't think I could contend with it today."

"Pity," Miss Chiltern commiserated. "Just like Albert.
Same thing exactly."

They were distracted by the sound of bagpipes and
dropped the subject of Sarah to talk about Davey, his
musical skill and his manly virtues. From Mary Chiltern's
fluttery insistence that there was no finer man in New
Castle, Felicity concluded that she, too, was not immune to
Davey's charms. Not long afterward Lyman Webster rang
the dinner bell and there was a rush to the tables.

It was almost three before the banquet ended and the last
platter was wiped clean. The young people dispersed and
their elders stretched out on the grass to doze or converse.
Providence was pounced upon by Eb Bordman, red-faced
and perspiring, who whispered something in her ear before
bearing her away for a stroll under the trees, and Felicity
was left behind to wonder about the silly notions of
romance that affected everyone's behavior. She was just
deciding never to be caught up in such idiotic nonsense
herself when Josiah Wrentham waved to her from across the
grass and came over to join her.

On the voting roll, Nathaniel Wrentham, Josiah's father,
was listed as a farmer although he had never, to anyone's

knowledge, planted so much as an onion on the ten acres Bedelia Grass had brought as her dowry twenty-nine years before. Wrentham's livelihood, such as it was, came from tending sick animals, and he generally took his pay in eggs, beef, corn, and hand-me-downs, an arrangement totally in accord with his lackadaisical nature and quite satisfactory to his compatible wife. The joke was that it was this same combination of negligence and affection that filled the Wrentham cradle eighteen times in not so many more years. Of the eighteen children Josiah fit in the middle with nine older and eight younger than he. In terms of how many were left at home, however, there were only twelve, and of these Josiah, at fifteen, was the eldest boy.

"I've been looking for you," Josiah told Felicity.

"Why?"

Josiah jammed his hands into his pockets and glanced over his shoulder at his family lounging nearby. "No reason."

Josiah and Felicity had attended school together until just that spring, when Miss Chiltern had pronounced them and their contemporaries "done," as if they'd been a tray of honey buns. In school Josiah had consistently surpassed Felicity. By his own admission he did his homework only when convenient, skipped school according to inclination, and laid claim to no greater ambition than to be a soldier and "fight in the wars." Still, when he was called on to locate the South China Sea, multiply fractions, or give the dates of Henry VII's rule, he was ready with the correct answer. It upset everything Felicity had been taught about the rewards of industry, and made her chronically mistrustful of him.

They walked along silently while Josiah cast around for something to talk about. Finally he said, "There's gossip going around that Hiram Sheffield may switch from Gans Ober's mill to your ma's."

"I know."

"Is it true?"

"It's not certain. Mama doesn't like the idea because she's afraid people will think we got the business unfairly."

"Because of Barbara being sweet on your brother?"

Felicity nodded.

"Ober had a fierce fight with Mister Sheffield a few weeks ago," Josiah noted.

"How do you know?"

"Pa was in the mill yard tending one of Ober's horses when it happened. They were arguing about how much money Ober was trying to charge Mister Sheffield. Pa said Ober tried to pull Mister Sheffield off his horse, and Mister Sheffield cut him with his whip, then rode off. If he'd of stayed, the Ober boys would have killed him."

"They're monsters, those boys," Felicity said feelingly, "especially Klaus."

Josiah nodded. "That's why the Websters didn't invite the Obers today. They were afraid of trouble."

"Between them and Mister Sheffield?"

"Or between Klaus and your brother. Klaus has been going around saying some ugly things about Barbara Sheffield."

"Mordie would fix him good if he heard it," Felicity conceded.

"I'd do the same if I ever heard anyone say anything nasty about you," Josiah declared.

Felicity stopped and turned to face him. "Oh really, Joss Wrentham. And wasn't it you who called me 'only a female'?"

"That was just teasing."

"Well, you won't have anything to tease me about once I win the swimming race."

"Forget the swimming race, Lissy."

"Certainly not. I intend to hold you to it. When shall it be?"

"Lissy, for Lucifer's sake, you can't swim."

"How do you know what I can or can't do? Name the date."

"What do I care what date?"

"Name it, Joss."

"You name it."

"All right. A month from now. The last Sunday in September."

"I'm the one who'll get in trouble for it," Josiah said stoically. "They'll say I put you up to it."

"You did."

"I didn't mean for you to take me seriously."

"You mean you didn't mean to take *me* seriously." Felicity suddenly lifted her hand to shade her eyes. "Joss, Mama's waving at me. I've got to go."

She hurried off, leaving Josiah to stare after her. "Drat," he mumbled, aiming a kick at a clod of dirt. "Drat and double drat."

· · *10* · ·

It was time to go home. In the midst of the good-byes Providence noticed that Winsome was missing.

"She's probably with Paul, Mama," Felicity suggested. "She's been following him around all day."

"Go look for her, Lissy. I don't want to leave Saree alone at home too long. Aaron, Mordie, help your sister look."

Felicity remembered having seen Paul and Winsome half an hour earlier leaning on the fence between the front yard and the meadow beyond. While Mordecai and Aaron went off in separate directions, she cut across the yard, climbed the fence, and crossed the meadow. On the far side of the meadow there was a narrow strip of woods dividing the Webster property from the road, and when Felicity got there she swept her eyes along the line of trees, thinking they might be sitting somewhere in the shade. She didn't see them. Then it occurred to her that they might be in the lambing shed where there were generally a few late-born lambs to be admired, and she started back.

A hair-raising shriek brought her to a standstill. The cry came from the woods behind her. An instant later she heard Winsome cry out, "Stop it! Stop it!"

Felicity whirled around and dashed along the rim of trees until she was parallel to the point where she believed the shriek had originated. She plunged into the woods, sweeping aside the foliage, and burst into a clearing where she saw Paul Webster struggling on the ground with Winsome. "Leave her be!" Felicity shouted. "Let her alone!"

"She tried to kill him," a voice quavered, and Felicity turned to find Winsome standing a few feet away. Then who was on the ground? She took a more careful look at the person kicking and clawing at Paul, then gasped. "Sarah?"

"She went for him," Winsome said tremulously. "She had a knife. She tried to stab him with it."

"How did she get here?"

"How should I know? She must have gotten out of her room. Lissy, what shall we do?"

"We'll go for Mordie and Aaron."

Paul had a firm grip on Sarah's wrists now, but she continued to twist from side to side in an effort to get free. "Hurry up, will you," Paul called out grimly.

"We'll be right back." Felicity dragged Winsome out of the woods and together they raced back toward the house. Halfway there they saw Mordecai and Aaron walking toward them. At first the twins gestured at them impatiently, but as the girls drew closer they saw their sisters' faces and broke into a run. "What is it?" Mordecai called out.

Quickly Felicity explained the situation and led them running back through the woods. When they reached Paul and Sarah they saw that Sarah was no longer trying to get up, but lay between Paul's knees staring up at him with wide, unblinking eyes. Aaron pushed Paul aside, took Sarah by her hands, and pulled her to her feet. "Saree," he asked gently as he brushed the dirt off her skirt, "are you all right?"

Sarah glanced at Paul, then glanced away without answering.

"Tell us, Saree," Mordecai urged. "What is it? What are you doing here? How did you—" Self-consciously, Aaron looked at Paul, then altered the question from "How did you escape" to "How did you come? Did you walk all the way?"

Her voice was barely audible. "Yes, I walked."

"It's nearly nine miles. You must have been walking for hours."

"Let's find Mama," Felicity proposed.

"Wait till I brush the leaves out of Saree's hair," Winsome fussed. "She looks a mess."

"You don't look much better," Felicity noted. "Your hair's tangled and you're missing a button off your bodice."

Winsome said pettishly, "I tried to pull her away from Paul. Can I help how I look? I told you she had a knife."

"A knife?" Mordecai exclaimed. "Where is it?"

Winsome pointed to some bushes, then went over and picked up Sarah's whittling knife. "Here."

"Give it to me." Mordecai tucked the knife in his belt, then said apologetically, "Paul, I'm sorry about this."

Paul shrugged. "No harm done. Hadn't we better get back before they decide we've been waylaid by redskins?"

Providence was standing next to the wagon, and it wasn't until the approaching party got fairly close that she realized there were six instead of five, and that the sixth was Sarah. She was so shocked that for a moment she was rendered speechless. It was Davey, already seated in the wagon, who said in surprise, "Is that Sarah with you? How did she get here?"

"She's all right, Ma," Aaron said reassuringly. Behind Sarah's back he shook his head to indicate that Providence shouldn't make a fuss.

Providence nodded back, then said quietly, "Saree? You decided to join us after all? It was such a long way. Your gown is soiled. Did you fall down?"

Sarah shook her head.

"We found her in the woods," Mordecai explained, waving his hand behind him. Then he said to his sister, "Come on, Saree. Let's go home."

It wasn't to be that easy. Sarah balked, taking a step backward and shaking her head violently. Her eyes were fixed on Davey.

Her fear of Davey was as incomprehensible to the family as were her other peculiarities, but there seemed nothing anyone could do to talk her out of it. Felicity stepped forward, took her hand, and said softly, "Come with me, Saree. We'll sit together in the back."

Sarah nodded and climbed into the wagon with her sister. Providence turned back to Paul. "We mustn't leave without wishing you well at Yale, Paul. We're sure you'll do your grandparents proud."

"Thank you, Mistress Greenhill." Paul's eyes were on Winsome. "I intend to do my best, though I expect I'll miss my friends here at home."

Later they found the door to Sarah's bedroom bolted and standing upright, but with a chink on the hinge side just wide enough to permit a slender body to slither through. She had obviously used her knife to pry off the hinges. Davey unbolted the door and reinstalled it, while Providence sat with Sarah in the parlor trying to reconstruct her adventure. But Sarah refused to talk about it, and finally Providence abandoned the questioning. As often as Sarah had run away, she'd never before tried to escape from her room, and this new behavior was frightening. Providence ended by taking the only precaution she could against a repetition. She refused, despite Sarah's pleas, to give her back her knife.

Sarah had frequently seen *the davey*'s lascivious gaze fall on Winsome and heard his lustful remarks veiled as compliments. Perhaps the others hadn't understood, but she had. *The davey* meant to seduce Winsome, and what better time or place, Sarah had concluded, than at at the Websters' party. He knew Sarah was his only adversary; the only one who recognized him for what he was and therefore the only one capable of interfering with him. So he had chosen a time when Sarah would be safely out of the way.

Once Sarah figured out what *the davey* was up to, she made plans to outwit him. She had behaved as they expected her to, refusing to attend the party and passively permitting them to lock her in her room. Then, after the wagon disappeared behind the trees, she had pried her door off its hinges and set out after them. She had finished carving the hawk, a guardian equaling, or perhaps surpassing, the power of her Indian. She considered carrying it with her, then decided to risk leaving it behind in order to travel light. The trip to the Websters, even without the burden of her Indian or her hawk, would take hours, and she must get there in time. *The davey*, she reasoned, wouldn't be able to try anything during the early part of the day, because that would be mostly taken up with socializing. They'd ask him to play the bagpipes, and he'd oblige. Then would come the eating, and it would certainly be late afternoon before *the davey* could absent himself from the festivities without his absence being remarked on.

More worrisome to Sarah had been the danger of being seen and stopped. More than once in the past she had been intercepted by well-meaning neighbors and delivered back into her mother's care. To thwart the possibility, she kept off the road and made her way across the intervening properties, climbing fences and trudging through the woods until she reached the boundary of the Webster farm.

It hadn't been long before Sarah had stumbled on Winsome and *the davey*. She hadn't stopped to think how odd it was that she should come upon them at that precise place and at that precise moment. She thought only of the grotesque scene she was witnessing. *The davey* had taken possession of Paul Webster's body—how clever of him to choose someone young and handsome—and he was sitting on the ground with Winsome in his lap. Her bodice was pulled down around her waist, and she was letting him suckle at one of her breasts while she curled round him with her head resting against his head, eyes closed and mouth slightly, dreamily, open.

He had put her into a trance, Sarah realized. Winsome would never have submitted to him unless she were powerless to do otherwise. But Sarah hadn't been powerless. She had rushed forward, thrown her arms around *the davey*'s neck, and pulled him away from her sister. Winsome had toppled backward and begun screeching (ironically, screeching not at *the davey* but at Sarah). Sarah had kicked and bitten and scratched *the davey*'s face before he finally got the better of her, straddling her and holding her down. Then, gazing up into his glistening eyes, she realized that he had tricked her. He had baited Winsome in her presence to lure Sarah out into the open, and to lure her away from her guardians. He had meant her to follow him and now he meant to kill her.

He would have killed her, too, Sarah knew, if it hadn't been for Felicity's intervention. Felicity commanded *the davey* to stop, and he had stopped. He had begun fading like an echo dying out into a whisper, and in that last brief instant when he stopped being Paul Webster and was not yet Davey Macneill, Sarah had become aware of something remarkable. *The davey* was capable of fear. He exuded it as sour as the bile in Sarah's throat when she saw what he was doing to Winsome. *The davey* was vulnerable, and if he was vulnerable, then he could not only be stopped from killing, he could himself be killed. She would do it. She would kill *the davey*, and once done, she would run away, this time successfully, to be free at last, free, alone, victorious.

What Sarah didn't know was that she had had a companion in the woods the day she went to the Websters. At the spot where she had first entered the woods, an Indian stalking a squirrel had seen her, hid from her, and then followed her.

Racing Bird, his younger Iroquois brothers, and the rest of their party were on a hunting trip and camped an hour farther north, deep in the forest, nowhere near property settled by whites. True, they had stumbled on white land a few weeks before, but, as Racing Bird knew, the whites would steal the souls of Indians with no more compunction than they stole the Indian's land, and they had cleared out quickly and put down again where it was safe.

Now, however, hunting on the edge of white territory, he had stumbled on the white woman. He had never seen any woman, white or Indian, quite so lovely. She was young. He judged her to be about his own age, which meant that she had seen about twenty-one summers. He would have been surprised to find that he had miscalculated by three years, so fresh did she seem, and so innocent. He was struck by her golden hair, which looked like strands of corn silk, and by her slender body that moved like an Iroquois girl's body, swift and graceful. But it was her face that mesmerized him. It was fragile-boned and perfectly formed, with huge eyes the color of the sky.

He tracked her through the woods and kept her in sight as she passed through the fields and climbed fences, then hid again when they encountered two more whites, a man about Racing Bird's age and a much younger girl. It had astonished him when the woman cried out in rage and rushed forward to attack the white man. The occurrence had been both unexpected and bewildering, all the more so because the woman hadn't spoken a word, but had simply thrown herself onto the man and begun grappling with him. She had pulled a knife from somewhere and attempted to stab him, and Racing Bird thought she would have succeeded had not the young girl darted forward, wrested the knife from her grasp, and thrown it away. Surely no natural woman would have fought like that—and without apparent reason.

Yet when the others came, a dark girl and two young men with identical faces, she became meek and permitted them to lead her away. It was a mystery so intriguing that Racing

Bird continued to follow them, not only back to the
gathering of white men, a risky business he ordinarily
wouldn't have undertaken, but along the path to home,
keeping to the side of the rutted dirt road as the wagon
rolled by. It wasn't until the group alighted from the wagon
and entered the house that Racing Bird turned back to the
woods, but even then he wasn't satisfied to see the last of
her and made up his mind to return.

· · *11* · ·

The days immediately following the party were peaceful,
the only noteworthy event being the commencement of
Felicity's swimming lessons. Everyone assembled in the
barnyard after supper one evening for the initial immersion,
which was to take place not in the wide stretch of
Horseshoe Cove but in the depths of the Greenhill's horse
trough. Felicity had improvised what she considered to be a
suitable bathing costume, and showed up in Mordecai's
one-piece woolen shirt and underdrawers, held by strings at
the knees and waist.

"Lissy," Providence admonished, "how can you display
yourself like that to your brothers and Davey?"

"I'm not showing anything different from what they've
got," Felicity answered. "Two arms and two legs. I don't
know why we females must always behave as if there were
something odd about our limbs."

"You could have worn your petticoat."

"I'd drown in my petticoat."

"Not in the horse trough, you wouldn't," Winsome
observed.

"I don't expect to confine myself to the horse trough
forever."

"Still," Davey interjected, "if you don't get in, you'll
never get started swimming."

Gingerly Felicity climbed into the trough and stood with her arms clasped around her chest. "The water doesn't look any too clean."

Davey flicked out a few pieces of straw.

"Isn't it too narrow?"

"It might be a tight squeeze for me," Davey replied, "but not for you."

"Either get on with it," Providence said impatiently, "or go upstairs and put on your clothes."

Felicity dropped to her knees, then to all fours, and finally she flopped down on her stomach.

"Here's what you must do," Davey instructed. "Hold your breath and put your face in the water. Count to two, then raise your head and take a breath. But when you raise it, raise it sideways like this." He illustrated. "Then put your face back in the water, then lift it out at the count of two and breathe again."

Felicity tried, pushing her head as far under as she could, then raising it high out of the water and gulping air.

"That's the idea. Now keep practicing that."

"It's hard work," Felicity gasped.

"Only till you get the hang of it."

"Davey, I think it might be better if I could learn to stroke while I'm learning to breathe. This isn't much different from ducking for apples."

"It's the best way to start."

"Davey, won't you take me to Horseshoe Cove? We can go early in the morning when no one's around, and you can swim there too. Wouldn't you like to?"

"If you're asking me if I'd like to get up out of my bed two hours earlier than usual to dunk in an icy bay, the answer's no."

"Please, Davey. Please say you'll do it."

"You're starting to turn blue, Lissy," Providence declared. "Come out of there now. That's enough for one day."

A few minutes later Felicity surveyed herself in the

bedroom mirror. Her hair was stringy and matted, her eyes were bloodshot, and her skin had puckered in a most peculiar fashion. If the first lesson were indicative of the ones to follow, learning to swim wasn't going to be so pleasant as she'd thought. But still, she would do it. One way or another, she would learn.

Hiram Sheffield stopped by the next day, cantering through the gates on horseback and hailing Providence, who was sweeping the front stoop. He was a large, successful-looking man of the variety who preach prosperity but balance acquisitiveness with charity. Sheffield supported a large family, gave to the poor, worked for the church, and was thereby forgiven his success by all but the most cynical of his neighbors.

Providence greeted him warmly. "Good day, Mister Sheffield. You picked a fine morning for a ride."

"It is that, but I'd have come out whatever the weather. I'm here with a purpose, Mistress Greenhill."

"Come into the house, won't you? Can I offer you some refreshment?"

"I wouldn't refuse a cool glass of water," he answered, swinging down out of the saddle.

A few minutes later, seated comfortably in the parlor, Sheffield confirmed the reason for his visit. "I've quit Gans Ober's mill, and I've come to ask if you're interested in doing business with me."

"We're a much smaller mill," Providence pointed out. "There are fewer of us to run the place. I'm afraid we couldn't accommodate you."

"The size of your mill isn't a deterrent. My crops are harvested on a rotating basis and in a variety of seasons. And with what I'll pay you, you'll be able to hire extra hands if you need them."

"If you're dissatisfied with the service Ober gave you, I can't imagine that we'd suit you. There are other, better equipped mills than ours, Mister Sheffield."

"I don't intend to detail my grievances with Ober, but I'll say I've come to dislike his business practices. That's why I'm proposing the switch. You have a reputation for honesty, Mistress Greenhill. You charge fairly and you deliver when you say you will."

Providence decided to be completely candid. "I suspect that you may have been persuaded to come to us by other factors."

"Such as?"

"Such as the friendship between Mordie and Barbara."

"I can ill afford to base my business decisions on such frivolities, Mistress Greenhill."

"There might be those who think otherwise."

"If you mean the Obers," Sheffield returned with a grimace of distaste, "I care nothing for what they think."

"Apparently Klaus is enamored of Barbara and jealous of Mordie."

"He has no reason to think he could ever find favor with my daughter, not with his reputation."

Providence said forthrightly, "It's my reputation I'm concerned with. Tempting as it is, I think it might be unwise to accept your patronage."

"Unwise? Most people would say you'd be a fool to decline."

"Better a fool than an opportunist."

"I won't take an answer now, Mistress Greenhill. Speak to Gans Ober, why don't you? Perhaps you'll find him as eager to be rid of me as I am to be rid of him."

Providence smiled. "I suspect that Barbara told you not to come home without my acquiescence."

"And your son?" Sheffield returned good-humoredly. "Hasn't he advised you to acquiesce?"

"Yes he has."

"Then take my advice. Go to see Ober before you make up your mind."

Providence delayed telling the twins about Sheffield's visit until they came in for the noon meal. When she said he'd been there Aaron dropped his knife and Mordecai howled as if he'd been stabbed with it. "Why didn't you call us up from the mill, Ma? What did he say?"

"You know perfectly well what he said. He offered to give us his business."

"He did that, did he?" Davey exclaimed in surprise. "I know you expected it, but I wasn't so sure."

"And you refused. Did you refuse, Ma?"

Aaron broke in before she could answer. "No matter how you feel about it, Ma, you shouldn't have turned him down without talking to us first."

"I told him that I thought people would misunderstand," Providence answered.

"Meaning the Obers," Mordecai interjected.

"I also said that we aren't equipped to handle such a large volume of business."

"We can hire another man, even two men if need be." Mordecai pushed himself away from the table and began to pace. "I'm telling you, Ma, it's not fair to pass it up without giving Aaron and me a say in it."

"Stop walking around me like a bear about to pounce, Mordie. Mister Sheffield suggested I talk to Gans Ober before I make up my mind, and I agreed to do so."

Mordecai stopped in his tracks. "Then it's not decided?"

"No, it's not decided."

The twins exchanged grins and clasped hands in a familiar gesture of accord.

Davey was the first to leave the table, and after he'd excused himself Providence called Sarah to join them. It was an established fact that Sarah wouldn't come to the table while Davey was there. Now, as Sarah sidled into the kitchen and slipped into her chair, Providence experienced a not unusual twinge of anxiety. At twenty-six Mordecai and Aaron were totally self-sufficient. Soon they would marry and start families of their own. In another few years Felicity and Winsome would do the same. But Sarah would always be dependent and need caring for. How difficult for them all and how sad for her.

Mordecai and Aaron rose to go back to work, and Mordecai broke into Providence's thoughts to say, "Ma, about the Obers. I'll go to see them with you."

"What?" she asked, still pensively regarding Sarah. Then focusing on what he said, she answered, "I'm not so sure that's a good idea."

"I want to see if Ober has the nerve to accuse us to our faces of stealing the business away from him."

"I don't want any trouble, Mordie."

"There won't be any. I promise."

"All right, then. We'll go tomorrow. Now let's hear no more about Mister Sheffield or the Obers. Saree, here, have a piece of cornbread."

· · 12 · ·

The outsized gate leading into Gans Ober's property was never shut and served no practical function except as a tribute to Ober's outsized ego. Beyond the gate the drive forked, leading on the left to an eccentric jumble of buildings that composed the family compound, and on the right to the mill with its stone foundation and its great paddles ponderously rotating in the millstream.

There was great activity in and around the mill as Ober's six sons went about their business. The activity was familiar to Providence and Mordecai, but familiar on a far smaller scale. Here there were dozens of barrels and sacks piled in the yard, and the clang and whirr of the grinding wheels was deafening. Ober, a rough man with a thick neck and broad shoulders, appeared in the mill's doorway as the wagon drew up in the yard. Providence realized that Mordecai must present a threatening appearance with his musket slung across his knees, and she called out a hasty explanation. "We saw no Indians on the road, thank the Lord. We're grateful we didn't need the gun."

Mordecai, taking the hint, placed the gun onto the floorboard before climbing down from the wagon and offering his hand to Providence. Together they walked over to Ober, who made no pretense of welcoming them. "What's on your mind, Mistress Greenhill?" he asked rudely.

"We'd like to speak to you about Hiram Sheffield."

"I've nothing to say about Hiram Sheffield."

"You know by now that he has proposed switching his business to our mill?"

"What of it?"

"We'd like you to know that we didn't influence his decision to do so."

"That's why you came here? To tell me that?"

"Yes it is. We don't want any hard feelings between you and us."

Ober's eyes darted to Mordecai. "What kind of fool do you think I am? Don't tell me your son didn't sweet-talk Barbara Sheffield into asking her Pa to make the switch."

Providence saw Mordecai stiffen and put her hand on his arm, but he shrugged it off and said in a level voice, "You and Mister Sheffield have been having trouble for a long time."

"There was no talk of him quitting my mill until now. And he wouldn't have pulled out so fast if he hadn't already made arrangements elsewhere."

"That's not true," Providence declared. "He came to us only yesterday."

"You think I believe that just because you said so?"

"We're telling you the truth, Mister Ober."

"I'll bet you are," a fresh voice chimed in. "Don't they look like they're telling the truth, Pa?"

Providence suddenly realized that, except for the slap of the mill paddles, the mill noises had ceased, and that all six of Ober's sons had gathered in the yard. Klaus, a ginger-haired giant, was leaning against the side of their wagon with his hands in his pockets and grinning maliciously. "We didn't come to fight," Providence told him.

"I know you didn't. You came to crow."

"No. We came to explain."

"So you explained," Klaus returned in an oily voice. "You never meant to steal Sheffield's business from us, just like Mordie here never meant to steal Barbara from me."

"Barbara was never your girl, Klaus," Mordecai cut in.

"Don't be too sure," Klaus suggested with a taunting grin. "Maybe she only tells you what she wants you to know."

Mordecai took a step toward Klaus, and Providence interjected quickly, "We're leaving." She stepped between Mordecai and Klaus. "We came here with good intentions, but apparently it was a mistake."

"It was a mistake, all right," Gans Ober informed her, "and it would be a bigger mistake to come again a second time."

Providence swung around to face him. "We haven't hurt you," she declared, "but I'm beginning to realize that you prefer to think we have. All right, then. I see no reason to refuse Sheffield's offer. We shall be doing business with him, and you may think what you choose. Come, Mordie, it's time we got back to the mill."

Mordecai's elation at his mother's sudden show of spirit overcame his own anger. He squared his shoulders and addressed himself to Klaus with a Gaelic cadence unmistakably acquired from Davey. "Good luck to you, Klaus. I'm wishing you good health and better luck with the ladies."

Klaus glared at Mordecai as if he'd have liked to leap at his throat, but his father restrained him with a sharp command to step aside. Klaus detached himself from the wagon, and Providence and Mordecai climbed aboard. Mordecai reached down for his gun, and as Providence clucked at the horse to start him moving, Mordecai once again laid the gun conspicuously across his knees.

They stopped alongside the road to eat the wedges of bread and cheese that Providence had brought along, then continued north for another six miles to the Sheffield farm, reaching the border five minutes before they sighted the farmhouse, a handsome brick building on the crest of a hill. Providence guided the wagon halfway up the long dirt drive and left it in a clearing where there was a tether rail and a trough of water for Jiffy.

They were met at the door by Ella Sheffield, Hiram's pretty wife, who greeted them cordially, but with her usual air of preoccupation. "Listen to that din in the kitchen," she complained as she led them into the parlor. "There are ten of them in there, my four, five hired men, and Hiram's aged mother who's quite . . ." Her voice trailed off, leaving Providence, who was acquainted with the elder Mistress Sheffield, to fill in the void.

"Strong-lunged," Providence supplied.

"Exactly. And the hired girl's sick and Hiram's out to the barn doing something or other, heaven knows what. Speaking of food, have you and Mordie . . . ?"

"We have. I carried our meal with us when we left home. We ate on the way."

"Cider then?"

"That would be refreshing."

Mistress Sheffield rushed out of the room, and a few minutes later Barbara Sheffield entered, carrying a silver tray laden with mugs of cider, a wedge of cheese, a slab of bread, a crock of honey, sundry utensils, and the announcement that "Tessie has a fever and Mama has to serve the pudding. She sent me to keep you company. She thought you'd like a taste of bread and cheese."

Providence started to explain again that she and Mordecai had eaten, but it required too much effort. Besides, she thought, knowing Mordie, he'd as soon eat again as not.

Mordecai, who had been behaving quite normally before Barbara entered the room, suddenly became tongue-tied and could barely blurt out a hello. He took the tray from her and began blundering around the room.

"Put it on the tea table, Mordie," Barbara instructed.

Mordecai disposed of the tray, then recovered sufficiently to say, "You know my mother, of course."

"Don't be silly, Mordie," Barbara returned with composure.

Mordecai gave an embarrassed laugh, misjudged the height of the chair next to the tea table, and sat down with a thump. The jar shook him back to normalcy, and within a few minutes he was spreading honey on his bread and telling Barbara about their encounter with Ober. "We told him," Mordecai concluded, "that we intend to accept your father's business and left him in a stew."

"Good for you," Barbara applauded. "He's a dreadful man. They all are, his sons, too, especially that clod of a Klaus."

Mordecai had purposely not mentioned Klaus, and now he merely said, "I've met better." He glanced at his mother who acknowledged his tact with a slight nod.

"I'm so glad you're going to accept Papa's offer." Barbara went on. "He doubted you would."

"We're going to make sure he won't regret switching to us," Mordecai declared. "We're going to do a good job for him. As a matter of fact, Aaron and I have been thinking about making some improvements in the mill." He glanced at his mother's amused expression and added hastily, "Not without consulting with you, of course, Ma."

"Lucy Wrentham was speaking of Aaron the other day," Barbara said. "She's planning a Sunday picnic to celebrate her nineteenth birthday next month, and she especially wants to ask Aaron. He'll accept, won't he? What I mean is, Lucy and I are planning to make it a foursome."

"A foursome?" Mordecai asked apprehensively.

"That is, if you and Aaron are willing."

Mordecai's poise again gave way, and he tipped over the honey crock while reaching for the cider. He righted the pot quickly. "I don't see why Aaron should say no."

"So shall I tell Lucy it's set?"

"Yes, why don't you?"

Providence shared a conspiratorial smile with Barbara while Mordecai dabbed at the puddle of honey on the table. Barbara was a charming girl and a clever one. It looked as if Mordie stood no chance at all of getting away without marrying her.

After a while Mistress Sheffield rejoined the group, and soon after that Hiram Sheffield, smelling of manure but otherwise as prepossessing as usual, ambled into the parlor. The last half hour of the visit was taken up with business, Sheffield confirming his faith in the Greenhill ability to serve him well and arranging to examine the mill facilities within the next week or so. His summer crop was already at the market, but soon his early fall crop would be ready for reaping, and he was eager to assure himself that the mill would be prepared to accommodate it. Providence promised him that everything would be done that needed to be done, and they sealed their bargain in wine, the self-confident Barbara and her fatally smitten suitor drinking from the same glass.

"I feel as if someone's spying on us," Felicity said nervously. "I wouldn't want Joss to see me."

"At six in the morning?" Davey returned. "Your friend Joss is lying in his bed dreaming of strawberry tarts. Now, you get yourself ready to swim."

Felicity, again wearing her brother's undergarment, waded back into deeper water and struck out parallel to the shoreline.

"One and breathe, two and breathe," Davey instructed. Then, as Felicity floundered, he shouted, "Kick, kick, kick." He grabbed her hands as she began to go under and pulled her upright. "Now, look, Lissy. Suppose I was pushing a wheelbarrow. Would I push it forward with my arms and then walk up to it?" He bent at the waist, stretched out his arms, then walked forward, straightening his back. "I'd look like a caterpillar doing that, wouldn't I? Well, in a way that's what you're doing. You breathe, then you stop breathing and kick, then you stop kicking and breathe. You got to do it all at once."

"It's hard, Davey."

"No harder than for fishes to walk."

Felicity had been at it from first light. The waters of Horseshoe Cove were still cold, and her teeth chattered as she stood hugging herself. "I am swimming, though, aren't I?" she challenged, trying to keep up her spirits.

"Not exactly. You're just not sinking till the count of five. Now try it again."

"Do it for me once more, Davey. Let me see how it goes."

Davey complied. He belly flopped into the water and churned out toward the middle of the pond, his bathing costume—knee britches and a shirt with the sleeves cut off—weighing him down and making him seem even more ungainly than his size and weight warranted. When he reached the halfway point, he turned ponderously and swam back. "There," he said, breathing hard. "Do you see how to do it?"

"You look like a whale flopping around in the water."

"I told you swimming's not natural to people. What do you expect? Now," Davey went on doggedly, "you see how you have to move and breathe at the same time. You try it."

Felicity said dubiously, "I think there should be more form to it, Davey. I don't see how I can win a race bobbing up and down like an empty keg."

"You can't win a race standing there shivering neither. Now, are you wanting to swim or are you wanting to get back in the wagon and ride home?"

Felicity sighed and pushed off, heading toward the center of the cove. She tried to imitate Davey's powerful stroke, slapping the water with her hands and kicking her feet. She swam a few yards, then, with an alarmed cry, collapsed and went under. Davey lurched forward and pulled her up by her hair, then tugged her back to shallow water.

"I'm not as strong as you," she spluttered. "I can't do it."

"Maybe we'd better leave it go for now."

"One last try, Davey."

"This time don't be swimming out over your head. Stick to shore."

Felicity launched herself into the water, but almost immediately breathed in when she should have breathed out, and came up choking. As she wiped the water out of her eyes she saw something move in the bushes. Before she had time to call Davey's attention to it, the bushes parted and a figure stepped out into the open.

But Davey had seen it too. "God almighty," he exclaimed.

It was a young Indian brave dressed in leather trousers and carrying a knife. He held up his hand in a peaceable gesture.

Felicity moved closer to Davey, and Davey said quietly, "Don't show no fear."

The Indian pointed with his free hand to his trousers and then began to divest himself of them. Davey, assuming the worst, quickly stepped in front of Felicity.

"What's he doing?" Felicity asked nervously as she peered out from behind Davey's back.

Under his trousers the Indian wore a loincloth, and hanging at the front of it, like a decorative codpiece, was a beaded scabbard. He stuck his knife into the scabbard, then stepped to the water's edge and dove into the pond. The water barely rippled as he sliced into it.

"Let's go," Davey muttered. "Head for the wagon."

"Wait, Davey," Felicity whispered. "Look at him. Look how he swims. I think he's been watching us. He's trying to show me how."

The Indian turned smoothly at the far bank and glided back through the water. When he reached the shallows he motioned to Felicity, then demonstrated his stroke by swimming slowly and gracefully along the shoreline.

"Look, Davey. He doesn't lift his head. He tilts it, and not all the way, either, like you said to do, but just enough to take in a breath."

The Indian accomplished his turn by twisting his body at the end of a stroke and picking up again with no break in the rhythm. When he came abreast of Felicity and Davey he stood up, pointed to his legs, then dipped back down and commenced swimming, this time holding his arms out in front of him to form a kind of prow and propelling himself only by the motion of his legs.

"He keeps his legs straight and his toes pointed," Felicity observed. "He doesn't kick the water either. He moves his feet in little flutters."

Davey took hold of Felicity's arm and shoved her toward the road. "That's enough now. Come on, we're getting out of here."

"We forgot our shoes." Felicity pulled free and ran back to recover their shoes, which sat neatly side by side under a bush. She picked them up, then paused for a last look at the Indian, who had now begun to swim for himself, turning his back on them and moving silkily into deeper water.

"Isn't he wonderful?" Felicity declared as she and Davey hurried back to the wagon. "I never saw anyone swim so well."

"Hop up there onto the wagon. You can put on your dress whilst we're riding back."

"Davey, what do you think he's doing here?"

"Later today the boys and I will have a look around the woods. If there's Indians squatting hereabouts, we'll see they take themselves off."

"He wasn't doing any harm, Davey. I don't think he's more than nineteen or twenty years old. Oh, for heaven's sake, I don't see why you're making such a fuss."

"You don't, do you? Well, you'd see why soon enough if he took a liking to your scalp."

Felicity and Davey would have been amazed to know that Racing Bird hadn't come upon them by accident. He had spent more than one night sleeping at the edge of the woods in view of the house, and when he saw Felicity and Davey leave before dawn, he had followed them. It wasn't they who attracted him, but their connection to Sarah, the possibility that they might, in some unforeseen manner, provide him with a clue to the mystery of this exotic white woman who seemed part human, part spirit. His attempt to befriend the man and the girl had been similarly motivated, and although the man had been hostile, the girl had not. Perhaps another attempt to make contact would bring him closer to learning what he wished to know.

· 13 ·

Davey and Felicity reported the encounter at breakfast. Everyone reacted differently to it. Providence, like Davey, felt that Indians in the vicinity presented a potential danger and insisted that word of the sighting be passed along to the neighbors. Mordecai and Aaron saw no more in it than evidence of an Indian trek from one hunting area to another, especially since the Indian had behaved in a friendly manner, with no hint of hostility. Winsome evidenced a lively curiosity, especially in regard to the Indian's looks and physique, while Felicity was convinced that fate had arranged the Indian encounter to coincide with her particular need, and wanted nothing more than to return to Horseshoe Cove in the hope of a second meeting.

"Absolutely not," Providence told her.

"But why not, Mama? Why must people always think the worst of Indians? If we were to give them a chance to be friends instead of chasing them away, perhaps there would be less trouble between us."

But her mother was adamant. "Where there are Indians, there's bound to be trouble."

And so, after breakfast and despite Felicity's objections, Providence and Aaron set out to make the rounds of the neighbors and to round up a party to scout the woods later that day. Felicity, instructed to wash the dishes after they left, banged around the kitchen until, predictably, she succeeded in chipping one of her mother's clay porringers.

A few days after the incident, Hiram Sheffield came to inspect the mill facilities, and a few days after that Providence hired two additional hands. One was James Wrentham, an older brother to Josiah, and the other was a man named Gustav Adler, a German immigrant recommended by Eb Bordman. Neither man would live on the premises. James Wrentham had a house and family of his own, and Gustav Adler boarded with Eb Bordman. The men would work ten hours a day, six days a week, which would go far to compensate for the heavier work load.

It wasn't long before the men and the mill were put to the test. Sheffield's second crop of wheat was soon ready for harvesting, and wagons began to roll into the mill yard one morning during the second week of September. Abraham Rouse had been there earlier, and there were already twenty sacks of meal tied, stacked, and waiting for collection. Now James and Gustav set to work to unload Sheffield's wheat into wheelbarrows and transfer the loads to the mill, where Davey and the twins would commence the strenuous task of separating and grinding. The labor continued until dusk when Davey finally called a halt. The two hired hands left for home, and Davey and the twins took turns showering under the rain barrel they had rigged up to a pole behind the mill. Later, at supper, the twins dozed off between pudding and tea, while Davey skipped his usual pipe of tobacco and retired early to his room over the mill.

The next day was as hectic as the one before, with only one break at midday, and the third day repeated the second. Then, late in the morning of the fourth day, one of Sheffield's drivers ran into the mill yard with the astonishing story that he'd been waylaid on the road and his wagon set on fire.

"Waylaid?" Aaron exclaimed. "Who by? Was it Indians?"

"Maybe. I suppose. I'm not sure," the driver answered vaguely. "They were dressed like Indians all right, with leather trousers and painted faces."

"Then they were Indians."

"They didn't exactly look like Indians. I can't say why."

"How many of them were there?" Davey asked.

"Five or six or more. I'm not sure. They were carrying muskets, but most of them hung back amongst the trees. One of them run out at me at the curve of the road about a half mile back. He threw a torch at the wagon. The horse reared. Tossed me right out onto the road without my gun, then bolted. I couldn't fight them with my bare hands so I took off, and I didn't look back but run like the blazes till I got here."

"They didn't go after you?"

"They would have caught me if they had. I was puffing like smoke out of a chimney."

"It doesn't sound like Indians to me," Aaron ventured. "Just letting you go like that."

"I agree," Davey interjected. "It makes no sense."

"It does to me," Aaron suggested. "It wasn't Indians so it must have been white men, and if it was white men, then I know which white men it was."

"The Obers," Mordecai supplied.

"That's my guess."

"Not so fast," Davey declared. "We've no proof it was the Obers."

"Why would redskins torch Sheffield's wagon?" Mordecai reasoned. "And when is the last time you heard of one Indian attacking while the rest stood by and watched?"

"It could have been white men," Davey returned. "Sure, I agree to that. But there's no saying it was the Obers. You've no proof it was the Obers and no call to accuse them."

There was no repetition of the attack, but discussion about it went on for days. The twins wouldn't be shaken from their conviction that Klaus Ober and his brothers were behind it, citing examples of the Obers' vengeful nature to prove the point. Hadn't Klaus once beaten up Charlie Temple for winning at horseshoes? Hadn't he and his brothers once unhitched the Websters' horse from in front of the church and scared it into running off? They had even once started a fire on the steps of Brank's Tavern because Brank had chased them out for being drunk. If that didn't prove which way their minds were bent, what did?

The twins had wanted to retaliate immediately, but Davey had talked them into consulting Sheffield, and Sheffield forbid it.

"Surely we're not going to let them get away with it," Mordecai argued.

"We've got no proof against them," Sheffield pointed out. "It's better to ignore them than to accuse them of something we can't prove. We'd just be encouraging them to try something else."

"That's not how I look at it," Mordecai said belligerently. "I'd like nothing better than to give Klaus reason to try something else. The next thing he tries will be the last thing he ever tries."

A week after the wagon incident, Josiah Wrentham came calling on Felicity. Providence, Sarah, and Winsome had gone into the back field to pick rose hips, and Felicity was alone when he rode into the yard astride Apple Dumpling, the Wrenthams' swaybacked mare. Felicity came to the front door to meet him.

Josiah slipped off the horse's back and wiped his face with his handkerchief. "Hot as Hades," he announced by way of greeting. "Apple lay down and tried to roll over on me twice on the way down here."

Felicity rubbed the horse's nose, and Apple Dumpling snuffled gently. "Put her under the maple, Joss. It's cooler."

"First I'd better stick her nose in the trough."

"Come on, then."

A few minutes later Apple Dumpling was watered, and Josiah had been served a glass of cider. "I've come to invite you to my sister's nineteenth-birthday party," he announced. "It's to be at Horseshoe Cove the last Sunday in September. Aaron and Mordie are coming. They can bring you with them in the wagon."

"The last Sunday in September?" Felicity repeated. "That was supposed to be the day of the swimming race. Did you purposely set the race for that day because you knew it wouldn't work out?"

"Drat it, Lissy, you set the date. I didn't. Anyway, I should think you'd have given up on the swimming race, especially after what happened to you at the cove."

"Nothing happened to me at the cove."

"An Indian spying on you in your lacy drawers? That's nothing happening to you?"

Felicity said indignantly, "He wasn't spying. He happened to be there. That's all. And I wasn't wearing lacy drawers. I was wearing"—she balked at describing herself in Mordecai's woolen underwear—"I was wearing something of Mordie's."

"Well, you're lucky that redskin didn't kill you."

"If you had seen him, you wouldn't say that, Joss. He was perfectly friendly. I would have stayed if Davey hadn't been afraid of him."

"I suppose you weren't afraid of him?"

"No, I wasn't. I hate it that people are always so mistrustful of one another. The Spanish are thieves, the French are sneaks, the Indians are savages. We're even mistrustful of our own kind. My brothers think the Obers are villains. They think we are. It makes me sick to think about it."

"It's not that bad," Joss said. "There are just as many people who get along as don't."

"I think it comes from being scared, Joss, like your being scared to race me."

"Drat it, Lissy," Josiah declared. "You can't swim. Girls

aren't built right for swimming. Their bodies aren't shaped for it, and they haven't the strength."

"You see what I mean? You're scared I'll win."

"I'm not scared of anything," Josiah returned exasperatedly. "I'm just trying to let you off easy. You think you can do anything you set your mind to, and you can't. Why do you always have to be so stubborn?"

"If you don't like it, you don't have to come calling."

"Look, I came to ask you to Lucy's party. That's all."

"Who else will be there?"

"Aaron and Mordie and Barbara Sheffield and five or six other couples, besides me and my brothers and sisters. The boys are going to go clamming while the girls pick blackberries. Then Pa's going to build a fire and we're going to roast clams and corn and eat the berries for dessert. I already asked Asa and Sam and now I'm asking you. Are you coming or not?"

"I'll come," Felicity said grandly, "but only on one condition. I want to go clamming with you, not berry picking with the girls. Do you agree?"

"What do I have to agree for? You'll do whatever you want anyway."

"And that's when I'll prove to you that I can swim," Felicity added triumphantly.

Josiah rolled his eyes heavenward, but wisely decided to hold his tongue.

·14··

Certainly it was wrong to disobey. But everyone was wrong about the Indians, and Josiah was wrong about her. She was perfectly well shaped for swimming, and she had found out by observing the Indian that swimming required more grace than strength. Given sufficient practice she'd swim as well as any man.

She left the house long before dawn, skirting the open yard as a precaution against the possibility that Davey or her mother might rise earlier than usual and see her. She headed for the grove of trees beyond the mill. By wagon, Horseshoe Cove was more than two miles from the house, but it was only a fraction more than a mile in a direct line through the woods. Once out of sight of her own property Felicity struck out boldly and with no attempt at stealth. If there were still Indians in the area, they might misinterpret the intentions of someone sneaking through the bushes. Not that she actually expected to meet any Indians. Davey, Mordie, and Aaron had combed the woods between the mill and the cove and found no evidence that Indians were camping there or had camped there anytime in the recent past. The Indian brave must have done what she was doing now, strayed from his companions to explore on his own. He'd probably walked very much farther than she to reach the cool, inviting water of the cove, and by now he was long gone.

She reached the cove in half an hour. It was still dark as she stripped down to Mordecai's modest undergarment and stepped into the water. She hadn't expected to be afraid, but there was something menacing about being alone in the blackness. She pressed her elbows close to her sides and held her clenched hands pressed up against her chest in a guarded and helpless gesture, swiveling her head to search, straining her eyes till they ached, no more capable of wading out of the water than of plunging into it.

She stood like that for a long time, making no sound, breathing lightly, and waiting for daylight. Then she heard a bird chirp and soon the chirp turned into a full-throated trill, and suddenly she could see the outline of the trees nearest her, no longer one solid mass but separate trunks and limbs. She could make out the willow tree with its leaves touching the water and the partially submerged log looking like a rough-skinned lizard. Now the full crescent shape of the cove became visible, as well as the scrub brush and brambles framing it and the rock on the far shore.

As her eyes probed the murky shadows beyond the rock, she became aware that there was something there that didn't belong. She tried not to blink for fear that the object would move or disappear, and continued to watch until gradually the object detached itself from its background, and she recognized the Indian. He was standing as quietly as she, staring back at her with the same air of suspense. The enormity of her panic only became evident as it dissolved, leaving her barely able to raise her hand in salute. The Indian returned the salute, then leaped lightly up onto the rock and dived into the water, to emerge a minute later directly in front of her. She jumped back from the splash of cold water, then recovered, smiled shyly, and said hello.

The Indian responded by beckoning her to swim with him. When he saw her hesitate he swam a few strokes to encourage her. Self-consciously she waded out until the water reached her chest, then began to swim, copying his form but unable to duplicate his effortless breathing. She tired almost immediately and searched out the muddy bottom with her toes. He stopped swimming and returned to join her. He demonstrated his method of breathing by pillowing his cheek on the surface of the water, then dipping his mouth up and down in a series of exercises that she imitated as best she could. After a few minutes he nudged her to swim again and kept her company. Now, for the first time, she was able to swim a dozen strokes, combining the body movements with the breathing, before again groping for a footing in the slippery bottom ooze.

She practiced for a time while he swam behind her or next to her and even sometimes beneath her, until, at last, he urged her to swim across the cove. She didn't think she could make it, but it wouldn't have occurred to her to refuse, and she struck out bravely. It was a long way, and somewhere partway across, she abandoned her efforts to swim gracefully and gave way to an awkward dog paddle. But she did reach the far shore, and the accomplishment was such pure and heady joy that she burst into gasping laughter as she crawled out of the water on her hands and knees.

After that meeting she joined the Indian every morning for the next six days. Then on the seventh day she returned home later than usual, too late to sneak up to her room unobserved. She hid her swimming garment under a bush. She could retrieve it later. Then she entered the kitchen. Providence straightened up from the fire and Davey looked up from the table as she entered. "I'm not the last out of bed today, am I?" she inquired brightly.

"Where did you come from, Lissy?" her mother asked. "Your hair is wet."

"I woke early. I washed my hair in the rain barrel, then I went to see if there were any deer in the back field."

"Didn't I tell you I didn't want you wandering around while there are Indians in the neighborhood?"

"Good morning, Ma," Mordecai called out as he entered the kitchen. "What's this about Indians?"

Providence pushed a damp strand of hair away from her cheek. "Where are the others?"

"Right here." Aaron came in pushing Winsome and Sarah in front of him. Sarah's entrance was Davey's signal to exit. He rose, wiped his mouth with the back of his hand, and announced his intention to feed the horses.

After he left Aaron said quietly, "Ma, you didn't bolt a certain door last night." He tipped his head toward Sarah.

Providence shook her head in annoyance. "I didn't? It's all this fuss about Indians. It's got me distracted."

Sarah mumbled something and Providence said sharply, "What about Indians, Saree?"

"He took the ax."

"What?"

Sarah didn't repeat herself but sat looking at her mother, waiting for her to register what she'd said.

"Make yourself clear, Saree. An Indian took our ax?"

Sarah's eyes flickered around the table, then she looked down at her plate.

Providence frowned and glanced questioningly at Aaron. "Do you know what she's talking about?"

Aaron shook his head and shrugged. He said to his sister, "Are you telling us you saw an Indian, Saree?"

Without looking up Sarah said, "This morning at first light, coming out of the mill. He was carrying one of our axes."

"Davey sleeps in the mill," Providence declared. "It's unlikely anyone could get in without Davey hearing him."

Mordecai said dryly, "A bear could get in bed next to Davey without him noticing."

"Bears don't steal axes," Winsome quavered.

Now they were all gazing at Sarah. "You say this Indian had an ax," Aaron queried. "How do you know it was ours? One ax looks the same as another."

"It was covered with pitch and the handle was broken off."

"You could see that well from your window?" Felicity challenged. "And in the dark?"

"It wasn't dark," Sarah insisted. "It was already light."

"She's not imagining it," Aaron interrupted worriedly. "There is an ax with a broken handle."

"Where is it kept?" Providence asked.

"It's on a hook back of the door. Maybe I'd better have a look."

"I'll go," Mordecai volunteered.

He was gone longer than expected, so long that everyone grew restless with the strain of pretending there was nothing wrong. When he came back, he came empty-handed. "It's gone. I looked everywhere. There are a couple of other axes right out in plain sight, but not that one."

"I don't understand," Providence reflected. "Why should

anyone steal a broken ax when there are sound axes to choose from?"

"Maybe because it was right by the door where someone could grab it quick and run," Aaron speculated.

Providence paled, then suddenly reached out to dig her fingers into Felicity's arm. "Do you realize that the Indian might have been out there when you were skipping around the field this morning? Now listen to me. I want you to promise me you won't leave the house again without telling someone."

"Mama, I don't believe it's true about the Indian."

"I don't care what you do or do not believe. Just promise me."

"It's so unfair to blame everything on the Indians."

"Do you promise?"

It was on the tip of Felicity's tongue to tell them about her friendship with the Indian, but her mother's frightened face discouraged her. She was trapped, with no other answer than the one demanded of her. "I promise," she said miserably. "I promise, Mama."

No one really wanted to go after the Indians. There were only a few thousand whites in possession of the narrow strip of land along the Delaware coast, while to the west lay the mysterious domain of no one knew how many savages. Were there half a dozen, a dozen, or an entire army lying in wait just beyond the white man's territory? Would it be wise for the men to abandon their homes and families and plunge into that wilderness, even into the fringes of that wilderness?

Unlike Aarón and Mordecai, most people believed it was Indians who had torched Sheffield's wagon, and they read additional trickery into the theft of the ax. The group first sighted weeks before had been decoys, a small but impudent party sent out to goad the whites into a confrontation. The same was true of the appearance of the audacious Indian brave down by Horseshoe Cove, the torching of the wagon, and the theft of the ax. It was commonly agreed that it would be a mistake to respond by going after them. The wiser course was to match patience with patience and wait out the provocations.

To the Greenhill household, defending one's own territory meant adding to the precautions already taken. The girls were restricted to the property; not only restricted to the property, but restricted to that portion of it that was in full view of the house and mill. There were half a dozen muskets in the house. The men cleaned and oiled them, and in order to publicize their preparedness, the four adult members of the household carried a musket with them whenever they left the house, even when walking between house and mill. No sneaking savage could misinterpret the import of that message.

There were additional precautions. Instead of having Davey move into the house, a strategy that now seemed shortsighted, Mordecai moved into the mill, sleeping downstairs while Davey slept in his room upstairs. That way there would be two men to defend the mill and two adults to defend the house. The chance of ambush was thereby lessened. Until the crisis was over, the adults would take turns standing watch at night as well as during meals, which were times of particular vulnerability.

Felicity was appalled by the turn of events. She, like her brothers, believed that the Obers were behind the harassment of Sheffield's driver, and although she didn't know who had stolen the ax, she thought it idiotic to blame the theft on Indians. She prayed that her Indian friend had already left the territory, or if not, that he was cautious enough to stay out of sight.

The Saturday after the theft was town day. It was usual for the men to rotate their visits to New Castle, and this time it would be Mordecai's turn to accompany his mother, while Aaron and Davey supervised the work at the mill. Ordinarily Sarah would be locked in her room while her mother was gone, but considering the unsettled situation,

Providence decided it might be better to leave Sarah in Davey and Aaron's care while she was gone. It seemed simple enough on the surface, but when Providence went to Sarah's room to propose it, Sarah reacted violently. "No," she exclaimed. "No, I won't go over to the mill."

Providence reached out to touch her, but Sarah hunched her shoulders and backed up against the clothespress. "Is it Davey, Saree?" Sarah's panicked expression made it clear that it was Davey. "He won't bother you," Providence assured her. "He'll be busy working. He won't come anywhere near you."

"No." Sarah slid past the press, felt for the wall, and inched around the room to her bed. She picked up her carved wood hawk and held it out, not as an offering, Providence realized, but as a shield.

"I can't leave you alone, Saree," Providence said firmly. "Winnie and Lissy are going to spend the morning at the mill and you must too."

"I won't, Mama. I can't."

"Well, you can't stay here."

"Then I'll go with you."

"To town? You're willing to do that? To go to town with Mordie and me?"

"Yes. Yes, I'll go."

Providence capitulated readily. The change of scene would be good for Sarah. "Get ready, then. Mordie is hitching up the wagon. Put on your bonnet and come along."

Sarah took her bonnet down from the wall peg near her door, but she refused to relinquish the hawk when Providence attempted to take it from her. Going to town was better than staying with *the davey*, but she was never totally safe anywhere, not without her hawk to guard her.

· *15* ·

The center of New Castle wasn't much more than one dirt road running parallel to the waterfront. It was certainly no rival for Philadelphia as a seaport, but it provided the commercial and social services necessary to keep the local inhabitants both civilized and sane.

Eb Bordman, portly and disheveled, was standing on the porch of his shop when Providence, Mordecai, and Sarah arrived. The sign above him, in badly spaced and faded lettering, read BORDMAN rather than BORDMAN'S SUPPLIES, or what might have been simpler without sacrificing accuracy, BORDMAN'S. Just plain BORDMAN, however, was the summation of its proprietor's character: blunt, ungracious, and devoid of charm. The two-room shop mirrored him physically, as well, with merchandise stacked floor to ceiling and spilling out both doors into the front and back yards. Eb looked at the threesome in the wagon uncertainly for a moment, then resolved the problem of how to handle what he perceived to be a delicate situation by saying, "Good day, Providence. Good day, Mordecai. I see who you brung along."

"Yes," Providence acknowledged evenly. "Sarah thought she'd enjoy the outing."

"Step down, step down. Mordie, I seen Barbara go into the cobbler's with her ma a few minutes ago. But no need to chase after them. They'll be along here after a bit."

They followed Eb into the shop, Sarah holding the hawk tightly clutched to her bosom. Eb swept one of his dozen cats off a rickety chair ("I'll sell that mouser for a penny . . . if you'll take a penny, ha, ha") and offered the chair to Providence. He added in a low voice, "Ask her if she wants to set on the barrel."

"Sarah isn't deaf, Eb," Providence reminded him.

Eb stopped short of saying what he was thinking: *No, not deaf, just daft.* He cleared off a couple of barrels and stuck a

105

boot scraper under one of them for Sarah to use as a step. "Nice bird," he told her heartily, patting the wood carving on its head. He smiled around at the others to show how well he knew how to deal with dimwits, then took the envelope Providence handed him. "For Beriah? It'll go out on Monday on the *Bristol Rose*. Should be there in a day or two unless the ship gets pirated. Now, what's on your list?"

Providence began reading it off while Eb assembled the purchases: dried fish, sugar, salt, nutmeg and cinnamon, a jug of molasses, China tea, rice flour from the Carolinas, Jamaican rum, and a small precious slab of hard chocolate to be combined with sugar to make cocoa. There was the fall and winter to prepare for, with so many yards of cambric, so many yards of wool, and so many of silk, all to be delivered to Lydia Coffin who was the local seamstress. It took a shocking amount of real coin to pay for clothes that might have been homemade, and Providence regretted that she'd never become an accomplished seamstress.

Mordecai chose certain of the items himself—tobacco for Davey, balls of twine, additional burlap, a pair of heavy shears, a dozen more necessaries—then gave them to Eb to tally. Sarah, Providence was pleased to see, remained composed. She sat quietly, not talking, but looking around interestedly, even replying politely to Eb when he asked if she'd like a peppermint lozenge. "No, thank you. I do not care for sweets."

When they finished shopping Mordecai loaded their provisions into the wagon, then spotted Barbara Sheffield marching up the dusty, unpaved street toward him. Her mother bustled along behind her looking frazzled and indignant. When Barbara caught sight of Mordecai she called out in an artificially cheerful voice, "I'm sorry we were delayed, but here we are."

"What delayed you?" Mordecai asked.

Barbara shrugged noncommittally, but Mistress Sheffield answered in a distraught voice as she joined them, "Klaus Ober, that's what."

Mordecai was immediately on guard. "What about Klaus Ober?"

"It doesn't matter," Barbara hastened to say.

"She's right," Mistress Sheffield wheezed. "He's just sour because Barbara never gave him a tumble."

"Mama, please," Barbara pleaded.

"Don't 'please' me, Barbara. It's the truth. I'm going in to get some salt from Eb." She climbed the porch steps and disappeared into the interior of the shop.

"What happened with Klaus?" Mordecai demanded.

"Don't make a fuss," Barbara said. "It was silly and unimportant. While Mama was busy at the cobbler's I went to buy some candles from Mr. Cox, and Klaus must have seen me because he followed me inside."

"And?"

"He said something about me getting Papa to quit their mill."

"You should have walked right out on him."

"I tried." Her voice was still unnaturally bright. "He blocked the door."

"Wasn't Cox there?"

"You know Mister Cox. He's such a coward. Anyway, Klaus said something to me, then Mama came along, and he let me go."

"What did he say?" Mordecai pressed.

"Ssh, there he is," Barbara suddenly murmured.

Sure enough, Klaus had just strolled out of Brank's Tavern a few doors down the street. He saw Mordecai and Barbara looking at him, and he lifted his hand in a cocky salute, then turned his back on them and began walking away.

"What did he say, Barbara?" Mordecai repeated. "If you don't tell me, I'm going to catch up with him and ask him."

"Let it be, Mordie."

"What was it?"

"It was about you and me." Her face got pink and she

added tremulously, "About how . . . how well we know one another."

Mordecai didn't bother to question her further. With a bound he leaped after Klaus. He flew down the street and grabbed Klaus by the back of his jacket, jerked him around, and smashed his fist into Klaus's face.

After the fight Providence declared that the only thing that saved Mordecai from being murdered was the fact that Klaus wasn't in town with his brothers. She wasn't impressed with the fact that Mordecai won the fight. She left the praise to Barbara. Nor was she concerned with the right or wrong of it, as was Mistress Sheffield. *He deserved what your son gave him. No one deserved it more.* All that concerned Providence was Mordecai's bloody face and the fact that he had been so foolhardy as to attack a man twice his size.

True, Klaus was much bigger than Mordecai and more than a match for him physically, but he had been no match for Mordecai's rage. In the first minutes of the brawl Mordecai had given as good as he got. Then Klaus made his second mistake, threatening Mordecai with "worse than I give Sheffield," clearly an admission that it had been he who had set the Sheffield wagon on fire. He paid for the remark with a bone-crushing blow to his nose, and the fight was over.

Moses Fairbank, the ironmonger, had rushed out into the road and helped Klaus to his feet, then dragged him into the apothecary shop. Providence led Mordecai into Eb's kitchen where she ministered to his wounds. "You were foolish to let him goad you into a fight," she scolded. "Don't you see that's just what he wanted?"

Mordecai winced as she wiped his face with a wet cloth. "He won't want it again."

"Don't be too sure. You don't think he's going to let it lay, do you?"

"You heard how he insulted Barbara, Ma."

"It isn't what he said to Barbara that made such sad work of your face."

Mordecai's lip was cracked and swollen and his grin came off as more of a grimace. He flexed his fingers painfully. "My face doesn't compare to his."

"Your mother's right, Mordie," Barbara said primly, but her sparkling eyes revealed her pride in him.

"He was spoiling for it," Mistress Sheffield insisted. "And anyway, there's nothing to be worried about now. You can see he's all right."

But Mordecai wasn't Providence's only worry. Sarah had become alarmed when the shouting began, and had taken prompt refuge in the withdrawn attitude so characteristic of her when she was upset. She was eyeing everyone with wary distrust and looking as if she'd bolt, given the slightest opportunity. Providence, afraid she'd do just that, maneuvered herself into a position between Sarah and the door.

As for Klaus, it was Eb who was the first to confirm Providence's foreboding. He came into the kitchen to report that the apothecary had patched Klaus up and that Stanton Rouse, one of Providence's near neighbors, had tied Klaus's horse behind his wagon and was taking him home to the mill. "His nose is broke and he's none too pleased," Eb announced. "He says, since you're so bent on trouble, he means to see you get it."

Mordecai, too uncomfortable to comment, grunted disparagingly, while Providence, not wishing to aggravate his distress, refrained from saying I told you so, and merely gave an almost imperceptible shake of her head.

The weather was unpromising, Davey thought, sweltering hot and threatening rain. He studied the wispy black clouds, worrying about the sacks of meal stacked in the yard waiting for pickup. If the arrangement with Sheffield worked out, he and the twins would build a protective shed before next year's harvest, but that wouldn't help today. There was going to be a storm, and Sheffield's wagons weren't due for another two hours. Davey hated to interrupt the grinding, but it was beginning to look as if they'd better tote the sacks back into the mill.

Felicity and Winsome sat on a grassy knoll between the mill and the woods. The heat made them listless and cranky, and they had whiled away the morning with half-hearted attempts to amuse themselves. "If you could be anyone you wish, Lissy, who would you be?"

"I'm quite content to be myself."

"Not me. I'd be a princess, or perhaps a poet like the poets Mama sometimes reads to us. 'I sing of brooks, of blossoms, birds, and bowers: / Of April, May, of June, and July flowers.' Or maybe I'd be a bird; a soaring eagle looking down and thinking how much grander I am than the people below."

"It's silly pretending to be someone you're not. You're always going to be plain Winsome Greenhill of New Castle, Delaware, so why waste the time imagining what it would be like to be a bird?"

"Just for the joy of it, Lissy. Besides, I won't always be Winsome Greenhill. When I marry I'll change my name. And so will you."

"I have no intention of marrying."

"And if I marry someone rich and powerful," Winsome went on, "I won't be plain Winsome Greenhill anymore either."

"If you wish to make believe, go ahead, but I have better things to think about."

"That's he trouble with you, Lissy. You're too practical to ever be any fun."

After a while Winsome proclaimed her intention of going to sit in Davey's room. "It's cooler there anyway," she said huffily, the "anyway" referring to her sister's refusal to join in her imagining game.

After Winsome left, the sky became even darker, and Felicity heard the far-off sound of thunder. It reminded her of how wrong Winsome was. Felicity wasn't immune to fun at all. She remembered how she and Winsome had loved thunderstorms when they were younger. When the wind picked up the two girls would strip to their undergarments and run outside to wait for the first splattering raindrops to turn into a deluge. The wilder the storm, the happier they were; the more thunder and lightning, the better they liked it. And their mother's repeated warnings to stay away from under the trees had only added a delightful element of danger to the adventure. She and Winsome would race around on the soggy grass, open their mouths to drink the rain, and dam the already swollen mill brook with their bodies to make it overflow. Then, when the storm ended, they would flop onto the ground, exhausted and fulfilled, to warm themselves when the sun reemerged.

"It's starting to blow up," she heard Davey call out. "Aaron, Gus, come help me move these sacks."

She watched as the men began to lug the sacks back into the mill, making no concession to the rising wind except to turn her face away from the swirling leaves and dust particles. It was while her face was turned toward the woods that she caught sight of the young Indian brave loitering near the edge of the trees. What was he doing there? Why was he showing himself so openly? As she stared at him she saw him raise his hand and beckon to her.

He shouldn't have come. She glanced quickly at Aaron and Jim Wrentham, the only men in the yard at that moment. They had their backs to her and she took advantage of the moment to rise and meander around the back of the mill. Once out of their line of vision she headed for the woods. The Indian was waiting for her, and when she came abreast of him she took hold of his arm and tugged him farther back among the trees. "You shouldn't have come," she said severely, knowing he couldn't understand the words but determined to make him understand at least the gist of what she was saying.

A stab of lightning and the ominous roll of thunder cut her words short. The Indian cocked his head and wiggled his fingers to imitate the rain, but Felicity was single-minded in her determination to make herself clear to him. "I have something to tell you," she began. "The farmers know that you and your companions are camping near here. That is, if you have companions. They believe that you're here to do the whites harm. There was an incident, you see. Some men who were dressed like Indians ambushed a wagon. They think—" She looked at his politely attentive face and wondered how she could get through to him. "Wait a minute." She dropped to her knees and picked up a twig. "Watch me. Look at this." She smoothed out a patch of earth, then used the twig to draw half a dozen stick figures, one of which she adorned with a head feather. She looked up at him inquiringly, and he nodded. She drew more stick figures facing the Indians and put a musket into the hand of one of them, for good measure showing a balloon of smoke billowing from its muzzle. "Now do you understand? You are in danger. You must go away from here."

He nodded and said something in his own language. Then he knelt down next to her and took the twig out of her hand. He erased her picture and scratched out a bow and arrow, a four-legged animal, a fish, a bird.

"I see," said Felicity in frustration, "but it doesn't matter why you're here. All that matters is why they *think* you're here." Another lightning bolt cut across the sky, and Felicity jumped at the almost simultaneous crack of thunder.

Racing Bird gazed at her thoughtfully. He knew all there was to know about Indians and whites and the animosities between them, but he didn't want to talk about that. He wished to talk about the woman he had come to call the Other. Almost all the glimpses he had had of her were through the window of her room, but the discoveries he'd made only fired his curiosity more. She was secretive and watchful. She seldom spoke, and she seemed set apart from those she lived among.

He had been close to her only once since that encounter in the woods. One night he had seen her leave the house, and he had followed her to the mill. He had been careful to stay out of sight as he watched her creep through the mill doors, but when she emerged she had stopped suddenly and turned to look at him. She held an ax in her hand, and Racing Bird had fingered his dagger, not certain whether she meant to attack him. But she had merely stood looking at him without speaking, then turned her back and walked away. He had suspected then, from her wariness, her silence, her composure, that she might be possessed of some sort of magic. And today he had been confirmed in his suspicion. He had seen her leave the house with the others of the family, and he had seen what she was carrying, a hawk carved out of wood, the Iroquois symbol of victory in battle. Why she had it, he didn't know, but that it held significance for him, he didn't question.

Rain sifted down through the leaves as the Indian used the twig to draw the picture of a woman in the dirt. Next to her he drew a hawk. Felicity shook her head. What was he trying to tell her? She lifted her hair off the back of her hot and sticky neck. It seemed hopeless. There was no way for them to communicate. She got to her feet, and he got up with her. "Please leave," she urged. "Please, please, leave before something terrible happens to you."

She turned away from him and began running back toward the mill as rain pelted the ground and burst like grapes around her feet. When she reached the open field she turned back, half afraid he might be following. But there was no one behind her. She was alone, and, thankfully, he was gone.

· · 16 · ·

"Why do you get to go to the party and not me?" Winsome complained.

"Because Joss asked me, that's why," Felicity answered.

"It's not fair."

"The Wrenthams couldn't ask everyone, Winnie. Mama's not invited. Davey's not invited."

Winsome thought it quibbling to bring logic into the argument. Surely her sister knew how much she loved parties. What possible difference could it make if there were one more person added to Lucy Wrentham's guest list. "You can say that Mama made you bring me."

"I don't tell lies, Winnie."

"But I want to go."

"I can't imagine what for. You're not friends with any of the girls, and the boys are too old for you."

"Paul Webster didn't think he was too old for me."

"You mean *you* didn't think he was too old for you. I couldn't tell you from one of his sheep the way you were following him around at his party."

Winsome felt suddenly on firmer ground. She might be two years younger than Felicity, but she was considerably more knowledgeable about boys. "That's how much you know. He told me he intends to court me as soon as it's seemly."

"Paul is gone and he'll be gone for years. You won't even know him when he comes back."

"Yes I will. He gave me this to remember him by." Winsome dipped under her collar and fished up a blue ribbon from which dangled a small gold ring. "It belonged to his mother."

"He gave you his mother's ring?"

"He begged me to take it." The truth was that Paul had bribed Winsome with the ring. He'd taken it out of his pocket and held the shining circlet just out of her reach.

I'll give you a present if you'll give me a kiss.

Where did you get it, Paul? Surely it's not yours. It's much too small to fit your finger.

It belonged to my mother. See, her initials are etched inside. L.W. for Letitia Webster.

So she had let him kiss her, and then after a while he had gone further. It had been wicked, but she hadn't minded. It had been so delicious to be fondled by those large, strong hands, to have her breast covered by his moist mouth, to enjoy the sensation of his tongue darting between her lips. What a pity Sarah had come along to spoil it. But at least by then he'd given her the ring and made his intentions clear. One day he would propose, and she would most likely accept. She would be the wife of the handsomest man in New Castle; a minister, a gentleman farmer, and someone everyone would look up to.

"He had no right to give you that ring," Felicity said reprovingly. "I should think he would have known better than to give away his mother's possessions. You ought to give it back, Winnie."

"I won't."

"I'm going to tell Mama about it."

"You'd better not," Winsome threatened. "Or else I'll tell on you too."

"Tell what? You've nothing to tell."

It was the moment Winsome had been waiting for. Relishing it, she said sweetly, "How would you like me to tell Mama you met that Indian on the sly?"

Winsome had burst into the room while her sister was dressing, and Felicity was still standing in her chemise and drawers. To conceal her shock Felicity picked up her petticoat from the chair and started to put it on.

"I saw you from Davey's window," Winsome went on. "It was the day of the storm. You went off into the woods with him. Don't pretend it isn't true. I saw you with my own eyes."

"It's none of your business."

"How could you? He's a dangerous savage. It's a wonder he didn't murder you."

"He is not a savage, and not all Indians are murderers. He's a friend."

"A friend, Lissy? Well, I never!"

Felicity took time arranging her petticoat, twisting the waistband to put the seam down her back. Finally she said calmly, "And if you tell on me, I'll never speak to you again."

"Then you'd better not tell about the ring," Winsome reiterated, this time with a little less bravado. "If you can be friends with an Indian, I guess I can be friends with Paul Webster."

"I don't intend to see the Indian again."

"You'd better not."

Felicity reached for her dress and slipped it over her head.

"Well?" Winsome demanded.

"You're not going to Lucy's party."

"I'm not talking about Lucy's party. I'm talking about the ring."

Felicity nodded and finally said what Winsome wanted to hear. "All right. I won't tell if you don't."

Since the trip to New Castle, Sarah had refused to leave her room. She wasn't permitted to have lighted candles unless someone were with her, so she spent the long hours of night sitting in total darkness. Her vigil required the utmost concentration, and she gave it obsessively, sleeping during the day when the sounds from the mill reassured her that *the davey* was occupied, and watching during the night.

But it wasn't quite night when her mother knocked on the door and came in carrying her supper on a tray. She handed the tray to Sarah and lit the candles, excusing the extravagance by saying that it would be dark soon anyway. Sarah knew perfectly well that lighting the candles was her mother's way of making herself feel less guilty, as was her insistence on sitting with Sarah while she ate. How Sarah wished she wouldn't. With her mother seated on the bed just next to her chair, she had no choice but to eat or be scolded for not eating.

"Eat while it's hot," Providence instructed. "Saree, food is important. We must eat to live." She supervised Sarah's consumption of each meal with the same irritating solicitude, breaking off in the middle of describing some inconsequential event to urge another swallow of blood pudding or another spoonful of blackberries.

Even that was easier to bear than the inevitable probing that succeeded the meal. "You haven't left your room for days, Saree. It was the fight, wasn't it? You were frightened by Klaus Ober."

"It wasn't Klaus Ober," Sarah answered.

Providence misunderstood, thinking Sarah meant that it wasn't Klaus who had frightened her, when she really meant that Klaus wasn't Klaus but *the davey*. "Then what was it?" Providence asked. "Was it the storm?"

"No. I'm not afraid of thunder and lightning."

"The Indians? There's no need to fear the Indians. It has been weeks since there has been any sign of Indians in the neighborhood."

"I'm not afraid of Indians, Mama. They take no strange forms."

"They what? They take no strange forms? What does that mean, Saree?"

When Sarah didn't answer, Providence rose from the bed, took Sarah's tray, and blew out the candles. "Perhaps tomorrow you'll come downstairs for breakfast, Saree."

Alone again, Sarah felt more secure. She was free now to take the precautions she must in order to fend off *the davey*. He had almost succeeded in tricking her. How frightened she'd been when she recognized him in the guise of Klaus Ober. So frightened that it hadn't been until she was on the way home, sitting tightly pressed between her mother and Mordecai in the wagon, that she'd realized he'd meant to frighten her into running away. And if she had run, he'd have followed. She mustn't fall prey to his trickery again. She must watch him and be ready to turn the tables on him if the opportunity presented itself.

She walked around the room checking to see that her guardians were in place. Those that faced her bed during the day were now turned to face the window. Her two most powerful talismans, the Indian statuette and the hawk, were placed directly on the windowsill. Then she dragged her chair to a spot where she could see the mill door and the yard that divided it from the house. She didn't bother to check the door. She had heard her mother throw the bolt. It was unlikely that she would forget to lock the door a second time, as she'd forgotten two weeks before. But it didn't matter. Once had been enough to give Sarah the opportunity to arm herself.

As a final preparatory act she knelt in front of the window, pried open the baseboard, and lifted out the ax with the broken handle and painted all over with pine tar. She had chosen it because it fit perfectly into the only space she had to use as a hiding place. Then she took her seat in front of the window.

The hours passed slowly. Sarah knew that her mother and *the davey* took turns standing watch during the early part of the evening, and that after midnight the twins alternated every hour until dawn. But for all their vigilance they hadn't spotted the Indian who had been trespassing on the property every night for weeks. Only she was aware of his presence, a spectral figure moving in and out of the shadows. Just before dawn, when Mordecai finished his last round and reentered the mill, Sarah saw the Indian step out from under a tree. She couldn't make out his features, but she had seen him so often that she recognized the slender body and the distinctive way he moved, so gracefully that he seemed to glide rather than walk.

She knew she was the object of his brooding gaze, as she had been for so many nights past. Why he came she didn't know, but that she was the reason he returned night after night was obvious. That he was a friend was unquestioned. That he possessed powers equal to *the davey*'s was self-evident, else how did he come and go so freely, unsuspected, undetected, invisible to everyone but her. She turned her head to regard the carving she had made of the Indian brave. Was it created from imagination or memory? From past experience or foreknowledge? Now, although she had never openly acknowledged the Indian before, she raised her hand and beckoned to him.

He watched her without moving, his face upraised and still. But when she beckoned to him a second time, he came, crossing the bridge and yard to halt just beneath her window. Now Sarah could see him as clearly as she'd seen him the night she passed within a few feet of him by the mill: tall and slender, barefoot and near-naked, carrying his bow over his shoulder with a quiver of arrows harnessed to his back. His skin was darker than her wood carving, but shinier, more like the coppery horse chestnuts she'd collected as a child than like polished wood. His hair was black, tied back with a cord, and held sleekly in place with an embroidered band across his forehead—nothing like her carving with its feathered headdress. But it was his face that confirmed her knowledge of him. She knew the feel of his chin, his nose, his brow. She had molded the cheekbones and the hollows at his temples. She had defined the lips and traced in the fine lines at their corners. He was, after all, her inspiration and her handiwork. She rose from her chair and pushed it close to the window, then knelt on the seat and stretched out her hands to him.

Racing Bird's heartbeat was wilder than drums and throbbed louder in his ears. Like a hunter tracking his prey to the edge of its lair, he had tracked this woman/spirit to the brink of revelation. When she reached out to him he floated upward on her magic, offering himself to her bewitchment. He couldn't see the color in her eyes, but he knew they contained the sky. His reach couldn't bridge the gap between them, but he knew her hands were light as air and strong as rock. She was sister to the earth and it was he, the son of chiefs, who had found her. "I wish you to come with me," he whispered to her in the language of the Iroquois.

Sarah, hearing the strange words and thinking them an incantation, was not surprised to see the yard turn suddenly light. The dark had been lifted like a cloth whipped off a pudding bowl, turning night into morning. Behind her Sarah heard her mother's bedroom door open and the sound of her footsteps on the stairs. Quickly she stood up and withdrew from the window, pushing her chair away. An instant later when she glanced out the window again, she saw that the Indian was gone. But she spoke to him anyway, words that in her own tongue matched those he had uttered moments before: "I wish to go with you."

· · 17 · ·

Winsome was relieved that the secret of her ring wouldn't be betrayed, but she was angry that Felicity had somehow gotten the better of her in regard to Lucy's party. She lay in bed the night before the party wondering how things had gotten so twisted around. She was annoyed with herself for having been so easily intimidated, and decided finally that it was Felicity and Felicity alone who stood between her and the outing. Well, she told herself, I won't stay home. I want to go, and I will go one way or another.

Winsome was the most selfish of Providence's children, with an inbred disdain for rules and a determination to flout them if they interfered with what she wanted. Wanting to attend Lucy Wrentham's party was no exception. The first problem she faced was how to get to Horseshoe Cove. She could walk, but it was hot out and if she walked she wouldn't be fresh and sweet-smelling when she arrived. No, she meant to ride. Recalling that there was a piece of canvas kept lumped in the rear of the wagon for rainy-day protection, she decided it would offer a way to conceal herself. With the twins and Felicity riding up front, they'd never notice her.

The second and larger problem was how to account for her absence. She'd be gone all day, and had to provide some excuse to her mother. If it weren't for the Indian scare, it would be easy. She would simply say she was going to walk to the Fairbank's farm to play with Asa's little sister, who hadn't been invited to the party either. However, since she wouldn't be permitted to leave the property, it wouldn't do. Besides, the family would be suspicious if she were to cheerfully resign herself to visiting Charity Fairbank instead of throwing a tantrum or sulking in her room. They expected her to kick up a fuss. Winsome considered the problem carefully, then decided that behaving as they expected might be the answer. There was nothing to be gained by throwing a tantrum, perhaps, but sulking in her room? That offered promising possibilities.

On the following morning Winsome stamped downstairs, flopped into her chair at the kitchen table, rattled her cutlery, banged her plate, then sat glowering at her sister until Felicity, exasperated, could stand no more and said impatiently, "Don't think I care in the least, Winnie, because I don't."

"I don't expect you to," Winsome returned. "Why should you care? You're going to the party. You're going to spend the day having fun with friends. You're not going to be left at home with nothing to do."

"There's plenty to do," Providence suggested matter-of-factly. "You can help me clean the house, and later on you can help me bake. It's about time you learned how to bake a pie."

"I don't call it something to do to make beds and bake pies," Winsome returned disdainfully. "Lissy's not going to learn to bake pies, is she?"

"I *know* how to bake pies," Felicity reminded her triumphantly. "I'm a good baker already."

"You think you're good at everything."

Aaron paused with his spoon in the honey crock. "It's not Lissy's fault you weren't invited, Winnie."

"She could have done something about it."

"What was she supposed to do about it?" Providence asked.

"She could have made Joss invite me."

"It's not Joss's party," Mordecai observed.

"What's that got to do with it? He asked Sam Rouse and Asa Fairbank. Joss knows me as well as he knows them."

"Now, look here, Winnie," Providence said irritably, "behaving badly isn't going to change things or make you feel better."

"Neither is baking pies."

"You can help me muck out the barn," Davey proposed.

"No, thank you."

"Are you going to eat your breakfast or not?" her mother demanded.

"I don't want it."

"Then excuse yourself and go up to your room."

"I suppose you'd like me to lock myself in my room like Sarah and never come out," Winsome challenged.

It was a remark calculated to hurt. Sarah had remained upstairs for seven days now, and Providence was at her wit's end trying to find some way to coax her down. "If you like, I'll march you upstairs myself," Providence replied angrily.

Winsome scraped back her chair and walked to the back stairs. "If you want me in my room so much, fine. I'm not coming down and I'm not going to let anyone in, so don't bother to knock."

"Good riddance," Felicity called after her.

"You don't really think she'll stay up there," Aaron scoffed. "Five minutes after we leave she'll be downstairs again looking for something to eat."

"I've had quite enough of Winnie,' Providence proclaimed. "Let her spend the day in her room and see how she likes it. She'll get no talking, no trays, and no sympathy either."

Upstairs, standing in front of her bedroom door, Winsome smiled with satisfaction, then stomped into her room and slammed the door. A few minutes later, wearing her visiting gown, she reemerged, shut the door quietly, and tiptoed to the front stairs.

Nathaniel Wrentham had unintentionally imitated the design of Horseshoe Cove by arranging half a dozen canopies in a curve around the space where he would later build his fire. He had devised the canopies out of bedsheets tied to tall sticks jammed in the sand, and although, as his wife pointed out, the canopies might not withstand an appreciable breeze, they would certainly serve their purpose adequately on a calm and sunny day such as this.

There were twenty-six guests invited to the party, a formidable group to entertain and feed for people of limited means. However, September weather was ideal for an outdoor picnic, still warm enough to allow for wading in the bay, yet not too warm for an afternoon campfire. There were clams aplenty, the digging of which would occupy the boys and feed the party. And to divert the girls there were, adjacent to the beach, late-blooming blackberries ripe for the picking. In other words, without much outlay, the Wrenthams had planned a festive occasion; one that promised pleasure and good company for everyone invited.

Because of the Indian scare, almost all of the young people had been prevailed upon by anxious parents to team up and come by wagon. Only one of them, Enoch Dell, had arrived on horseback. Sam Rouse and his sister, Anne, brought Barbara Sheffield. Matthew Taft drove Alice Sibbes and Timothy Brace; Nancy Rhodes and Rebecca Pool had come with Philip Goodbody and Asa Fairbank. The twins and Felicity reached the picnic site almost simultaneously with the rest of the guests and happily joined the commotion.

Winsome had fallen asleep in the back of the wagon, but she woke with the noise. In order to heighten the dramatic effect, and lessen the possibility that she'd be taken home, she waited for the twins to unhitch the horse and tether him to a tree before she tossed off the canvas and jumped to her feet. "Good morning," she called out brightly, bestowing a self-satisfied smirk on her astonished sister and brothers.

"Winnie!" Felicity exclaimed.

"How did you get here?" Aaron demanded, ignoring the obvious.

"Damn," Mordecai said in disgust. "I thought I heard something in the back of the wagon. I should have stopped to see."

"That was a really stupid thing to do, Winnie," Aaron admonished. "What's Ma going to think when she finds out you're gone?"

"I said I wasn't coming out of my room today," Winsome reminded him.

"You know very well Mama wouldn't let you go all day without eating," Felicity scolded. "She'll be scared to death when she finds you gone."

The discussion that ensued was heated, noisy, but relatively brief, with Aaron saying finally, "Well, Mordie, which of us is it to be? Do you take her home, or do I?"

Mordecai said gruffly, "I'll take her." He patted the horse's head and began untying his reins, at the same time casting a rueful glance across the clearing toward Barbara Sheffield.

"Wait a minute," Winsome pleaded. "You don't have to take me. If Mama's angry, she'll send Davey."

"Mama doesn't know where you are," Felicity declared.

Winsome cast around for a reasonable lie. "She will if she goes into my room. I . . . I left her a note. I told her what I was going to do. I asked her to please let me stay."

"Is that the truth?" Mordecai challenged.

Winsome, knowing that he wanted to believe her, called upon her skill at playacting to convince him. "I said I wouldn't complain about being punished. I even said I'd do Lissy's chores along with mine for a whole month if Mama let me stay." This last claim was something Winsome tacked on to appease her sister, who was the only one of the three still glaring at her. "So you see, Mama might let me stay. And if she doesn't, she'll send Davey for me, which means you needn't bother either way."

"Davey's got better things to do," Felicity remarked.

"So have I," Mordecai added, directing another soulful glance at Barbara Sheffield.

"I could take her," Aaron said dubiously.

"Lucy would be disappointed," Winsome argued, inspired by the sight of Lucy walking toward them.

Aaron half-turned and Lucy waved. She was wearing a new frock, pink muslin embroidered with green leaves, and she had green ribbons threaded through her blond braids. Not so high-spirited as Mordecai's Barbara, she was nonetheless extremely pretty as she came up to greet them. She welcomed the group warmly, including Winsome with the rest, and it was this ready acceptance of an additional guest that decided the issue. Aaron and Mordecai exchanged shrugs and Felicity shook her head in disapproval, but no one said anything further about taking Winsome home.

The first hour of the party was given over purely to socializing. Barbara and Mordecai, Aaron and Lucy, and others among the guests who were sweethearts occupied themselves in conversation, while the less romantically committed indulged themselves in games of blindman's bluff or sack racing or "skying a copper"—that is, tossing pennies for heads or tails—or hide and seek. Felicity accepted Joss's invitation to pair off for the sack race while Winsome turned down both Asa Fairbank and Sam Rouse, dismissing them summarily with the explanation that she didn't play with children.

Winsome had something else in mind. She had her eye on Enoch Dell, the handsome nineteen-year-old son of John Dell, the horse trader. At the moment she spotted him, Enoch was engaged in conversation with Alice Sibbes. Winsome's eyes narrowed as she studied the pair: Alice leaning against a tree and looking adoringly into Enoch's face, Enoch smiling down at her. Alice was pretty, Winsome thought, but not nearly as pretty as she. It shouldn't be difficult to catch Enoch's eye.

"Winnie? Good morning. When did you get here?"

Winsome turned to find Timothy Brace at her elbow. Timothy, a big, awkward, plain-featured young man, was habitually alone at parties and always eagerly seeking company. Winsome said pointedly, "Why, Timothy, hello. I was just thinking how odd it is that Enoch is taking up Alice Sibbes's time instead of you."

Timothy looked perplexed. "What do you mean?"

"Everyone knows Alice is sweet on you."

Timothy's homely face lit up with hope. "Who told you that?"

"Rebecca Pool."

"I don't believe it."

"I suppose you don't, else you wouldn't leave her to Enoch Dell."

Timothy scrutized Alice and Enoch doubtfully, then ventured the comment that if Alice liked him, she'd never made any attempt to show it.

"Do you like her?" Winsome asked.

Timothy said gruffly, "As much as I like anybody, I suppose."

"Because," Winsome went on unperturbedly, "if you like her, you've never shown it either." It was fairly safe for Winsome to assume that Timothy did like Alice, or at least that he would like her given any encouragement. Poor, lumbering Timothy couldn't afford to be discriminating. "Timmy, I think Lissy's looking for me. I'd better go see what she wants."

Shortly afterward Winsome saw Timothy sidle between Alice and Enoch with a greeting that was at once too deferential and too familiar, then launch into loud conversation. A look of glazed resignation crossed Alice's face and Enoch, murmuring an excuse, began to walk away. Winsome intercepted him. "Enoch, wait."

"What? Oh, hello, Winnie."

Winsome noticed that Alice was glaring at her, and she tossed her head as she took Enoch's arm. "Could I walk a way with you, Enoch?" She dropped her voice to a whisper. "Isn't he awful? He's been following me ever since I got here. Maybe he'll leave me be now that he's found Alice."

When it was time for the boys to clam and the girls to go berry picking, Mister Wrentham informed them all that there would be prizes. For the most berries picked there would be linen dress collars embroidered by Mistress Wrentham, and for the most clams dug, whittling knives. Felicity's announcement that she would clam rather than pick caused consternation on the parts of Mordecai and Aaron, who flatly forbade it. "You've got nothing to wear," Aaron gave by way of excuse.

"Yes I have."

"If you're talking about my underdrawers," Mordecai declared, "they'll not do. I'm not going to have my sister wading around in my underdrawers."

"I fixed them. I've sewn a skirt onto them. It took me two nights sitting in my room to finish in time."

"My underdrawers with a skirt sewn on? I'll say not."

Felicity took her case to the Wrenthams. "No harm in it that I can see," Mister Wrentham told the twins. "She might get wet, but the sun will dry her out soon enough."

"She's not proposing to traipse around in her bare skin," Mistress Wrentham added. "If she has something to wear, why shouldn't she clam? For that matter, any of the boys who would like to berry are welcome to do so."

The Wrenthams carried the day, and Felicity went behind a bush to slip out of her dress. Underneath she wore Mordecai's woolens, with a brief petticoat sewn onto the waistband that made it resemble a pair of aproned underdrawers. If not exactly becoming, the costume was at least modest, even Mordecai admitted that it was unrecognizable as underwear.

The clammers were to work in teams of two with a bucket between them, and it seemed natural that Josiah should partner Felicity. They walked around the crescent of beach to a spot well away from the other clammers and entered the water. The water was clear and sandy in its depths but slimy in the weed-filled shallows, and they waded out gingerly, towing the bobbing bucket between them. They began feeling for the smooth-domed clam shells, burrowing down into the bottom sand with their toes and reaching underwater to retrieve the clams and drop them into the bucket. The cove was a favorite spot for clammers, and the pickings were poor. After twenty minutes they had found only four clams. "I guess we didn't choose such a good spot," Josiah noted. "At this rate it'll take us an hour to pick up half a dozen."

"We don't have to stay here," Felicity suggested. "Let's cross the spit and clam on the other side."

Josiah didn't like the idea and shook his head. "It gets deep too fast over there. Besides, the spit is rocky. There's hardly any beach, and I'm not keen to cut up my feet crossing it."

"We'll walk around in the water."

"The rocks jut out too far. The water's deep."

"Then we'll swim."

"You can't swim, Lissy," Josiah reminded her.

"I can so." Felicity gave him a push to get his attention. "I can swim, Joss. And it's only a short distance around the point."

They were very near the mouth of the cove. A jumble of moss-covered rocks marked the point. And Felicity was right; it wasn't very far around them. Nevertheless, Josiah was still hesitant.

"I said I can swim," Felicity repeated impatiently, "and if you won't come with me, I'll go alone."

Aaron suddenly called out "One dozen!" and Mordecai, his partner, answered with "One dozen and one!"

"There," Felicity declared excitedly, "they're ahead." She let go of the bucket and began slogging toward the open bay. Just short of the rocks she stopped in chest-deep water, ducked under, and emerged holding up a clam. "I told you," she said delightedly. "It's going to be better on the other side."

Reluctantly, Josiah trudged after her. "A lot of good it did me to roll up my pants," he complained. "It'll take all day to dry off."

Felicity peered inside their bucket. "We've got five clams," she said. "Put them in your trousers pocket, and I'll hook the bucket handle over my shoulder."

"I'll hook the bucket handle over *my* shoulder," Josiah amended. "You just concentrate on swimming."

Felicity waded out until she was parallel to the rock outcropping, then began to swim. The water was calm, but she wasn't quite as confident in practice as she made out in speech. She stuck close to the rocks, preferring to risk scraping an elbow or knee to panicking with nothing to grab onto. Josiah was just behind her as she rounded the point. She wanted to get all the way around without having to stop, but it was farther than she'd supposed, and she realized she couldn't make it without stopping to catch her breath. She reached out to grab onto a rock, and at the same instant she heard Josiah say sharply, "Wait, Lissy. Stop."

Since she had no choice anyway, she clung to the rocks, breathing heavily, while Josiah treaded water next to her. "Indians," he whispered. "There are Indians on the other side of the spit."

Felicity peered over the rocks. There were, indeed, Indians squatting at the water's edge. She counted ten of them, and she wasn't surprised to see that one of them was the Indian brave whom she had befriended. It was apparent that the Indians had also been clamming. There was a mound of clams in front of them, and they were prying open the shells with their knives and eating the clams raw. A few yards away, lying in the grass, there were bundles of layered animal hides strapped together with leather thongs.

"Come on," Josiah urged, "we've got to warn the others."

"They're not doing any harm, Joss."

"If they knew there were whites here, they'd come after us."

"Do they look like a scalping party to you?"

"How do I know what a scalping party looks like?"

They watched as the Indians silently and methodically reduced the pile of clams to a shamble of shells, then rose, gathered up the shells, and carried them into the water for dumping. They washed their hand and faces, then began gathering up their belongings. "They're getting ready to return to their tribe," Felicity whispered.

"If I had a musket, I'd speed them along."

"Don't say that, Joss. They look peaceable enough."

"One of them could be the Indian who scared you the day you came down here with Davey. Have you thought about that? Come on, we're going to tell Mister Wrentham."

Felicity held him back. "No, Joss. Look, they're leaving. Let them go."

The Indians had shouldered their bundles and were walking toward the woods. Felicity noticed that it was the young Indian brave who took the lead, with the others dropping into line behind him, and she wondered if he held some special status among them. It was rather sad to think that she would never know any more about him than she knew now, and she gazed after him wistfully as he and the others disappeared into the woods.

"Somebody should go after them," Josiah insisted. "They may be planning trouble."

"Don't be an idiot," Felicity snapped. "They've obviously been on a hunting expedition, and now they're headed home. Anyone can see that."

"Maybe, but I still say we should let the others know."

"It will ruin the party for everyone."

"It's already ruined for me."

"Joss, if you tell, you'll never be my friend again."

"Drat."

"I mean it, Joss. I really mean it."

Josiah was finally forced to concede the unlikelihood of the Indians conducting a massacre weighed down with animal hides, and against his better judgment was persuaded to say nothing. It was a victory for Felicity and one that gave her satisfaction, but no great pleasure. The Indian brave was gone, and she hadn't had the opportunity to say good-bye.

Things weren't working out as Winsome planned. Her strategy to get Enoch's attention had succeeded, but her attempt to hold it fell flat. He was polite, but patronizing, immune to her looks and bored by her conversation. When finally he suggested she go look for someone "to play with," she walked off in a huff.

Things didn't improve later when, unfortuitously, Winsome was paired with Alice Sibbes for the berry picking. Alice was obviously no more pleased by it than Winsome, and for the first few minutes in the berry patch they worked side by side without speaking. The pails were large (it was Mistress Wrentham's practical decision to have the girls pick a sufficient quantity to stock her kitchen larder as well as feed the picnic), and the work monotonous. After a while activity lagged, and Alice broke the silence by saying peevishly, "Who invited you today, Winnie?"

"Lucy."

"No she didn't. I asked her."

Winsome, sensing the start of something unpleasant, kept silent.

"You like the older boys, don't you?" Alice said next.

"What boys?"

"Paul Webster, for instance, and Enoch Dell."

Winsome felt at a disadvantage. She was three years younger than Alice and not very adept at sidestepping unwelcome questions. "What business is it of yours?" she said defensively.

"I saw you talking to Enoch. What were you talking to him about?"

"Nothing in particular."

"You were whispering in his ear."

"Leave me alone," Winsome answered ungraciously. "I don't have to tell you anything."

"Was it about me?" Alice persisted.

Winsome wondered what she was expected to know about Alice that was worth repeating to Enoch. "I don't tell tales."

"Because if you heard something about me, from, say, Paul Webster, something unkind, well, it's simply not true."

So that was it. Winsome began to feel a little less intimidated. "Why are you afraid of what Paul Webster might say?"

Now it was Alice's turn to become wary. Seeing that they were standing apart from the others, she said in a low voice, "Don't tell me Paul didn't get fresh with you, Winnie. I saw you the day of his picnic. When you came back from walking with him you were pulled to tatters."

"That's not true," Winsome answered. "Paul isn't like that."

"Oh yes he is. He's a nasty pig. I wish I had known it before I let him call on me."

"When did he call on you?"

"He came calling a few months ago. Later he said nasty things about me to Rebecca Pool. I thought he might have talked to you too."

"I don't believe you. I think it's rude to say such mean things about Paul."

Their discussion, carried out in soft voices, nevertheless attracted the attention of Lucy Wrentham and Rebecca Pool, who had moved closer to them. "Did I hear you mention Paul Webster?" Rebecca called out.

Neither Winsome nor Alice was eager to include anyone

else in their conversation, but some sort of answer was expected. "We were talking about the Websters' picnic," Alice answered.

"Oh that," Rebecca remarked. "That was the day I fell out of the hayloft and sprained my wrist. I was just as glad to miss the picnic."

"The only thing good about that day," Lucy added candidly, "was celebrating Paul's departure."

Alice couldn't keep herself from nudging Winsome and murmuring, "You see? I told you."

"You're being unfair," Winsome declared. She felt as if they were ganging up, not on Paul Webster but on her for being favored by Paul Webster. "Paul is a very agreeable person."

"You *like* him?" Rebecca said incredulously.

"I like him and he likes me."

Lucy laughed. "Oh, yes, I'm sure he likes you. He likes all the girls, especially from the neck down."

"Lucy!" Rebecca exclaimed in mock horror.

"Well, it's true, isn't it? One afternoon last year he came calling on me. When Mama left the parlor he tried to kiss me, right in front of Daniel and Phoebe too. Then he put his hands on me. Don't ask me where."

"You never told me about that, Lucy," Alice interjected.

"I had to slap him, and even then he didn't leave until I said I'd call Papa. Papa would have made him—"

"Halt!" Mistress Wrentham called loudly from among the bushes. "It's time to halt!"

Alice poked Lucy and Lucy nudged Rebecca. "That's exactly what Papa would have said," Lucy whispered, giggling.

Winsome eyed them with disgust. How could they talk about Paul like that? She was tempted to tell them that whatever they thought of Paul, his intentions toward *her* were honorable, that he'd even given her tangible proof of his affection in the form of his mother's ring. Forever afterward, she was thankful that she didn't speak. It was only two or three minutes later, as the girls made their way back to the beach, that Lucy said, "You know, there was something else I never told anyone about Paul Webster. He stole a ring of mine, a gold ring with my initials inscribed."

"He did?" Alice asked in a shocked voice. "Are you sure?"

"I was sewing when he came calling. I had taken off the ring and put it on the lid of the sewing box. Later it was missing. I didn't dare accuse him, but I'd seen him looking at it, and I'm sure he took it in revenge for my slapping him. It wasn't worth anything to him except that its loss would hurt me."

Winsome felt the color suffuse her cheeks. Not Letitia Webster, but Lucy Wrentham. That's who the initials referred to. She reached up instinctively to touch the ribbon around her neck. Thank heavens she was wearing the ring tucked inside her dress and not outside where it most surely would have been seen. What a ninny she'd been, what a stupid, silly fool.

· · *19* · ·

Midday came and went, and still Winsome didn't come downstairs. Providence began to feel bad, reminding herself that if Winsome were spoiled, it was she who had spoiled her. She hoped that hunger would draw Winsome out of her room for the midday meal, but neither the odor of sizzling sausage nor the kettle's singing was lure enough to bring her down. Finally, after Davey finished eating and left the house, and Sarah had been brought her tray, Providence knocked at Winsome's door. There was no response, and Providence rapped harder. "Winnie? Winnie, if you want your dinner, come downstairs."

She waited for a moment, then pushed on the door,

somewhat surprised to find it unlatched. Winsome's bed was rumpled, the doors of her wardrobe were open, and the dress she'd worn to breakfast lay in a heap on the floor as if she'd melted inside. "Whatever—" Providence picked up the dress, shook it out, then looked around the room in perplexity. Winsome's room was small, originally a nursery attached to the master bedroom, with only one exposure, a window that faced the front yard. Providence went to the window and looked out. When she saw Winsome wasn't in the yard, she began to feel uneasy.

She looked at the dress she was holding, then tossed the dress onto the unmade bed and began rummaging through the wardrobe. It took only a minute to ascertain which dress was missing. It was the yellow cambric, her visiting gown, that was gone. Providence glanced at the bonnets on the shelf above. Sure enough, the yellow skimmer was gone as well.

Providence shook her head. Winsome wouldn't dress up for no reason. In logical sequence Providence's thoughts proceeded from Winsome to the twins to Felicity and finally to Lucy Wrentham's picnic. That was it, of course. The performance at the breakfast table, the bad temper, the manipulations, the angry retreat, had all been part of a plan—rather a clever plan for Winsome, Providence was forced to admit—but absolutely unforgiveable. Certainly she must have known she'd upset everyone, but, as usual, Winsome had been more interested in her own pleasure than in the trouble she might cause. What's more, Providence suddenly realized, she had left the property. Winsome knew how dangerous it was to wander the countryside unprotected, yet she had deliberately disobeyed Providence and set out for Horseshoe Cove on foot.

Frightened now, Providence went looking for Davey. She found him in the barn and told him what had happened.

"By now she's most likely there," Davey said calmly. "So don't worry yourself."

"I don't think she is there. If she had shown up, one of

the twins would have brought her home again. They wouldn't have let her stay knowing how I'd worry."

"Winnie's a quick lass to make up a story. She probably figured something out to tell them."

"No, Davey. No, I don't think so. You've got to go look for her."

Davey, for all his reassurances, was looking worried himself. With an effort to minimize the situation he said lightly, "Well, I'm just as glad to leave off the mucking. Give me a minute or two to saddle up the horse, and I'll ride over to the cove and fetch her."

Given the ride to and from Horseshoe Cove, plus the time it would take Davey to pry Winsome away from the party, Providence estimated that he'd be gone for at least thirty to forty minutes. It might be longer if he had to stop to speak to the Wrenthams. After he left, Providence wandered around the house restlessly, then decided to walk down to the gate to wait for them. She took a musket with her, but she was preoccupied and forgot that she was leaving Sarah unattended, and with her door unlocked.

The deviation from Sunday routine had made Sarah suspicious. When the twins and Felicity left the house, then Winsome disappeared, and finally *the davey* had ridden out of the yard, she concluded that the reckoning was at hand. She had been in a state of preparedness for days, knowing *the davey* was waiting for that one unguarded moment to pounce, but her senses had become blunted by exhaustion, and she began to wonder if she would recognize the moment when it came. Now she had recognized it, and there was nothing left to wonder about except her ability to meet it.

She suspected that since *the davey* had sent the others off, he would also send her mother away before coming after her. Sure enough, soon after *the davey* left, her mother came out of the house carrying her musket. Sarah watched as she walked down the dirt drive and disappeared around the curve leading to the road. Then she got up and went to the door, opening it a crack to listen for anything out of the ordinary. The house was quiet. She rearranged her guardians, putting some in a half circle around the open window and some facing the door, then retrieved the ax from behind the baseboard and put it and the hawk on the windowsill. All her precautions made, she again took up her post by the window.

Finally he came. She spotted him at the edge of the woods, partially camouflaged by the trees. She got up quickly and backed away from the window. He would be disconcerted to see the window empty for the first time in weeks. She flattened herself against the wall and spied on him as he struck out across the field that lay between the woods and the mill. He entered the mill yard, stopped to look around, then cocked his head to listen before climbing the outside steps of the building.

Picking up the ax and the hawk, Sarah went downstairs and slipped out the kitchen door. She circled the house and then darted across the backyard to the mill brook. Not bothering with the bridge that could be seen from *the davey*'s window, she hiked up her skirts and waded through the calf-deep water, then once on the other side sought the protection of the building wall. She clung to the wall as she crept toward the stairs. Then, realizing that she would be hampered by the hawk, although she still needed its protection, she stopped, put down the ax, and stood the hawk in the grass facing *the davey*'s door.

"Well, if it ain't the crazy girl."

Sarah whipped around to face the open door of the mill. *The davey* was standing just inside. It didn't surprise her to see that he'd again taken on the guise of Klaus Ober, complete with a dirty gray bandage patched across his nose, but she didn't know how he had come down the stairs without her seeing him.

"I spotted you from the window," he said, jerking his chin upward. "I thought they kept you locked up."

Sarah made a tentative move toward the ax, but he anticipated her and reached out to grab her arm. "I thought you was up to something. That's why I snuck down to surprise you." Still holding her arm, he pulled her into the mill. "How'd you get loose? Where's your ma?"

There seemed no point in answering, so she didn't. *The davey* knew perfectly well where her mother was.

"I guess she went to the Wrentham's picnic along with the rest. What about Davey Macneill? Ain't he here lookin' after you?"

Sarah tried to pull free, but *the davey* tightened his grip. "All the better if he ain't. It makes it that much easier. I only have to worry about keepin' you quiet."

"I'm not afraid of you," Sarah blurted. "There are stronger forces than *the davey*."

She felt his hand tighten on her arm, and she winced as he twisted her arm behind her back. "What did you call me?"

She tried not to answer, but she cringed as he dug his fingers into her arm. "*The davey*," she whispered.

"Davey? You think I'm Davey Macneill? You're as daft as they say."

"I haven't told," Sarah said. "I've kept the secret, but that doesn't mean I don't know what you are or what you intend to do to me."

He frowned, then suddenly his frown cleared, and he smiled a chilling smile. "So that's it, is it? That's what Davey Macneill's hiding behind that holy pure act. He's taking his pleasure from the crazy girl. And maybe from the girl's ma too. That's the rumor goes around from time to time. Now it looks like the rumor's not half the truth of it."

She tried again to free herself, but he was holding her too tightly. "I come to burn down the place," he informed her, "but I'm in no particular hurry now I see there's nobody here but us."

He pulled her closer and tried to kiss her. She twisted her head away and felt his moist lips on her cheek. "Later on, you tell them it was Davey. You say Davey was just taking his pleasure of you. You hear me? That's what you tell them."

Sarah tried to fend him off, but her struggles were futile. She caught the scent of him as he pulled her onto a pile of wood and grain sweepings. It wasn't only the sour odor of sweat she smelled, but the ancient, fetid odor of sin. It overwhelmed her and inebriated her so that she lay helpless as he fumbled with her clothing and swarmed over her with his seeking hands.

She lay as if drugged while he stripped her and arranged her limbs, arms over her head, legs outspread. She watched him as he exposed himself, and she received him without a murmur, even after the initial thrust when, master at the Devil's work, he forced himself deep inside her. Then, gradually staring into his glazed eyes, she realized that his power, as well as his evil, was flowing into her body. She could feel him grow weaker and herself grow stronger. It became imperative to suck him dry, to absorb the evil and make it her own. He grunted with surprise as she wound her legs and arms around him, imprisoning him within her. He tried to move, but she held him still, dug her nails into his back, gazed at him with wild, elated eyes, and then forced him to climax.

"Whore," he growled hoarsely. "Damned whore." He wrestled free, pulled back his fist, and struck her full in the face; then sat back on his haunches, recovered his balance, and staggered to his feet.

She tasted blood in her mouth and fought her faintness to keep her eyes fixed on him as he swayed over her. "Tell them Davey done it," he said. "Understand?" He kicked her in the side and forced her to answer. "Who done it?"

"The davey."

"That's right. It was Davey done it." He buttoned his trousers, and she turned her head to watch as he walked back into the recesses of the mill. Moments later she smelled something burning. Flames licked up from the grain bin, and *the davey* stood with his back to her, watching. Shakily, she got to her feet, and without bothering to wipe away the blood running down her chin, went for her ax. Now, she told herself, it was her turn.

· · 20 · ·

The Indians had burned down the mill and kidnapped Sarah. Providence soon discovered that one of Sarah's woodcarvings was also missing; the hawk she'd carved out of white ash. The image it brought to mind of Sarah clutching the hawk as a terrified child might clutch a doll only added to the horror. But nothing was so shocking as Winsome's revelation that Felicity had known there were Indians loitering near the property. At first Providence hadn't believed her. She thought the story was something Winsome made up to lessen her own guilt, but Felicity confessed and Winsome was vindicated. Yes, Felicity had known about the Indians. She had met the Indian brave on more than one occasion.

"Didn't you know it was wrong?" Providence demanded. "Didn't you understand the danger? Didn't you realize that you were providing them with opportunities to spy on the mill, to choose their moment to strike?"

The answers to those questions were obvious, succinct, and inexcusable. Even after her mother calmed down and tried to make amends to her for the impromptu outburst, Felicity remained inconsolable. She had, through her thoughtlessness, brought about a calamity of such outsized proportion that she deserved neither understanding nor forgiveness. For days afterward she would hide in her room like a wounded animal curled in its den.

The twins, Davey, and a party of neighborhood men searched for Sarah that first day, but the search proved fruitless, and hard on its heels came word that Klaus Ober was also missing. There were those, knowing Klaus's intemperate ways, who thought he'd simply taken off, but majority opinion had it that he, too, had been set upon by the Indians and either murdered or taken captive. A more extensive search was organized, and the second expedition rode deeper into the wilderness north of New Castle to look for Sarah and Klaus. This expedition was composed of fourteen local men, including four of the Ober boys, as well as Aaron, Davey, and Mordecai. It was a search that was to end in still another tragedy.

Ironically, three days after they first set out, the party was attacked, not by the Indians they were tracking, but by a band of white outlaws. Two of the men were killed in the ambush; Asa Fairbank's uncle, Caleb, and Herman Ober, one of Klaus Ober's brothers. In addition, seven more were wounded, one of them mortally, and that one was Davey Macneill.

The twins brought Davey home, still alive but delirious and with wounds from two bullets that had penetrated his chest and nearly severed his left arm. That he survived the journey back seemed miraculous and gave hope that he might recover. Providence sat with him day and night, bathing his wounds and spoon-feeding him with soups and teas and concoctions of beef blood and brandy, and for a time he rallied. They all prayed for him, and it seemed to them that their prayers must be answered since God in his mercy could not pile anguish on anguish, or expect them to bear more than they had already bore in their loss of Sarah. But although Davey held on for nearly a month, stamina alone was insufficient to overcome his terrible debility, and on the second day of November in the year of 1744 he died.

Beriah arrived two weeks afterward. He had postponed his wedding until summer and left his print shop in charge of his future father-in-law, who would see to its supervision until his return. Providence protested that he mustn't neglect his well-being for theirs, but she protested weakly because having him at home helped immeasurably to fill the lonely gap in their lives. His presence was a comfort. As the eldest son he commanded automatic respect, but he was appreciated beyond that for his mature judgement and his mastery of practical considerations. They looked to him to take charge.

And take charge he did. The mill must be rebuilt and the Greenhill credit reestablished. He called on their customers—the Rouses, the Websters, the Pools, and the Sheffields—to ask for their support. All of them agreed to help with the restoration of the mill, and some of them, Hiram Sheffield in particular, lent money.

At first the family, still stunned and grieving, left it to Beriah to make all their decisions for them. But his strength soon conveyed itself to them, and they all began to pitch in, so that gradually some semblance of normalcy was obtained. By mid-December the mill was rebuilt. By mid-January Beriah began to talk about returning to Williamsburg, promising to rejoin the family late in spring for another visit.

As it was to turn out, however, it wouldn't be Beriah who rejoined them, but they who would join him, since Providence had already begun to consider moving to Williamsburg with Felicity and Winsome. Living would be hard in New Castle now that there were debts to pay, no money for hired hands, and only Aaron and Mordecai to recoup their losses and feed them all. Winsome, always so carefree in the past, had developed an absolute terror of going anywhere, and Felicity, the biggest worry of all, could not be shaken from her state of melancholy. All in all, it seemed to Providence that it might be a wise move to start their lives afresh in another city. When, in March, Mordecai proposed marriage to Barbara Sheffield, and Aaron, not to be outdone, proposed marriage to Lucy Wrentham, Providence made up her mind. Beriah would come for the double wedding in June. Afterward they would go to Williamsburg to attend his wedding, at which time she, Winsome, and Felicity would remain to take up residence.

* * *

A dozen times a day Racing Bird sought her out to reassure himself of her presence. A dozen times a day he offered a prayer of thanks to the gods for letting him be the one to deliver her to the tribe.

It had been he who had first caught the stench of smoke that day and insisted on diverting the march to investigate. The others, wary of whites, had held back until he insisted, and they had followed reluctantly, hiding behind the trees to watch the flames billow and rise, obeying him because he was the son of a chief, but doubting his wisdom.

They doubted him no longer, not since the moment they had seen the spirit / woman walking toward them with the hawk and the bloody ax in her arms. Her golden hair had hung loosely over her shoulders, and her smoldering eyes had testified to her power. In silent acknowledgment of him as leader she had walked directly to Racing Bird and handed him the ax. No words had been necessary. The bloody ax, the hawk, the fire; they were symbols of victory in warfare, divine symbols that were objects of worship, Iroquois symbols. Racing Bird and she had gazed at one another, speaking without words, pledging themselves to the world of their brothers and sons. And when Racing Bird had finally turned and gestured to his men to follow, it was with the knowledge that she would follow as well.

And so a dozen times a day Racing Bird sought her out. She wasn't a mortal woman, but she was, he thought, in many ways like mortal women: beautiful, mysterious, and infinitely desirable. So desirable that he wished to possess the substance as well as the spirit of her. Perhaps one day this gift would be granted him, but if not, he would still continue to thank the gods who had brought him closer than most men to the secrets of immortality.

Williamsburg 1755

. . . .

*Blessed is he whose transgression is forgiven,
whose sin is covered.*

> *Psalm 32:1*
> A *Psalm of David*

When Winsome caught a glimpse of herself in the chinoiserie mirror over the mantel, she also caught a glimpse of Darby Littlefield watching her. She had been wise, she thought, to choose the yellow silk, which made her dark hair and eyes seem all the darker, and which stood out so shimmeringly among the drab purples and lifeless grays of the other women's gowns.

"Here." Littlefield plucked a pink rose from a vase, raked off the barbs with his thumbnail, and handed it to her. She tucked the stem into the front of her bodice so that the blossom lay between her breasts.

"I should have liked to plant that rose myself," he murmured.

"The garden's not yours to cultivate, Mister Littlefield."

"I fear you don't take me seriously."

"How can I on such short acquaintance?"

"Perhaps, then, we should get to know one another better. I have rooms at the Red Mask Inn, Miss Greenhill. Do you know it?"

"I know *of* it, Mister Littlefield."

"I should like you to be my guest at tea one day."

"It would hardly enhance my reputation to do so." She smiled to show that she took no offense, that she understood that the invitation was not meant to be taken seriously.

Littlefield was a recent arrival in Williamsburg, having come from England to claim land his father, the Duke of Kenilmoor, had purchased from the Ohio Company. He wasn't handsome. His face was pockmarked and pale beneath his powdered wig, and his affected weariness made him seem somewhat effete, but he was wellborn and he was wealthy, an irresistible combination. Aside from Lawrence Collier, owner of Green Meadows, the largest tobacco plantation in Virginia, there was no bachelor in the room to match Littlefield for eligibility, and that included the man to whom Winsome was betrothed, Bartholomew Smythe, merchant in farm tools and mill machinery. And since Collier, as everyone knew, cared less about women than he did about tobacco profits, Littlefield was the better marriage prospect. *Too bad*, Winsome reflected, *that I'm already engaged*. Then she added speculatively, *Although nothing, of course, is irrevocable*.

Darby soon excused himself, and a moment later Bartholomew reclaimed Winsome. "I think it's time we left, Winnie. My parents and my sister are just going."

Winsome cast a critical eye at Bartholomew's plump and chronically flushed face. "It's still early," she answered. "I don't see why we have to leave just because your parents are leaving."

"I thought we might walk home. I'd like to spend a few minutes alone with you."

What he really wanted, Winsome knew, was to inveigle her into accompanying him to some secluded spot so he could kiss her, and she was in no mood to be slobbered over. "Not yet, Bart," she told him. "I don't intend to be among the first to leave."

Bartholomew dropped his voice to murmur peevishly, "Darby Littlefield was flirting with you."

"Don't be silly."

"Jane Fitzroy has her eye on him, and Littlefield is here at the Fitzroys' invitation."

"Why tell me about it?"

"Doesn't he know that you're spoken for?"

"I suppose he doesn't."

"You should have told him, Winnie."

"For pity's sake, lower your voice. Here come the Fitzroys."

Their hosts strolled over to ask if they were enjoying themselves, and Winsome assured them that she and Bartholomew were most pleasantly occupied. It was certainly true of her, and not just because of Darby Littlefield.

The Fitzroys were part of a small circle of vastly wealthy landowners who oversaw their Virginia estates part of the time and lived in handsome town houses the rest. It was an exclusive society and not easily penetrated. But Bartholomew's father, unrefined and self-made, had managed to get himself elected to the Williamsburg Assembly, and tonight marked the Smythe family's entry into society. Winsome was thrilled to be included. She glanced around at her surroundings, the high-ceilinged drawing room, the painted walls, the Oriental rugs, the inlaid woods, and the richly embroidered upholsteries. She meant to live like this herself one day.

"You are Beriah Greenhill's sister, are you not?" Mister Fitzroy inquired. "He is considered to be the best printer in Williamsburg. I understand he learned his craft from Benjamin Franklin in Philadelphia. Remarkable man, Franklin. Likes to invent things. A little too outspoken for my tastes, but influential. He has, at least, the sense to know that the colonies need protection. If it were left to the Quakers, Philadelphia would have been overrun by the French and the Indians long ago."

Winsome, with no great knowledge of Benjamin Franklin, and even less of the state of the colonies, smiled self-consciously and tried to think of some appropriately graceful reply. She was saved the necessity by Darby Littlefield, who rejoined the group with a slender, elegantly gowned, haughty-looking girl on his arm. "Indians?" Littlefield exclaimed. "Naturally one hears about Indians, but it's almost impossible to believe they actually exist."

"You've only been in the colonies for two months," Mister Fitzroy reminded him. "All you know of the continent is what you've seen in the civilized city of Williamsburg. Wait a bit. When you travel north to the Ohio Valley you'll see another world entirely. That's Indian country, and you can be sure they'll find some way to let you know it."

"The Indians have also been known to conduct occasional raids on our outlying hamlets," Mistress Fitzroy added, "so you can be sure we don't doubt their existence."

"I suppose they can be an annoyance," Littlefield conceded in a bored voice.

"An annoyance?" Bartholomew shot back. "Winnie used to live in New Castle. The Indians burned down her family's mill and abducted her sister. Would you call that an 'annoyance'?"

"I think you take too harsh a view of what was merely a careless remark," Littlefield replied.

"And I think your so-called carelessness is aimed to offend."

The embarrassed silence that followed was broken by Mister Fitzroy, who suggested that Littlefield accompany him and his wife across the room to meet the governor. They strolled away, Jane Fitzroy still clutching Littlefield's arm as she tossed a supercilious grin back over her shoulder at Winsome.

Winsome said angrily, "Why did you speak to him like that?"

"You know why."

"Did you see Jane Fitzroy's face? She was pleased to have me humiliated."

"If so, it's because she resented Littlefield's attentions to you."

"Take me home, Bart."

"I thought you wanted to stay."

"Well, I've changed my mind."

"How can you tell the child such frightful tales?" Nedda fussed, "and on the eve of his birthday too."

Providence was accustomed to Nedda's leapfrog logic and undismayed by it. "He's not apt to have nightmares over a story he's heard dozens of times. Are you, Berry?"

Little Berry shook his head and adjusted himself into a more compact package on Providence's lap. "Go on,

Grandmama, tell the part where the bear says, 'If you don't take me to the honey tree, I'll squeeze the lifeblood out of you.'"

"I'm not going to listen to another word," Nedda declared.

"Let's leave that story for now," Providence suggested, coaxing the child out of the protest she was forming. "Let's talk about your birthday. Let's try to guess what your presents will be."

"Now you propose to give the surprises away," Nedda criticized. "I'll not be a party to it." She got up from her chair and flounced out of the room.

Providence sighed. She tried to make allowances for Nedda, at least when it came to little Berry. Nedda had endured the tragedy of three stillbirths before successfully delivering a healthy son, and now at thirty-seven, her child-bearing days were apparently over. It was no wonder she doted on her son, but Providence still wished she would try a little harder to be pleasant. She was so unvaryingly critical of everything and everyone.

"A jackknife?" Berry chirped.

Providence, eyeing the chair Nedda had vacated, answered, "Perhaps not a jackknife."

"Marbles?"

"If there were marbles, what kind would they be?"

"All colors and sizes with . . ."

Conversing with Berry didn't require Providence's full attention. She spoke to him and at the same time let her thoughts wander. She must write to the children, to Mordecai and Aaron and their wives. *Nedda is her usual high-strung self, which is, in its way, reassuring. How are you, Barbara? And you, Lucy? And my grandchildren? How badly has the weather affected you? February was an ugly month, but March looks brighter. Here there is nothing but talk about the French and the probability that we shall be fighting them over the Ohio territory before long. I know you are all safe there and that my sons will not*

*be called upon to fight, but all this war talk is disturbing to a
mother's peace of mind . . .*

"A pony."

"I'd not count on a pony, Berry. There's really no place to
keep a pony."

"A dog, Grandmama. Do you think a dog?"

*As you know, little Berry celebrates his sixth birthday tomorrow,
just a week after his father's fortieth. I've bought him the new boots
he covets, shiny black replicas of his father's. I know he'll love the
whistle and the slingshot you sent, although Nedda will probably
confiscate the slingshot before he ever has a chance to use it.*

*Felicity is well. I told you when I last wrote that she has been
talking about finding employment. She insists that marriage isn't
inevitable in the way of birth and death, which is quite true, but to
my mind no justification for her indifference to every man who
calls on her. To hear her complain one would think she were
damned by her beauty rather than blessed with it. I'd give her up
for a spinster except for her innate common sense.*

*Winsome, on the other hand, is almost totally lacking in that
attribute, although now that she's engaged I have hope that she will
actually marry. Bartholomew Smythe is an ideal match, a young
man who is ambitious and hard-working. I'm afraid his father's
money is more important to your sister than any considerations of
character, but fortunately Bartholomew is someone of whom we
may all be proud. The wedding is to be in August, and it will be a
relief to me to have your sister settled.*

"Grandmama, I think I may receive a whistle."

Providence looked down into her grandson's face. He
resembled his father, but there was Jonas there, too, in the
tender brown eyes and sweet smile. How much love and
how many griefs had gone into the molding of that dear
child. "I wouldn't be surprised at all if you were to receive a
whistle."

"Papa," little Berry burst out energetically, "Grandmama
says she thinks I'll receive a whistle."

Providence looked up to see Beriah standing in the parlor
doorway with Nedda's moist and anxious eyes peering out

from behind his shoulder. He winked and said, "Your Grandmama's often right." Then added, "Ma, Nedda says you're going home now."

"It's past the baby's bedtime," Nedda said defensively. "I thought you were probably getting ready to leave."

Providence set little Berry on his feet. "I should go now. I'm eager to hear about Winsome's evening."

"Where is she, Ma?" Beriah asked.

"She and Bart are attending a supper party at the Thomas Fitzroys'."

Nedda slithered back into view. "Really?" she said interestedly. "Fancy Winnie being invited to the Fitzroys'."

"It's a party in honor of a gentleman named Darby Littlefield, I believe."

"The son of the Duke of Kenilmoor? I've heard about him. I wonder if he likes Williamsburg."

"Williamsburg may be no substitute for the Royal Court," Beriah remarked, "but I'd be surprised if he found it dull. There's novelty in it, if nothing else."

"Boots, Grandmama?" Berry burst out with sudden inspiration. "Boots like Papa's?"

"You'll have to wait and see." Providence swooped down to give him a hug and kiss. "You wouldn't want to disappoint your mama by learning it all beforehand, would you? Nothing's half so dull as knowing what tomorrow's apt to bring."

·· 22 ··

"Mama, why should I depend on Berry to keep me? As for the twins, you know yourself that the mill hasn't prospered this year. How can I take money from them?"

"I ran that mill for years, Lissy, and after the mill burned down we took no share from it until the boys showed a profit again. Surely we needn't be ashamed of taking some small share now."

"Mama, I've heard you say more than once that you dislike being supported by your children."

"Perhaps. But I'm practical enough to adjust to necessity."

"Bother necessity. Necessity is simply another way of saying one must observe the proprieties."

"And heaven forbid you should observe the proprieties, Lissy."

There was a physical as well as temperamental resemblance between mother and daughter. Felicity, like Providence, was tall and slender, with an olive complexion, remarkable violet eyes, and thick, richly waved black hair. But while Felicity's hair glistened with red highlights, her mother's was touched with gray. Individually they attracted second glances. Together they caused heads to turn. Now, oblivious to the curious looks of passersby, Felicity held her mother's arm and propelled her along the balmy April streets at a pace just short of a trot. "What am I to do, Mama? I'm a young woman. Am I to be passed on from my brothers to my brothers' sons like a family heirloom?"

"Don't tell me again that you won't marry."

"I've said a hundred times I won't marry. I don't wish to marry. I prefer to be independent."

"One day you'll change your mind."

Felicity's determination not to marry wasn't new, and although Providence hadn't taken her seriously during her adolescence, she took her seriously now. But she didn't believe Felicity's insistence on spinsterhood had anything to do with her desire for independence. Rather, Providence believed, it had its source in Sarah's abduction ten years before. Felicity had never shaken off her guilt regarding that tragedy, or the inevitable disillusionment that the guilt engendered. At twenty-five Felicity was beautiful, feminine, desirable, and hopelessly cynical about her chances for happiness. It worried Providence more than she would permit herself to admit.

"I've been saving money for five years now, Mama, money Berry's given me and the twins have sent me. I have enough to pay the rent for the first three months, and by then I should be able to pay the rent from my earnings. And I can bake, Mama. You learned from Papa and I learned from you, and I do it well."

"Papa worked for a baker for a number of years before he opened his shop in Philadelphia. It takes experience and skill to succeed in trade."

"Berry did it."

"Berry was a skilled printer when he came to Williamsburg."

Providence found it difficult to argue in the midst of a headlong rush down Francis Street. She was relieved when Felicity finally called a halt. "There it is, Mama."

They were standing in front of a two-story building, freshly painted, with a wooden sign fashioned in the shape of a musket above the door, and with the name Oatland inscribed on it. "This is a gunsmith's," Providence pointed out.

"Not the gunsmith's, Mama. The cottage behind."

Providence peered down the narrow alley next to the gunsmith's. At the end of it, about sixty feet back from the sidewalk, was a ramshackle cottage with broken shutters and a door hanging off its hinges. A barrel, obviously set out to catch the runoff from Oatland's rain gutter, partially blocked the alley's entrance. Providence's reaction was dismay, not only because of the condition of the place, but because she recognized it. "Isn't this where . . . isn't this the place they call Meg's coop?"

"No longer. Mister Oatland paid her to leave when he moved into the gunsmith's shop."

"You propose to rent a cottage whose former occupant was a prostitute?"

"The rent is reasonable, and it's just the right size for my purpose."

"How can you think of occupying a house of such notorious reputation?"

"It's not the house that has the reputation, Mama. It's the former occupant. I'm sure Meg Buckles took her reputation with her. Come and look at it. I don't think the door's locked."

Providence followed Felicity up the alley and through the lopsided door. The odor inside the building was foul, calling up pictures in Providence's mind of the disreputable Meg with her wild hair and eyes, her shabby clothes, her coarse language, and her crabbed fingers forever scratching at herself. The house was only fifteen feet wide, but it ran back some forty feet and consisted of two rooms, one behind the other. The front room had one window fitted with oiled paper rather than glass, and a fireplace set in the wall that divided the rooms. The filthy, smoke-blackened hearth contained a charred wooden lug pole and a dead fire of ash. When Providence went close she saw the remains of a rat, with crushed head and singed fur, lying among the ashes, and she turned away with a shudder.

"Look in here, Mama," Felicity called.

The back room had a little more to recommend it. There was a back door and two more windows dingy with dust. A bare pallet was set next to the rear brick wall of the fireplace, and an overturned footstool with a tattered tapestry cushion lay near the door. "Appalling," Providence said flatly.

"It only needs cleaning up. Come look at the garden."

The "garden" consisted of a fifteen foot square of barren clay and a tall fence surrounding it. "It looks like the yard at the debtor's prison," Providence remarked.

"It looks like the Garden of Eden to me, Mama."

"I can only observe that you have a vivid imagination."

Felicity laughed and kissed her, then turned her head toward the door. "Ssh, it's Mister Oatland," she whispered.

They listened to the sound of boots tramping through the empty rooms, terminating with the appearance of a tall, thin stalk of a man in the doorway. "Well," Mister Oatland said without preliminary. "Are you taking it, Miss Greenhill?"

"Yes, I am, Mister Oatland."

"You understand the terms and agree to them? The rent is to be delivered promptly the first of each month. The house is to be maintained in good order. . . ."

Providence raised an ironic eyebrow.

"There's to be no immoral or unlawful business conducted on the premises—"

"I hardly think," Providence interrupted, "that it's necessary to introduce such a provision."

"Who are you?" Oatland demanded.

"I am Miss Greenhill's mother."

Mister Oatland dismissed her with a disparaging grunt. "Renewal of the lease after one year is entirely subject to my discretion. Now, who's to sign the agreement for you?"

Felicity said in a puzzled voice, "Why, I'll sign it myself."

"I want a man to sign it."

"Why is that?"

"So far as I'm concerned, no document signed by a woman is legal or binding."

Felicity drew herself to her full height. "It's to be my house and my business, and it will be my money paying the rent. I shall sign the agreement."

"It don't take more than a helpless crying female to relieve herself of the obligation and me of my income. You told me your brother's Beriah Greenhill, the printer, didn't you? Let him sign for you."

"Listen to me, Mister Oakland. I'm prepared to pay you right now for the first month's rent, and I shall do so right after you and *I* sign the contract."

Oatland shook his head.

"You're being unfair," Felicity exclaimed.

"Fair or not, I don't take a woman's signature."

Providence suddenly grabbed Felicity's arm and pulled her toward the door. "Good day, Mister Oatland."

"She don't want the place?" Oatland asked.

"Oh, Mama," Felicity murmured miserably.

Providence pointed a finger at Mister Oatland. "Two tiny, dark rooms in a rundown house at the end of an alley? Frankly, I cannot imagine what possessed my daughter to say she'd take it, especially considering the reputation attached to it. How long will it be before people forget that the house was occupied by a woman as unsavory as Meg Buckles? It's filthy. It stinks. It will take back-breaking work to make it habitable. The shutters and doors are falling off their hinges. There's a rain barrel blocking the entry to the alley. I suspect that the chimney's clogged. No, I think you'll have to find someone else willing to pay you to live in this hovel. Come, Lissy."

"Just a minute," Oatland commanded. "I promised her the house and she can have the house. All I ask is that she have someone, a man, that is, vouch for her promise to pay."

"She is no longer interested, Mister Oatland."

Oatland mumbled something, and Providence asked him to repeat it. "I said I'm agreeable to calling a chimney sweep, and I'll remove the barrel."

"What about the shutters and doors?"

"I never said I wouldn't fix them."

"You haven't said you will."

"It goes without saying."

"That's not very businesslike, Mister Oatland."

"Mama," Felicity interrupted, "wait a minute. Mister Oatland, will you take three months' rent in lieu of a man's signature?"

Oatland was ready to capitulate, and all three parties to the discussion were aware of it. Providence tipped the scale by saying, "Three months' rent is more than you'll get if the place remains unoccupied."

"If she don't pay prompt," Oatland warned, "she'll be out the next day. I'll take no excuse and give no favor. Is it understood?"

"It's understood," Providence returned.

"Perfectly understood," Felicity added. "You'll have your rent on the first day of every month."

Oatland looked from one woman to the other, nodded curtly, and finally rumbled out a grudging "Done."

Felicity made Winsome sick with all her talk of staying single. She had once had the remarkably bad taste to say that her maidenhood was not for sale, and to say it within Bartholomew's hearing. Winsome still blanched whenever she remembered it. Now she was talking about going to work. What work could she do? Did she intend to teach school or hire out as a servant? There wasn't much else open to a woman. It was difficult enough to explain away her blithe disinterest in marriage without also having to make excuses for the fact that she actually wished to be employed.

This morning Felicity had talked their mother into going off with her on some mysterious errand connected to this latest obsession of hers. Winsome preferred not to think about it. However, she was just as happy to have her sister and mother occupied. It kept them from asking what she intended to do with her day. It was warm for March and Winsome chose to wear an unlined cape and a pair of low-heeled sandals. She combed her hair into a neat chignon and donned her prettiest spring hat, a flat-crowned straw skimmer with plue and yellow bows clustered under the broad brim. Then, before setting out, she perfumed herself with rose water and pinched her cheeks to bring the color into them.

It took nearly an hour to walk to the Red Mask Inn, which lay outside of town on the Richmond Road. Once there she strolled slowly past the inn, turned back and strolled past again, this time pausing in front of the gate to adjust her hat strings. She repeated the procedure twice more, and the fourth pass was rewarded by the sound of Darby Littlefield's voice calling out, "Miss Greenhill? Good day."

She looked up and saw him standing in the open door of the inn. He was wigless and jacketless and held a glass of ale in his hand. "Why, Mister Littlefield, is that you?"

"What are you doing so far from home, Miss Greenhill?"

Winsome looked around as if she'd just wakened from sleep. "The Red Mask? Have I really come so far? I had no idea."

By that time Littlefield had come down the path to join her. "I saw you outside the gate and thought you might be coming to see me. Then you walked past and my hopes were dashed. You can well imagine how pleased I was when I saw you come by again."

"I was on my way back home."

"Then I suppose there's no hope you'll join me in my rooms for tea?"

Winsome's eyes were demure under their fringe of lashes. "You're very wicked, Mister Littlefield."

"Not very, Miss Greenhill." He smiled and Winsome thought to herself that he was really more attractive than she'd given him credit for. At the party she had found him pallid, almost too delicate-featured to be manly, but now the patrician nose and close-set eyes, the high forehead and wavy brown hair, combined to give him an appearance of character, even of nobility. "If I can't induce you to have tea with me," he went on, "perhaps you'll consent to let me walk a way with you."

"I can't see any harm in that."

"Give me a minute to fetch my jacket."

Winsome had thought everything out in her mind beforehand, what to do if she succeeded in flushing him out of his lair and what to say if he proposed to join her in her walk. It pleased her to find events matching her expectations, and she laid a delicate hand on his arm as they walked, encouraging him to talk, asking him his impression of the colonies, complimenting him on his observations.

They were still some half mile from the edge of town when Littlefield pointed to an unpaved cow path bisecting the cobbled road and suggested they stroll that way. Winsome didn't wish to dirty her skirts, but thought it behooved her to acquiesce. She picked her way along the dung-strewn path behind him until he stopped and she came up short behind him. "Look there," Littlefield directed.

There seemed to be nothing to look at except a fenced-in field containing a single rather doleful-looking cow. "Do you like it?" he asked.

Winsome leaned down to pick a thistle off her skirt. "I've never been particularly drawn to cattle."

He laughed. "The cow is pastured here by a local family who pays for the privilege. I'm not calling your attention to the cow. I'm calling your attention to the house."

Winsome saw it then, the bare framework of a house on the far side of the field.

"It's mine," Littlefield said.

"You own this land?" Winsome asked in surprise. "I thought your property was somewhere out in the wilderness."

"This is one of two parcels my father purchased. This one is small, only two hundred acres while the other is two thousand, but it's a nice bit of property."

"And you're building on it?"

"I've decided that I'd like to have a civilized base near a respectable-sized town. Would you like to see it close up?"

"I'm not very good at fence climbing."

"Never mind." Littlefield swooped her up in his arms and deposited her on the far side of the fence, then leaped over and took her hand to lead her across the field.

At close range the house seemed much larger than it had appeared from a distance. It was a three-story structure that would, Littlefield explained, contain twelve rooms when it was completed: two parlors, summer and winter, dining room, kitchen, library, and six bedrooms. Littlefield led her across the rough boards of the ground floor and pointed out where the windows and door would be and which rooms were which. "This is the entrance hall and here is the dining room. This is the winter parlor, and here in back, the summer parlor. The master bedchamber is directly above."

"There's a splendid view of the mountains," Winsome noted.

"There will be a splendid view of the rose garden as well, that is, the rose-garden-to-be." He moved close, standing just behind her. "The beds at Swithin Fell are laid out in a circular pattern; white roses in the center, then pink, then red roses on the outer rim."

"Swithin Fell?" Winsome repeated. "Is that the name of your home in England?"

"Swithin Fell Castle in Kenilmoor."

Castle. Winsome's heart fluttered at the thought of herself as mistress of a castle, wife to Darby Littlefield. She realized suddenly that it wasn't such a farfetched notion, and the realization took her breath away.

"You smell of roses," Littlefield murmured, his lips close to her neck.

Winsome stepped away and turned to face him. For a moment she hesitated. "Mister Littlefield, I . . ." Then she took the calculated risk. "Perhaps I should have spoken sooner, but I didn't realize that on such short acquaintance you would . . ."

He was looking at her expectantly, slightly puzzled, as she plunged ahead. "I should have told you sooner that I'm betrothed. I'm to marry Bartholomew Smythe in four months' time."

Littlefield said calmly, "When I first noticed you at the Fitzroys' party, that fact was pointed out to me."

"You knew and yet you went out of your way to make my acquaintance?"

"You did nothing to discourage me."

Winsome was disconcerted. What kind of man was he to admit such a thing? More to the point, what kind of woman did he think she was? There was an edge to her voice as she said, "I shouldn't have come walking with you. It was a mistake."

"Surely you must have had something in mind when you passed by the Red Mask today?"

"Certainly not. How would I?"

"You passed by four times. I was watching."

Winsome gasped and would have fled except that Littlefield blocked her retreat. "I like you very much, you know," he murmured.

"You have no right to speak to me like that."

If you're going to be angry, then you might as well have something to be angry about." Before she could stop him, he put his arms around her and kissed her. It was a rough kiss and not, Winsome thought with chagrin, altogether the kiss of a gentleman. But not altogether unpleasant either. She pushed him away.

"I was wrong to let you bring me here. I insist that you take me back."

"Are you sure that's what you want, Winsome?"

"And please do not address me by my given name. Under the circumstances—"

"Under the circumstances," he cut in with a disarming smile, "you can decide never to speak to me again or address me as Darby. The first is safer, but the second more rewarding."

Things weren't going quite so smoothly as Winsome had envisioned, but Littlefield excited her, and she thought it would be a pity to give up so easily when there was suddenly so much at stake. She considered the choices he'd suggested, then said with composure, "Show me again where you intend to plant the rose garden, Darby."

· · 23 · ·

That evening Felicity told Winsome her plan, and the house on Nassau Street erupted. Felicity dashed from room to room, while Winsome pursued her. "To think that Mama allowed it!" Winsome shouted. "I can't believe she allowed it. What will people think?"

"Why should it matter to me what people think?" Felicity returned. "For that matter why should it matter to you? Bart's father was once a fishmonger. That's how he started, and he's proud of it. The Smythes are certainly not going to find anything to criticize in my being a baker."

"Stop running away from me, Lissy."

"Then stop shouting at me."

Providence intervened, but not even she could effect a truce in the face of such commanding histrionics, and the house reverberated until finally, in desperation, she threw the bolts and doused the lights.

Nedda's reaction the following day was equally dramatic. It was Sunday and Providence and Felicity attended church alone, Winsome having decided to disregard the God who had demonstrated such disregard for her. After church, as was their usual habit, Providence and Felicity walked to Nicholson Street to visit Beriah and Nedda, and when the first opportunity presented itself, Felicity made her announcement. "I have news. I have decided to enter into trade."

Nedda mouthed the words silently. "Into trade?"

"That's right, I'm going to open a bake shop."

"But why?"

"Because I know how to bake, and I think I can succeed as a baker."

"Where?" Nedda demanded. "Surely not here in Williamsburg?"

"I've rented the vacant cottage behind the gunsmith's shop on Francis Street."

Beriah frowned. "The only vacant cottage I know of on Francis Street is Meg's coop."

"Yes, that's the one. It's the house Meg Buckles used to occupy. I signed the agreement yesterday."

"Meg Buckles?" Nedda intoned faintly. "You have rented Meg Buckles' house?"

"I have."

Nedda turned to Providence. "Surely you raised objections?"

Providence said briskly, "Meg Buckles has been gone for over three months, and there will be a conspicuous sign over the door conveying the information that there is now a bake shop on the premises."

Nedda leaned back in her chair and began fanning herself with her handkerchief. "A baker. I should have thought you would forbid it."

"I'm a grown woman," Felicity told her. "I don't need permission."

Nedda sat up again and leaned forward in her chair. "And how, may I ask, do you expect to pay the rent?"

"I have money, Nedda."

"Money you received from Beriah, I presume?"

"Money I've been saving for a long time. What's more, it's because I don't want my brothers to support me that I've decided to support myself."

"But why, Lissy?" Beriah interrupted. "Surely you know that I'm proud to take care of you."

"I do know it, and I'm grateful. But I've decided that I'm quite capable of taking care of myself and prefer to do so."

"It's one thing for a woman to work if she's forced to work by a combination of adversities," Nedda chimed in again, "and quite another for her to shame her family by announcing to the world that she must support herself."

"I don't think I'm shaming my family, Nedda, and if I'm shaming you, then there's nothing I can do about it."

"Home is a woman's province. Not the world. Certainly not a bakery on Francis Street. You should be thinking about getting married."

"You don't really care whether or not I marry. You care only that I do what's expected. Well, let me tell you something. I'm unlikely to marry, and I'm equally unlikely to do what's expected. If I were to do what's expected, I should do nothing at all. I should go on rising each morning with no prospect of filling my day; dress, breakfast, and putter about the house knowing there will be no deviation from my boredom, no diversion in my life, because there are no diversions for an aging spinster."

"An aging spinster, indeed. I think you take pride in being perverse, Lissy."

"Not like the pride you take in it," Felicity snapped.

"Do you hear her?" Nedda exclaimed. "Do you hear what she thinks of me? Her own sister-in-law who cares so much about her?"

"You don't care about anything but appearances, Nedda," Felicity returned. "You're too shallow to care about people."

This remark from Felicity met with a prickly silence that Beriah broke by saying, "That was unnecessary, Lissy. I'm sure you didn't mean it."

Felicity was about to tell him that she most certainly had meant it, but Providence caught her eye and shook her head. She said instead, "I lost my temper. I'm sorry, Nedda."

"I should hope you would be," Nedda said sanctimoniously.

Later, on the way home, Providence scolded Felicity for speaking as she had, suggesting that it wasn't worth antagonizing Beriah to put Nedda in her place.

"But she's impossible, Mama. I can't imagine why Berry ever married her."

"I would venture," Providence returned wryly, "that he has asked himself that same question from time to time over the years. Whatever the answer, it doesn't change his situation. Or ours. Nedda is family, and families must be tolerant of one another's foibles."

"You might as well call a lion a kitten as call her shrewishness a foible."

"Nevertheless, she isn't at her best under stress, and you did give her a shock."

"In that case, I'll try not to shock her again, Mama."

But there was still another shock in store for Nedda, and

it wasn't long in coming. Felicity, thinking more and more that she would need help running the bakery, invited her mother to go into partnership with her. It would, she pointed out, postpone the need for a hired girl and provide Providence with a challenging outlet for her energies. She would earn money of her own, and her presence would lend an air of substance and respectability to the project that might otherwise be lacking.

At first Providence declined on the grounds that Nedda and Winsome would be even more distraught than they already were if Providence should join Felicity in her venture. But the logic of Felicity's proposal was irrefutable. Felicity could use help, and the help Providence was capable of providing would be superior to that of a mere hired girl. Besides, the thought of being active again was irresistable. Felicity had been entirely right the day she suggested that her mother hated being useless as much as she.

Oatland was not a charming landlord, nor was he particularly civil, but he turned out at least to be a man of his word. Within a week of Felicity's signing the lease for Meg's coop, he had brought in a sweep to clean the chimney and hired a man to repair the exterior, so that when Felicity and Providence saw it next it had properly hung doors and neat, freshly whitewashed shutters. Felicity had decided to hang a bake paddle over the front door and, for good measure, she commissioned a signmaker to inscribe the words on the paddle as well. That way there would be no confusion whatever about what was dispensed within. Next the two women set to work to transform the interior of the house, airing out the rooms and scrubbing everything in sight: ceiling, walls, floors, and windows.

Nedda's objections notwithstanding, Beriah conscripted his printer's apprentice to lend a hand, and in his spare time the apprentice repaired floorboards, sealed seams, waxed floors and applied whitewash to the walls and ceilings. Then a carpenter was called in to build a counter and shelves in the front room. The house, dominated by the surrounding houses, received little direct sunlight; only the backyard was open to a patch of sky. Beriah overrode Felicity's objections to his contributing money to improve the situation and paid a glazier to replace the oiled paper with panes of glass, so that for a generous portion of each day there would be light enough to see without having to resort to candles. Beriah also usurped another responsibility, bringing in a local bricklayer to construct the bake oven. When the bricklayer finished his work there was a large double oven jutting into the back room with two iron doors and a flue connected to the central chimney.

The front room, which would serve as the shop, could accommodate little more than the wooden counter, but it was made cheerful with crisp window curtains and interior window boxes planted with ivy. A settle and an armchair were brought into the back room, along with a twelve-foot trestle table whose top was a board cut from a single piece of lumber, a corner cupboard, and a large hutch. Rows of shelves were built along three of the four walls and curtains were hung at the windows. There was an alcove right next to the oven, and Providence suggested that the cosy alcove be utilized as a warm niche for the bread rising. A large tub was bought and placed there for that purpose. During the renovations Felicity and Providence spent their nights improving their skill at quantity baking, and the Greenhill larder, as well as the larders of some dozen or more neighbors, benefited from this concentrated activity. Before long the sign was hung over the bakery door—THE BAKE PADDLE, FELICITY AND PROVIDENCE GREENHILL, PROPRIE-TORS—and the doors officially opened.

Winsome had always been fussy about her appearance. Now she was obsessive, spending hours arranging her hair; treating her complexion with Lady Molyneux's Italian Paste, and Venetian Bloom Water, buffing her fingernails;

experimenting with oils, pomades, and colognes; and scrubbing, starching, and pressing her clothes with the heavy charcoal-burning sadiron.

Her energies were directed toward one all-important goal: enticing Darby Littlefield. He had already made it clear that he was interested, and she was determined to turn his interest into a serious bid for her hand. Why should she settle for Mistress Bartholomew Smythe when she could be Mistress Darby Littlefield and eventually the Duchess of Kenilmoor. The Duchess of Kenilmoor. Just saying it aloud thrilled her.

The situation, however, was delicate. She mustn't give Darby the impression that she would deceive Bartholomew for the sake of a light flirtation. At the same time she mustn't frighten Darby away by doing anything rash, like breaking her engagement. She agreed to see Darby, but only in public where there could be no question of impropriety, and no repetition of their first clandestine meeting, which Winsome felt had worked somewhat to her disadvantage. She wanted Darby to love her, but if love were to lead to marriage, he must respect her as well.

They met on the Duke of Gloucester Street or on the steps of the church on England Street, or at the corner of Nicholson and Capitol, always pretending to run into one another by chance and always behaving with stiff formality. It pleased Winsome's sense of the dramatic to act out these seemingly innocent scenes, and Darby's impatience with the arrangement encouraged her to think he would press his suit all the more vigorously.

But there was a drawback to this elaborate pantomime. It risked observation by the wrong people, and eventually it led to trouble. When Jane Fitzroy went out of her way to visit Jennie Smythe one bright, warm Friday morning in April, it wasn't simply a social call. Nor was it the lovely weather that caused Jennie to clap on her bonnet and leave the house a few minutes after Jane's departure. Jennie marched straight to the office of Albert Smythe and Son, and a few minutes after, Bartholomew stalked out of the office and headed for Nassau Street.

Winsome had just washed her hair and was sitting on an overturned bucket in the backyard drying it when she was startled to see Bartholomew lope around the side of the house. "Bart? What ever are you doing here?"

Bartholomew had braced himself for the interview, but he couldn't control his voice, which came out high and clipped. "I knocked at the front door, but you didn't hear."

"Is something wrong? You look so strange, Bart."

He threw the question at her. "How well do you know Darby Littlefield?"

Winsome was caught off guard. She hunched over her knees and stared up at him. "I know him," she replied. "You know him too. We met him at the Fitzroys'."

"Is that the only time you've seen him?"

She studied his face, trying to decide how much he knew, then said tentatively, "I've met Mister Littlefield in the street once or twice."

"I understand you met him three times this week alone."

"Who told you that?"

"Do you deny it?"

"I have no idea," she answered coolly. "I don't keep count of the times I meet someone in the street."

"You saw him on Tuesday in front of the silversmith's, where you and he stood talking for near half an hour. You saw him again on Wednesday by the steps of the chruch, so engrossed that you neglected to return Jane's greeting."

"Jane?"

"Jane Fitzroy."

"Oh, that Jane," Winsome said disparagingly. "The Jane Fitzroy who abhors me."

"Was she lying?"

"She wasn't lying, but neither was she telling the truth. She twisted something innocent into something vile, and she wasted no time carrying it to the one it would hurt. Did she also tell you that I conversed with William Farbolt on

Monday, or that Amos Dewey stopped me in front of the butcher's shop?"

Winsome realized, when she saw Bartholomew wince, that she shouldn't have brought up the name of Amos Dewey, but it was too late to take it back.

"I thought you promised me not to speak to Dewey?"

"It was he who spoke to me."

"To what purpose?"

"I didn't stay to hear. I snubbed him and went by."

"I should have shot Amos Dewey for the lies he told about you last year," Bartholomew said bitterly.

"Jane Fitzroy and Amos Dewey are both loathsome. They're too loathsome to take seriously. As for Mister Littlefield, I barely know him, Bart. That's the truth."

Bartholomew was wavering. Winsome could sense the uncertainty. "Don't be silly about this, Bart. If I were to meet Darby Littlefield a dozen times a week, it wouldn't mean anything. Heavens, if there were something between us we shouldn't parade it on Capitol Street in full view of horrid females like Jane Fitzroy."

Winsome held out her hands to him, and after a moment he pulled her to her feet and kissed her. His kiss was no more agreeable than usual, but for once it didn't bother her.

·· 24 ··

The first few weeks of business were slow because the shop, tucked away as it was at the end of an alley, was easily overlooked. Friends came, of course, and so did adjacent shopkeepers and neighbors, and men expecting to find Meg Buckles, then returning with the hope of engaging Felicity's attention. But this limited clientele wasn't enough to turn the bakery into an instant success. "Gilbert's Bake Shop on Waller Street is getting all the business," Felicity complained.

"People need inducement," Providence speculated.

"What sort of inducement, Mama?"

"Something they can get here that they can't purchase from Mister Gilbert."

"Such as?"

"The Dutch in New York have a pastry they call a cruller."

"A what?"

"A cruller. I think the word "crull" means curl in Dutch. Anyway, it's a twisted bit of dough that's fried in deep fat rather than baked, drained, then sprinkled with sugar. It's delicious. I wonder if we could make them here in the bakery. We'd have to take turns at it, watching to see the fat stays the right temperature and that the crullers don't burn. But I think it might be worth the trouble. What do you think?"

"If you can duplicate the recipe, Mama, I can learn to bake them."

And so, one day during the fifth week of business, the Bake Paddle added "Dutch curl cakes" to its line of breads and muffins. That same evening, while Providence and Felicity were counting their money, the doorbell jangled and the shop door opened to admit a late customer. "Ah, a snug retreat from this chill and godforsaken city," he declared in a mellifluous voice.

They looked up to see a strange young man dressed in a red brocade jacket, flounced yellow jabot, and green vest. He was carrying two bundles of papers, one under either arm, so that he was forced to shut the door with his shoulder. "'If thou wilt outstrip death,'" he proclaimed, "'go cross the seas, and live with Richmond'—in this case Williamsburg—'within the reach of hell.'"

"I beg pardon?" Felicity said in bewilderment.

"Shakespeare. *Richard III*. Slight alteration of the dialogue. No matter. Tell me, what have you got to feed a hungry actor?"

"We've got what you see; bread and curl cakes."

He was hungrily eyeing the crullers, and Providence invited him to sample one, while she and Felicity exchanged amused glances. He put down his pile of notices on the counter, picked up a cruller, and demolished it in two bites. "Umm, delicious."

Closer scrutiny revealed the colorfully garbed stranger to be a pale but even-featured young man with a sly, somewhat waggish smile as well as frayed collar and cuffs. "You're not a resident of Williamsburg, are you?" Providence noted.

"I'm not. I'm a scout, madam. Rather like your Indian scouts. I go before to deal with the savages. No insult intended."

"Where are you from then?"

"England originally, New York now. Tom and Walter say there's no point packing a trunk for three nights in Philadelphia, so we plan on coming here next before going back to New York."

"You're speaking of your acting troupe?"

"Not my troupe. Thomas Kean and Walter Murray's acting troupe. Do you think you might put one of these notices up in your shop?"

"I see no harm in it," Felicity answered agreeably.

"I thank you, fair lady. Now for another of those curl cakes. How much?

Felicity grinned. "Half a penny for two, so you've another free one coming."

"Most civil of you, I must say." He plucked a second cruller from the tray, ate it, then bowed. "Pardon my rudeness. My name's Flower. Robby Flower at your service."

"How do you do?"

"The question," he promptly returned, "is how do *you* do? It's late in the day for all these breads and cakes to remain unsold, isn't it?"

"We've been in business for only a month," Providence felt compelled to explain. "We've yet to establish regular customers."

"You may never," Flower suggested bluntly. "It was only my sharp sense of smell led me up that dim alley. Your shop's hard to find." He dug into his pocket, came up with a ha'penny, and laid it on the counter, then dove into the tray for his third and fourth cruller. "You've got to announce yourselves to the public. Put out notices. Tack 'em up everywhere. Give out samples. Shout in the streets. Have you a name?"

"The Bake Paddle," Providence told him.

"'The Bake Paddle for curl cakes and crumpets!' How does that sound?"

"Well, we don't make crumpets."

"Then leave it at curl cakes, but let people know. That's what you've got to do."

He was gazing longingly at the cruller tray, and Providence offered him another one free. "Consider it payment for your good advice, Mister Flower."

"Never say no to an invitation," he replied cheerfully, taking his fifth cruller.

"When is the troupe coming to town?" Felicity asked.

"We're coming in May, straight from a successful run in Philadelphia, opening in Williamsburg on May tenth. We'll be here during the summer months, then back to New York in time for the winter season. It's all in the notice there; *Richard III*, Farquhar's *Beaux' Stratagem*, one or two others. I'll make sure you ladies get in free if you come round backstage. What's your name?"

"Greenhill."

"I'll remember it. Thanks for the curl cakes. Now, don't forget what I told you. Don't wait for them to come to you. You go out and pull 'em in. Take it from me. That's the way."

It seemed like sound advice, notwithstanding the rather disreputable source. Anticipating Nedda's response to their decision to advertise, they decided not to ask Beriah to print up the notices. Instead they went to Raymond Strickland's print shop. Silas Remington, the blacksmith's apprentice, tacked them up around town to good effect, the following Monday attracting sufficient customers to buy all but five of the five dozen crullers they'd made. When they closed shop on the following Saturday they had sold all their baked goods, including crullers, muffins, and bread. "If anyone saw us," Providence noted as she locked the doors, "they'd think we were celebrating a catastrophe instead of a profitable week of business." She flopped down on the stool behind the counter. "We made money, Lissy. Can you believe it?"

"It's good," Felicity agreed, "but we'll never get rich on curl cakes. Mama, I've been thinking. Whan that actor, Mister Flower, comes back to town, I'm going to ask if we can hawk our curl cakes at the theater."

"What? Do you have any idea how much more work that would be? Aren't we exhausted enough as it is?"

"It will be worth it. We'll attract additional customers and make more money. Then we'll hire additional help. It's what you did years ago when Hiram Sheffield switched his trade from Ober's mill to ours."

"Hawking pastries in the theater? You actually want to do that? I can see your sister now—to say nothing of Nedda—arriving at the performance of *Richard III* to find us with trays slung round our necks shouting, 'Sing out for your curl cakes! Here they are! Ha'penny apiece!'"

Felicity giggled wickedly. "It might be worth it just to see Nedda's face. Isn't it a delicious thought?"

"The only thought I can entertain right now is to wash the trays, tie on my bonnet, and go home to bed."

Nedda arrived on Sunday morning just as Providence, Felicity, and Winsome were preparing to leave for church. Winsome opened the door, leaping aside as Nedda charged into the hall holding aloft a large sheet of printed paper. "This is too much," she cried.

"What's wrong?" Winsome asked in a frightened voice.

"You mean they didn't tell you either? I found this tacked up on the oak tree in front of the rectory."

"What is it?"

"Look at it." Nedda shoved the notice into Winsome's hand. "They didn't even go to your brother to print them. They knew he'd draw the line at that, so they went to Raymond Strickland. Then they paid Silas Remington to nail these screech sheets all over town."

"These are public notices," Winsome murmured.

Providence and Felicity had come to the top of the stairs, and Nedda snatched back the announcement and waved it at them. "Everyone knows about it. That is, everyone knew about it but me. 'Why, Nedda dear, isn't that your mother-in-law? Isn't that your sister-in-law? I thought Berry was doing well? Oh, it's not that? Then is it a family disagreement? Not that either? Well, then, what is it, dear?'"

"Did you tell them what it is?" Felicity challenged.

"How could I? I was struck dumb."

"I'm sorry I missed that magic moment," Felicity returned calmly.

"'Come By and Buy,'" Nedda exclaimed. "'The First Curl Cake Free! Felicity and Providence Greenhill, Proprietors of The Bake Paddle!'"

"What's wrong with it?" Felicity asked. "I thought it was well phrased."

"The name Greenhill in letters six inches tall? May I remind you that my name is also Greenhill."

"I'd rather you wouldn't," Felicity answered politely.

Providence poked Felicity with her elbow. "Come now, Nedda, it's not really that bad, is it?"

"Mama," Winsome chimed in, "how could you let Lissy persuade you to put them up?"

Providence and Felicity descended the stairs to confront their accusers at eye level. "I should think it would be obvious," Providence told them. "We did it to encourage people to patronize the bake shop, and the reason we went to Raymond Strickland was to save Berry the ordeal of having to deal with you, Nedda."

"You knew I'd be offended, and still you did it," Nedda declared. "It's not enough to invite snide comment about Berry's inability to support his family; you had to tack up the name Greenhill on every street corner in town for good measure. Do you have any idea how humiliating that is to us?"

"And to me," Winsome added. "How will I hold up my head in society?"

"In society?" Felicity returned. "Since when have you been a member of society?"

"You know very well that the Smythes have begun to travel in better circles."

"If you're worried about the Smythes, you needn't be," Providence said impatiently. "The Smythes aren't bothered in the least by what we're doing. As a matter of fact, Bart's mother was one of our first customers. She couldn't have been more encouraging."

"Not everyone is as tolerant as the Smythes, Mama."

"That's true," Providence interjected, "but we're not doing something we're ashamed of."

"No, you're not. You're doing something I'm ashamed of."

"Listen, Winnie," Felicity said bitingly, "you of all people shouldn't accuse us of doing something improper."

"Why me of all people?"

"Have you forgotten Amos Dewey?"

"Amos Dewey lied about me. I never did the things he said."

"I know that, but for all his money Amos Dewey has a grimy reputation, and grime rubs off. Walking out with Amos Dewey was improper, far more improper than Mama and I trying to earn an honest living."

"You're twisting things again, Lissy, like you always do," Winsome burst out. "Let me by." She pushed past her sister and mother and clattered up the stairs to slam the door of her room.

"Lissy," Providence said quietly, "we were discussing the bakery, not that unpleasant incident last year."

"I lost my temper, Mama. I'm sorry."

"Oh no you're not," Nedda shot out. "You're never sorry about anything. You always think you're right and everyone else is wrong. You don't care who you hurt so long as you get your way. Me, Winnie, your brother, it doesn't matter in the least to you."

"That's not true," Felicity declared angrily. "I don't tell you what you may or may not do, and you have no right to judge my worth by your standards."

"No one except a hermit can ignore the fact that one's behavior reflects good or ill on others."

"I've never hurt anyone, Nedda."

"Really? Well, your sister Sarah would be here if it weren't for you. Everyone knows it. Surely you know it too."

The words bounced off the walls and reverberated in their ears like clanging bells. Even Nedda stood absolutely still after she'd spoken, as if the shocking words had come from someone else.

"How could you say such a cruel thing?" Providence said finally.

Nedda leaned back against the door, and her voice dropped to a weak whisper. "I suddenly feel quite faint."

"As well you should."

"Naturally you'd take her part."

"I think you'd better go, Nedda."

"I'm going to tell Berry you commanded me to leave."

"Tell him whatever you wish."

Nedda stood there uncertainly for another moment, then tottered to the door and fumbled with the door latch. She stepped outside, then turned back for a tremulous but well-aimed parting thrust. "No matter how much you deny it, Lissy, it's still true. It's simply that no one ever says it aloud. And if you *do* end up a bitter old maid, well then, it's no better than you deserve."

She left without closing the door, and Providence walked across the hall to close it herself, then turned back to say, "Lissy, you mustn't mind. She's such a—" The rest of the sentence remained unspoken because Felicity, too, had fled.

· · 25 · ·

Winsome's romance with Darby wasn't progressing as rapidly as she wished. So far he hadn't yet told her that he was in love with her, and he hadn't asked her to break her engagement to Bart, a request that would be tantamount to a proposal. From the first he had complained about the strictures she imposed on their meetings, saying that he disliked meeting so publicly and saw no necessity for it. How were they to get to know one another so long as they remained at arm's length? Was she merely amusing herself with him? Did she not trust him? Was she afraid of her own feelings? What was it that prevented her from allowing him to get close enough to touch her?

Winsome might have asked the same questions in regard to Darby's reluctance to declare himself, but, of course, she didn't. And now, almost imperceptibly, her hold on him was slipping away. Darby was becoming less attentive and more preoccupied. At their last meeting he had only spent ten minutes with her before excusing himself on some errand or other. Winsome was beside herself with worry, convinced that she had jeopardized her chances by appearing aloof when she had meant to appear demure.

The problem became simply a question of how to renew his interest in her, and the answer was quite clear. With or without a commitment, she must finally arrange to be alone with him. She justified the decision by telling herself that she had misjudged him in one major respect. She had thought him the same as all the other young men she knew, when he was, in fact, quite different. He was to the manor born, and, like other aristocrats, had little use for the proprieties. Men like Darby Littlefield made the rules, not followed them. It wasn't a mistake she'd make a second time.

She didn't show up when they were to meet next on South Henry Street. It took courage to stay home, but she gambled on Darby's curiosity to bring him to her. They had set the time for meeting at two o'clock, and when two came Winsome stood in the hall watching the clock strike the hour. She was still standing there at two-fifteen and at twenty-five after two. By two-thirty she was beginning to fidget, but at twenty-five to three she heard the rap of the door knocker and breathed easier. She counted to ten before going to the door, and pretended surprise when she saw him on the doorstep. "Darby? What are you doing here?"

"Where have you been?" he demanded impatiently. "I stood in front of the apothecary for half an hour waiting."

"I understood we were to meet at two."

"Yes? Well, it's closer to three now."

Winsome glanced at the clock in the hall. "Oh, Darby, I'm so sorry. I didn't realize."

Darby stepped into the hall, and Winsome shut the door behind him. "You see, I've dropped the key to the desk, and it's lodged in a crack in the floor. Mama will be so angry."

"You left me standing in the street for the sake of a key?"

"I said I'm sorry. I don't know how I could have been so absentminded."

Darby shook his head exasperatedly. "Where is it?"

Winsome preceded him into the parlor and pointed to the rounded head of a key protruding from between the floorboards. Darby dropped down to one knee. "It's jammed between the boards. I can't get a grip on it." Grumbling, he took a folded knife out of his pocket, worked it down into the floor crack, and with some effort retrieved the key and handed it to her, then got to his feet and dusted off his trousers. His next words shocked Winsome, even though she had half expected them. "Winsome, I don't think we should see one another again after today."

"Darby, I told you that I lost track of the time."

"It's not because of that. It's because I'm tired of playing the fool. I haven't seen you alone and in private once since the day you came to the inn, and I've no more patience left for meeting on street corners."

"You're seeing me alone now."

"Not by invitation."

Winsome said quietly, "Yes, by invitation. Please stay. Please sit down and talk to me. I want you to."

A slow smile creased Darby's face. He glanced at the decanter on the parlor table. "Is that sherry?"

"Yes. Please have some."

He picked up the decanter, poured the sherry into two glasses, gave one to her, then took her hand and led her to the sofa. "I assume that your mother and sister are presiding over the bakery?"

It was the first time he'd ever mentioned the bakery, and Winsome found herself unable to look at him as she mumbled in embarrassment, "Yes, they are," then hurriedly switched the subject. "Darby, perhaps I've been wrong about us. I've been so mixed up, wanting to be with you, but knowing it's improper."

"It hardly makes the situation any more proper by faking propriety."

"No. No, I suppose it doesn't, but I needed time to decide."

"To decide what, Winsome?"

"About us," she said vaguely, still hoping he would take the initiative.

He shrugged, then said something unexpected. "I've had a letter from my father urging me to visit our property in the Ohio Valley. I'll be leaving in a few weeks."

"Why didn't you tell me?"

"I would have." He picked up her hand and laced his fingers through hers. "Anyway, would it have made a difference?"

"Yes. No. I don't know. In what way different?"

"Would you have invited me to visit you sooner?"

"What has one thing to do with another? I don't see how our situation is altered by you going."

"Then it wouldn't have made a difference."

"I didn't say that, Darby."

"It's not very kind to toy with my affections, Winsome. I still don't know what you feel for me."

Winsome withdrew her hand. "The first overture should be the man's."

Darby's look of amazement was exaggerated. "What more can I do? Ever since the night we met I've made it plain that I want to know you better. It's you who go on insisting on these farcical encounters in one public place after another."

"You haven't asked me to break my engagement to Bart." There. She'd said it. She studied his face closely to try to read his reaction.

He leaned back, stretched out his legs, then said languidly, "So that's it. You want me to state my intentions."

"Is that so surprising?"

"Not so much surprising as unfair."

"Unfair? You think I'm being unfair to you?"

"No. I think stating my intentions would be unfair to you. You must realize that I'm about to undertake a perilous journey. Suppose I don't come back? What would happen to you then?"

"Are you saying that it's your concern for me that keeps you from speaking?"

"That's right."

"But my wedding is to take place in August. If I'm not going to marry Bart, I must tell him now."

"No, there's time. I'll be back by the end of July. Wait until then."

So he did love her, and he did mean to propose. She tingled from the implication in those three words, 'Wait until then.' "Yes," she told him breathlessly. "If that's what you want, of course I'll wait."

Darby stood up suddenly and took the sherry glass from her hand. He put it down on the table, then pulled her to her feet, put his arms around her and kissed her. Winsome returned the kiss, apprehensive but excited as he drew her back down onto the sofa and began to fumble at the bodice of her gown.

She put up token resistance, but he overcame her protests with the force of his ardor, making her feel childish to refuse him. Her struggles became weaker as his skilled hands sought to rouse her. "Your breasts are beautiful," he whispered, and soon, "Your body is lovely, so pale and perfect."

She had never seen a man naked. Her experience with Amos Dewey had been furtive and incomplete, carried out at night in the back of a carriage with no leisure for scrutiny or exploration. Now she watched as Darby disrobed, and was shocked by his thin, wiry frame and raw masculinity. She wanted to look away, but was afraid to let him know that she was repelled.

"I've wanted to make love to you since I first saw you," Darby said, kneeling over her. "I knew I would, you know. I knew you'd give in to me sooner or later. Now I intend to have you to my heart's satisfaction, completely and quite thoroughly."

Winsome cried out as she received him, closing her eyes and tensing her back. She'd planned for this, planned it carefully down to this moment. Her submission would bind him to her with the same irrevocable ties that bound lovers from the time of Adam and Eve. Why then, she wondered, did she feel so violated and betrayed?

* * *

Providence came in through the kitchen door to find Felicity pouring batter into a large rectangular pan. There were two other batter-filled pans resting on the kitchen table. "What are you doing?" she asked. "Don't you bake enough all week without having to skip church to bake some more?"

"I'm making pastries, Mama."

"Everyone at church asked for you. I had to say you stayed home because you were indisposed."

"I'm sure the Reverend Sackville won't think me a sinner. Where's Winnie?"

"I left her at Nedda's."

"I don't know how you can go on visiting Nedda, Mama."

"I don't intend to be deprived of my son and grandson because my daughter-in-law is sometimes difficult. It's time you got over being angry and came along too."

Felicity stopped what she was doing to glare at her mother. "No, Mama. No I won't. I won't set foot in that house ever again."

"That's foolish, Lissy. We have to make allowances for Nedda. Her mind's an unhappy tangle, all caught up in itself, like a spider trapped in its own web."

"I don't need to get tangled up in it too, Mama."

"Family is family, Lissy. Now, what did you say you're doing?" Providence eyed the baking pans curiously. "What do you mean, you're baking pastries?"

"They're miniature cakes and tarts. I thought we could add them to the curl cakes."

"Who in Williamsburg would ever want such things?"

"I think many people will want them. Instead of having to slice a cake into wedges, one need only to arrange the individual pieces on a tray. Utensils aren't necessary, either, since one eats them with one's fingers."

"No one *buys* cakes," Providence said skeptically. "People bake their own. What woman would present her guests with cakes purchased from a shop? Either they bake them themselves or have their servants bake them."

"That's because there aren't any cakes to buy. Now there will be."

"Such preciousness may suit the French Court, but I think the housewives of Williamsburg will find it frivolous, to say nothing of the work we'd set ourselves."

"We'll only make them up for the Saturday trade, for people wishing to serve them to company at Sunday tea."

"Pastries," Providence murmured. "Well, let's first see how they turn out."

· · *26* · ·

The pastries turned out well. Felicity and Providence decided that since they were something of a novelty, they would begin by charging only six pence the dozen. If the pastries were well-received, they would eventually raise the price. Soon new notices were tacked up around town. *A variety of individual miniature cakes and tarts, iced and decorated, six pence for the dozen, available on Saturdays and in quantity for special occasions from the Bake Paddle on Francis Street. Felicity and Providence Greenhill, Proprietors.*

On the Thursday after the notices were posted, the bakery was visited by a rotund little man carrying a notice that, from its tattered state, gave evidence of having been ripped down from wherever it had been tacked up. "My name's Bundleman," he informed them. "I work for Darby Littlefield."

"How do you do," Providence greeted him. "How may we help you?"

"I'd like to sample your cakes and tarts with an order in mind, provided they suits."

Felicity said obligingly, "Take your pick, Mister Bundleman. Which one would you like to try?"

"All of 'em" he answered grandly. "I'm talking about a substantious order."

Providence and Felicity exchanged glances as he helped himself. One of each added up to eight separate pastries: three kinds of tart made with dried cranberries, dried pumpkin, and dried apples, and five cakes; plain, spice, cream, honey and prune. Bundleman took a considering bit out of a blueberry tart, chewed it and swallowed it, then put the uneaten portion down on the counter. He took up the next confection and bit into it; then the third. After he'd sampled each of the eight he finished off the remainders, finally flicking a handkerchief out of his pocket to dab at the corners of his lips. "Except for the punkin, which ain't to my liking, I'd say they was tasty. We'll be needing ten dozen delivered two weeks come next Saturday."

"Did you say ten dozen?" Providence repeated carefully, with another flickering glance at Felicity.

"That's right. And I'll expect a special price."

Felicity suggested with composure, "Four shillings, six pence the lot, Mister Bundleman."

Bundleman did some mental arithmetic, then nodded. "Satisfactory," he said. "Supper's at eight, so we'll expect delivery around seven. You can stop by the Red Mask on the following day for your money."

"We would expect to be paid first," Felicity told him.

"You ain't questioning Mister Littlefield's credit, are you?"

Providence gave Felicity a poke, and Felicity said, "No, of course not. Sunday following will be acceptable."

Bundleman gave the counter a rap with his knuckles to conclude the deal. "Ten dozen pastries, two weeks come Saturday, excluding the punkin, at four and six the lot."

John Bundleman was an opinionated man with an unwavering belief in absolutes. Had Providence and Felicity understood this they would never have worried about selling something on account. To Mister Bundleman, paying for what you get was as taken for granted as getting what you pay for (in this case ten dozen pastries with no punkin). He had made his way up from stableboy to kitchen drudge to wardrobe keeper to personal servant through a combination of ambition and strict self-discipline, and he had raised Darby Littlefield from a lad. He might not be a gentleman's gentleman, but he was a gentleman's prize, principled, loyal, and indispensable. He lived by strict rules and expected everyone else to do the same.

A number of Bundleman's rules concerned themselves with issues of honor. A man is obedient to his father and respectful of his mother; a man never turns tail on an enemy, never betrays a friend, never tells on a lady. It was, therefore, distasteful to hear the name Winsome Greenhill bandied about in his master's parlor.

Bundleman had returned to the inn and had entered the parlor to find Mister Littlefield entertaining an acquaintance. "I told you that Winsome Greenhill would be worth cultivating, did I not?" the visitor was saying.

"You did indeed," Littlefield conceded.

The name caused Mister Bundleman to pause. He had just come from The Bake Paddle. Hadn't he seen the name Greenhill on the bakery sign? He couldn't recall the given names, but he was sure the last name was Greenhill. How many Greenhills could there be in a town the size of Williamsburg? Could they be talking about the younger of the two women he'd just been interviewing? If not certain, it was a distinct possibility. She was beautiful enough to be fair game.

Neither paid any attention to Bundleman as he slithered past, entered his bedroom, and shut the door. Among Bundleman's rules there was one against eavesdropping, but it hardly applied to this situation since the voices were far too loud to escape hearing no matter how hard one tried.

"So she finally succumbed," the visiter declared. "I told you she would, given some little encouragement."

"I hope I'll be able to get rid of her as easily," Littlefield ruminated. "She has ambitions, that one. She whispers marriage in my ear as if she actually believes I'd entertain notions of turning a baker's daughter into a duchess."

"I know what you mean. She hopes to use her pretty face to lure a rich husband. She tried the same with me."

"Too bad she has nothing more than her pretty face to recommend her," Littlefield said.

Bundleman, sitting on his bed, shook his head disapprovingly. He had been right. They were talking about the girl from the bakery.

"What do you say when she speaks of marriage?" the visitor asked.

"I've told her not to break her engagement in case I lose my scalp in the wilderness."

"Sly," the visitor said appreciatively. "She can't cause you any trouble so long as she has a fiancé to answer to, and Bartholomew Smythe is the perfect dupe."

"It doesn't really matter. I've just about had my fill of Winsome Greenhill," Littlefield went on. "I'll see her once or twice more, then simply fail to show up at her house one day. That will mark the end of it."

The two men laughed, then the visitor said, "I have a cousin from New York arriving for a visit any day now. Her name is Eleanor Whitehill and she's coming with her father, my uncle, Cyrus Whitehill. Would you care to meet a lady for a change?"

"I'd like nothing better, Amos. Perhaps I can prevail upon you to bring her to my supper party."

"Miss Greenhill won't be there?"

"Heaven forbid. By then I hope to be free of her."

"In that case I shall certainly bring Eleanor. I'm sure she'll be delighted to come."

"It's settled then. I look forward to it."

Bundleman sighed. Dalliances were expected of a healthy, vigorous man like his employer, but joking about his conquests was reprehensible and bragging about breaking the heart of a respectable, if misguided, girl was an abomination. That weakness of character was something that Bundleman could hardly condone, and yet loyalty made him seek a scapegoat for Littlefield. It wasn't

Littlefield who was to blame, but the environment, this rudimentry colonial society, rich in opportunity but poor in tradition and breeding, a society in which bounders like Amos Dewey flourished and which sometimes weakened men like Darby Littlefield.

On the same day that Bundleman visited the bakery Felicity heard that Kean and Murray's acting troupe had arrived in Williamsburg and was boarding at the Market Square Tavern on the Duke of Gloucester Street. She knew from the notice tacked up on the bakery wall that *Richard III* would mark the opening of their engagement on Friday, a week hence, and she decided to visit the inn that evening.

"Not alone, you won't," Providence told her. "You'll take Winnie along for company."

Winsome was, to say the least, unreceptive to the idea, but Providence prevailed, saying, "It isn't seemly for a woman to enter a public house alone. You're going with your sister, like it or not."

So in the end it was Felicity in company with Winsome who marched down the Duke of Gloucester Street to the tavern. The Market Square Tavern was less elegant than the Red Mask, but busier, catering as it did to less affluent wayfarers—tinkers, itinerant painters, drovers, and settlers moving through on their way north or west to stake out land claims. The front door opened directly into the taproom, a large chamber with a dozen or more occupied tables, including one at which there was a party of five boisterous army officers. One of them, tall, blond, and blue-eyed, stood with raised glass toasting a tableful of ladies—Felicity judged them to be actresses by their flamboyant makeup and dress—who applauded the tribute with equal enthusiasm. A large sign over their heads read NO INDIANS, NO NEGROES, NO WHORES.

Felicity spotted Robby Flower sitting on a stool at the far end of the room next to the table of officers. He was serenading the other patrons on his Jew's harp, and stopping occasionally to take a pull from a tankard of ale on the floor next his feet. He looked up when Felicity and Winsome walked over to him, acknowledged them with a nod, but continued to play until he'd finished the tune and collected the coins that splattered the floor around him. Then he said amiably, "You're the curl-cake bakeress, aren't you?"

"You do remember," Felicity answered. "I'm Felicity Greenhill and this is my sister, Winsome. Winnie, this is Robby Flower."

"How do you do," Winsome said primly.

"Oh, pretty well." Flower slid his arm around Winsome's waist, gave her a squeeze, and then released her. "Could I buy you a mug of ale?"

"No thank you," Winsome informed him coldly.

"I've come with a proposition," Felicity interrupted.

"I'm always open to a proposition," Flower allowed cheerfully.

"I took your advice. I had notice printed up advertising the curl cakes and I've done well with them this last month. Now I'm making miniature cakes and tarts. I'd like to sell them at the theater."

"I've not had much experience with miniature cakes, but I've had a tart or two in my time," Mister Flower rejoined, winking at the table of eavesdropping officers.

One of them, the young man who had offered the toast to womanhood, suddenly leaned forward and touched Felicity's arm. He started to speak, but Felicity ignored him and continued her conversation with Flower. "Will you introduce me to Mister Kean and Mister Murray? I'd like to propose an arrangement with them."

"Kean's sitting right over there," Flower replied. "Come, I'll be glad to introduce you."

"Wait," the blond officer spoke out, but Felicity pretended she hadn't heard and followed Flower across the room, dragging Winsome with her.

Kean turned out to be a good-looking man and as sharp as his name. Felicity told him why she'd come, and after hearing her out he pronounced himself willing to consider the proposal. "I'd not object to it," he said, "so long as you don't interfere with the performances."

"I'll close the stall while the curtain's up."

"What stall?" Kean asked. "There is no stall in the entrance hall, and there is no room to store your pies and cakes."

"We can find a corner for a counter. You have able-bodied men in your company. Perhaps they can arrange something for me. I'll serve the customers from trays and store my hampers backstage."

"We perform two nights a week, Friday and Saturday."

"I can accommodate to that schedule."

"And we'd expect some share in your profits."

"Why?" Felicity asked in surprise. "I don't expect to share in yours."

"People will come to see us with or without refreshments. I daresay you couldn't attract a similar crowd on the strength of your cakes and tarts."

"How much would you expect?"

"Half the profits," he answered.

That she might have to pay for the privilege of hawking her wares in the theater hadn't occurred to her, and for a minute she was taken aback. Recovering, she said firmly, "That would not be acceptable. I'll give you one-tenth."

"One-third."

"One-eighth."

"One-quarter, Miss Greenhill, and no less."

It was finally settled at one-quarter and arrangements made for Felicity to be at the theater for opening night. She shook hands with Mister Kean and then with Robby Flower. Somehow during the parting amenities Robby Flower managed to slip his arm around Winsome's waist again, but this time she brushed him away indignantly.

Minutes later, as she and Felicity emerged from the inn,

a voice called out to them, and they turned to find themselves once again facing the young officer. "What do you want?" Felicity asked irritably. "I thought we made it plain that we're not interested in making your acquaintance."

"Lissy, I'm Joss. Don't you recognize me?"

Felicity stared at him in disbelief. "Joss? Joss Wrentham?"

"No one else."

Felicity took in the square chin, the strong mouth, the steady blue eyes. "It is you. Winnie, it's Joss."

He was smiling at her rather foolishly, and for a minute she smiled back with equal awkwardness, then she rushed forward and threw her arms around his neck. She was nearly as tall as he, and he braced himself to keep from being bowled over. "Whatever are you doing here, Joss?"

"I arrived yesterday. I've joined the Virginia rangers. I intended to call on you this weekend. You're still at number four, Nassau Street, are you not?"

"We are. Winnie, for heaven's sake, it's Joss. Aren't you going to say hello?"

"I will if you give me the chance," Winsome answered. She stepped forward and, speaking over Felicity's shoulder, asked curiously, "Where did you find money enough to buy yourself a commission?"

"Winnie," Felicity admonished through gritted teeth, "is that all you can think of to say?"

"Well, Lucy never wrote that you'd become an officer. The last we heard is that you were fighting under the command of William Pepperell, Joss."

"That was some time ago. When we captured the French fort of Louisburg on Cape Breton, I was cited for heroism. It was no more than fortuitous circumstance—I was only sixteen and raw as they come—but I was promoted in the field two ranks, from private to sergeant. Then I was made a second lieutenant after we stopped the French from recapturing Louisburg. After that I was promoted to first lieutenant for the same reason that Pepperell was knighted; consolation for the Treaty of Aix-la-Chapelle."

"The treaty restoring Louisburg to the French," Felicity noted ironically.

Josiah nodded. "Since then, of course, the situation has done nothing but worsen. The French have swarmed all over the Ohio Valley, and we have no choice except to fight again. We've a new commander in chief coming any day now, Major General Edward Braddock. Once he arrives we'll be going north again."

"But for now you're here," Felicity exclaimed happily. "When will you come to see us?"

"Is Sunday convenient?"

"Sunday for supper. Come at seven."

"I'll be on your doorstep."

"I can't wait to tell Mama."

· 27 ·

Josiah arrived promptly at seven, looking well turned out in a freshly pressed uniform and polished boots, and was ushered into the parlor to be greeted and fussed over. Supper was a pleasant hour taken up with reminiscences of the old days in New Castle. As they talked, Providence made a mental note to write Lucy to let her know how well her brother was. *I'm sure you will be proud to learn that he's a first lieutenant now. He tells us that he hopes to visit you and the rest of his family as soon as he's able, perhaps before the year is out.* She was tempted to make something of the fateful chance meeting between Josiah and Felicity, but decided not to jinx the possibility for romance by commenting on it in the letter. Let fate deal as it would with that issue.

She wasn't beyond giving fate a nudge, however, and after supper she hustled Winsome into the kitchen, leaving

Felicity and Josiah alone. "How did you come to join the Virginia rangers?" Felicity asked.

"My cavalry unit was disbanded a few months ago, and I heard there were two companies of Virginia rangers being organized, so I came down."

"You like the army, don't you?"

Josiah regarded her quizzically. "You sound as if I shouldn't."

"I'm not a Quaker, Joss, but I think it's wrong to bear arms. Will George Washington command the company?"

"No. Our commander is another Virginian named Lawrence Collier. I understand he's a rich bachelor much in demand by the ladies. Do you know him?"

"I've seen him, but I'm not acquainted," Felicity answered. "We hardly travel in the same circles. He owns a plantation on the banks of the James River. It started as a small farm worked by his grandfather and father, but he has gradually increased it to immense size and is now reputed to be the richest man in Virginia. I'm surprised he's willing to leave his tobacco interests to go to war."

"He's a friend of your lieutenant governor," Josiah explained. "They say he accepted the commission at Dinwiddie's request. Dinwiddie feels strongly that if the French aren't stopped, they'll eventually invade Virginia."

"I hear the French have an efficient army, and that they've enlisted the aid of the Iroquois."

Josiah nodded. "We also have an informal alliance with the Indians, but we don't use them so well. The French bribe them with false promises and seduce them with visions of wealth and glory."

"As much as I detest killing," Felicity said, "I detest the Indians more."

"You used to speak more kindly of them."

"That was before they took Sarah and murdered her."

"I'm sorry. It's been so long. I had forgotten."

"I wish I could forget, but there's always something . . . or someone," she added bitterly . . . "to remind me." Seeing Josiah's pained expression, she added quickly, "I was speaking of my sister-in-law, who delights in such morbid reminiscences."

"The lure of catastrophe?"

"The satisfaction of causing pain, I'm afraid."

"The Indians don't always kill their captives, Lissy. I know of a case where a white captive, a woman, was adopted by the Iroquois. I saw her myself once."

"You did?"

"Yes. She was in the company of a party of braves. Her skin was darkened by the sun, so that her complexion was like that of an Indian. But she was a white. The Indians aren't always brutal or barbarous. They're capable of compassion too; as much as any white man."

"I know, Joss. Please let's not talk about it any more just now."

Josiah was only too eager for a change of subject, and they talked of other things until Providence and Winsome rejoined them for a parting glass of sherry. Then Felicity accompanied Josiah to the door. "Please come again," she told him.

"I will if you invite me."

"How may I reach you?"

"Leave a message with the innkeeper at the Market Square Tavern. He'll see that I get it."

They wished one another good night. Felicity closed the door and leaned her head against the doorjamb. *Does Joss regret the lives he's taken,* she wondered, *or is it easier to kill a stranger than to kill one's sister?*

The week following was busy, with Felicity and Providence putting in long extra hours baking. Then on Friday morning Nedda arrived at the bakery in a flurry of indignation, having just learned about the arrangement to sell pastries at the theater.

"It was your idea, Lissy. Don't deny it. You're doing this purposely to spite me. Berry and I have taken a box with the Tagglestons and the Bentons for this evening's performance. John Taggleston is a successful merchant and Catherine Benton is cousin to Governor Dinwiddie."

"We know who the Tagglestons and the Bentons are, Nedda," Providence interrupted. "Get to the point."

"The point is that we've only just begun to socialize with them. How are we expected to explain the spectacle of Berry's mother and sister selling cakes and tarts in the aisles, shouting 'Cakes and tarts, ha'penny apiece'?"

"We aren't going to sell our goods in the aisles," Providence soothed. "We've set up a stall in the lobby."

"However you do it, it's undignified. It's a humiliation to us. How are we to deal with it?"

"You might stay home," Felicity suggested dryly.

"You'd like that, wouldn't you? You'd like to prevent Berry and me from widening our friendships or aspiring to better our lot. You take perverse pleasure in degrading us."

"Stop saying 'we' and 'us,'" Felicity suggested. "It's only you who are unhappy with what we're doing. Berry isn't bothered in the least."

"Berry may be too loyal to show it," Nedda retorted, "but don't tell me he'll not be embarrassed to have his mother peddling sweetmeats in the lobby while he sits like a gentleman in one of the boxes."

She had made her point, and although Felicity refused to acknowledge it, Providence was disturbed by the thought that Beriah might be made uncomfortable by her presence in the theater. "Perhaps it would be better for me to remain home this evening," she conceded.

Felicity objected vehemently, saying, "Pay no attention to her, Mama. I can't manage alone. You have to come."

"Winnie can take my place."

"You know how much she'll like that."

"Perhaps she won't like it, but she'll do it if I insist."

The argument continued to crackle for a few minutes more until Providence made up her mind to the partial concession, Nedda was resigned to her partial victory, and

Felicity was left to her defeat. "Well, you got your way, Nedda," she said shortly. "There's nothing else to keep you here, is there?"

"I assure you I wouldn't have come here at all if there hadn't been good reason."

"How is it that your good reasons are unvaryingly mean-spirited and selfish? All that ever interests you is *your* dignity, *your* pleasures, *your* aspirations. You care nothing at all for other people's desires, I suppose because you care nothing at all for other people."

Nedda's lips puckered with distaste. She flounced to the door and pulled it open, then turned back to say, "*Your* only attribute is knowing yourself how hideously common you are. If you have any sense left at all, you'll marry while you're still pretty enough to find a man willing to overlook your hopelessly vulgar, lower-class tastes."

"I don't look to any man for my salvation. If I marry at all, it will be to please myself, not save myself."

"In that case," Nedda said shrilly, "I suppose we will be expected to welcome a chimney sweep or a cow-chip peddler into the family one day."

With that final observation Nedda departed, setting the shop bells to jingling as she slammed the door behind her.

Winsome resigned herself to the one evening of servitude, but not happily. Joseph Savery, the carter, deposited her and Felicity, along with their eight pastry hampers, just outside the stage door on Waller Street at six-thirty, then rattled off, leaving them to fend for themselves. "He might at least have carried the hampers inside," Winsome complained. "That's what comes of being a free 'nigra.'"

"It has nothing to do with being a Negro," Felicity said. "He's late for another job on Mill Street. Come, we'll each take an end and carry them in one at a time."

Their entrance backstage was a plunge from calm into chaos. An actor wearing a ruffled shirt, velvet cape, and high-crowned hat rushed by barefoot, carrying his boots and stockings in his hand. A moment later a woman ran past clutching her breast and declaiming, "'I had an Edward, till a Richard kill'd him; I had a Harry, till a Richard kill'd him!'" They could hear hammering onstage, someone was shouting for the Sheriff of Wiltshire, and they were nearly bowled over by two children dressed in velvet knickers. A moment later an important-looking personage paused in the midst of displaying his "'bruised arms hung up for monuments'" to shout, "Out of the way, ladies. Move that basket out of the way."

"We'd like to," Felicity told him. "Where can we—"

"Not here," the man thundered as he stalked off. "Can't you see there's no room?"

"Apparently no one is going to assist us," Felicity said decisively. "We shall have to take care of ourselves." She looked around for a secure haven. "We'll pile them up behind the door, Winnie."

It took nearly half an hour to lug in the hampers, stack them, and arrange the first half-dozen pastry trays. Felicity didn't want to leave the hampers untended, so Winsome remained with the hampers while she carried the trays one by one up the side aisle to the lobby. Kean had seen to the construction of a stall—a pair of two-foot-wide boards laid across three upended barrels—and Felicity lined up her trays on the makeshift counter.

The customers weren't long in coming. A portly gentleman bought two pastries for himself and his wife, and was followed by others so that Felicity soon found herself conducting a brisk trade, doling out cakes and tarts and taking in coins while she greeted strangers and exchanged pleasantries with acquaintances. She saw Beriah raise his arm to wave to her as he and Nedda entered the theater, but before Felicity could wave back, Nedda had taken a firm grip on her husband's elbow and pulled him up the stairs leading to the boxes.

Meanwhile, backstage, Winsome sat on an overturned crate and observed the frantic activity. She was fascinated by the actors, their intensity and their absorption in what seemed to be nonsensical activities. They reminded her of herself as a child pretending to be a princess or a bird or an angel. How she had loved dressing up in her mother's clothes or in costumes and jewels she would improvise from scraps of fabric or strings of berries, never guessing that there were adults who earned their living from such childish make-believe.

After a time Felicity returned to refill her trays and to turn over the first batch of coins into Winsome's keeping. Then, just before the curtain rose, she carried the freshly filled trays back to the lobby to be ready for the first intermission. Winsome couldn't see the stage from her position near the back door, but she could watch the entrances and exits and listen to the speeches. The first was delivered by Thomas Kean, who emoted the lines "Now is the winter of our discontent . . ." to thrilling effect. Winsome didn't quite understand the meaning, but the words were beautiful. As the lines were spoken she repeated some of them under her breath: *"the lascivious pleasing of a lute," "this weak piping time of peace."*

During Act I, Scene II, Robby Flower, elegantly attired as a nobleman, emerged from a room at the back of the theater, passed by Winsome without acknowledging her presence, paused for a moment in the wings, then burst upon the stage declaring, "Have patience, madam. There's no doubt His Majesty will soon recover his accustomed health." He sounded different on stage than he did face-to-face, Winsome thought. Not seeing him but just listening, one might almost believe he was a gentleman. But, of course, he was just made of "scraps of fabric and strings of berries," all sham and no gentleman at all.

A few minutes later Flower came back into the wings on his exit line, "Madam, we will attend your grace," and sauntered over to stand in front of Winsome. "Have you a sweet for the earl, brother to the queen?" he asked.

"Have you a halfpenny?"

"No, only a smile for a beautiful lady. Won't that buy me something?"

"Here then," Winsome said begrudgingly handing him a mashed raisin cake. "Now please go do your begging elsewhere."

"I've a sweet tooth, no doubt about it," Flower murmured. "I fancy these sugary confections, and I could just as easily fancy you if you'd let me." He ate the cake and wiped the crumbs from his lips, then said, "Tell me, Miss Greenhill, would you like to be an earl's lady?"

"Not an actor earl, thank you."

"It's the nearest most of us come to carrying a title."

"How true, Mister Flower," she returned, carefully withholding any external sign of the delicious secret she harbored.

"But romance isn't the exclusive property of royalty," Flower added. "As I say in the play, 'Thine eyes, sweet lady, have infected mine.'" He reached for another cake, but Winsome slapped his hand away.

"That was Mister Kean's speech," she reminded him, "not yours. And if I recall it rightly, the answer was 'Would they were basilisks, to strike thee dead!'"

Flower's grin broadened. "You've a quick memory."

"And a quicker temper, Mister Flower. You might remember that before you try to steal another cake."

"It's not just cake I'm after, Miss Greenhill."

"Whatever you're after, you're wasting your time with me."

"I think you'd like me if you got to know me."

"I've no intention of taking such a risk, Mister Flower."

An agitated guardsman suddenly strode up and slapped a cloak over Flower's shoulder. "You're the first murderer tonight, Robby. Hurry up or you'll miss your cue."

Flower divested himself of his hat and pulled the cloak's hood down over his head, mumbling, "What are they up to?

'O, spare my guiltless wife and my poor children!' and so on and so on. All right, here I go."

Winsome glared at his retreating back, then muttered to herself, "It's Lissy's fault I had to come here and endure the attentions of that . . . that . . . that actor."

· · 28 · ·

Winsome was shocked to learn from a casually dropped remark from Felicity that The Bake Paddle would supply pastries for Darby Littlefield's supper party the following Saturday evening, a party Winsome had known nothing about. Darby had formed the habit of visiting Winsome on Tuesdays and Fridays. He was scarcely inside the door on Tuesday afternoon before Winsome brought up the subject of the party, only to have him shrug it off. "It's nothing; a little supper party to honor Robert Dinwiddie, the lieutenant governor. You know he's also a director of the Ohio Company, and it's politic that I cultivate his friendship."

"I'm not to be invited?"

"Don't be ridiculous. How could I invite you?"

"But you're leaving in only two weeks, Darby. Surely you could have invited Bart and me."

Darby said irritably, "That would be in the poorest of taste, would it not?"

"It would be quite natural to invite us so long as you're inviting Bart's father and mother."

"The Smythes? No, I haven't invited them either. Smythe may be a member of the Assembly, but they tell me he started as a fishmonger, and to my way of thinking the stink of fish still clings to him."

The remark shocked and silenced Winsome. If the Smythes weren't worthy of Darby, how could he think that Bart was worthy of her? How could he ask that she remain engaged to Bart? It had been a thoughtless remark, but a revealing one. She brooded after Darby left, and brooded all that evening, an evening spent in Bart's company at the Smythes'.

Bart's father was an intelligent man, but he was also, as Darby had pointed out, boorish and uncultivated. His speech was ungrammatical, and the scope of his interests was confined to discussions of machinery and tools or, in more expansive moods, the evils of trade embargoes. Never had Winsome been so aware of his rough edges, and at the supper table she eyed Bart, as well, with distaste. He might be a little more polished than his father, but essentially there was little to choose between them, and his mother was little better. Socially inept, she applied more enthusiasm than skill to playing the lady. Jennie, Bart's twenty-year-old sister, was not only plain to look at but completely charmless, and too stupid to realize that it was her father's affluence that accounted for her popularity. Her father bought her whatever she wanted—clothes, perfumes, baubles, and trinkets without end—and when the time came, he would buy her a well-placed husband too.

As Winsome looked at the family ranged round the table she began to think it remarkable that she had expended so much effort on winning a place for herself among them. She never would have bothered with the Smythes if Amos Dewey hadn't threatened her reputation by talking about their shared intimacies. Winsome had made a mistake trusting Amos. She had tripped up as she so often tripped up, at that moment when her romantic fantasies overcame more practical considerations. Amos had bowled her over with his romantically wicked reputation and his compliments, and he had nearly been her undoing. It had been necessary to protect herself, and Bart, with his lumbering affection and absolute faith in her, had provided easy refuge. Then, too, Bart's father had just been elected to the Assembly, which seemed to bode well for the Smythes' position in society. She should have realized they never would be accepted by their betters. The stink of fish still clung to the name Smythe.

Bart, noticing Winsome's preoccupation during the evening, brought it up on the walk home. "What's wrong, Winnie? You barely spoke tonight."

"What do I know about drills and awls and angle measures? That's all your father ever talks about."

"You weren't receptive to Mother's plan to invite your family to supper next week, and when she brought out the linens she's embroidering for you, you showed no interest at all."

"I said they were pretty."

"You scarcely looked at them. You weren't very nice to Jennie either. Sometimes I think you dislike Jennie."

"What could there possibly be to dislike about Jennie?"

They walked in silence until they turned the corner onto Nassau Street, then Bart said unhappily, "I wish I knew what it is that's upset you."

Winsome held off the reply until they reached the house. Then she said calmly, "Bart, I don't wish to marry you after all."

"What?"

"I don't wish to marry you."

He stopped and pulled her around to face him. "What is it? What have I done?"

"I've changed my mind, Bart."

Bartholomew startled her by asking, "Is it that business with Darby Littlefield?"

"What do you mean?"

"Are you upset because I accused you of seeing him?"

"No," Winsome answered, relieved that he actually knew nothing about her and Darby. "It has nothing to do with Mister Littlefield."

"Then it's my jealousy. I told you I was sorry, didn't I? It was stupid of me to listen to gossip. But when Jennie told me that Jane had seen you and him—"

Winsome hadn't known that Jennie was the one who had

relayed Jane Fitzroy's gossip to Bart, but it was of no particular importance now. "I said it has nothing to do with Darby Littlefield or with your jealousy, either, for that matter. It has only to do with me, with my lack of feeling for you."

The street was dark, with only the moon for illumination. Bart bent forward to search her face. "I love you, Winnie," he pleaded, his eyes bright with misery.

Winsome probed her emotions for some scrap of sympathy. Instead, her determination to disentangle herself from Bart prompted her to say coldly, "But I don't love you, and I can't marry a man I don't love."

She was horrified to see that he was beginning to cry, and panic made her crueler. "Nothing will change my mind. I don't wish to marry you, and I don't intend to marry you. Surely that's perfectly clear. Good night, Bart."

"No. Don't go. Wait. Can't we talk?"

"There's nothing more to talk about."

He tried to hold her back, but she pulled loose and ran up the front steps, hurrying to get inside and close the door to avoid pursuit.

Of course, the engagement wasn't that easily terminated. Winsome's announcement, made moments after she entered the house, confounded her mother and sister and triggered an interrogation that Winsome cut short by fleeing the parlor and locking herself in her room. She remained there until Providence and Felicity left for the bakery on Wednesday morning, then resumed her normal pattern of activity—cleaning house, shopping, and preparing supper—as if to prove to everyone's satisfaction that there was no need to treat the event as a crisis.

She was less successful than she hoped. That evening her mother came into her bedroom for a private talk that lasted for an uncomfortable hour, during which Winsome was unable to satisfy her mother's curiosity as to why she had broken with Bart, offering nothing more enlightening than her doggedly repeated statement that "I realize I don't love him, Mama."

Then, shortly afterward, the Smythes arrived; father, mother, and betrothed. Felicity occupied them in the parlor while Providence tried to persuade Winsome to come downstairs. Failing that, Providence joined the Smythes and there was a hushed huddle in the parlor, ending with Bart suddenly rushing into the hall and up the stairs, only to have Winsome shut the bedroom door in his face. The Smythes left soon after, showing signs of belated acrimony. They had done what was required. The burden of guilt now lay with the Greenhills.

By Thursday evening word had spread, and Nedda charged into the house demanding an explanation. She had heard the news but couldn't believe it. Had it been a lover's quarrel? Was it prenuptial nerves? What had ever possessed Winsome to toss away the prospect of an excellent marriage? Winsome clung to the explanation that she didn't love Bart, scarcely an excuse acceptable to Nedda, but one that found an unexpected ally in Felicity and resulted in yet another row.

"It wouldn't surprise me if you put Winnie up to this, Lissy," Nedda exclaimed, "giving her the impression that there's some shame attached to a woman's dependency on husband and home, discouraging her from making what would have been a most advantageous marriage."

"There is something wrong with marriage if there is nothing else," Felicity maintained.

"Else? What else?"

"Love."

"Love," Nedda repeated disparagingly. "Love is all very well in its place, but it's hardly a substitute for the security of a well-placed marriage. If you want to end your life as an impoverished old maid, that's your privilege, but it's a sin to encourage Winnie to ruin her life as well."

"Did you marry Berry because it was advantageous?" Felicity challenged.

"I thought Berry would do well one day, and I knew I could inspire him to succeed. What I didn't anticipate was having to deal with his impossible family."

"If we can put up with you, Nedda, which requires endurance of heroic proportion, then surely you can put up with us."

The interview concluded, as always, with Nedda leaving in a huff, but the diversion had served the purpose of finally laying to rest the subject of Winsome's broken engagement.

Winsome intended to tell Darby on Friday that she had broken her engagement. With no obstacle between them they could now announce their affections—and intentions—openly, perhaps at Darby's party on Saturday evening, the possibility suiting Winsome's flair for the dramatic. But on Friday her plans were upset when a boy brought her a note saying that pressing business would prevent Darby's visit that day. What was she to do now? How was she to relay the news?

A ready-made solution offered itself when Felicity expressed concern over having to entrust Joseph Savery to the task of delivering the pastries to the Red Mask. "We can't go with him, Mama, because we have to be at the theater. What if something goes wrong? Someone should really go along to look after the hampers."

"Perhaps Winnie can go."

Winsome offered token resistance, knowing it would be expected of her, but soon relented with the grudging admission that, no, she hadn't anything better to do.

The pastries were packed into twelve square hampers, eight for the theater and four for the party, and on Saturday evening Winsome helped her mother and sister carry them out to Joseph Savery's wagon. Felicity and Winsome settled themselves on the floor of the wagon holding the hampers steady, and Providence sat up front with Joseph. The theater was the first stop. After Felicity and Providence unloaded their hampers Savery turned the horse toward the west end of town, holding the horse to a walk so as not to jiggle the hampers that were left.

By the time they finally drew into the inn's stableyard, Winsome was fidgety with impatience. She saw several horses and carriages she recognized. One belonged to the lieutenant governor and bore the governor's crest, one was the Fitzroy's carriage, and a third belonged to the Deweys, a large black-and-gold affair with four polished brass lanterns hanging front and back.

Joseph pulled the wagon up to the kitchen door, helped Winsome alight, then helped her to carry in the hampers. As was usual whenever Joseph entered by the kitchen door, he was royally welcomed. Savery was a free Negro. His father had been half brother to Daniel Savery, one of the richest white landowners in Virginia, and Daniel had freed Joseph's father on his twenty-first birthday. Joseph didn't socialize with the white Saverys, but he shared the protection of the Savery name, as well as the Saverys' lordly self-assurance, spoke eye-to-eye with whites, and was the envy of those Negroes who were held as slaves.

The cook and her four helpers, all noisy, fat, middle-aged daughters with satiny black faces, were owned by the innkeeper. They had no hope of ever being free unless they were to marry a free Negro with money enough to buy their freedom as well. Now they surrounded Joseph, pushing him into a chair and thrusting a pewter mug into his hand.

The cook slapped a plate of pigs' feet and cabbage onto the table in front of him. "Eat up," she commanded. "I'll wager you've not et since morning." She jerked her thumb toward Winsome. "Who's she?"

"She's the bakery lady's daughter," Joseph explained. "She come to look after the pastries."

"The what? Well, let her start unpackin' then."

Winsome wasn't pleased to be ordered about by a slave, but complied rather than make a fuss. "I'll need some platters."

The cook signaled to one of her daughters, who gave Winsome two large pewter trays.

"What is these things?" the cook asked curiously as Winsome began unpacking the pastries.

"You can see what they are," Winsome said shortly.

The cook picked up a raisin cake and turned it this way and that. "A little cake," she concluded.

"Put it down, please."

The cook sniffed it, then nibbled it. "Raisin cake. Couldn't be no more than three raisins in a cake that size."

"Now that you've taken a bite," Winsome said ungraciously, "you might as well finish it."

The cook laughed. "They's a curiosity. I never seen cakes and pies the size of biscuits. Joseph, you seen these runty things?"

Joseph nodded amiably, drank down his beer, and stuck out the mug, which was immediately replenished by one of the cook's daughters.

The cook ate the little cake, ran her tongue over her lips to savor the sugary aftertaste, then reached for a second cake. This time Winsome slapped her hand away. "I told you not to touch them," she said sharply.

"Listen now, missy, don't you be fresh with me."

Winsome put down the tart in her hand and said angrily, "I suggest you finish this chore yourself."

"Me?" the cook declared. "Not me. I got my hands full here." She pointed to a sideboard loaded with food. "Four sucklin' pigs to carve up and put back together, chopped beef pudding, fish aspic, cabbage relish, figs to glaze. No, not me. You're supposed to take care of the cakes, girl."

"Don't call me girl."

Savery intervened. "You're lucky she don't call you every which name, you don't do the job you sent here to do."

"I've already done more than I was expected to do. This is slave work, and I'm not a slave. I'm leaving now."

"You can't go without me," Joseph informed her, "and I ain't done eating."

"You were hired to deliver four hampers to the inn, not to act as my chaperon," Winsome told him.

The cook rolled her eyes in amusement and said, "She right 'bout that. You ain't responsible for what this white girl do."

"Besides, she go by herself, you can stay here with us," one of the daughters cajoled. "You ain't got no reason to hurry off now, has you, Joe?"

Winsome didn't wait to hear Savery's reply. She marched out of the kitchen and down the hall to the inn's foyer, and from there slipped into the ladies' parlor, a small sitting room set aside for the comfort of female guests to the inn. She availed herself of the momentary privacy to remove her cloak and drape it around her shoulders, then remove her hat. Under the cloak she wore a party gown fashioned of tiers of ruffled pink silk flounces, with green velvet ribbons laced through a pleated low-cut bodice. Hoops supported the skirt and the taffeta petticoat, and her delicate, high-heeled slippers (rescued from her drawstring purse) were made of green silk. Her tasseled ivory fan (also fished up out of her purse) opened to display a parade of multicolored butterflies fluttering across a green silk field, and her hair, once the dull bonnet was removed, was splendidly coiffed with green velvet bows tucked here and there among her elaborate curls.

Winsome was going to the party.

· · 29 · ·

The taproom was full of noisy patrons, but when Winsome peeked into the large dining room, she saw that it was empty. Darby must have paid dearly for its exclusive use. The dozen or so round oak tables that composed the room's usual furnishings had been pushed against the walls and supplanted by boards laid across trestles to form a large U-shaped dining table set for what appeared to be about fifty people.

Winsome pictured the table surrounded by Virginia's upper crust with Darby and herself at its head. It would be a moment of exquisite triumph. She took a proprietary view of the arrangements, checking the plates and silverware for cleanliness and the lamps for a sufficiency of oil. Of course the inn wasn't as elegant as their house would be when it was finished, but even a temporary domicile must reflect some aura of grace.

When she turned back into the hall she noticed Ferris Halley coming in the door. Halley was a rich merchant, but notorious for his debauchery and therefore seldom entertained by the respectable families of Williamsburg. Winsome wondered if Darby were aware of his reputation and decided she must caution him at the first opportunity.

She started for the stairs, but stopped when she heard someone call her by name. She turned and saw Robby Flower, Jew's harp in hand, standing just inside the front door. "What are *you* doing here?" Winsome demanded.

"I'm here to entertain."

"To entertain at Darby Littlefield's party?"

Flower nodded. "Littlefield came into the theater a few days ago to reserve a box for next Saturday's performance of *The Beaux' Strategem*, and while he was there he mentioned that he was looking for a musician to play tonight. Naturally I spoke up."

"Naturally."

"It's *Richard*'s last night. I bribed one of my fellow actors to take my role. How do I look?"

He was wearing green: tight britches, silk shirt, velvet vest, and a long-tailed cap with bells at the tip. Winsome said, "You look a far cry from a nobleman."

Flower rubbed together his thumb and two fingers. "Littlefield's paying me enough to make it worthwhile to play the fool for one night."

"I'm really not interested in how much money he's paying you, Mister Flower."

"What are you doing here, Miss Greenhill?" Flower asked.

"What do you think I'm doing here?"

"By the look of you I'd say you were one of the guests."

"How very astute of you."

"You never told me you know the duke dandy," Flower remarked.

"What occasion had I to mention my friendship with Mister Littlefield?"

"Just how friendly are you?" Flower had the audacity to ask.

Winsome answered curtly, "Friendlier than you and I shall ever be."

"Well, be careful. That kind keeps dalliance and duty separate."

Winsome hadn't escaped the unpleasantness in the kitchen only to be set upon by the horrid little actor in his ridiculous jester's costume. She picked up her skirts and fled up the stairs.

Darby had opened the parlor and both bedrooms to accommodate his guests, but there wasn't sufficient space to allow for easy circulation. Winsome had to squeeze past people blocking the door and strain her eyes over people's heads and shoulders to see. She spotted Mister and Mistress Dewey at the far side of the room and Amos standing with his back to her talking to Jane Fitzroy. Amos might be taken in, but Winsome was experienced enough in the courtship game to know that Jane, staring up at him attentively, was more apt to be calculating his worth than weighing his words.

She recognized some of the other guests: Governor Dinwiddie talking with Lawrence Collier, the rich bachelor who had broken a dozen hearts with his steadfast refusal to bring a bride home to Green Meadows; the Rutherfords; the Answells; the Carruthers; all of whom she knew only by sight. She saw the William Waverlys, whom she had met years before when she and their son, Thomas, attended school together, and a moment later her attention was caught and drawn to Daniel Savery, Joseph's uncle. How odd that one should be white and one should be black; that one should be up here dressed in velvet and lace, and the other sitting below in striped ticken and homespun.

Her eyes continued to sweep the room until she located Darby in company with Thomas Fitzroy and a young woman whom she didn't know, a brunette like Winsome but slighter of build and paler in coloring. She was quite pretty, Winsome was forced to admit, in a frail, rather pinched way, but she lacked vivacity and, to Winsome's eyes, she dressed abominably. Winsome ran her eyes over the filmy high-necked white gown with its lace-trimmed jacket and long tight-fitting sleeves. There wasn't a bead or a bow to be seen, not a flounce on the skirt, not a pleat, not a gather. If she were as drab as she looked, Darby would be doubly glad to see Winsome there.

Just as she started to push her way through the crowd, a plump little manservant put his hand on Darby's arm and whispered in his ear. Then he turned to the room and announced that dinner was served. Immediately, the guests began to converge on the doorway, forcing Winsome back into the hall. She was being borne away with no opportunity to announce herself to Darby; jostled, pushed, and finally impelled to turn and descend the stairs along with the others. She would have separated herself from them in the downstairs hallway, but she tripped on the bottom step and someone caught her arm and guided her firmly through the door into the dining room. When she turned her head to see who it was, it turned out to be Ferris Halley. "Your companion?" Halley inquired.

"I beg your pardon?"

"Your dining companion? Shall we leave a place for him?"

By then Winsome, awake to her predicament, wanted only to escape. "I have no companion," she said. "Please excuse me."

"You are here alone?"

"Yes. That is, no. I'm a friend of Mister Littlefield, but I'm not here as one of the guests."

"I see," Halley returned silkily. "I think I understand. Come, sit down next to me." He blocked her way with a chair, leaving her no choice but to sit down, then pulled out the chair next to her and slid into it. "I cannot believe that Darby has kept you a secret."

"What?"

"My name is Ferris Halley. Who are you?"

Winsome looked back to the doorway jammed with guests, then directed her gaze toward the kitchen passage. If Savery were still in the kitchen, she would prevail upon him to drive her home after all. She reached up to feel for the edges of her cloak and realized with a start that the cloak was no longer covering her shoulders. She must have dropped it on the way downstairs.

"Your name is . . . ?" Halley persisted.

"Winsome Greenhill." Winsome saw Amos Dewey enter the room and walk over to converse with the Rutherfords, who had seated themselves directly in front of the kitchen passage. Then she saw Darby walk in with the pale brunette. Winsome turned her head away as they passed, but heard him address the young woman as "my dear Miss Whitehill." She rose quickly but sat down again when she saw Robby Flower in the doorway. He caught her eye and winked, then lifted a chair onto one of the round tables next to the door, sprang up onto the table, and settled himself in the chair. Almost simultaneously the plump little manservant closed the dining-room door and Winsome realized that she was trapped.

Darby and his companion took their seats at the head of the table, and Amos Dewey and Jane Fitzroy joined them. Winsome, seated only a few yards distant, turned her face and found herself eye-to-eye with the detestable Halley, who dropped his voice to an intimate whisper and said, "Now, tell me, Winsome, how is it I missed you? I thought I knew every doxie in town."

Winsome stared at him in horror.

"Are you new?" he went on. "Did Darby import you for his own private use?"

"How dare you?" she said hoarsely.

"Come now. I've no objection to you for a dinner partner. On the contrary, I'm delighted to be seated next to someone with whom I can converse without constraint."

"We've one place too few," someone called out, and there was a momentary flurry while the mistake was corrected. A moment later Robby Flower began to play, and the cook's daughters marched in bearing the platters of food. Halley patted Winsome's arm and reached out to toy with her sleeve. "Well, you haven't answered. Where did Darby find you?"

Winsome answered sharply, hoping to put him in his place. "Mister Littlefield didn't find me anywhere. I met him at the Fitzroys' where he and I were both invited guests."

"Don't tell me Fitzroy is the one found you. He's slyer than I thought."

One of the cook's daughters leaned down to present the tray to Winsome, her black eyes widening slightly in surprise, then narrowing knowingly. She deliberately brushed Winsome's shoulder as she thrust the platter between her and Halley. Halley speared a piece of pork and tasted it before digging into the platter and filling his plate. "There's nothing sweeter than suckling pig," he declared loudly, then lowered his voice to add in a lascivious aside, "I'll wager you taste as sweet."

His fingers crept into her lap, and she reached down to push his hand away. She might as well be manacled to the table for all the freedom she had to escape his vile assault. In desperation she addressed the lady on his far side. "You are Mistress Waverly, are you not? I know your son, Thomas."

"Do you really?" Mistress Waverly responded coolly.

"Yes. We went to school together."

"That must have been some time ago." Mistress Waverly shifted her shoulder just enough to make it clear that she had no further interest in talking to Ferris Halley's companion.

Halley was sucking his greasy fingers. When he reached out to caress Winsome's hand she whispered fiercely, "Stop it. Don't touch me."

"Darby's not looking," he said playfully. "And even if he were, he'd not begrudge me a little sport." He picked up his wineglass, took a gulp, then said solicitously, "You're not eating. Here, have a bit of pork." He picked up an oily piece of pork with his fingers and waved it under her nose.

It was more than Winsome could bear. "Stop it," she cried. She knocked his hand away, and in her hurry to rise, knocked over her chair as well. The fork flew from Halley's hand, dislodging the bit of pork. Mistress Waverly screeched as it struck her, leaving a grease stain on her bodice, and Halley regarded Winsome in surprise.

"How dare you!" Winsome exclaimed. "How dare you!"

Halley, grinning widely, seemed more enchanted than dismayed by her behavior until he suddenly found himself jerked around and held aloft by the fabric of his lace jabot. An instant later Robby Flower struck him on the jaw and he sprawled onto the table, a groggy intruder among the crockery. He tried to get up, but Flower struck him a second time saying, "Stay where you are. You're more at home lying on the table than sitting at it. Stick an apple in your mouth and you'll pass for pig."

"What do you think you're doing?" Darby's imperious voice demanded. He hadn't risen from his chair, but his face was livid with anger, and he was looking straight at Winsome.

"I'm teaching this porker his place," Flower answered with aplomb.

"I hired you to entertain, not to manhandle my guests."

"He meant no harm," Winsome asserted, returning Darby's gaze steadily. "Mister Halley insulted me."

Darby said coldly, "Mister Halley is here at my invitation. To the best of my recollection, you are not."

Winsome didn't believe she had heard him correctly. She stood facing him as the color drained from her face, unable to explain and totally demoralized.

"So, unless you came at Mister Halley's invitation, you really have no right to be here. Do you agree?"

He was actually waiting for her to reply. Winsome, too tongue-tied to speak, stood staring at him.

"If you have nothing to say for yourself," Darby continued, "I suggest you leave."

Winsome found her voice and said in anguish, "I wanted to speak with you in private. That's why I came."

Darby's smile was cynical. "You chose rather a gaudy costume for a private interview, Miss Greenhill."

"Darby, please—"

"I don't know why you felt you had the right to intrude on my gathering, but I fear it has to do with some misguided notion that we are better acquainted than we are; better acquainted, I might add, then we shall ever be."

Winsome began to tremble, and her eyes filled with tears. She looked at Amos Dewey, who was smirking and whispering into Jane Fitzroy's ear, then at Darby's companion, who said softly, "Don't be harsh, Mister Littlefield. The girl is crying."

"I'll call my manservant and have him escort you home," Darby said, responding to Miss Whitehill's plea, but in an unforgiving tone.

It struck Winsome all at once that his dismissal of her was final, that he wasn't merely sending her home from a party to which she held no invitation, but that he wanted to be rid of her forever. She slumped against the edge of the table and would have collapsed onto the floor if Robby Flower hadn't grabbed her arm.

"You've had your say, Mister Littlefield," Flower declared. "Now I'll have mine. You're as grand a rotter as any I've seen on the boards, which proves there's no play equal to life. 'Were I the Moor, I would not be Iago,' eh? I'm on to you, Mister Littlefield. 'Heaven is your judge, not for love and duty, but seeming so, for your peculiar end.'"

"That's enough," Darby snapped.

"It's not enough, but it's as much entertainment as you

paid for, and as much entertainment as you're going to get. Take my arm, Miss Greenhill." Flower laced Winsome's hand through his arm and held her firmly as they turned away from the table.

"The next time I see your insolent face," Darby called after Flower, "I'll put my fist to it."

"I hope that's a promise, Mister Littlefield," Flower responded cheerfully. "I'm sure there's them who'll pay a bob or two to see you licked."

Years later, long after the incident had grown blessedly hazy in her mind, Winsome would still vividly recall the silence of the room, and how when they started toward the door, the silence was broken only by the jaunty jingle of the bells on Robby Flower's cap.

· · *30* · ·

Sleep would have invited nightmares, so Winsome hadn't slept. She had spent the night pacing the floor of her room like a sentry before the gates. Not even that frenetic activity, however, prevented the onslaught of terrible thoughts. It had actually happened. Darby had refused to acknowledge her. He had faced her across a room full of people and asked her to get out. He hadn't raised a hand to help her. Quite the contrary, he had encouraged her humiliation.

She was ashamed, unbearably so when she recalled the detached stares of Darby's guests. They had behaved like spectators at some frivolous entertainment arranged in their behalf. The snide smiles bestowed on her by Jane Fitzroy and Amos Dewey were branded into her memory as effectively as if they had been burned into her flesh. Darby's female companion saying, *Don't be cruel. Can't you see she's crying?* had been Winsome's requiem. The sound of the bells on Robby Flower's cap had been her death knell and would be with her for the rest of her life, as would the slam of the dining-room doors and the eruption of voices behind it.

In the hallway Winsome had tried to break away from Robby Flower and run out the front door, but he had prolonged her misery by holding tightly to her arm and preventing her escape. He had dragged her down the passage to the kitchen, where she had stood, nakedly exposed as a poseur, before the cook, her four daughters, and Joseph Savery, who was sitting where she had last seen him, mug still in hand. Even then Winsome might have rallied had they attacked, but she had been denied even that saving grace. Instead they had stood looking at her with the same air of uninvolved interest as had Darby's supper guests. She was a dead squirrel by the side of the road, a casualty, a somewhat unappetizing curiosity.

It turned out that Robby Flower had walked to the inn, and he asked whether the innkeeper should be consulted in regard to hiring a carriage to take him and Winsome back to town. She had been forced to stand by while Joseph Savery explained that it was he who had brought her in the first place, and under what circumstances, before going on to say that he considered it no more than fair that he take her back home. Robby Flower would be welcome to go along, no charge exacted.

It was the cook who called attention to Winsome's missing cloak and hustled off to look for it. When she returned she had it over her arm, and she placed it around Winsome's shoulders. Then she guided Winsome to the kitchen door as if it were understood that she were beyond functioning on her own. On the way home she sat squeezed between the two men while they traded banalities over her head—gravediggers oblivious to the corpse. And when they reached the house on Nassau Street she scrambled over Robby Flower's lap and fled to the door, unable even to say thank you for having been rescued.

Winsome had been too numb to fully comprehend her

situation at first, but now she comprehended it all too well. She hadn't lost Darby. She had simply never had him. While she thought she was manipulating him, he had been manipulating her. She wasn't sure how much the guests the night before had understood, but at the very least it would be all over town that she had invited herself to Darby Littlefield's party, created a scene in which the most notorious womanizer in Williamsburg figured, and had been asked to depart. At the worst there would be those who deduced that Darby was better acqainted with her than it appeared, and that his cruel treatment was attributable to the fact that he had been enjoying favors in private that he had no wish to parade in public. Either way, when word of her mortification filtered down to friends and acquaintances through the offices of Jane and Amos, she would become an object of ridicule to all of Williamsburg.

Then, too, there were Winsome's mother and sister. Her mother had always thought less of her than she thought of Lissy. Now her mother's low regard would be confirmed. As for Lissy, how she would gloat over Winsome's downfall! How she would exult in the thought that it wasn't her eccentric attachment to spinsterhood and career that had, in the end, given the Greenhill family a bad name, but Winsome's besmirched reputation. Winsome's despair was absolute. She could never face people. Her life was over. She didn't have the nerve enough to end it all, but she would never again show herself in public.

Winsome had already retired when Felicity and Providence got home from the theater, and the next morning she came down late for breakfast, her face blotched and her eyes swollen. In answer to her mother's concerned query she complained of a headache, said she had no intention of going to church, and then refused to be pressed by Felicity for a description of the previous night's festivities. No, she hadn't noticed who was there or how many or what would be served. No, she hadn't seen Darby Littlefield. No, she

hadn't anything interesting to tell them. In answer to
Felicity's persistent questions, she reported that the pastries had been safely delivered and laid out on trays by
Winsome's own hands. As to whether they were well
received, she had no idea. She had no interest in discussing
Darby Littlefield or Darby Littlefield's party. All she
wanted to do was go back up to her room and lie down.

That evening Josiah was coming to supper again, and
Felicity wanted to get her business out of the way early so
she would be free to make supper preparations. After
church she left Providence with Berry and Nedda and
started for the Red Mask. It was the first time in weeks that
she had enjoyed a really long walk, and she was exhilarated
by her freedom, buoyed by a sense of well-being. She was
making a profit from the theater concession, and if the
pastries had been a success at Littlefield's party she would
be able to anticipate business from the gentry. Soon,
perhaps, she would have an additional oven installed in the
bakery, provided Mister Oatland permitted, and she might
even take on a baker's apprentice to tend to the menial
tasks. Yes, she felt good. For the past week especially she
had been possessed by overwhelming energy and self-
confidence. She felt she could do anything. It was rather
like the lift one got at the end of a long winter; an eagerness
to get on with one's life.

As she entered the Red Mask her nostrils were assailed
by the aroma of stale ale, and she squinted against the
change from sunlight to dark. The front hall was empty, but
before she could look for help, the innkeeper poked his
head out of the taproom and told her in answer to her
inquiry that Mister Littlefield's parlor was number seven,
upstairs to her left. She climbed the narrow staircase and
rapped on number seven. After a moment the door was
opened by a sallow young man whom she assumed was
Darby Littlefield, but who didn't look as she'd expected. In
wrinkled shirt and trousers he more resembled a street
vagrant than a gentleman. His lips were parched and

cracked, his eyes red-rimmed, and his breath, even from a respectable distance, was execrable.

"Well," he greeted her, "I told Bundleman to bring me back something to improve my temper. I never expected him to display such resourcefulness."

"I'm Felicity Greenhill," she announced coolly.

"Greenhill? Felicity Greenhill?" The name seemed to have a deflating effect on him. His welcoming smile shriveled and he said shortly, "Come in then. I don't want to talk about it in the hall." He backed up to admit her. "I'll tell you right now, Miss Greenhill," he remarked as he shut the door, "that I consider it an unfortuante incident, and not one for which I'm to blame."

Felicity couldn't account for his remarkable change of mood, but assumed it had to do with the pastries. "Did something go wrong?" she asked. "My sister told me she delivered the cakes and tarts and then left. She assumed they would be satisfactory."

"Is that what she told you? All she told you?"

"Why, yes. Is there more?"

"Miss Greenhill, why are you here?"

"Mister Bundleman told me to come. He said I was to collect my money this morning. However, if there was something wrong with the pastries . . ."

Darby took a step closer, and Felicity forced herself to endure his sour breath without making a face. His face had cleared and once again his tone lightened. "I haven't quite recovered from the effects of last evening. You must forgive me. I didn't get to bed until dawn. The pastries were quite satisfactory. As a matter of fact, there was considerable comment about them, all of it flattering."

"I must say I'm relieved, Mister Littlefield, although I don't quite understand what you meant when you spoke of an unfortunate incident."

"Again my apology. I'm afraid I mixed you up with someone else. Stupid of me. The effect of overindulgence. Now, how much money are you owed?"

"Four shillings, six pence. That's the sum Mister Bundleman and I agreed on."

Littlefield excused himself and retired into another room, then emerged a minute later to press a half-pound note into her hand. "Keep the half pound," he suggested magnanimously. "The pastries were worth it."

"I don't accept gratuities, Mister Littlefield." Felicity opened her purse, took out five shillings, six pence, and laid the coins on the nearest table. Littlefield nodded, then opened the door to usher her out. "Good day, Miss Greenhill."

"Good day, Mister Littlefield."

The man's behavior was more than a little odd, Felicity thought, unless such erratic changes of mood were commonplace among nobility. She hurried downstairs and started out the front door, but was suddenly brought up short by the entrance of Bundleman, who blocked her path. "Oh, Mister Bundleman, good day."

"Good day, eh? That's what you call it? You call it a good day, do you?"

There seemed nothing appropriate to say in answer, so she simply smiled inanely.

"I'd like to have a word with you, Miss Greenhill." Bundleman crooked his finger at her. "Come outside. No reason to make a spectacle of yourself twice in a row."

Felicity was mystified. What was he talking about? She followed him outside, where he turned, wagged his finger in her face, and said sternly, "It ain't right."

"What isn't?"

"It ain't right what you been doing."

For an instant Felicity thought Bundleman was referring to the fact that she was a baker. It seemed preposterous, but she could think of no other explanation. "Why should it matter to you what I do?" she returned in a puzzled voice.

"Maybe it shouldn't, but I'm a man of principle, Miss Greenhill. I don't like to see girls go wrong. When you went up there just now did me master tell you again he don't mean to see you?"

"Why should he do that?"

"I heard him say it two weeks ago, missy. He's been having his sport with you, that's all. And some sport it's been. Taking advantage of you and talking about it to anybody who'd listen."

"I don't know what you're talking about."

"And," Bundleman continued, "what he says about you ain't something you'd feel good to hear. He knows you been trying to snag him, and it gives him a proper laugh. Now, listen to me, it was lucky for you that actor stood up for you last night."

"What actor?" Felicity interrupted.

"The way it appears to me, all you got to say is that Robby Flower brung you. Stick to that and you may be able to save your reputation yet. Flower may be one of the lower cut, but he ain't riffraff. He's a man of principle, like myself. Of course, there's the problem of your fiancé. I don't know what you're going to tell him, but I hear he's a dull sort who'll swallow anything."

"Mister Bundleman, please stop talking. I don't understand any of this, and I am most desperately eager to do so."

"If you've any sense at all," Bundleman went on, "you'll marry that young fellow you're engaged to. What's his name? Smythe, is it? Marry the young fellow and be done with it; that is, if it ain't already too late. Take my advice or leave it, but leastways remember it. One day you'll tell yourself, 'Mister Bundleman was right, and he meant it for my own good.' Know your place and stick in it. That's the best way."

He marched back into the inn and shut the door behind him, leaving Felicity standing in the road. She didn't know what he was talking about, but she had begun to suspect. He had certainly dropped enough clues to let her know the direction of his advice. If she wanted the complete story, she must visit the only person who could give her an accurate account. Resolutely, she set off down the road in the direction of the Market Street Tavern.

·· *31* ··

"I don't know how she could have been such a fool. More than a fool. She's perverse. She's bent on ruining her life."

"I suspect you're right about her being foolish," Robby Flower said thoughtfully, "but it takes more than one foolish mistake to ruin a life."

"What you've told me is so degrading. How could she ever have trusted the man?"

Robby Flower had been breakfasting with four of his cronies when Felicity burst into the Market Street Tavern. He had intercepted her halfway across the room and led her back out the door and across the stableyard into the harness shed, where they stood conferring. "Of course," Flower said, "I'm guessing at some of it, but I've seen a few things, and I'm quick at figuring. To my mind, she trusted the wrong man, trusted him enough to let him have his way with her."

"Mister Flower? Surely you don't think it went that far?"

"A man like Littlefield, he'd have no other reason for wasting his time with the likes of your sister."

"What a terrible thing to say."

"I'm not tactful, but I'm honest, and that's the way I see it. You shouldn't be too judging of her. There's no doubt she was taken in, made promises to."

"Surely she should have known she'd never win him by permitting him to . . ." Felicity was unable to go on.

"Offhand," Robby Flower remarked matter-of-factly, "I can't think of a better way."

"Better?"

He shrugged. "More logical then. The trouble is, she's not bad enough. There's women who are experts at getting their own way, even from bastards like Littlefield, but not your sister."

"You seem to know her well on such short acquaintance. Surely you haven't—"

"Not at all. Don't go thinking that. Don't think worse of her than there is to think, and don't put me in the same class with Darby Littlefield."

"I'd like to kill Darby Littlefield."

"Somebody may do that someday. In the meantime, I think I'm up to teaching him a lesson he'll not quickly forget."

"A lesson? There's nothing to be gained by confronting him, it that's what you're thinking. It would only result in additional pain for Winnie."

"No reason she has to know," Robby returned. "This satisfaction will be for you and me alone."

"For you?" Felicity asked. "Why for you?"

"I'll state my case plain, Miss Greenhill. I have intentions toward your sister, and unlike Darby Littlefield, my intentions are honorable."

Felicity started to speak, but he held up his hand. "You're about to say she'll not look on a poor actor as an encouraging prospect, but you'd be surprised at how persuasive I can be."

"That isn't what I was going to say."

"Do you find something in me not to your liking?"

"On the contrary, I like you very much. It's not that. It's Winsome and what she is."

"You mean what she's done. What she is, is something else. I've only seen her a few times and never except to be turned away, but I know a match when I meet one. She's got imagination, ambition, and spunk, just like me. She's lovely, she's lively, and I guess there's no question now but that she's loving."

"Mister Flower!"

Flower held up his hand again as if to ward off her indignation. "I didn't mean to offend. You've got to remember that actors are the same as everyone else in most respects, that is, we're loyal to our own and the majority of us are honest, but none of us has any particular regard for chastity. On the other hand, the kind of villainy Darby Littlefield lets loose on the world, that's something we can't abide."

"Whatever you're planning, Mister Flower, you mustn't break the law."

"Robby Flower break the law? What do you take me for? I don't intend to take my bows on the gallows."

Felicity smiled ruefully. "Thank God for that. You're too rare a gentleman to lose."

"Do you really think so, Miss Greenhill?"

"I really do."

"Tell me, then, are you agreeable to putting me in your sister's way?"

"I don't understand."

"I can't woo the girl without seeing her, and so far she's not been overly encouraging. If you'll put me in her path, I promise you'll never need worry about her again."

"I can't help you win her, Mister Flower," Felicity answered, "but I suppose there's no harm putting you in her way."

Flower grinned. "Since we're going to be seeing a lot of one another, do you think we could call us by our first names?"

"I think I'd like that."

"In that case, Lissy, I'll let you in on a little secret. Littlefield's coming to the theater next Saturday evening, at which time me and my mates are going to deal with him. The plans are already made."

"Who are your mates?"

"Two of my fellow actors."

"Surely you haven't told them about my sister and Mr. Littlefield?"

"Would I be such a cad? All they know is that I've quarrelled with him and that I'm seeking satisfaction."

"Satisfaction? Not a duel?"

Robby said pridefully, "No doubt I could best him in a duel, having faked them often enough, but that's not my intention."

"What is your intention?"

"You'll see, Lissy. You'll see."

As soon as Felicity got home she informed her morose sister that she had invited Robby Flower to supper that evening, then waited for the explosion. It wasn't long in coming. "You invited him to our house?" Winsome exclaimed. "Why? Why did you do that? The man is insufferable."

"I bumped into Robby Flower today in the street. We stopped to talk, and then I remembered that Joss is coming this evening. Robby Flower has been helpful to the bakery, and I liked him, and I thought it would be pleasant to invite him as well. So I did so."

"You call him Robby now?"

"That is his name."

"Well, I'll not entertain him. I'm not coming out of my room."

"You wouldn't wish to hurt his feelings, would you?"

Winsome fell monentarily silent. She had been sick with fear that someone at the Red Mask might have let something slip to Felicity about the night before. Thank God that apparently hadn't happened. But how dangerous was Robby Flower? Especially if he had taken offense with Winsome the night before. After all, she hadn't thanked him for coming to her aid. She said grudgingly, "I couldn't care less whether or not I hurt his feelings, but I suppose you'll keep after me until I say yes, so I might as well give in. But don't expect me to be more than civil."

"Civil," her sister returned with composure, "will be an improvement over your usual behavior."

Later that day Felicity decided it was necessary to tell

her mother about Winsome. However, she was careful to withhold what she believed to be the extent of Winsome's shame, merely describing the previous night's debacle as the foolish caprice of a headstrong girl. "You know how much she admires a certain style of life, Mama, how much she longs to be part of it. Perhaps she thought that one guest more or less would go unnoticed."

It was just as well that Felicity spoke to her mother when she did, because Nedda arrived with the news that afternoon. Fortunately, Winsome was upstairs locked in her room when Nedda barged through the door to unburden herself of the gossip she'd heard at church. "You know and you're not disturbed? Don't you realize what people are saying? They are saying that Winsome has been chasing Darby Littlefield for months, that the poor man has been utterly beset by her and too much a gentleman to speak up."

"I doubt that Littlefield is too much a gentleman for anything," Felicity commented laconically.

"That's why she broke with Bart. She took it into her head that she'd rather set her cap for Littlefield, and has made his life wretched by following him all around town, pretending to meet him by accident, marching up and down in front of the Red Mask, and generally conducting herself in the most brazenly unbecoming manner."

"The story sounds a little exaggerated," Providence said soothingly. "It's difficult to believe that the man was as sorely put upon as all that."

"What you're suggesting," Nedda returned irately, "is that Littlefield may have encouraged her when it's obvious that he did not."

"Not at all," Providence returned. "I was suggesting that Winsome may not have been chasing him so much as fantasying about him. Perhaps she was looking to escape her betrothal to Bart and Darby Littlefield offered her an excuse."

"If we're looking for excuses, I'd say yours deserves the

prize. Winnie certainly didn't imagine herself into her party dress any more than she imagined herself into the dining room of the Red Mask last night. I don't hear you saying anything, Lissy. What do you think of it?"

"I say it's fortunate people aren't saying that she and Littlefield were carrying on behind Bart's back."

"It's like you to say something like that," Nedda shrilled. "It's not bad enough to have your sister ridiculed? You're thankful she has been branded a whore?"

"I'm pointing out that it may be better for her to be ridiculed than drummed out of society altogether."

"She has been drummed out of society, at least out of the upper reaches of it, and us along with her."

Here it comes, Felicity thought, the inevitable switch from singular to plural.

"Do you have any idea who was at that party last night? Governor Dinwiddie, the Rutherfords, the Carruthers, the Answells. Lawrence Collier was there, too, the richest landowner in Virginia. If ever we aspired to better things, we can forget it now. None of those people will ever invite any of us into their homes."

"Frankly," Felicity told her, "I have no desire to take tea with Lawrence Collier."

"You, you, you. Don't you ever think of anyone but yourself? Must I forever be condemned to the society of shopkeepers because you, and now your sister as well, are hopelessly common?"

"On, no," Felicity groaned. "Not that again."

"I do think, Nedda," Providence interjected, "that we are getting rather away from the subject of Winnie. In my opinion, Winnie has already suffered enough for what was obviously very stupid behavior. I don't think we need worry that such an embarrassing incident will ever be repeated. The sooner forgotten, the better it will be for her and for all of us."

"If it's ever forgotten," Nedda declared.

"If it's not," Felicity said sweetly, "it will be because you won't be able to resist reminding us."

Felicity's words were all but lost in the flurry of Nedda's indignant departure.

Winsome opened the door to a spruce and smiling Robby Flower, extravagantly overdressed in mauve velvet suit, embroidered pink vest, and white ruffled silk shirt. She greeted him with what she hoped was precisely the right shading of courteous disinterest. "How do, Mister Flower. Won't you come in?"

"There's not much point being on your doorstep if I don't come in," he answered practically. He had his hand behind his back, and once inside the door he whipped it around to present her with a nosegay of huge blue and yellow pansies. "I made them," he informed her immodestly. "They're velvet and silk. No smell, but no wilt either."

Winsome brought him into the parlor to join Providence, Felicity, and Josiah. The first awkward moments were bridged by a discussion of the weather, the theatrical season in Williamsburg, the discomforts of army life, and Robby's talent for flower making. "I learned it from my ma, and I put it to good use in my profession. You should see the balcony scene when we play *Romeo and Juliet*: purple wisteria, climbing red roses, and vine leaves you have to rub between your fingers to tell they're not real."

The two men took to one another. Josiah was charmed by Robby's gaiety, and Robby was drawn to Josiah's amiability and to his willingness to let Robby dominate the conversation with anecdotes invariably centered on himself. Robby's mother—tact prevented anyone from asking about his father—had worked as cook and seamstress for a traveling carnival. His earliest memories were of being swaddled in sequins and gauze, while being playfully tossed from one to another of three acrobats named Archie, Winks, and Bandy. And among his playmates were a pair of twins who matched him in height and weight, but who had wrinkled little-old-man faces and confounded his eight-year-old sensibility by smoking pipes and talking in high, squeaking voices about "homely virgins of desperate expectation."

It was Robby, expansively drawing Josiah out and oblivious to his warning frown, who introduced the subject of Indians. "Josiah," he said, "you've not spoken of the savages. I know the French are using them, and some of the British as well. Have you dealt with them?"

"I have."

"What's it like facing the painted faces and feathered tomahawks?"

"The same as facing army uniforms and polished swords. Unpleasant for the most part."

"I've heard stories of whites taking their own lives rather than be captured."

Josiah glanced at Felicity, who was staring down into her lap, then across the table at Providence, who said quietly, "We've faced such a tragedy. My daughter, Winnie and Lissy's elder sister, was abducted by Indians many years ago."

Robby pressed his forehead with the heel of his hand. "Robby Flower, you're a fool," he said feelingly.

Providence smiled sympathetically. "No, you're not. You couldn't have known."

"It's not always like that," Josiah felt obliged to interject. "They may be ferocious, but they're also human, with as great a capability for compassion as any white." Deliberately, he turned to address himself directly to Felicity. "I told you there are whites living among the Indians. I mentioned one woman I myself have seen."

"A white woman living as an Indian?" Winsome asked interestedly.

"A white woman who had lived with the Iroquois for many years. She's actually one of the tribal leaders. I've heard many men tell me thay've seen her, and I saw her myself once, just before battle, among a company of braves."

"Do you mean to say she bore arms?" Winsome asked in surprise.

"No. They believe she's endowed with some sort of

magical power; a medicine woman, a spirit god, I suppose. Another soldier and I saw her about a year ago when we were on patrol near Fort Necessity. She rode a white horse at the head of a dozen braves decked out for war, and she held a hawk carved of wood in her hand as a sort of talisman. I understand she's called Fire Hawk by the Iroquois. She stopped near our hiding place, conferred by sign with two of the braves, both of whom were also astride white horses, then rode off with them."

Providence leaned forward. "Joss, did you say she carried a carved hawk?"

Josiah noded. "Yes. To the Iroquois the hawk represents strength and power. It's one of their animal gods."

"What did this carving look like? That is, how big was it? Could you see it clearly?"

Felicity suddenly turned to her mother with a startled look. "Mama?"

Providence put her finger to her lips.

"I don't really remember," Josiah answered. "We were lying flat on our bellies behind some bushes with nothing on our minds but keeping low."

"But you did see the hawk."

"Oh yes, I saw it." He frowned, then held his hands apart to indicate the approximate size. "It was maybe two feet tall, made out of a light-colored wood, ash I would guess. The wings were partially open. I remember that."

"What did she look like?" Felicity chimed in. "Can you remember, Joss?"

"Only that she wore an Indian headdress and was wrapped around with a heavy shawl. It was difficult to tell about her features. She was a middle-aged white woman, that's all."

Felicity reached out to clutch her mother's hand. "Mama, you heard him. The Indians worship the hawk. No doubt there are similar carvings in every Iroquois village."

It was a statement, but is was also a question, as her

mother was well aware. "It's less than likely, Lissy," she said.

"Yet," Felicity continued, "she must belong to someone, somewhere?"

"She belongs to the Iroquois," Josiah declared, driving home his point. "A white woman alive and living among the redskins."

"Yes," Felicity murmured. "Oh, yes."

· · *32* · ·

The six days following Robby and Josiah's visit passed slowly for Felicity, who could think of little else but the fact that Sarah might still be alive. But when she broached the subject to her mother, Providence refused to acknowledge the possibility. "I won't have you revive these morbid thoughts of Saree. It's unhealthy."

"But you yourself were the one who was first struck by the idea."

"I admit that Joss's description of the carved hawk put me in mind of her. However, that was before I learned that the hawk is a common object of worship among the Iroquois."

"The description was so exact."

"So far as it went."

"The Indians who were hanging around New Castle were Iroquois, Mama."

"There are very many Iroquois in this part of the country."

"Mama, if there's any chance at all that it's Saree, wouldn't it mean something . . . everything . . . to know she's alive?"

"I don't know. I honestly don't know whether I prefer to think of her as alive or dead."

"Mama!"

"To think of her alive," Providence persisted, "means thinking of how she lives and what she has become. In many ways that's more painful to me than to believe that she's gone to her rest."

"But if we could bring her back?"

"What you want, Lissy, is to make everything all right again. That can't be. There's no way to move back in time."

"But I was the one responsible for what happened to Saree."

"Perhaps you were in a sense, but no more responsible than circumstance, no more than Winsome for running off that day or me for leaving Saree unattended. Saree is gone, Lissy. There's no way to resurrect her or the years that have passed since."

Felicity said no more to Providence after that conversation, but Sarah continued to dominate her thoughts all that week until Robby Flower's plan to give Darby Littlefield his comeuppance provided a welcome respite.

Farquhar's *The Beaux' Stratagem* drew a large crowd, and Felicity was kept busy satisfying its collective sweet tooth. She saw Jane Fitzroy and Amos Dewey when they entered the theater, then lost sight of them. A few minutes later she was approached by Ferris Halley, who purchased a cake, then lingered to inquire about the possibility for "even more delectable diversions" after the theater. Fortunately for Halley, he was jostled out of hearing before Felicity had time to reply.

Darby Littlefield was one of the last to arrive. Felicity caught only a glimpse of him and of the lady he escorted, but the glimpse sufficed to show her that the young woman was pretty and tastefully turned out, and that she was cloyingly attentive to Littlefield. They were accompanied by a stern-faced older gentleman she overheard Littlefield address as "Mister Whitehill."

At five minutes to seven the theater bell was rung, and three minutes later the lobby area was deserted. Felicity stacked the empty trays, tucked the money box under her arm, and as the curtain rose, made her way up the side aisle into the wings. She and Providence had developed a routine of alternating turns in the selling booth and backstage. Felicity had done the precurtain selling. Now she would remain backstage during the first and second intervals while her mother took her station out front.

Felicity watched Act I from the wings, but felt no sense of involvement with what transpired onstage. The play was a comedy in which Robby played the part of Will Boniface, landlord of the inn, with a daughter named Cherry and an abiding passion for ale. "I have fed purely upon ale. I have eat my ale, drank my ale, and I always sleep upon ale." The action was of interest to her only from the point of view that every sentence uttered moved the first act that much closer to its conclusion. Finally, the curtain speech given, the actors exited and the curtain fell. Robby pranced offstage to join her. "We have a full house," he announced happily.

"Where is Mister Littlefield?"

"Come, I'll show you. He and his party are in the first box, stage right. I reserved a spot for you." He led her across the stage behind the curtain and settled her on a stool just inside the proscenium arch. "They're just the other side," he whispered. "You'll not be able to see them, but you'll not need to. You'll hear them, and that's all that matters."

"Robby, I hope—"

"Don't worry," he whispered as he slipped away. "Just leave it to me."

A moment later Felicity cocked her head as she heard Littlefield speak on the other side of the curtain. "Are you enjoying the play, Miss Whitehill?" he inquired.

"Oh yes," she replied. "I've seen it twice before, but I'm always amused by it."

"And you, Mister Whitehill?"

"I prefer something with a little more substance, Mister Littlefield, *Henry VI* or *Macbeth*."

"*The Beaux' Stratagem* is pure froth," Darby admitted agreeably, "but appropriate for the ladies. It's less draining than Shakespearean tragedy." The smile which Darby bestowed on Miss Whitehill, and which Felicity could not see, was parenthetical, letting her know that it was she, and she alone, who aroused his concern.

"I, for one, prefer Shakespeare," Jane Fitzroy remarked, "and I'm not in the least put off by tragedy."

"Provided the subject matter is love," Amos Dewey teased. "I've never known a lady who didn't prefer *Romeo and Juliet* to *Richard III*."

"Tell me, Mister Littlefield," Mister Whitehill asked, "have you seen the play in London?"

"I attend the theater in London, of course," Darby replied, "but we have our own theater at Kenilmoor Castle, and I attend there more often. I cannot count the times I've seen *The Stratagem*."

Darby noted the quick look Eleanor Whitehill darted at her father, but was undisturbed by it. He had meant to impress her, and was pleased that he'd succeeded. Title, wealth, and privilege were more important assets, he knew, than a handsome face when it came to wooing a lady. And he was smitten with Eleanor. He hadn't as yet admitted the fact to anyone, but in the past week he had come to think of her as a strong candidate for the eventual title of Duchess of Kenilmoor. She would be eminently suitable on a number of counts. She made an attractive appearance, she was intelligent, and she was a lady. Her grandmother had been lady-in-waiting to Queen Anne and had married Lord Abington Walpole, second cousin to former Prime Minister Robert Walpole. Her father's connections were equally distinguished, touching on such illustrious names as Drake and the First Earl of Chatham, William Pitt. Even in this primitive outpost Eleanor had been raised by a governess, could speak French and play the spinet, and wonder of wonders, amused herself by cultivating a formal rose garden. There was, of course, the drawback of her father, who was a moralistic prig and who appeared to have taken an immediate and, to Darby's way of thinking, unreasonable dislike to Darby. But Mister Whitehill would be hard put to discover any serious fault with which to charge his prospective son-in-law. Of that Darby was quite certain.

"Then I suppose," Eleanor was saying lightly, "*The Stratagem* is rather a bore for you."

"I may have seen it often," Darby improvised gallantly, "but never in such charming company."

A few feet away Felicity grimaced, but Mister Whitehill's exception to the remark—"I would hate to think, sir, that your life had been so uniformly dull up until now"—made Felicity wonder if that gentleman weren't also skeptical of Littlefield's sincerity.

A sudden clanging near to hand made Felicity jump, and a moment later Jane Fitzroy suggested, "There's the bell. Let's turn our chairs back to the stage."

Felicity looked around anxiously. What had happened to Robby? The din on the other side of the curtain increased as wandering theater patrons returned to their seats, then decreased to a scraping of chairs on the wooden floor. Backstage the actors had begun to take their places. There was only a minute to go before the curtain rose on the second act. Something seemed to have gone wrong. The confrontation wasn't going to take place after all. Felicity stood up and took a step away from her stool, but was arrested by the sound of a child's voice, reedy but loud, exclaiming, "There he is! That's him! That's Mister Smallmeadow. Lookee, Charlie, there he be. He's the one, ain't he?"

Felicity held her breath. Another voice, a little older but still the voice of a child, chimed in with, "That's him, all right. Pa, that's the the one we told you about. That's him, Mister Smallmeadow."

"Smallmeadow, you say?" a third voice boomed. "Where? Which one is he? Is he that old man? I thought you told me he was young?"

"Not the old one, Pa," the younger voice cried out. "It be the other one, the one sitting twixt the lady in yeller and the lady in blue."

Felicity recognized "Pa" as Robby, but with a gravelly quality added to his voice. She pulled back an edge of the curtain and peeked out. She couldn't see Darby Littlefield or his party, who were screened by the proscenium frame, but she could see the trio of speakers who had risen from their seats in the third row of the orchestra. Robby had disguised more than his voice. He had given himself a beard and a mustache and exchanged his usual colorful garb for loose brown trousers, black boots, a leather vest, a homespun shirt, and a wide-brimmed, high-domed hat. The two little boys on either side of him, whom Felicity recognized as *Richard III*'s little princes, now wore osenbrig knickers and clean, somewhat oversized blue workshirts. Their hair was slicked back and they managed to present their pink-cheeked, innocent faces to the house before concentrating their attention on Darby Littlefield's box. As Felicity watched, Robby swept off his hat and held it to his chest while he shaded his eyes with his hand. By then every other head was turned to Littlefield's box as well.

"Are they looking at us? Felicity heard Mister Whitehill inquire in a puzzled voice.

"Right at us," Jane Fitzroy said curiously.

"I've something to say to you," Robby announced. "You. Yes, you. You know who you are, Smallmeadow."

"Are you addressing me?" Darby demanded imperiously.

"Nobody else."

Felicity heard the impatience in Littlefield's voice as he returned arrogantly, "I have no idea who you are or what you want. Kindly direct your attention elsewhere."

"He says he ain't the one, Willie," Robby declared. "What do you say?"

"He's the one, Pa," the smaller of the two boys replied. "He give Charlie and me each a shilling to get in the carriage with him, just like I told you. He said he wanted directions to the High Road."

"This gentleman's name is Littlefield," Amos Dewey intervened helpfully. "It is not Smallmeadow."

"Now, ain't that a coincidence," Robby proclaimed, giving time to let the coincidence sink in.

"This is ridiculous," Darby exploded. "You are outrageously rude. You are offending me, and you are embarrassing the ladies."

"He locked the carriage doors," Willie declared. "He told the driver to take the low road down by the bay."

"What are they talking about?" Eleanor Whitehill inquired nervously and in an undertone.

"I have no idea," Darby answered. "They have obviously mistaken me for someone else."

"You told us you like little boys. You said we should be nice to you, and you'd give us each another shilling."

"In the interest of the ladies," Darby said in a strangled voice, "I think perhaps we should leave."

Felicity listened to the creak and shuffle as they began to gather up their belongings and push back their chairs.

"The driver's name was Bundleman," little Charlie announced. "Ask him if his driver's name ain't Bundleman, Pa."

"Mister Littlefield," Mister Whitehill suddenly boomed resonantly, "if I'm not mistaken, your manservant is named Bundleman?"

Activity in the box ceased. "This is bizarre," Darby said loudly in way of answer.

"I'll say it is," Robby called out, waving his arm like a barrister inviting the spectators to pass judgment. "You know what you are, *Mister Tinypasture*, you're depraved. Why don't you tell everyone how you like to use little boys?"

"How dare you!" Darby cried.

"You wanted us to take off our britches," young Charlie reminded him, then paused to allow for audience response; a simultaneous intake of air into a hundred lungs. "And when he wouldn't, you started to grab for Willie."

Here and there Felicity heard an indignant feminine squeal.

"Oh yes, you did. You was rubbing your hands all over him. You stuck him betwixt your knees, you did. You was trying to shove your hand in his drawers, you was."

"Be quiet!" Darby shouted. "Be quiet, I say."

The audience was beginning to mumble. To Felicity it sounded like gathering thunder.

"I smacked you, and you smacked me back, right acrost my cheek. You was all red in the face, just like now. You ripped Willie's shirt, and you was wiggling around in the seat like you had the lice—"

Felicity heard someone strike the railing of the box with a fist, and then heard Eleanor Whitehill's quavering voice pleading with her father to take her home.

"Then Willie kicked you, and I got the door open, and we jumped out."

This time there was a gratified mass sigh, and Felicity saw Robby squeeze the older boy's arm to forestall an incipient bow.

"Those filthy little beggars," Darby cried out in anguish.

Now there was frantic conversation from the box. *Come, Eleanor—Yes, Papa—This is idotic—They're lying, I tell you— Amos, please take me home—*Then Amos saying in a stage whisper, *Darby, for God's sake, let's get out of here.*

"They're lying, I tell you," Darby repeated. He shook his fist at Robby and the two little boys and shouted down to them, "I don't know what your game is, but you'll not get away with it. I'll see you flogged through the streets!"

Disapproving clucks and grumbles from the audience.

Somewhere from the back of the theater a voice broke in to say, "You know what their game is, Darby. They're trying to shame you into paying."

The voice belonged to Ferris Halley, and an answering voice piped up to offer the opinion that if Darby Littlefield counted Ferris Halley as a friend, then what the boys were saying was most likely true. This sentiment apparently was shared by the majority of the audience, who erupted, unbelievably, into spontaneous and deafening applause.

There was a noisy scramble as Darby and his party fled. Felicity saw Robby grab the boys' arms and hustle them out the side door into the theater alley. Then, as she climbed down from the stool to cross to the stage door, she saw Thomas Kean part the curtains and step out onto the stage to quiet the audience. It wouldn't be easy, she thought. *The Beaux' Stratagem* couldn't hold a candle to *The Robby Flower Stratagem*, a drama that would be gleefully talked about and reviewed for months to come, much to the satisfaction of everyone except its principal player.

· · *33* · ·

Winsome heard about the incident involving Darby three days after Darby left Williamsburg. It shocked her, but she believed it. It took no great stretch of the imagination to conceive him capable of such base depravity, and condemning him reestablished her own equilibrium. Why should she think herself stupid or feel demeaned because she had been victimized by a man so utterly perverse?

Apparently Winsome wasn't the only one to hold that view. The incident at Darby's supper party took on altered signficance in light of the theater incident and Winsome's role was reversed. Now she was looked upon as the injured party, gossip having it that Littlefield had cruelly humiliated an innocent girl whose only fault lay in her mistaken assumption that he cared for her. Even Amos Dewey found it politic to excuse Winsome and deny any friendship between him and Littlefield. And the only other two who knew the truth, Robby and Felicity, were pleased to have the unpleasantness so satisfactorily resolved.

Robby had begun calling on Winsome, and although her initial response to the visits was unenthusiastic, she gradually began to warm to him; especially since each time he came, he bore some little gift—a set of silver buttons, hair ribbons, a variety of trinkets that inspired Providence to refer to him as "the courting crow." "I'm expecting him to build his nest on the front doorstep any day now," she told Felicity.

As Winsome's spirits improved, Felicity's spirits deteriorated. She wasn't able to rid herself of the nagging suspicion that Sarah might be alive, and it didn't make things easier when her mother mistook her frequent preoccupation for the symptoms of love. "It's Joss, isn't it? You're very fond of him."

"Yes, Mama, I'm fond of him. But not in the way you think."

"Joss is steady, manly, and solidly planted in the good earth of respectability. He'll make a fine husband."

"I don't want him for my husband. He's an old friend, but he's not a man I could marry."

"I think he's falling in love with you."

"If so, then he's bound to be disappointed."

"I don't understand you, Lissy. I swear I don't."

Nor does Joss, Felicity thought to herself. He makes no allowances for the fact that a woman might yearn for more than to keep house or raise children.

"It's a woman's place," he had said at their last meeting. "After all, men can't bear children, can they? You can't picture me offering my teat to a mewling infant, can you?"

"No. You're physically unable to nurse an infant. But I'm not unable to earn my keep, and I do."

"Surely you'll not want to go on doing so once you're married?"

"I'll always want to do something, Joss. I'm not a domesticated animal. I'm not a cow to spend my days cropping grass and dropping calves."

"God assigns us our destinies," he had contended.

"God rules our spirit, Joss, not our choices."

Josiah's well-intended but subjective interpretation of God's will was bothersome to Felicity, not only because she couldn't envision herself fulfilling God's purpose if it were at odds with her own, but because she had devised a plan, a plan that had begun as wishful thinking, advanced to firm resolve, and that would eventually require Josiah's cooperation for its successful implementation. What if his narrow views were to prevent him from seeing things her way, she wondered. How would she persuade him to change his mind? She looked for ways to broach the subject of Sarah, but Joss's unsentimental reaction to any idea he deemed impractical made her hesitate. "Why not simply leave Ohio to the French?" she asked one day.

"And let them overrun the valley and every other part of the territory? That would be suicide for the British."

"Can't the territory be evenly divided between the French and the British?"

"The Ohio territory links Canada to New Orleans, and the French are determined to have it. They've built forts; Le Boeuf and Venango and Fort Duquesne on the site where we were defeated last year. I think that's where Braddock will attack. I expect that when the company moves out it will be to meet Braddock somewhere near there."

"Is it far?"

"Three or four weeks' march. Difficult terrain. All wilderness. But we've done it before. The colonial troops are experienced at trekking, and once we connect with Braddock's forces we'll carry them through. We'll take the French with ease. There's no great danger to us. It's the French who'll suffer the losses this time."

"The Iroquois will be fighting alongside the French, you think?"

"I know they will. And they'll die with the French. I promise you that."

"I'm thinking of the white woman you told me about, the one who lives with the Iroquois. Won't she be in danger?"

"Don't waste your sympathy on her. She may be white, but she's an Iroquois now."

"Couldn't she be rescued?"

"No doubt she no longer wishes to be rescued."

"I don't believe that, Joss. I'm sure that given the choice, she would wish to be reunited with her family."

"Lissy, why all this talk about war and killing and being taken captive? I can think of more pleasant topics."

Felicity relented, and for a time said no more about Sarah. But then, one day six weeks after Josiah's arrival in Williamsburg, he told Felicity that his company would be moving out. He had received the news himself with mixed feelings of elation and depression, looking forward to the march, but loath to leave Felicity. "I'll miss you, you know. It will be hard to leave, especially on such short notice."

"How short, Joss?"

"We'll be breaking camp at dawn on Tuesday."

"Day after tomorrow?"

Josiah nodded. "Braddock's at Alexandria. We'll not meet him there, however. We'll be moving in a parallel line at his left flank, and we'll join with him later."

"Where are you going?"

"You know where. There's no great secret about it. We're going north to Duquesne." He saw her look of dismay and was peculiarly elated by it. "I'll be coming back, you know," he told her.

"Yes, of course you will. But Joss, won't there be ladies traveling with the troops? Wives, sisters, mothers of the officers, perhaps?"

Josiah, placing his own interpretation on the query, said firmly, "I don't approve of it myself. Soldiers who are going to fight are hampered by the presence of females. No, there will be no ladies this time, at least not with the rangers. Besides, there wouldn't be time to—"

"I'm merely asking," Felicity interrupted. "I'm simply curious to know. After all, it must be difficult for men to be months and miles from civilization without the comfort of womanly affection."

"I didn't say no women. I said no ladies. There are always the women."

"Camp followers, you mean?"

"That's the tactful name for them."

"How will they travel?"

"On horseback like everyone else."

"How will they be accommodated? That is, will they eat with the men? And where will they sleep? Do the troops offer them protection?"

Josiah had not expected to be interrogated on the subject of whores, not when there was so much else to talk about. He said impatiently, "No more questions, Lissy. There's something else I wish to talk about."

Felicity put out her hand to touch his arm. "There's something I wish to talk about too. Sarah."

"Sarah? Sarah who?"

"My sister Sarah. I don't think she's dead."

Josiah frowned, confused by what he took to be an arbitrary change of subject. "What reason have you to think that? Has someone brought word of her?"

"Yes. You have."

"Drat it, Lissy, why do you find pleasure in baiting me? Or are you merely trying to stop me from telling you how I feel about you?"

"Not now, Joss. This is more important. I think the white woman you saw with the Iroquois is Saree."

Not even he was sure whether his reaction was to the allegation about Sarah or to Felicity's suggestion that his feelings were of no consequence, but he said harshly, "That's idiotic. Idiotic and typically female."

For once Felicity didn't pick up on the disparaging reference to her sex. "Listen to me. You told me the woman is middle-aged and Saree would be thirty-five and no doubt looking older. You said she carried a hawk carved of wood. Well, Saree owned such a hawk, just the size you indicated, and with its wings partially outspread. We found the hawk missing after she was taken. You told me they call the white woman Fire Hawk. I believe they named her that because of the hawk she was carrying when they abducted her. It was her most treasured possession. She treated it as they would, as something sacred."

"Such carvings are common among the Iroquois, Lissy."

"Then if, when they took Saree, she were carrying her hawk, that's all the more reason why they might have spared her life. I've thought about it very carefully, Joss. Sarah was never . . . never like the rest of us. She was otherworldly and strange. She spoke little and seemed always to be listening to sounds we couldn't hear. She never behaved as expected, never showed anger, fear, or pleasure as we did. To the Iroquois, who are superstitious, she may have seemed to possess supernatural qualities. It makes sense that they wouldn't kill her, that they might even believe her to be one of their gods."

Josiah, impressed with her argument but still unconvinced, said, "Even if it were true, there would be nothing to be done about it."

"Don't say that. There must be some way to rescue her."

"Not with things the way they are now. The Iroquois are armed and vigilant. There's no way to get near them."

"You're going to get near them."

Josiah suddenly realized what she wanted. "Lissy," he declared, "there's nothing I can do to help you. I have no power to direct action against the Iroquois."

"Could you not speak to your commanding officer?"

"Collier? No, I couldn't. I wouldn't dare. Our mission is to take Fort Duquesne, and the strategy for the campaign rests in the hands of Braddock. The rest of us, Collier included, must follow orders."

"But if you see her again?"

"It isn't likely, but even if I do, I'm powerless to act."

"If I were there, I would find a way to help her," Felicity said fiercely. "I'd *make* Braddock do something to help her."

"But you won't be there, Lissy."

Felicity studied his face, trying to make up her mind whether or not to confide her plan to him. Had he been more receptive to her request for help, she might have told him everything, but now it seemed too risky. It would have to be postponed until such time as he was powerless to stop her. "No. I won't be there," she conceded.

Josiah reached out to take her by the shoulders. "I'm sure it's not Sarah. But even if it were, you would have to content yourself with the thought that she's as well and happy as she can ever be."

"Content myself with that thought? You don't know me very well."

"Not for lack of trying, Lissy. There's nothing I want more than to know you well."

"You're such a good person, Joss," she said softly. "I can't remember a time when I didn't feel affection for you. But this isn't the time to speak of anything more. Let it wait. Let it wait a little."

Providence was thinking about her children. Berry and the twins suffered from Jonas's strong-headedness, while Winsome had taken from her father something of his recklessness. It had been left to Felicity to inherit from her mother not only her looks but also what lay hidden just beneath the surface. For although Providence had long ago ceased to think of herself as impetuous or headstrong or passionate, so complacently had she fit into the secure life she'd fashioned for herself, there was no doubt that those qualities were as much a part of her as the blood that ran in her veins, and it was those qualities she had passed on to Felicity. She thought now, as she stood at her bedroom window, that of all her children perhaps Felicity was the least blessed. Then for the second time she raised the letter she had in her hand and held it to catch the morning light so that she could make out the words.

Dear Mama,

I would have preferred to tell you face-to-face what I am about to commit to paper, but I could not because you would have stopped me from carrying out my intentions. For many weeks now I have been thinking about Saree, believing she is still alive. Joss's description of the white woman living among the Iroquois fits her too perfectly to be coincidence. I believe you think as I do, although you have been careful not to commit yourself to the possibility for fear of causing me pain.

I have decided to look for Saree. I know you will be frightened learning this, but you mustn't be. It is not such a fearsome undertaking as you might suppose. I will be traveling under the protection of the colonial troops, with Josiah as my confederate and guide. He has agreed to help me discover Saree's whereabouts, and as a first lieutenant with men under his command, he will be able to bring to bear the necessary force to free her. Do not be angry with him. I swore him to secrecy.

Joss estimates that our journey north and back will take four to six weeks, and if the French are engaged and defeated as easily as he expects, I shall be home again by early August. I am personally in no danger. I will be nowhere near the battle, nor risking my own scalp at the hands of the Indians either. Joss says he would never permit me to go were he not confident of my safety.

Mama, I have hired a girl to help in the bakery. Her name is Pudding, a free Negress and niece to Joseph Savery. Joseph tells me she is not ill-named, being somewhat thickheaded, but he tells me that she follows orders well, is a happy little creature of seventeen, and best of all, that she will be happy with whatever wage you wish to pay. Expect her at the shop this morning at eight.

I know you will feel deceived and ill-served at first knowing what I've done, but there was no other course for me. I have always held myself to blame for Saree's capture, and I will not rest until I make amends. I know you will forgive me when I bring Saree home and we are once again united as a family. Pray for Saree, for Joss, and for me, Mama.

Your loving daughter,
Lissy

Wilderness 1755

· · · ·

Delight thyself also in the Lord;
and he shall give thee the desires of thine heart.

Psalm 37:4
A Psalm of David

Obtaining a horse wasn't difficult, although it and the other supplies took all the savings Felicity had managed to accumulate since opening the bakery. She bought the horse and saddle, as well as the saddlebags, from Curler's livery on North Street, purposely choosing an establishment some distance from home with a proprietor who was a relative stranger. Felicity knew how to ride, but she was no expert on the subject of horses. She had to take at face value what Curler told her when he discussed such fine points as fetlocks and wind, and she had no idea what to look for when Curler showed her the horse's teeth. However, the horse was a mare named Cocoa, with melancholy eyes and an appealing gentleness that made acceptable Curler's claim that "She's a lovely bit of flesh, no lovelier at any price."

When it came to picking the saddle Felicity surprised Curler by rejecting the sidesaddle he showed her and, instead, chose a man's saddle. It would be more practical for the rough riding she'd be doing, and what it lacked in comfort it would make up in a secure seat. She owned a riding habit and could utilize the boots and riding gloves, but the habit itself, blue broadcloth with a matching plumed hat, was inappropriate for a trek into the wilderness. She decided on men's trousers under a sturdy homespun skirt, a man's padded jacket, and a man's wide-brimmed hat; items readily available at Selwin's dry-goods store on South Henry Street.

There wouldn't be much room in the saddlebags, Felicity realized, and she would have to limit herself to essentials. A gun would be one of them. There were two muskets at home to choose from, and gunpowder could be purchased from Mister Oatland, the gunsmith. She decided she could pack no more than one change of outer clothing, two of undergarments, and an absolute minimum of the other female necessaries. She would need a blanket, a water flask, and eating utensils. The food itself wasn't a worry. Once she joined forces with Josiah he would provide for her. However, she would be on her own for the first two days and needed some basics; a bit of dried beef, some dried fruit, and a supply of the dry, saltless ship biscuits that Joss referred to as hardtack. Those would be rations enough to see her through.

She found an excuse to absent herself from the bakery on Monday long enough to buy her supplies and deliver them directly to the livery stable, thus avoiding piquing her mother's curiosity. Curler's curiosity was appeased by the explanation that she intended to travel under the protection of the colonial troops as far north as Fredericksburg, where a "sick aunt" awaited her arrival.

Monday night was hot, and she slept little. Curler delivered the horse by prior arrangement on Tuesday morning in front of the stable, watched her mount, and waved her on her way just as the first light striped the horizon. It would be another sweltering day, but the sky was clear, with no sign of rain, and it felt exhilarating to be utterly free and in command, with no one to answer to and no responsibilities other than the one; to find Saree and bring her home. There was, of course, the problem of facing Josiah, but since Felicity didn't intend to present herself to him until nightfall of the second day of the march, there would be little he could do then to send her back to Williamsburg.

The encampment was about two miles north of the Red Mask on Richmond Road. Josiah had told Felicity that the company, consisting of two platoons loosely numbered at fifty men each, lacked military discipline but was experienced in combat. Most of them, including Joss, had been in the Ohio Valley the year before when the French drove out the British and Colonial troops who were trying to construct a fort there. And many of the men had also fought ten years before at Cape Breton. They were, according to Joss, professional soldiers; adventurers looking for excitement in the army, just as they had looked for excitement when they decided to migrate to the colonies. Farmers and family men with some stake in the land were in the minority, which Joss felt was just as well, for although they fought with purpose, their hearts were divided, and they didn't make the best soldiers. It was a ruffian army, Felicity concluded, but perhaps a ruffian army was needed to deal with the French and with the red savages.

By the time she reached the campground the field was swept clean of tents, the campfires had been doused, and the first of the long double line of horses and pack mules had begun to move out into the road. Felicity didn't see any sign of Josiah, but she did recognize Captain Lawrence Collier sitting astride a sleek black stallion and issuing commands to his men. She felt a twinge of envy looking at him. Collier was only, perhaps, ten years older than she, but so much surer of himself. He was admired because he had worked himself up from genteel farmer's son to wealthy plantation owner. He had cultivated the tastes of the affluent and had been accepted as a distinguished and successful member of the Virginia establishment. He was independent, respected for his opinions, and bachelorhood added rather than detracted from his reputation. And why? Because he was a man. At best her own self-sacrifice and accomplishments were regarded as eccentricities. And why? Because she was a woman. Worse yet, Collier had been given the choice of whether or not he wished to be here, and commended for his bravery in choosing to come. Her presence, on the other hand, had been accomplished through stealth and deceit, and would be severely criticized when it was discovered.

But this was no time for reflections on the unfairness of life. Felicity waited at a distance until the tag end of horses and men were in the road, moving in formation up the High Road, then pressed her knees into Cocoa's flanks to make her pick up the pace. She had, by then, begun to look for the women, and soon she saw them—a dozen or more females who had been riding next to and among the soldiers, but who had now begun dropping to the rear. They were a scruffy lot, scavengers in face paint and cheap beads, and she kept a wide distance between herself and them during the hours that followed.

When the command echoed down the line for the first respite Felicity stopped where she was, some quarter mile to the rear, and sat down by the side of the road to eat her solitary meal of dried fruit. She felt deprived as she washed down the chewy, tasteless scraps with water from her flask, especially watching Cocoa graze contentedly among the tender grasses. The horse was in far better shape than she. Four hours in the saddle had exacted its price. Her hip bones and the tip of her spine were bruised and aching. The muscles of her inner thighs were pulled and sore, the flesh of her thighs was rasped with saddle burns, and the sun had baked her face and scorched her lips. Beyond the discomfort was the exhaustion. She had never been so tired. But just as her eyelids began to droop, the cry came to remount.

She didn't notice at what point they left the road, perhaps because the road had narrowed by slow degrees until it became a trail just wide enough to accommodate a single horse and carriage. It wasn't until the trees began to close in and the defined formation of horses and riders became raggedy that she realized they had struck off the High Road and were entering the forest. Now she drew a little closer to the horses ahead of her. She judged it to be ten hours or more since they had started out, and she was worried that the moment might come when she could ride no farther and must call for help. If that moment came, she wanted to know she would be heard.

Just before dark the riders came to a clearing that turned out to be a lake girdled by a broad strand of stony mud flats, and it was here that the command was passed down to halt and make camp. Felicity's legs were wobbly when she dismounted, and she was dizzy with fatigue. She rested her forehead against the saddle for a moment, then forced herself to loosen the cinches and lift off Cocoa's saddle and the saddlebags. There was no way to go on avoiding the troops. They were everywhere, fanning out in a wide arc along the lake front and unloading their gear wherever there was space, but for the moment, at least, they were less interested in her than she was in them. She chose a spot for herself that offered some privacy, arranging her belongings at the far side of a tree screened three-quarters around by holly thickets, and then took hold of Cocoa's reins and led her down to the lake.

At the water's edge Felicity removed her boots, then waded into the water up to her knees, pulling Cocoa along with her. While Cocoa drank, she did, too, cupping her hands to bring the water to her lips, then splashing water on her face and on the back of her neck. The heat remained oppressive, and Felicity's face smarted from the effects of the sun earlier in the day. She had considered bringing a sun mask, but had rejected the genteel accessory because she thought it might set her apart and make her conspicuous. Now she was sorry, especially since she had seen at least two or three of the other women wearing them. Again she dipped into the water and patted her cheeks and forehead and parched lips. Finally she sloshed back out of the water, picked up her boots, and made her way across the stony beach, disregarding her sodden skirt dragging in the mud. She was brought up short by a hand on her arm. It was a woman who stopped her, a youngish woman with a pockmarked face and deep-set, mistrustful eyes. "So you made up your mind to join us, did you? We was wondering how long you'd trail behind like somebody's mongrel bitch."

"What I do is my business," Felicity answered shortly.

"I've never seen you before. Where do you come from?"

"Williamsburg."

"The devil you do."

"I don't care whether you believe me or not," Felicity returned in a tired voice.

"I know every whore in Williamsburg town, and you're not one of 'em."

"I've not bothered you," Felicity told her, "and I'd rather you don't bother me."

"Who is she, Clara?" a second rough voice joined in.

Felicity shifted her gaze to the newcomer, an aged yet ageless crone whom she recognized as Meg Buckles, the bakery's previous tenant.

"I don't know. She says she's from Williamburg, but if she is, then she's somebody's private doxie."

"I'm my own mistress," Felicity said.

"That's a trick, ain't it?" the woman named Clara joked. "And one I'd like to learn."

Felicity started to pass them by, but Meg grabbed her arm. "What's your name?" she asked.

There seemed no point in lying. Felicity said curtly, "Lissy."

"How come you been hanging back all day? Why didn't you ride with the rest of us?"

Felicity considered what to say, but before she could say anything, a soldier walked up behind Clara, and reached around to cup her breast with one hand while pinching her buttocks with the other. "I'll be lookin' for you a little later," he said genially. "You got a space needs fillin'."

"Yeah," Clara returned promptly. "My money pouch." She flipped the pouch hanging at her belt, then gave him a friendly rap as he walked away.

"Well, Lissy?" Meg repeated. "I ast you a question. How come you didn't ride with us ones?"

"I wasn't feeling well," Felicity answered. "I don't feel

well now." It wasn't a lie. Her legs were suddenly weak again, so much so that she laid her arm over Cocoa's back to support herself. "Please leave me alone. I want to go back and lie down."

"We ain't stoppin' you," Meg pointed out.

But as Felicity moved away, Clara called out warningly, "It's your choice to stick by yourself, but you'll think better on the first time a half dozen or so of them cocks decides it wants your arse."

Felicity didn't reply. She slogged back to the place where she'd left her belongings and tied the horse at loose tether. Then she crawled behind the tree and rested her head on her saddle. It was dark now, but dark or light, it didn't matter. Her gritty eyelids closed, sound faded, and within seconds she was asleep.

She woke to a jab in her side and found Meg Buckles glowering down at her. "Wake up," Meg ordered gruffly. "Open up your eyes."

"Stop it," Felicity mumbled. "Please leave me alone."

Meg curtseyed. "Oh, do pardon. Next time I'll knock on your door, milady."

"Next time leave me be."

"If it's alone you want," Meg asserted, "then go back to sleep. In a few minutes there won't be a white man in callin' distance." She turned her back and shuffled off.

Felicity became gradually aware of the nervous pawing of horses' hooves, the tread of boots, and, here and there, a brusque command. The light was still pale, but she had been able to make out Meg's features, which meant that dawn was breaking and the troops preparing to resume the march. She rose quickly, emerging from her secluded bower to find herself in the midst of activity as campfires were stamped out and equipment and supplies organized. She would have to hurry or be left behind. She sought out a private spot behind a bush to relieve herself, then made her way down to the lake to wash.

There were mosquitoes buzzing around her head, and she waved her hand in front of her face in a fruitless attempt to stave them off. She noticed that her hands were covered with bites, and that there were lumps all over her face and neck. It was bad enough, she thought, to suffer sunburn and muscle ache without adding the itch of insect bites. This red, swollen, stiff-jointed self was what she would present to Josiah at the end of that day's march; hardly a persuasive image or one to inspire affection.

She was parched and drank some of the lake water, thinking to herself that she must bring the horse down to drink, and that at the same time she would refill her flask for the day's ride. Then something else occurred to her. She didn't recall having seen Cocoa when she went past the place she was tethered. Picking up her skirts she flew back across the flats, up the sloping embankment, and through the trees, her heart pounding as she stared at the place where the horse had been. The earth was ridged with the marks of Cocoa's hooves, and Felicity could see that during the night she had nibbled away a half-moon of vegetation from the base of the tree. Now she was gone. There seemed to be horses and people everywhere as she began to run from one group to another in panic. She wondered if Meg might have let the horse loose out of spite, but when she tracked her down, Meg said indignantly, "What do you think I am? I wouldn't leave no one horseless in these savagery woods."

"Listen," Felicity told her, "I thank you for waking me. I shouldn't have spoken to you the way I did."

"That's right, you shouldn't of, but I still don't know nothing about yer horse."

Felicity continued to dash here and there, growing more desperate minute by minute. Soon the command to move out would be given and she'd be left behind. Then suddenly she felt a tug at her skirt and looked down to see a soldier sitting crouched on the ground and grinning up at her. Just a few yards behind him two horses muched oats from a heap of grain that was piled on the ground. Felicity gave a cry of relief. One of the horses was Cocoa. The reins were still around her neck, but there was a chunk of bush entangled in one end dragging on the ground. Felicity started toward her, but the soldier grabbed her skirt and held her back. "Stay a minute," he invited. "Let's take a look at you."

"That's my horse," Felicity said anxiously.

"I know it's your horse. I seen you watering her last night."

"I'd like to take her."

"Now, there's a coincidence," he returned suggestively. "My mind's running in the same direction."

Felicity had known she'd have to fend off unwanted overtures, and she'd rehearsed for it. "I'm not of a similar mind," she told him with dignity.

"You're not what?" he asked incredulously. "Say, what kind of whore are you?"

"No kind," Felicity answered coolly.

"The hell you ain't." He reached up, pulled on her arm, and tumbled her down between his legs, knocking off her hat and pulling her hair loose. Then he twined his fingers in her hair to hold her head still, and kissed her. His breath stank, and his beard was like a carpenter's rasp on her sunburned face, but even more horrifying was his attempt to force open her lips and thrust his tongue into her mouth. She began to pound him with her fists, struggling wildly and flailing at him until finally he released her.

"You're disgusting," she said, panting.

"And you're crazy," he said in a dazed way as he flexed his bruised shoulders.

She got to her feet and rushed over to retrieve Cocoa. A few minutes later and at a safe distance she spat into the dirt to rid herself of the taste of him, then leaned her head against Cocoa's flank while she controlled the queasiness that had overcome her.

"Clara guessed you ain't no whore," a gravelly voice announced.

Felicity twisted her head to return Meg Buckles's steady gaze. "I didn't say I was."

"A raw recruit," Meg added with a snaggle-toothed leer. "Well, you won't be that for long."

·· *35* ··

Felicity rode with the women that second day. After the incident with the soldier she felt safer among them, at least for the time being. That night she would put herself securely into Josiah's hands, and after that he'd watch out for her. Meg introduced her to the other women, conveying to them her own assumption that Felicity's status was that of apprentice whore. Felicity said nothing to contradict the assumption, believing it would antagonize them to think she might simply be making use of them. The prostitutes numbered fourteen in all, ranging in age from Meg, the eldest, down to Fern, a pretty child of eleven or twelve, daughter to Clara, a tired-looking woman not much older than Felicity herself. Then there was Kate with the withered arm and Elga, to whom all the others deferred, a tall, pipe-smoking mulatto with a wild halo of kinky black hair. The other names and faces were something of a blur to Felicity, but would sort themselves out gradually as the days passed.

It was cooler riding through the woods than it had been on the High Road, and although Felicity was saddle-sore, she sat the mare better and handled the reins more skillfully than she had the day before. The command to halt came a little before noon near a stream where they could water their horses and refresh themselves. By then Felicity was famished. Her last complete meal had been supper two nights before, with nothing but dried fruit and water since then. She ate all her dried beef and hardtack, then shared what was left of the dried fruit with Meg, who plumped up the bits of apple and pear in a mug of water before eating them, and reciprocated with a bit of rock candy.

Felicity was grateful to the old hag for being civil to her, although she soon found out that her civility had its limits. When she attempted to question Meg about herself, Meg made it clear she meant her business to remain her own, "I disremember" being her stock answer to every question: where she came from originally, whether she had ever been married, whether there was family somewhere. The only revelation she made freely was that her own whoring days were over, and that now she functioned chiefly as adviser and comforter to the others.

She was disreputable-looking, with a foul mouth and vulgar sense of humor, but she was friendly and quick with helpful suggestions. She showed Felicity how to boil down bits of bark to make an astringent solution that would repel insects. She pointed out that a mud poultice laid on the palms of the hands and permitted to dry would fill in the raw splits opened by hours of handling the reins. And she suggested to Felicity that a knife up one's sleeve was quicker to stop a man than "a lot of smart talk about not being in the mood." Felicity, with some sense of irony for who had become her mentor, nevertheless listened attentively and profited from Meg's instruction.

That afternoon word came down the line that Indians had been sighted along the trail. By the time it filtered down to the women the details were lost, and no one knew where the Indians had been sighted, how many of them there were, or whether they comprised a hunting party or a war party. The report itself, however, was enough to draw the women into tighter formation and discourage stragglers. They had made a sharp right turn some hours back and were now riding through hillier country, and when they stopped at nightfall it was near the banks of a narrow river called the North Anna.

Felicity was eager to start looking for Josiah, but it seemed more judicious to wait until after supper. Elga rode among the women issuing orders and dividing the chores; some to gather firewood, some to visit the soldiers to beg food, some to fetch water. Felicity was told to clear a space for the fire. When that was done someone carrying two forked sticks and a straight stick proceeded to construct a lug pole, from which someone else suspended a pot filled with water. Then the women who had gone foraging among the soldiers began to drift back bearing their offerings; a handful of beans, two potatoes, a half-dozen carrots, an onion, a turnip, a porringer filled with barley, and from little Fern, the pièce de résistance, a couple of knuckles of cured ham. Felicity's mouth watered as each item was unceremoniously dumped into the pot, and forty minutes later, when Elga doled out the stew, she was as demanding as the others in claiming her share.

She ate ravenously and had just tipped her plate to let the last few drops of broth dribble into her open mouth when she felt a hand steal around her neck, cup her chin, and jerk back her head. She dropped her plate and raised her eyes to see a face, grotesque in its upside-down position, suspended just above her own. It was the soldier who had kissed her that morning. She pulled loose and leaped to her feet, aware of the women watching her as she turned to face him. "You shouldn't surprise someone like that," she said shakily. "Next time call out."

"I came looking for you. We got some unfinished business."

"I'm eating my supper."

"Not no more you're not."

"Make him show his money," Meg advised from her place on the opposite side of the fire.

The soldier reached into his pocket for a coin and pressed it into Felicity's hand.

"Make him show his cock," Fern added mischievously, her angelic child's face gleaming in the firelight.

"Get it out in the open," another bawdy joined in, "where we can all admire it."

"I ain't going ass up for nobody's pleasure but my own," the soldier informed them, then wound his arm around Felicity's waist and began dragging her away to the cackle of obscene laughter.

Felicity was appalled. She tried to wriggle free. "I prefer to walk at my own pace."

"For a whore you've got an odd way of talking," the soldier commented without loosening his hold.

"Please stop. You're hurting me."

He continued to pull her along until they were out of sight of the other women. Then he released her. Quickly she shoved the coin back at him. "Here, take it. I don't want your money. Find somebody else to wrestle with."

"Why, you rotten little slut," he growled. "Who gave you the right to say no?" He made a lunge toward her and missed. She tried to run, but he closed the gap in seconds, crooked his arm around her neck, and pulled her violently back against him. She remembered Meg's advice about the knife, but she hadn't yet taken her knife out of the saddlebag and was defenseless. "Try to tell me no? You'll be glad enough to say yes when I'm done with you." He jammed his knee into the small of her back and tightened his arm around her throat. "Too good to lift your skirts for me, are you? Well, let's see if you'll lift them for your life."

Felicity was terrified. She couldn't strike out at him and she couldn't cry out because of the pressure on her larynx.

"Filthy whore," the soldier muttered. He pushed her down onto her hands and knees, then straddled her, laying his full weight on her so that she collapsed onto the ground.

Then he shoved her cheek into the dirt and with his free hand between his legs began pulling up her skirt. "Stop," she gasped. "Stop it. Leave me alone."

"You won't do it for money so I'll take it for free," he declared hoarsely.

Felicity screamed, or tried to scream, but the sound was cut short when he struck her in the face with his fist. She began to sob, then suddenly heard the sound of a voice ordering the soldier to release her. "What is this?" the voice demanded. "What are you doing?"

The soldier released her and scrambled to his feet. "Nothing, Captain Collier. She's one of the whores. We're just having some fun."

"You there," Collier demanded. "You female. Are you all right?"

Felicity sat up and tried to catch her breath. "Yes," she managed to say. "Yes, I'm all right. Please, I want to see Josiah Wrentham."

"Who?"

"Lieutenant Josiah Wrentham."

She sat in a patch of moonlight, fully visible to Captain Collier, but he, astride his black stallion, was an obscure shadow against the black backdrop of trees. "What business could you possibly have with one of my officers?"

There was a silence during which Felicity became painfully aware of the captain's scrutiny and of her own disheveled appearance. "I know him," she said urgently. "He's a friend. Please tell me where he is."

"He's gone," Collier informed her.

"Gone where?"

"He led an advance party north this morning. He's no longer with the company."

"No longer . . . ?"

"You heard me. Now hear this as well. You, too, Private. I don't want trouble between the females and my soldiers. The next incident like this will end with the soldier in irons and the whore left behind to deal with the savages."

"But wait," Felicity pleaded. "Listen to me."

"That goes for officers as well as privates, miss. I don't care how many officers you know. Now, you heard my advice. I suggest you take heed of it."

Felicity walked away from the soldier, but she wasn't sure whether or not he would come after her a second time, so she crept under a bush in the woods and spent the night in hiding. She was frightened; more so than she had ever been in her life. With Josiah gone there was no one to turn to, no one willing to believe who she was. She didn't know how she was to survive, nor did she know what to do about Sarah. It had all seemed so simple when she knew she had Josiah to count on. He was in love with her, and that made all things possible. But now, alone, not even able to rescue herself, how was she to rescue Sarah? She couldn't think. Blessedly, exhaustion took over and she slept heavily throughout the night, postponing the necessity for deciding anything.

She woke at first light with the startled sensation that all was not well, then recalled her unresolved situation with despair. What was she to do? Should she try again to tell Captain Collier who she was and what she was doing there? It seemed like the only logical solution to her dilemma, even though Collier was not apt to be sympathetic. But it was not something she could do right away. She must choose her time carefully to coincide with a time when Collier had no other matters pressing.

With no great enthusiasm she rejoined the women, chagrined to find them in various stages of undress, some shamelessly bare-breasted, some in underdrawers and chemises. Meg was completely dressed above the waist but naked from the waist down, while rubbing her buttocks with some sort of clouded solution out of a jar. She waved the jar at Felicity. "Here, take some." Seeing Felicity's puzzlement she added, "It ain't nothin' but salted water, but it toughens the arse and makes the riding easier."

Felicity's backside was sufficiently sore to make the offer tempting, but she would have died rather than expose any private parts of her anatomy. She declined politely.

"Where you been?" Meg asked.

"Nowhere."

"Not sayin', eh? Well, it's yer own business where you spend yer nights. What went wrong with that jack last night? He come back and said yer refused him. Took it out on Bertha. Blacked both her eyes and near twisted her arm out'n its socket."

"Oh no," Felicity murmured.

"Elga had to run him off before he beat up on us all."

"Was he looking for me?"

"I suppose he were, but he made do with Bertha. How come you refused him? He paid yer, didn't he?"

"I . . . I gave him back his money."

"Did he ask yer to do somethin' nasty?" Meg persisted. "What did he ask yer to do? Suck cock?" She misread the expression on Felicity's face and added bluntly, "It don't do to be squeamish. In that case yer should of asked fer an extra shillin'."

"I'd rather not talk about it," Felicity mumbled.

"It's all part of the job. What did yer expect? Hand-kissin' and by-yer-leave?"

"I'm sorry about Bertha," Felicity said miserably. "I'll tell her so."

"Don't tell her nothin'. Just do yer job next time and don't leave it to no one else to take yer kicks."

Felicity suspected that Meg had been appointed to speak for the group, and the message was clear. The women were a loose but interdependent confederation. There were rules to be obeyed, and Felicity would be expected to obey them. "I'll remember what you said," she assured Meg.

It began to darken during the morning's ride, and by noon the sky was filled with black clouds. The midday halt was brief, just long enough to stretch the legs, gnaw on whatever rations had been put aside from the previous night's meals—in Felicity's case there was nothing—and give the horses a rest.

Felicity kept to herself during the break, maintaining a distance between herself and the others by pretending to be occupied picking burrs out of Cocoa's mane. She was agonizingly self-conscious about the occurrence the night before. She didn't remember who Bertha was, but the glimpse of a woman with swollen, greenish-brown bruises surrounding both eyes left no doubt as to her identity. The unfairness of what had happened only made Felicity feel worse. She hadn't been responsible for Bertha's beating, yet she was guilty of it.

The rain began early that afternoon and continued all day, gradually turning the spongy earth to mud and drenching horses and riders. It had been pleasant at first to receive the cool, cleansing drops on one's face and hands, but after a while cool turned to clammy and the slogging ride became a sodden ordeal. By the time the order was passed down to make camp, Felicity was chilly, hungry, and fatigued. If ever she were going to make contact with Collier, it had to be now.

She ignored the call to halt, intending to ride forward to the head of the line, but as she passed the women Meg rode her horse into Felicity's path. "Whoa there," she called. She reached out and took the reins out of Felicity's hands. "Elga says you, Annie, Gerda, and Kate is to get the food. Best go about it right quick. We're starved."

Felicity's stomach knotted. "Me? Beg for food?"

"It ain't beggin'. The soldiers expect to share with us. Try to get a piece of meat if you can."

"How?"

"Ride up to someone and ask fer it. If need be, promise somethin'. Not to do it fer free, but maybe a little somethin' extra." Meg ran her tongue over her lips and winked.

Felicity knew she could never approach the soldiers in the blatant guise of a prostitute asking for a handout, but there was no way to say no to Meg. She nodded, reclaimed the reins, then spurred her horse and rode forward. Dusk was premature, having deepened early after the stormy afternoon. It was difficult to differentiate between officers and men as they hurried about their tasks or huddled around scraps of damp, smoking wood, but Felicity reasoned that Collier would be somewhere at the head of the line, and she picked her way past the others without attempting to sort them out.

Collier's tent was easy to spot. It was larger than the others and set apart from them with a sentry posted in front. Felicity rode right up to it before dismounting. She dropped the reins over Cocoa's head and started to walk forward, but was stopped by the sentry, who thrust his musket in her face. "What do you want?"

"I wish to see Captain Collier."

The sentry's face was suspicioius beneath his dripping hat brim. "If Collier wants a female, he'll send for one."

"I'm not a—"

Collier's voice interrupted from within the tent. "Hill, what's going on out there?"

The sentry pursed his lips as if readying some sarcastic reply, but dropped his voice instead and muttered, "Wait here, you."

He ducked into the tent and reemerged a moment later to hold open the tent flap for her. Felicity slipped through into the soft glow of candlelight illuminating a dry canvas floor, luxuries that filled her with sudden self-pity. "I'm Felicity Greenhill," she blurted out through trembling lips.

Collier sat on a cot holding a map on his lap. He was in his shirt sleeves, and his boots, like her own, were thick with mud. But he looked comfortable and dry, and Felicity envied him with all her heart. For the first time ever she saw him up close, a man in his middle or late thirties, somewhat craggy and uneven-featured but saved from homeliness by wide-set gray eyes and a handsome mouth. He regarded her silently: a filthy and rain-drenched female wearing a shapeless man's hat; sunburned, callused, and swollen with insect bites. Then he said politely, "Excuse me for remaining seated. The tent roof is too low to permit me to stand. You say your name is Greenhill?"

"Yes. I'm . . ." Felicity knew he expected her to say that she was one of the whores, and she wanted to disabuse him of the idea. At the same time it seemed bizarre to identify herself as a lady. "I'm a baker," she said.

She saw a flash of white teeth. "You're not looking for employment, I trust. We've not much use for a baker here."

"I'm a friend of Josiah Wrenthan. That is, we're related by marriage. He's brother to my brother's wife."

His eyes narrowed. "Wait a moment. Are you the female—"

"Yes, I am. The one you mistook for a whore. I expected to travel under Lieutenant Wrentham's protection. My presence among the other women is inadvertent."

"Greenhill?" Collier mused. "Greenhill. There was a Greenhill at Darby Littlefield's party a month or so back. Are you—"

"No, I'm not." She didn't elucidate, realizing it wouldn't help her case to identify that other Greenhill as her sister, but she added, "Beriah Greenhill, the printer, is my brother. Surely you know who he is."

"Would you mind removing your hat?" he asked.

Felicity did so, presenting him with a discolored cheek-bone so puffed up that it partially closed one of her eyes. Apparently, however, there was enough of the other showing to satisfy him. "No, you're not the one. She was browned-eyed, with a softer, younger look. Well, tell me why you're here. What do you want?"

"I came to ask for your protection until Josiah returns."

"Under the circumstances I can only suggest you make the best of your situation. Perhaps you can find some other man to look after you. Lieutenant Wrenthan isn't the only man susceptible to a woman's wiles."

"Please try to understand. Josiah is not my lover, nor I, his. He is a relative. You see—this is difficult to explain but I must try—I came because of my sister."

"You seem to be blessed by a plentiful supply of relatives."

"Many years ago my sister was abducted by the Iroquois. Recently Josiah told me about a white woman fitting her description held by the Iroquois who inhabit the region near Fort Duquesne. I decided to come look for her. I thought Josiah would help me, but I knew he wouldn't permit me to travel with the army, so I followed on my own, intending to reveal myself to him when we were a safe way out of Williamsburg. I never dreamed that Josiah wouldn't be here among the troops."

Collier smiled. "You expect me to believe such a story?"

"It's the truth."

"Are you certain you didn't follow Lieutenant Wrentham with some other purpose in mind? Are you sure he's a—what did you call him—a relative by marriage? I understood that he's a stranger to Williamsburg. He told me that he was born and raised in New Castle."

"Yes. So was I. My family and I moved here ten years ago. That is, my mother, my sisters and I moved here. Two of my brothers remained behind in New Castle."

"Did you not say that your brother is Beriah Greenhill, the Williamsburg printer?"

"Beriah is still another brother. I have three." She looked at his skeptical expression and said despairingly, "How can I make you believe me? Please listen. We had given my sister up for dead. Then when Josiah told me about the white woman living among the Iroquois I became hopeful that she might still be alive."

"And so you came to rescue her. And how did you plan to bring about this rescue?"

"I hadn't planned. I thought I would find a way."

Collier shook his head, then said crisply, "I don't believe you. Miss Greenhill, if that's your name, I'm fairly certain that no young lady of decent background would leave her home, indeed, would be permitted to leave her home for such a dangerous and totally impractical mission. Nor do I think Lieutenant Wrentham is related to you by marriage or by blood or by any other tie, unless it be libidinous in nature. And even if there were a sister being held captive by the Iroquois, there would be nothing to be done about it, at least not now, and not by me. This company of men is not at the disposal of young women in search of adventure."

Felicity despaired. "What am I to do if you won't help me?"

"I ask the same question. What am I to do? I'm an army officer, not a chaperon. I have no time to waste looking after females. My job is to command a company of soldiers. I cannot be expected to feed and shelter and protect every whore disappointed in her expectations and regretful of having attached herself to a body of rough-and-ready soldiers."

"How many times must I repeat that I am not a whore?"

"I'm no more interested in hearing your protests than you are in offering them. I have matters to attend to, Miss Greenhill, matters of importance." He turned back to the map spread across his knees.

Felicity stood for a moment trying to grasp the fact that she had been dismissed, then turned on her heel and rushed back out of the tent.

Felicity faced the harsh reality that she must care for herself or perish. The imperatives of survival were immediate; how to protect herself and how to feed herself being the most pressing. She was indignant with Lawrence Collier for not believing her when she told him why she was there, but she was more frightened than indignant. Until Joss returned she would be at the mercy of the troops, dependent upon them for sustenance and vulnerable to their lascivious overtures.

She hadn't intended to return to the women, but if she were to eat that night there was no alternative, and the immediate problem became where and how to make her contribution to the pot. She started back on foot, leading the stolid Cocoa through the mud. The rain had eased, but it still continued to fall, and the dozens of small campfires she passed spit and smoked under impoverished blanket awnings. At intervals during the day she had heard guns being fired, and once she'd spotted a pigeon drop out of the sky, but she hadn't appreciated the foresight of those hunters until now, seeing the birds and small game cooking over the fires. Still, she hadn't the nerve to beg even though she began to salivate when she caught a whiff of meat roasting.

She was within a few hundred yards of the women, and still empty-handed, when she saw a soldier feeding a pair of horses, and nearby, a second soldier poking a fire to life. There were three plucked pigeons lying on the ground next to the fire and she eyed them greedily; three pigeons for two men. Surely they could spare the extra. Almost without thinking she stooped, picked up a small stone, and tossed it at one of the horses, which whinnied and reared as it felt the sting to its flank. The other horse began to prance nervously, and the man tending them called for help. The second soldier darted to his aid, and while they were occupied Felicity scooped up one of the pigeons and fled.

The resultant pigeon stew, thickened with potatoes contributed by Anne and additionally stretched by a slightly moldy but still edible cabbage supplied by Gerda, was delicious and gave Felicity no qualms. Nothing she had ever eaten tasted better, and, she thought, stealing was certainly preferable to selling her favors. Now if only she were dry and warm and able to enjoy a good night's sleep. When the meal was over she took Meg at her word— "They'll not fuss with us tonight. It ain't no night for screwin'"—and settled herself close to the fire, where within minutes she was asleep.

Her first inkling of something amiss came just before dawn when she was startled into wakefulness. The rain had stopped, the fire was out, and the other women were still asleep. She raised her head, but saw nothing out of the ordinary. Still, she felt uneasy. Her first thought was that the soldier who had attacked her two days before had come looking for her again, but seeing no one she decided that she'd been disturbed by some small scrabbling creature in the underbrush.

She stretched out her arms, and with no expectation of falling asleep again, lay staring up at the sky. She thought about Lawrence Collier and felt her face grow warm with recollected humiliation. She knew how unconvincing her explanations must have seemed to him, especially in light of her deplorable appearance and condition. Yet the crux of his skepticism hadn't lain in her appearance but in the rules that dictated womanly behavior, rules that didn't apply to him.

A gentleman might appear disreputable and still remain a gentleman. He might associate with the rabble without being branded a ruffian. He needn't seek permission to leave home or to risk his life for something he believed in. He was free to choose, free to justify and defend, free in myriad ways denied a woman either by law or by prejudice. She remembered again his last words to her: "I have matters to attend to, Miss Greenhill, matters of importance." Why hadn't she answered that she had matters of importance to attend to as well?

She turned her head. What was that? Hadn't she heard something, a sigh, a whisper, a rustling in the leaves? She held her breath to listen, but decided after a moment that it had been her imagination. Nevertheless, it was a relief when the sky brightened and she heard a discernible sound, the chirping of birds. Then, abruptly, there was another sound. She heard a cry ring out, a cry that started low and rose to a screech. Felicity sat bolt upright, as did Meg and two or three others. "Oh lord," Meg called out. "Oh lord, they're on us!"

Felicity had never heard anything like it. "What was that?" she said, her voice quavering.

"It were a redskin," Meg told her, jumping to her feet and looking around in terror.

The rest of the women were getting to their feet with dazed faces. "Where did it come from?" Clara demanded of Felicity.

"I couldn't tell," she answered. "I don't think it was close by."

"Are you sure it's Indians, Meg?" the child, Fern, asked in a frightened voice.

"It ain't the first time I heard that sound," Meg confirmed.

"Nor me neither," Elga joined in. Elga rose, spit on her hands, and pushed back her masses of unruly hair. "But there's no call to panic. They ain't going to attack."

"How do you know?" Felicity asked.

"Because they don't give warning when they do."

Other voices had risen beyond them. Gruff commands were being issued, and there were imperative cries for action. Then another shout went up, this one a hoarse cry for help, answered an instant later by an anguished oath. Then suddenly, everywhere, people were running. "Meg's right," another woman bawled. "Oh, merciful God, what will become of us?"

Elga, as leader, was the first to go looking for an answer, and Felicity, not wishing to rely on Elga to report back, followed. They joined a group of white-faced soldiers carrying muskets, and she heard one soldier ask another if they were under attack.

"It's a raid, not an attack," was the answer.

Felicity didn't comprehend the difference until she saw the milling crowd part to make way for two soldiers carrying a body from which protruded a feathered lance.

"A raid," Elga repeated. "They must of come into camp during the night."

Felicity was horrified. "How? Weren't there men on guard?"

"They can't be everywhere," was the laconic reply.

They pushed their way closer and saw another body being carried off. Felicity caught sight of the man's bloodied face and head. "Took his scalp," Elga muttered. She turned to a nearby soldier. "How many did they get?"

"Thirteen."

"All dead?"

"One's alive, but barely."

Another bystander muttered, "If he don't die first, Collier will hang him for letting those redskins steal their guns and horses."

The two women moved closer to the scene of the massacre. The bodies lay where they had been murdered, not in one concentrated spot but haphazardly sprawled among the trees, where the Indians had dispatched them one by one as they lay sleeping. It seemed remarkable to Felicity that the Indians could have succeeded in murdering thirteen men without arousing the rest of the camp, but then she recalled that not an hour before she had awakened with the ominous feeling that there was a presence nearby. Her waking may have saved her life.

"Here's Collier," Elga whispered.

Collier arrived on the scene flanked by two of his lieutenants. He was a full head taller than either, and they had to move quickly to keep up with his long stride. He surveyed the scene, then went over to talk to the men tending to the sole survivor. One of them shook his head and then both soldiers rose and walked away. Collier turned and, in a voice that carried easily to everyone present, said, "Lieutenants Arbor and Webster will have these men buried immediately. Their personal effects will be collected; money belts, jewelry, any small items that we can carry back to their families. The rest will be buried with them; clothes, saddlebags, boots. I don't want their saddles left to those bloody Indians, either, so they'll be buried as well."

"Ain't we goin' after 'em?" someone called out.

"No," Collier answered grimly.

"You mean we're just going to let those murderin' bastards get away with it?"

Collier didn't reply, and Felicity, roused to sudden, inexplicable rage, heard herself cry out, "How can you let those savages go? Don't you care that thirteen men were murdered?"

"Shut up," Elga whispered. "Don't rile him."

"Thirteen men murdered and you don't propose to bring their murderers to justice?" Felicity challenged. "All that interests you is burying their saddles?"

Collier turned his head to see who had spoken. When he caught sight of Felicity he sauntered over and said calmly, "Miss Greenhill, the Indians would like nothing more than to have me send a party of men after them. If I were to do that, there would be thirty dead instead of thirteen."

"You have guns, don't you? And these men are experienced fighters."

"They're no match for Indians in these woods. The

Indians came into camp without being seen or heard. They massacred thirteen men who lay within yards of their comrades. They left with thirteen horses and thirteen muskets and now, no doubt, they're waiting in ambush for whatever party may be dispatched to deal with them. I told you last night that my job is to command a company of soldiers, and I intend to do it without interference from you. You're tolerated here through my benevolence. Be sure you continue to deserve it." He turned to his officers and said curtly, "Report to me when my orders have been carried out." Then, with no further words to Felicity, he strode away.

"So that's it," Elga murmured. "I never thought it would turn out to be something like that."

"What are you talking about?" Felicity asked impatiently.

"Why you kept to yourself when we first rode out. Why you refused to diddle that soldier. Where you was the night before last. How come you have the nerve to talk to the captain like that. You're the captain's whore."

Felicity opened her mouth to protest but stopped when she heard the deference in Elga's voice. "Me? The captain's whore?"

"You ain't denying it, are you?"

Felicity hesitated for a moment, then said quietly, with a finger to her lips, "No, I'm not denying it. But, Elga, keep it to yourself. He wouldn't want it spread around."

Felicity knew, of course, that Elga would never keep such an intriguing tidbit to herself, nor did she want her to. All she meant to accomplish by asking for Elga's silence was to inhibit the other women from asking questions. She knew the ploy had worked when she found herself the object of their furtive attention; attention tinged with a new aura of respect. Even Bertha, who had suffered for Felicity's refusal to service the amorous soldier, went out of her way to be friendly. Felicity was relieved to have found a means to protect herself from harassment. She knew her troubles were far from over, but at least she could remain among the women without being expected to perform as one of them.

From then on Felicity rode with the women but slept alone at night, carefully maintaining the illusion that she slept with Captain Collier by bedding down as close to his tent as she could. It required skill to elude the sentries, but once accomplished, the proximity to Collier had the additional advantage that no one would dare venture within the captain's purview, so she was safe from intrusion. She quickly settled into a routine that was bearable, if not comfortable. Word of her special relationship to Captian Collier had by then filtered through the ranks, and she found herself able to move about without fear of molestation.

She didn't concern herself with the possible consequences of her ruse until she realized that while she was now safe, she was also mistrusted. The troops feared her privileged status. Josiah had described the soldiers as men who were, for the most part, ne'er-do-wells, and he hadn't exaggerated. By far the majority of them were uneducated ruffians with no taste for honest work, who endured army regulations only because they would do anything for the chance to fight, and who, between military encounters, fought among themselves. Felicity had been witness to half a dozen confrontations started over nothing but fought with murderous intensity. And these were the men who had decided that as "the captain's whore," she posed a threat. It would be ironic she thought, if she had secured her virginity at the cost of her life.

As the days passed Felicity came to know all of the women; not only Meg, the cheerful crone, and Elga, the leader, but all the other women as well. They were remarkably prosaic despite their calling. Gerda, Anne, and Bertha were middle-aged, cantankerous, and gossipy; Grace, Kate, Nell, and Mattie were young and hopelessly romantic; and Tiba and Heavensent, mulattoes like Elga, tended to guard their dignity above all else. She felt sorry for Fern, still a child despite her woman's experience, and she disparaged dull Clara, whom she blamed for Fern's unhappy lot. But of them all, only Ella, a hopeless and brain-fogged drunkard, fit Felicity's concept of the prostitute, and even she was more pathetic than distasteful.

Felicity continued to contribute her share of food every third or forth day. Stealing was a constant challenge, and she patrolled the camp to pick up what she could, never too much from any one place and never the same place twice. She carried a musket, and for a while she thought she might hunt, but she attempted it only once, firing at a plump, tuft-eared rabbit and sobbing with relief when the shot went wild. She did, however, learn to track the hunters and soon made a practice of it, snatching up the dead quarry and sneaking off with it whenever she could safely manage to do so.

She also learned to utilize the whores as unsuspecting accomplices. The first occasion came about inadvertently. She had been skulking behind the trees looking for an untended fire when she came upon two soldiers taking their turns at Heavensent. One soldier, with his trousers around his ankles, fondled himself while calling encouragement to the other, who was panting and thrusting away between Heavensent's obligingly spread thighs. Felicity wasn't ignorant of how the act of copulation was accomplished, but she was shocked to observe the brutality of it and redirected her gaze. It fell on the contents of a saddlebag spilled out on the ground at her feet. A tin of tea lay within reach, and she picked it up and walked calmly away with it, not even bothering to hide it under her skirt. After that she missed no opportunity to attend what she privately came to call "the bawdy brawls."

Collier had doubled the number of night sentries after the Indian raid, and there was no more overt trouble, but there was almost daily evidence of Indians along the trail. Sometimes it was a recently abandoned campfire, the remains of a deer that had been skinned and butchered, or an arrow affixed to a tree trunk. But sometimes it was a bloodthirsty screech that woke them during the night with the chilling reminder that they were vulnerable to attack no matter how many sentries there were to give warning. Whenever that happened Felicity woke seeing Sarah, not as she must be now but as a young woman with golden hair and haunted eyes, cradling a hawk in her arms and screaming like one possessed. Was she out there somewhere just beyond reach? Frightened and wondering, Felicity would find herself unable to fall back asleep.

Felicity saw Collier frequently, but she stayed well out of his way, explaining to those who asked that he insisted upon it.

"I can't say as how I'm surprised," Meg noted. "He's a cold bastard, ain't he? No wonder he's never married. How's he in bed?"

"Like anyone," Felicity answered noncommittally.

"In, out, and over, yer mean? He's a tall un, ain't he? I bet he has a spigot to match."

Day by day they were getting closer to their destination, traveling now through mountainous terrain and hearing daily rumors that they were to meet with Braddock's army at a place called Thicketty Run, a petty branch of the Sewickly Creek. The rumors had a stimulating effect on the troops, who daily became more demanding on the women. A number of the women complained of being ill-treated and a few bore bruises that attested to it. One night it was Fern's turn. She had gone off, as was her habit, with a jaunty walk and a promise to bring back a purseful, but she returned whimpering, with a blackened eye and a split lower lip. Clara tried to comfort her, but it was practical Meg who did the nursing, concocting a poultice of wet sassafras leaves to bathe her face and, as it turned out, her back and buttocks as well. Felicity was shocked, but Meg dismissed the incident with a shrug. "The more licks she takes early, the better she'll learn to take care of herself."

Felicity began to anticipate Josiah's return. She prayed she could convince him to help her in the short time that would be left, admitting to herself that it might require more on her part than a demand on their friendship. If necessary, she decided, she would promise him anything in return for his loyalty, even marriage if that was what he wanted.

One afternoon they halted near a small deep-water lake, and Felicity saw her image reflected back to her in the lake's mirrorlike surface. She barely recognized the harridan she'd become. How could she hope to win Josiah's support looking as she did? There were scratches on her face from riding through thickets. Her hair was matted with tangles. She compared the white skin of her upper arms with the dark skin of her forearms and hands. She was dark as mahogany. Her clothes were torn and filthy. Her fingernails were broken. She had callused hands and feet. She had scabs on her shins and knees and the bruise on her cheek was still discolored. She knew the plainer she looked the less apt she was to attract attention and she'd not made a great effort to remain presentable, but not all the sloven-liness was intentional. She had forgotten to pack soap, and the fragile tortoiseshell comb she'd brought had broken in her saddlebag. She had neither scissors nor hair ribbons nor lotions, and there hadn't yet been a stop long enough to allow for the washing and drying of clothes. Something, she knew, must be done to rectify the situation.

That evening there was a full moon. Felicity settled into a hollow beneath a bush near Collier's tent and bided her time. It hadn't been her turn to collect foodstuffs that evening, but she had made the rounds anyway. Now, tucked close to her, wrapped in her spare clothing, were some string, a bar of lye soap, a wide-toothed comb, a piece of soapstone, and a tin of salt. The hours went by slowly, but finally it was time. Carrying the bundle she crawled out from under the bush and headed away from the camp,

making a wide circle that brought her to a point more than
halfway around the lake. She checked to make sure she was
alone before stepping out from the protection of trees onto
the narrow shoreline. Then she unwound her bundle and
dumped everything out onto the ground. Moving quickly,
she stripped and gathered up all her clothes. She wouldn't
be able to dry everything completely, but there was a
breeze, and if she wrung out the wash thoroughly and
draped it over the bushes it would be no more than damp
by morning.

She carried the clothes to the water's edge and washed
them, then set to work on herself, sitting in the shallow
water and lathering herself head to toe, then utilizing the
soapstone to smooth her calluses and the roughness on her
elbows. Even under the least difficult circumstances her
thick, waist-long hair presented a challenge. She had been
wearing it pinned up under her hat and hadn't bothered to
take it down after her comb had broken. Now it was so
heavily snarled that she had to comb it out strand by slow
strand, pulling at the knots and blinking back her tears. But
finally she ran satisfied hands down the silky tresses before
plaiting two long braids that she tied with string. Next she
opened the tin of salt and cleansed her teeth, then swished
fresh water in her mouth to eliminate the taste of brine.

It was the middle of the night, but she wasn't tired and
the lake was tempting, so she stood up and entered the
water. When it lapped around her shoulders she began to
swim, taking long, lazy strokes that carried her out into the
center of the lake. She was taken with the eerie feeling that
she had been there before. She knew the water, the
moonlit night, the fringe of lakeside trees that were
outlined against the moon-bright sky. The silence was
profound, the night mysterious. Then, too painful a
recollection to bear, it pierced her nonetheless, Horseshoe
Cove and the Indian brave, the repetition of her joy and of
her folly. It was too sharp to be merely imagined.

She knew there would be no rock on the far shore, but she raised her head to scrutinize the flat rim of clay and the screen of trees beyond and saw him standing there watching her, a tall and slender wraith conjured up from illimitable stores of memory and guilt. Or was it memory? The lake and the moon and the trees were actually there, as was she. The confusion between past and present became a momentary enchantment as the quiet figure regarded her. She glanced back to the spot where she had entered the water, judging the distance and wondering whether it was possible to flee the specter of the past. There was magic in the night, in the sparkling beam of moonlight on the water that led from him to her, in the way he stood motionlessly staring.

Then suddenly everything turned dark. She looked up and saw a cloud pass over the moon like a hand passed over the eyes, and when an instant later she looked back to shore, she saw that the man—a trick of the eye, a game played on the senses—had vanished.

· · 37 · ·

The troops tended to maintain their individual positions in the line, and gradually Felicity grew to know many of them by name, especially the more intimidating of them: Ridge Beckwith, a burly man who was a crack shot despite being one-eyed, and Sessy Gray, whom Meg characterized as "ugly sober and uglier drunk."

Felicity had also learned that the name of the soldier who had first accosted her was Ned Grubbe, and that although he gave her no more trouble to her face, behind her back he called her the Devil's hex, and attributed every misfortune, including the death of the thirteen soldiers, to her ill omened presence. Needless to say, there was nothing

Felicity wanted less than to become involved with any of these men, and yet it happened and happened under violent circumstances.

It was mid-afternoon of a steaming hot day when Felicity saw Ridge Beckwith split off from the other riders and cut into the woods carrying his musket in the crook of his arm. It was again Felicity's day to contribute to the larder, and she decided to follow him. Beckwith was a hunter who killed for sport as well as food and seldom bothered to pick up every quarry he dropped, thereby making it easy to filch something for the pot. Felicity turned Cocoa off the trail and waved to Meg who, assuming she was responding to a call of nature, bawled after her, "There be persinus ivy in there. Watch yerself."

Off to her right Felicity could hear Beckwith forcing his way through the foliage, but she couldn't judge how far she was from him until he fired his first shot. She waited for it, then urged Cocoa forward. The second shot was closer, and she dismounted, tossing the reins over Cocoa's head, and tiptoing forward. Soon she was close enough to catch a glimpse of horse and rider in profile, and she crouched down as Beckwith took aim and fired again. This time she saw something break the leaves as it tumbled out of a tree, and heard Beckwith mutter, "That was three." He cocked his head to listen, and although Felicity couldn't hear anything herself, Beckwith turned in her direction and fired. A pigeon plummeted down a foot or two from the spot where she was hidden. She was elated and reached out to recover the prize, but was arrested by the sound of another horse crashing through the woods. She poked up her head to see Ned Grubbe rein in his horse. He was scowling, and there was tension in his bearing as he called out Ridge's name.

"Damn," Beckwith growled, "you'll spook the birds. What do you want?"

"Don't tell me you can't figure it out," Grubbe returned pugnaciously. "I come about one of the whores."

Under cover of their voices Felicity had recovered the dead pigeon and begun to creep backward to safety, but Beckwith's next words stopped her. "If you're talking about Fern, you picked the wrong time."

"She told me you warned her away from me," Grubbe challenged.

"What if I did? She said you hurt her."

"What I do with that whore is my business."

"Does that include beating her?"

"I didn't beat her," Grubbe shot back. "I knocked her around a little, sure, but there's no law against it."

"I say nobody beats up little girls," Beckwith returned calmly.

"She's not a little girl. She's a whore and one you've rammed more than once. So what's the difference?"

"The difference is I don't hurt her, and you ain't going to hurt her again neither. If you touch her, I'll make you sorry you ever seen her. Or me, either, for that matter."

Grubbe answered in a surly voice, "I don't scare that easy, Ridge. I come to tell you to stay out of my business from now on."

"Leave her be, and we'll have no quarrel."

"You keep butting in, Ridge, and I'll give you what I give her, but with my pistol instead of my fists."

Felicity saw Beckwith pat his musket. "You better practice your shooting then, Ned," he said in a level voice. He swung down off his horse and began to walk toward the place where Felicity crouched, but before he got close enough to see her Ned Grubbe said hoarsely, "I don't need no practice, you bastard."

Felicity heard the shot before she spotted the pistol in Grubbe's hand, and by then it was too late to warn Beckwith. He pitched forward and fell face down among the leaves. Grubbe dismounted, walked over to kick Beckwith's motionless body, then took aim and fired another bullet into the back of his head. Felicity watched in horror as Grubbe replaced the pistol in his belt, remounted his horse, and rode back the way he'd came. She looked down at the bloody pigeon in her hand, gagged, and tossed it away, then got up and ran over to the place where Beckwith lay. His head was smashed and pulpy, with bits of flesh and hair spattered on the ground and on his clothing. She gulped in air, then stumbled away a few yards before she gave way to her nausea, dropping to her knees and vomiting up the sour bile that was all that remained of breakfast, before being able to rise again and look for Cocoa.

A halt had already been called by the time she returned to the troops. Seeing her, Elga waved her over and shouted to the others that she had returned.

"Where have yer been?" Meg cried. "It can't of took that long to shit. We thought you'd been killed too."

"Then you know?" Felicity said incredulously. "You know what happened?"

"Sure we know. Ned Grubbe went to report it to Collier."

"He did? Have they sent someone to bring back the body?"

"Not yet," Elga answered. "Not till Collier gets a proper party together."

"It's a miracle you come back," Tiba cut in. "We thought you was took for sure."

"Fer sure," Meg echoed. "You seen the redskins, did you?"

"What redskins?"

"What redskins? You mean you didn't see them? Jesus God, Ned come ridin' up not five minutes past sayin' that him and Beckwith got set on by Indians. We thought fer sure they'd got to you too."

Felicity regarded Meg blankly.

"They murdered Ridge Beckwith," Fern joined in. "Ned Grubbe said they shot him. They shot at Ned, too, but he got away."

"No," Felicity protested. "No, you've got it wrong."

"Oh no we ain't," Meg insisted. "Ned told us hisself."

"No, wait. Listen. Grubbe shot Beckwith." Felicity looked at the women, especially at Fern, whose face was still painfully discolored and swollen from the beating Grubbe had given her. "They argued and Grubbe pulled a pistol. There were no Indians. I was hiding nearby and I saw what happened."

The women were staring at her wonderingly, but there was no skepticism in any of their faces. They believed her. "Lordy," Meg whispered. "You seen it?"

"Yes, I saw it."

"It's a blessin' Grubbe didn't see you. He didn't, did he?"

"No."

"What was they arguin' about?" Clara chimed in.

Felicity was careful not to let her eyes stray to Fern. "It doesn't matter. What matters is that Grubbe lied. I'm going to tell Captain Collier."

"What?" Meg screeched. "Oh no yer not. Tell Collier, indeed! If you tell Collier, every soldier in the company'll be after yer. Listen to me, people kill one another each and every day and get away with it. Ain't that right, Elga?"

"Meg's right," Elga confirmed.

"Don't stir up trouble for yerself," Meg went on. Behind her, the other women bobbed their heads in affirmation.

"But the man's a killer," Felicity declared.

"Ain't that enough to tell yer to lay off yer hands?" Meg reasoned. "You've got to forget it, and we're goin' to forget it too. Ain't that right?"

This time not everyone nodded. "I hate him," Fern suddenly burst out. She broke loose from the others and came to clutch at Felicity's skirt. "Tell, Lissy. I think you should tell."

Felicity looked at the small bruised face, and paying no further attention to the dissenting voices, spurred Cocoa into a jog. "Come back," Meg yelled, but Felicity ignored her and kept going.

She found Collier halfway down the line watching Lieutenant Arbor ride off with a party of men who included Ned Grubbe. Felicity dismounted and said urgently, "Captain Collier, I must talk to you."

"Not now, Miss Greenhill."

"It's important. I was in the woods a few minutes ago. I saw what happened."

"You observed the Indian attack?"

"It wasn't Indians. It was Ned Grubbe. He shot Ridge Beckwith."

Collier said in a skeptical voice, "Grubbe is the man who assaulted you, is he not?"

"What does that matter?"

"You tell me, Miss Greenhill."

"If you're implying that I'm making the story up, I'm not. I've not spoken to Grubbe since that incident, nor has he spoken to me. I was in the woods and I overheard the two men arguing. It was about the beating of one of the women, that is, about a little girl not yet twelve. Ned Grubbe had beaten her. He's like that. He hit one of the other women, too, perhaps more of them. They don't generally talk about such mistreatment, but it happens sometimes, and apparently more than sometimes at Grubbe's hands. Beckwith obviously knew about it and told Grubbe to stop. Grubbe became incensed and shot him."

"Beckwith made no attempt to defend himself?"

"He was walking away. Grubbe shot him in the back, then after Beckwith fell down Grubbe shot him again in the head. Go and see for yourself. You'll see I'm telling the truth."

Collier stared at her without speaking.

"Surely you don't still doubt me?"

"No," he said finally. "I don't doubt you. Still, there's nothing I can do about it. I have no proof against him."

"You have me. I've just told you that I saw him do it."

"Your word is meaningless, especially since your trouble with Grubbe is common knowledge."

"Don't tell me you mean to let everyone think that Beckwith was killed by Indians? It's unthinkable."

"It's expedient."

"How dare you speak of expediency with a man lying dead and a killer free to kill again."

"I dare anything, Miss Greenhill. I am, after all, the man in charge here."

"Damn you!" Felicity exploded. "You're no better than they are!" She whirled around and stamped off while Collier, a thoughtful expression on his face, watched her go.

The other women were relieved when they heard the outcome of Felicity's interview, and Elga spoke for them all when she said they must pretend it had never happened. But if they could tolerate the injustice, for Felicity it was an act of bitter resignation. She had done what conscience demanded, but when she looked into Fern's unhappy eyes, she felt like a traitor.

Word passed down the line that the Indian party had been small, only three red men who had struck and fled, according to Ned Grubbe. Felicity wondered why no one commented on the fact that Beckwith's musket hadn't been stolen and that his scalp and had been left intact, but the inconsistencies passed unnoticed, or at least uncommented upon, and Beckwith's body, like the bodies of the previously murdered men, was buried in an unmarked grave to prevent desecration.

A short time after they resumed the march a pair of soldiers rode back to flank the women. Collier had taken note that the females at the end of the line were particularly vulnerable to attack and must be guarded. Felicity wasn't deceived by his sudden solicitude. Collier knew as well as she that there were no Indians in the vicinity. He was simply taking precaution against the possibility that she might create some disruption with regard to Ned Grubbe.

They had been climbing through hilly territory for the past few days. It was the most arduous part of the trek so far, with a rash of mishaps along the way. A soldier was hurt falling off his horse, Kate sprained her ankle sliding on loose rocks, and then a horse fell and broke its leg, necessitating its being shot. Felicity averted her eyes as she rode by the men hacking away at the still steaming flesh, but solaced herself with the thought that the women might have steak that night if luck prevailed. It did prevail, Meg sallying forth in search of food and returning in triumph bearing a chunk of meat that must have weighed five pounds. "Don't ask me what I done for it," she informed them cheerfully, "but it's somethin' I ain't done for quite a spell."

Another few days of thinning vegetation and air brought them out onto a high plateau above the wilderness surrounding them. Felicity had never stood on a mountaintop. Aside from the ocean with its huge but monotonous perspective, her world had always been shortsighted. Now for the first time she saw the seemingly endless land that surpassed in grandeur anything she might have imagined. They camped on the mountaintop that night, Felicity wakening to the howls of wolves like portents of doom echoing from hill to hill, and then she wakened a second time to the distant roll of thunder. In the morning there were heavy clouds hanging over the valley like swatches of bunting, and the troops began their descent with the prospect of walking into rain.

They did finally run into rain, a deluge that compounded their discomfort when they had to cross Sewickly Creek, whose overflowing banks were ankle-deep in mud. Ropes were strung at the narrowest point and equipment floated across on hastily improvised rafts. There were only ten yards or so for the horses to swim, but the strong current carried them a way downstream before they regained their footing and brought their riders safely to the far bank. By then the rain had stopped, and the midday halt was called. Word was passed along that the halt would be longer than usual. "Collier sent a party ahead to scout the territory and locate Braddock," Elga reported. "They're to meet us here, then guide us to Braddock by the quickest route."

She was talking about Josiah, Felicity realized. Thank God she'd see him soon. They had left Williamsburg on June eleventh, but Felicity had lost track of time since then. She didn't know the day of the week or the date. Was it July 1 or 2 or 3? She wasn't sure of anything except it was still 1755. But then dates seemed inconsequential out here where there were no civilized events to mark. What mattered was that she would finally see Joss. The thought filled her with an anticipation that, sadly, was not based on affection but on the determined belief that he would help her find Sarah and effect a rescue. That she had made up her mind to marry Joss if she must was taken for granted, but that she might actually learn to love him never entered her mind. Sarah was all, especially now that circumstances—and Lawrence Collier—had compounded the obstacles. There had to be a way, and if she couldn't manage it on her own, she and Joss would manage it together.

"Well," Meg declared, "since we're goin' to be here for a spell, I think I'll go dry my bones in the sun."

Felicity decided to do the same. Spotting some bluffs a short distance upstream, she rode Cocoa through the shallows and dismounted at their base. The cliffs facing the river's edge were steep, but when she circled them she saw that the slope was gentle on the other side and the climb an easy one. She left Cocoa to graze and made her way up to a level place among the rocks, sat down, spread out her skirts, and removed her hat, then leaned back on her elbows to get the maximum benefit from the sun's rays. She closed her eyes and slept. Her troubled dreams were a kaleidoscope of bizarre images: rotting bodies with pustules erupting into bloody flowers; crackling thunder, and sinuous clouds enveloping and choking her, then turning into acrid smoke that spiraled out of the doors and windows of the mill; her desperate pleading with Sarah to throw the hawk onto the fire; and finally the tall, stern figure of Lawrence Collier saying, "It won't do. You shouldn't be here, Miss Greenhill."

The voice that awakened her was appropriate to the dream, and she opened her eyes to see Collier looking down at her. "You shouldn't separate yourself from the others," he reprimanded. "It isn't safe." He held his hands out to her and without thinking she took them and permitted him to pull her to her feet. She was tall, but only eye level to Collier's coat collar, which disadvantaged her.

She answered acidly, "Judging by the guards with which you've surrounded me, I assume you don't think it safe for me anywhere."

"The guards are for all the women."

"Or so you say."

Collier looked down over his chin at her. "You tend to be incautious, Miss Greenhill. You make a habit of wandering away from the troops."

"One occasion hardly constitutes a habit."

"What about the day you followed Ridge Beckwith into the woods? And then there was the night when I almost mistook you for an Indian and shot you."

"I don't recall such a night."

"You were swimming."

Felicity drew in her breath sharply. "That was you?"

"Fortunately for you that was I. I say fortunately because I might as easily have been an Indian myself or someone like Ned Grubbe. In either case a female alone, unprotected, and quite entirely naked might have had some cause for worry."

"You had no right to look at me unclothed," Felicity informed him indignantly.

"I'm guilty of looking at you, Miss Greenhill, but I didn't undress you, nor was I responsible for you being in that inappropriate spot at that inappropriate hour."

Self-conscious at having to gaze so far up at him, Felicity took a step backward to put some space between them. The step brought her perilously close to the edge of the cliff, and Collier reached out to pull her back to a firmer footing. Felicity shook off his grip. "And what, may I inquire, were you doing there at that inappropriate hour?"

"The same as now," he answered easily, "protecting my doxie."

"How dare you!"

"No, Miss Greenhill. How dare you? I'm not the one who talks of an intimate relationship between us. That's your doing."

Felicity was too stunned to deny it. "Who told you?"

"Certain tactful references make it clear that I'm not thought to sleep alone. I haven't contradicted the rumors because they do me no particular harm, except perhaps to interrupt my sleep from time to time."

"I don't understand."

"Your proximity to my tent at night. Did you not know that you frequently snore?"

"I? Snore?"

"Like a hibernating bear, Miss Greenhill."

Illogical as she knew it to be, Felicity was angered by the thought that Collier had been deceiving her when all along she thought she had been deceiving him. "Don't expect me to apologize," she declared rebelliously. "It was you who forced me into making up the lie by refusing to help me."

"I'm not such an ogre as you suppose," he returned. "In fact, against my better judgment I've begun to feel some sense of responsibility for you."

"It's too late," Felicity said fiercely. "I don't need you any longer." She lifted her braids onto her head and jammed the hat on over them. "Joss will be back any time now and he'll look after me."

She swept past him and started back down the rear slope of the cliffs, but Collier called out, "Wait," in a voice that struck her as sounding suddenly constrained and sober. She turned back to him with a curious look.

"I didn't happen on you just now. I came looking for you."

"You what?"

"Miss Greenhill, Lieutenant Wrentham and his party will not be rejoining us after all."

Felicity felt a choking sensation and raised her hand to her throat. "Why not?"

Collier nodded to the woods behind her. "Two of my men stumbled over their bodies about an hour ago."

· · 38 · ·

Felicity was to find out later that Joss and the two men under him had contacted Braddock's forces which were on the move and headed toward Thicketty Run. Josiah's scouting party was on its way back to intercept Collier's company when they were ambushed. A communication from Braddock was found among Josiah's effects that confirmed Thicketty Run as the spot where the two forces would join one another. Collier, acting with this knowledge and feeling some urgency to secure his men's safety, resumed the march within half an hour of having informed Felicity of Josiah's death and burial.

Of the subsequent journey Felicity was to remember little. She had never in her life fainted, and she didn't faint when Collier told her that Joss was dead, but she succumbed to another form of unconsciousness in which normal functioning became dependent upon habit rather than sensibility. In a somnambulistic state she took leave of Collier, returned to the women, and resumed her place in line. But if outwardly calm, she was inwardly distraught. She had been so wrapped up in plans for rescuing Sarah that she hadn't stopped to consider the realities of her situation. Even witnessing at first hand the ugliness and brutalities of warfare hadn't impressed her with the possibility that war could directly touch Joss or her. For the first time since leaving Williamsburg she was unsure of her mission, not only of its possibility for success but of its wisdom. What was one life saved when weighed against so many more lost?

Four hours after starting out the troops arrived at the site where Braddock and his forces were camped. Collier's men were a small motley band of provincials dressed like woodsmen riding among Braddock's colorfully uniformed troops with exuberant shouts. Men and equipment were everywhere: tents, wagons, artillery in the form of howitzers and twelve-pounders and the smaller mortars known as coehorns, barrels of foodstuffs, and even kegs of ale. To Collier's men, deprived of comfort for so many days, Braddock's army seemed replete with luxuries, and although they were soon to find out their first impression was exaggerated, for the moment they enjoyed a jubilant euphoria.

Collier was the first to dismount and salute Braddock, who had come forward to greet him. Braddock was a man in his late fifties, severe in appearance but splendidly dressed in white knee-length trousers, a white shirt ruffled under the chin, and a white vest with gold buttons. His red coat was trimmed with tasseled epaulets, each one containing a single star, and he wore a flowing wig under a tricornered hat. His sharp nose and piercing eyes gave him an imperious look suitable to the role of Major General and Commander of all His Majesty's troops on the North American continent.

Elga, riding next to Felicity, leaned across her pommel to say, "I hear his name comes from the Saxon for broad and oak. I say he's well named," her comment eliciting no reply from Felicity, who was wrapped in gloom and totally unaware of having been addressed.

The rest of the day was spent settling in. Among Braddock's troops was a boisterous band of prostitutes eager to socialize and filled with information to pass on to the newcomers. They, along with Braddock and two regiments, the 44th and the 48th, had left Alexandria on June 18 and had been traveling since then on a course that roughly paralleled Collier's and caused them equal hardship. The route had taken them through rough country, sometimes confining them to five miles' progress a day because a road had had to be cleared in order to accommodate the wagons and heavy artillery. Blocks and tackle had been used to lower the equipment from steep cliffs, and the journey through thick forests of white pine had been dark, lonely, and monotonous. They hadn't suffered encounters with the Indians as had Collier's company, but many of the soldiers had become sick from a diet too reliant on salt-preserved foods, and there had been deaths from dysentery as well as from accident.

As for plans for engaging the French, no one was sure when Braddock meant to mount his attack. It was suspected that it would be very soon since they were now within two days' march of Fort Duquesne. Indian scouts had been sent out to survey the territory, and it was assumed that when they returned the march toward the fort would resume, although no one could say with certainty what the day or the hour.

Felicity didn't expect Collier to single her out again, and it was therefore a surprise when, a little after dusk, a soldier brought the message that he wished to see her. "My," Meg brayed, "he's gettin' bold now, ain't he? I guess it's the last lovin' he expects to get afore going after the Frenchies."

Felicity attempted to decline the command invitation, but Collier's emissary was firm. "It'll be my head if I don't bring you back, so you're comin'."

Felicity entered Collier's tent to find two table settings laid out on a packing box and Collier seated on one of two camp stools. "Come in, Miss Greenhill," he invited. He waved to the seat opposite his. "I thought you might be induced to share my supper."

"Thank you," she answered coolly, "but I'm not hungry."

"You must eat."

"It's of no consequence."

He reached back to lift a metal strongbox off his cot and held it out to her. "I thought you would like to have Lieutenant Wrentham's personal effects."

She took the strongbox, then complied numbly when Collier again gestured to the seat opposite. Collier said, "Braddock tells me that the Indians who killed him were probably scouts sent out to reconnoiter by Contrecoeur."

"Contrecoeur?"

"Monsieur de Contrecoeur, the commander at Duquesne."

"Oh."

"I scarcely knew Lieutenant Wrentham, but I thought him an exemplary soldier."

"I never knew him as a soldier, only as a close friend. We were children together in New Castle. But then I've told you that."

Collier cleared his throat, then said awkwardly, "There's a letter in the strongbox. It confirms what you've told me."

"You read it?"

"It was originally in his pocket with a communication from Braddock."

"I see."

"You are untypical of most women, Miss Greenhill. I'm afraid I misjudged you."

"It's of no consequence."

"I wish to make amends."

"By inviting me to dine with you?" Felicity asked in an ironic tone.

"No, but I wish you would dine with me."

Felicity shrugged, too weary to make any further excuses. Shortly afterward, Collier's batman entered the tent carrying their meal. Under other circumstances Felicity would have been grateful for the slab of vension, the roast potatoes, and the glass of Madeira. As it was she could do no more than make a pretense of eating while Collier continued to try to make his position clear.

"I'm not a professional soldier," he told her. "My experience on the battlefield is negligible and my responsibilities are great, which may, in part, account for the fact that I was negligent in regard to you."

Felicity was beyond mere politeness. "Why, if you are not a professional soldier, are you commanding a company of soldiers?" she asked bluntly.

"Because I know the Indians. My family was one of the first to farm in Virginia. My grandfather and my father fought the Indians for every inch of land they settled. Twenty-two years ago, when I was sixteen, they ambushed and murdered my mother and sister. My father and I went into the woods after them. We tracked them for a month, during which time we caught sight of them only twice; once when they put an arrow through my hand"—Collier held up his hand to show a scar on his palm—"and once when they killed my father. I went after them again, not once but half a dozen times, and in the process learned how to fight them. I fought them in the woods and I fought them on my own land, and in the end I held the land and increased it. My knowledge of the Indians is very specialized, and if it's not warfare in accordance with army traditions, it's what's called for now. That's why I'm here."

He was looking at her ruefully, and she suddenly found herself close to tears, whether from sorrow or weariness or disillusionment she couldn't be sure. "I'm really not hungry, Captain Collier," she blurted out. "Please excuse me."

"Wait, Miss Greenhill. In a few days we expect to engage the French. Once we've secured the fort I'll make arrangements to see that you're given safe escort back to Williamsburg."

Felicity nodded, then got up and left the tent. She was in no state of mind to rejoin the women. She slipped into the shadows under the trees behind Collier's tent and pushed her way through the foilage, seeking some place to be alone. After a few minutes she was brought up short at the brink of a small ravine and decided she'd come far enough. She sat down with Josiah's strongbox on her lap and snapped it open. There was enough light left to examine its sparse contents: a purse containing a few pounds in notes and silver, a comb, identification papers, a letter from his mother, a silver toothpick, a watch and fob, a box of snuff, and lying at the bottom, a folded piece of paper. The message it contained was brief.

To Felicity Greenhill, number four, Nassau Street, Williamsburg. Dear Lissy, This letter will never reach you unless something happens to me, and therefore I am under no inhibition to censor my words. Surely you know that I am in love with you, or more precisely that the love that has lain dormant in me since we were children together in New Castle has been revived. It is something I must be sure that you know. That you feel no more than friendship toward me must now be accepted as unalterable fact, though I had hoped to live long enough to inspire you to greater affection.

There is something else I want you to know. Had I been able, I would have sought out the white woman living with the Iroquois. Although I believe it unlikely that she is your sister, I . . .

There was no more. The word "sister" was palely inked, and the word "I" only a scratch on paper. It was more than Felicity could bear and she began to cry, drawing up her knees and muffling her sobs by pressing her mouth against the thick fabric of her trousers.

Much later a sound coming from the floor of the ravine caught her attention and she lifted her head. Three horsemen were riding through the ravine, Indians with feathered headbands astride ponies that gleamed white in the shadows. Two were men and the third was a woman dressed in a beaded buckskin dress and a shawl. It was impossible for Felicity to make out her features or the color of her skin and hair, but the object she carried crooked in her arm was unmistakable. It was a hawk carved out of wood, about two feet tall, with wings partially outspread. They rode by looking neither right nor left, so ethereal they might have passed for ghosts had there not been the sound of the horses' hooves to give them substance, and so ephemeral that Felicity had barely registered their presence before they were gone.

Felicity spent the night at the edge of the ravine. She knew it unlikely that the Indians would pass that way again, but she lingered anyway, feeling some mystical connection between Joss's letter and their appearance. She was caught between hope and fear, wanting desperately to formulate some plan of rescue, but unable to do more than contemplate the probability of failure.

In the morning, rejoining the women, she learned that Braddock's Indian scouts had returned the night before after penetrating to an area half a mile from the fort. They had seen no evidence of a hostile force except for one Frenchman out hunting whom they had dispatched on the spot, and the way now seemed clear for the advance. Braddock had already given the order to resume the march.

No evidence of a hostile force? But that wasn't true, Felicity thought. There was evidence aplenty. Hurriedly she left the women and went to look for Collier. She located him among his troops, astride his horse and in the company of three strange officers. "Captain," she called, "please wait." Collier held his horse in check as she ran up to say breathlessly, "I have something to tell you."

One of the other officers asked impatiently, "Who is this woman?"

"Her name is Greenhill, Colonel Halket," Collier answered.

"One of the . . .?"

"No. The . . . er . . . relative of one of my officers." He leaned down to say quietly, "Can't it wait, Miss Greenhill?"

"No, it cannot. It has to do with the Iroquois."

"What did you say?" Halket again intervened. "What's this about Iroquois?"

Felicity turned to him. "There are Iroquois in the vicinity of our camp. I saw them."

"You saw them? When?"

"Last night. There are three of them who passed through the woods not a dozen yards from where I was hidden. One of them was white. That is, she's a white woman who lives among the Iroquois. They look on her as a medicine woman or magic spirit."

"Do you know of such a woman, St. Clair?" Halket asked.

"I've never heard of such," another of the officers commented. "Have you, Lieutenant Gage?"

The officer thus addressed answered, "No, Major St. Clair, nor do I believe there is such a woman."

"I don't care what you believe," Felicity said rudely. "She does exist. The Iroquois look to her to work her magic for them in battle. Don't you understand? I'm trying to tell you that the French and Indians are forewarned of your coming and prepared to fight."

"Forewarned?" the officer named St. Clair repeated with a gruff laugh. "Of course they're forewarned. You don't suppose we expected to surprise them, do you? We could never have moved two thousand men up from Virginia without being observed."

"He's right," Collier pointed out. "No doubt they've counted us down to every last wart and wen."

"But none of that matters," Gage noted. "Despite what they know they can't withstand our attack. They're undermanned, with insufficient arms to defend the fort. They have no choice but to surrender."

"Please listen to me," Felicity insisted. "If our troops were to take this woman hostage, it might discourage Indian participation in a counterattack."

"What is this nonsense?" Halket exploded. "Why are we discussing strategy with this female? Haven't we enough to do without entertaining the fantasies of hysterical women? Collier, since you know the wench, you deal with her." Halket jerked his horse's head around and cantered off, gesturing to Major St. Clair and Lieutenant Gage to follow.

"Please make them pay attention, Captain Collier," Felicity pleaded, reaching up to take hold of his arm.

"I can't," he said. "I haven't the authority. Besides, it would be impractical to delay our march in order to search the woods for three stray Indians."

"They aren't strays. They could be the key to saving countless lives."

"Or to losing them if it turned out to be another ambush. I think I understand what it is you're really after, Miss Greenhill, and I sympathize. However, there's nothing I can do to help you."

"If you won't listen to me, I'll go directly to Braddock."

"Braddock is hardly the type to countenance any interference with his plans, especially from a—"

"A woman," Felicity supplied.

"I was about to say 'a civilian.' Miss Greenhill, it is highly unlikely that the woman you saw is your sister, even less likely that she could be wrested from the grasp of the Iroquois. And even if we were to rescue her, who knows if it would aid our cause? It might simply impel the Indians to even more bloodthirsty behavior than we've already witnessed. Give it up, Miss Greenhill. I can offer you no better advice."

"I don't want your advice, Captain Collier. I don't want anyone's advice."

"So I've noticed, Miss Greenhill. So I've noticed." Collier touched his fingers to the rim of his hat, then rode off leaving Felicity with hands so tightly clenched that when she opened them a few minutes later she found two sets of raw half-moons dug into her palms.

· · *39* · ·

Braddock had been following an Indian track north, but that day he left the track and led his army to a body of water called Turtle Creek, intending to cross the creek twelve miles above its confluence with the Monongahela. When the troops reached the creek's eastern branch, however, they found themselves at the brink of a steep descent, unnegotiable for the artillery and wagons, and Braddock was forced to redirect the march to a more vulnerable position on the shores of the Monongahela.

Word soon came down the line that there had been further trouble. A few British stragglers had been waylaid and slain by Indians. As if that weren't enough, a party of Braddock's men, confused and angry over the slaying, had murdered Braddock's Indian scouts, one of whom was the son of a chieftain named Scarroyaddy. Braddock was furious, so much so that he had been heard to chew out Halket, along with the others of his officers, and to swear vengeance on the provincial incompetents he felt had been foisted on him.

It was decided to go no farther that day, and a halt was called before dusk. Felicity had abandoned hope of persuading Collier to help her, but she wasn't ready to give up hope of rescuing Sarah—if it were Sarah—by some other means. She waited until dark, then chose the most likely vantage point to watch for the Iroquois, a grove of trees between the river and hills that would offer the Indians safe cover as well as a quick means of retreat were they to come again.

There were, of course, sentries on patrol, but she slipped past them and walked to a spot a few yards inside the woods where she would have an unobstructed view of the camp but would be screened by the low-lying bushes that grew there in profusion. She placed herself at the base of a tree and settled in for what would be a long vigil, made longer by her self-imposed immobility. The slightest sound, the mere shifting of weight, might alert the Indians to her presence.

What she didn't bargain for was the soporific effect of immobility, darkness, and quiet, all of which combined to put her to sleep. It was hours later when she was stirred into wakefulness by the sound of breathing that wasn't her own, and she opened her eyes in terror as a hand was clapped over her mouth. "Quiet," a voice whispered.

Captain Collier's face hovered inches from her own, and she pressed her hand to her heart to still its thumping as she followed his gaze to take in the three horsemen who glided among the trees a few hundred feet away. As they watched, the horsemen drew their reins, dismounted, and silently crept forward to scrutinize the campsite. It was difficult to see them, but after a moment they began to speak, their soft words uttered in the Indian tongue. One of the voices was lighter than the others, unmistakably feminine. Felicity strained to hear, but if it were Sarah speaking, she couldn't tell from the pitch or tone.

The Indians stood with their backs to Felicity and Collier, and it occurred to Felicity that this might be the moment to act. But when she tried to convey this to Collier by gesturing toward the Indians and then toward the pistol in his holster, he merely shook his head and held her all the tighter. Then quite suddenly, as if some higher power were taking heed of Felicity's wishes, a shot rang out from the direction of the camp. However, it was the woman, rather than either of the braves, who grunted and reeled back clutching her shoulder.

Felicity lurched forward, but Collier wouldn't let her go, and she watched in horror as one of the Indians dashed for the horses while the other, with soothing words, put his arms around the woman to support her. The woman straightened up and responded to his murmured words with a command that was unmistakable in its authority, but which he apparently refused to obey, continuing to hold her until her horse was brought and then helping her to remount. There was shouting from the direction of the camp, and more shots were haphazardly fired into the woods, one of them hitting the tree just above Felicity's head. Collier pulled her down and covered her with his body, and there they remained until the firing ceased. When finally Collier released her, the Indians were gone.

Later, back in Collier's tent, he told her that it had occurred to him that she might take it upon herself to seek out the Indians a second time, and that when the women informed him that they hadn't seen her for hours, he had gone looking for her. "The woods were the logical place to set up a blind," he remarked, "especially for a strategist such as yourself."

"But how did you find me? I took such pains to hide myself."

"That was easy," Collier said. "I told you before that you snore, Miss Greenhill. If I hadn't stoppered you when I did, the Indians would have done so, and in a manner far more drastic, I'm afraid."

"I'm glad you saw her for yourself," she told him. "Now you must tell Braddock that her presence presages resistance to the British assault, and urge him to take her captive."

"Braddock knows about her already."

"He does?" Felicity returned in amazement. "You told him then?"

"Major Washington told him."

"George Washington? Is he here?"

"He arrived this afternoon to act as Braddock's aide-de-camp. The fellow's barely twenty-three years old and not someone Braddock is apt to take seriously, more's the pity, but he was full of talk about what Braddock should and shouldn't do. He kept us in council for over six hours this afternoon."

"But what about the white woman? What did Washington say?"

"Halket brought the subject up. You must have piqued his curiosity yesterday. Washington said he's heard about the white witch living among the Iroquois, although he has never seen her himself. He confirmed your assertion that the Iroquois look to her for the source of their strength in battle."

"And how did Braddock respond?"

Collier shrugged. "He said he has no patience for the customs of savages. He says that no heathen magic can match the power of a thousand British troops advancing behind their colors."

"Then he's a fool," Felicity exclaimed.

"I couldn't agree with you more," Collier said unexpectedly, "though not for the same reason. He told us today that he intends to cross the river at its upper elbow, then recross the stream just below the mouth of Turtle Creek. Washington advised him against it, and so did I. We both warned him that it was dangerous to expose the troops that way. We spoke of ambush. We suggested he wait for Dunbar to bring up the second regiment, but he refuses. He's determined to press forward. He claims that there are French reinforcements on their way to Duquesne and that it would be unwise to hold back. Washington and I both told him that it's not the French he need worry about but the savages."

"But if you were to take the white woman, you might render the Indians impotent."

"I told you before that such a move, even if feasible, might have the opposite effect. The only sensible move is the one Washington suggested and I seconded. We must fight like the Indians fight, from behind cover rather than out in the open. Washington argued with him, but one might just as easily argue with the Colossus of Rhodes. Braddock is implacable in his opinions and blindly self-confident."

Felicity felt weak, as if her insides had shriveled away. She was sitting on Collier's cot, and she suddenly bent forward to cradle her head in her arms. "But what about Sarah?" she said hopelessly. "Who will save her? She needs help, especially now that she's hurt and can't fend for herself."

Collier, seated on a camp stool before her, reached out to place his hand on her shoulder. "You're wrong, you know. The woman we saw is in no need of help, at least not from us. Even if she is the sister you're seeking, she wouldn't willingly leave the Iroquois to rejoin you."

"Don't say that. It's not true."

"You saw what happened when she was wounded. You saw how the braves leaped to her aid."

"She's my sister. She belongs with me, with us, with her family."

"You are obsessed, Miss Greenhill, obsessed with your role of savior and determined to ignore the truth. Your sister no longer exists except in memory, and memories can't be resurrected in flesh and blood. That woman whom you wish so ardently to rescue is not your sister, and I maintain that that is true even if once she did answer to the name of Sarah Greenhill. She's an Iroquois, as surely as if she had been born an Iroquois. To separate her from her tribe would not restore her to her previous life. It would merely destroy her."

Felicity raised her head. "Even if you're right, and I'm not ready to concede the possibility, it is still imperative that I determine whether or not the woman is actually my sister."

"There's no way to satisfy such a desire," Collier told her.

"If I could see her again, perhaps in daylight. It's obvious that she and her companions are somewhere close by. If I could find them—"

"If you were to attempt such an excursion, you would be killed before you rode a mile. No, Miss Greenhill, it would be suicide for you to seek them out again."

"Have I come so far to fail so miserably?"

"You're alive and unharmed. That's something to be grateful for. Now, listen to me. Tomorrow morning we follow the Valley of Long Run to pitch camp between the Monongahela and Crooked Run Creek. From there we'll secure the two river crossings, and on the following morning we'll march on the fort. Soon you'll be out of this and on your way home."

Felicity bristled. How could Collier assume that home mattered more to her than fulfilling her purpose in coming there. She got up from the cot and said coldly, "I appreciate your efforts to insure my safety, Captain Collier, but from now on I prefer to manage my own affairs."

"As you wish, Miss Greenhill. But I suggest you proceed more cautiously in the future, or you'll have no affairs to manage."

The following day—July 8 according to Elga—marked the next to last move, with the troops assembling at the point where the first crossing of the Monongahela would take place. It was a level piece of ground below some bluffs about twelve miles from the fort, and orders went out that the women, along with a reserve force of some four hundred men, would station themselves on the heights to wait out the assault. Felicity complied with the order, but she had made up her mind that she wouldn't remain behind when the forward march was called. If the witch woman were not too badly wounded, she would be somewhere in the vicinity of the battle that day. And Felicity, with no plan in mind but determined to make one last effort to set her mind at rest regarding the woman's identity, was determined to be there too.

During the predawn hours Lieutenant Gage and a band of soldiers, including Collier's company of Virginia rangers, set out to make both river crossings and to secure the British position on the far shore of the second crossing. Felicity, from a vantage point on the ridge above them, watched them go; Gage calling out the order to march, and Collier, a tall, erect figure, riding next to him. About an hour later St. Clair led a work party to clear a road for the main body of troops. And at dawn Braddock, with the bulk of the army, including horses, artillery wagons, and supplies, made the first of the two crossings, west to east. Felicity set out with this group, indistinguishable from the other provincials in her homespun britches, leather-fringed jacket, and wide-brimmed hat.

Once the last of the soldiers and equipment reached the far side of the river, the troops headed for the second ford. Halfway there a warning shot called attention to a party of Indian braves at the crest of a nearby hill. Felicity glanced up quickly, but they had disappeared as quickly and as stealthily as they had appeared, while the cry of "French redskins" echoed down the line. It wasn't yet noon when the troops arrived at the second crossing, but the river was wider and more treacherous at this point, and it took nearly three hours to move all the men and supplies across. They were now reunited with Gage and within seven miles of Fort Duquesne. An aura of excitement, like the onset of fever, had taken hold of the troops, and they milled around restlessly waiting for Braddock to issue his final instructions. Until then the advance had been orderly if ragged. Now, however, Braddock commanded the regulars to array themselves in dress uniform and told the drum and fife corps to make ready. The troops would move on the fort in battle formation.

There was a fantastical quality to the scene, attributable to the contrast between the wild landscape and the display of martial pageantry. Felicity saw Collier riding back and forth among the rangers and noted that he was dressed like his men in civilian clothes that were drab in comparison to the scarlet and gold of the regular troops. She saw Washington, a tall young man, dark-haired and personable despite his pockmarked face and rather too prominent jawline, conferring with Braddock. They seemed to be in disagreement over something because she saw Braddock speak sharply to Washington, then ride away while Washington, looking after him, shook his head in disgust.

It hadn't occurred to Felicity to wonder what would happen to her once the fighting began, but now with the terse call to arms she comprehended the exposed position she was in. The army was drawn up in the open where it would be difficult to hide once the final advance was begun, and she decided to seek cover. A quick investigation showed her that the flats where Braddock and his men were deployed were flanked on both sides with gullies and ravines, and she sought protection in one of them, riding ahead nearly a mile, then tethering Cocoa among the trees and taking refuge behind a cluster of rocks where she could observe without being observed.

A short time after she arranged herself the band was struck up, and a resounding cheer split the air. Felicity raised her head, then gave a gasp as she saw, crossing her line of vision, three riders on white horses. They rode at a leisurely pace across the flats, disappearing behind some trees about half a mile to her left. For an instant, with more desire than common sense, she considered going after them, but was stopped by the advancing troops who entered the field from her right. Gage and the drum and fife corps were in the lead, while behind them, sparkling rank on rank, came the soldiers with their polished boots and gleaming weapons.

A peripheral move to her left, a shimmer in the distance like the roll of surf toward shore, caused her to glance in the opposite direction. The illusion of surf was shattered as she saw a body of Frenchmen and near-naked savages materialize on the horizon. She could see that the Indians, garishly painted and armed with tomahawks as well as guns, were vastly in the majority. There seemed to be five or six hundred of them in comparison with the hundred or so Frenchmen. At the head of this exotic army was a white man wearing a colorfully fringed hunting shirt with a silver gorget or breastplate on his bosom, and Felicity watched in dread anticipation as he waved his men on.

As if it were some bizarre cotillion, the two armies closed the gap until they were only a few hundred yards apart. Then, abruptly, the Frenchman in command stopped, swept off his hat, and waved it over his head. The ranks broke and astonishingly, within seconds, the horde of Indians had vanished into the surrounding woods, leaving only a semicircle of Frenchmen to face the British. The Frenchmen opened fire and half a dozen British soldiers fell. Then Gage gave the command to return fire, and a moment later Felicity saw the French leader struck. He toppled like a pigeon shot out of a tree. Suddenly, everywhere, there were explosions of gunfire, men shouting, and the sound of horses whinnying in terror. Felicity spotted Collier rallying the rangers, then lost sight of him, but saw Gage ride by, and then a few minutes later, St. Clair, who took aim on a Frenchman and dropped him with a bullet in the chest.

The scene was so chaotic that at first Felicity couldn't

make any sense of it. The British uniforms were brilliant, the British soldiers aggressive, and there were so many of them in the field that she assumed they were carrying the day. But after a time she realized that the Indians were firing from ambush and that the French had begun to imitate their Indian comrades by seeking cover and firing from behind the protection of trees and rocks. The British, glittering targets, maintained their open position and were paying for it with their lives. Felicity's stomach knotted as she saw one after another go down. Why didn't they realize what was happening? Overcome with horror, she began to scream at them to take cover. "Don't you see? Don't you see?" Her screams were inaudible even to herself beneath the clash and roar of battle.

She wanted not to look, but it was impossible to turn away as soldiers attacked one another in a fury and cried in agony as they fell. The British and French fought with guns and swords and even daggers, ripping and slashing at one another, white against white in a murderous frenzy, but the larger force of the Frenchmens' army was beyond range of swords and shielded from fire. The Indians, hidden in the wooded ravines, were inflicting ruinous damage on the British, who were helpless to defend themselves against an enemy they couldn't see.

Eventually Gage began to urge his men to fall back, but their retreat was blocked by a second wave of soldiers arriving from the river, and the situation worsened. Now Felicity saw Lieutenant Colonel Burton enter the fray, swinging his sword with fury and bewilderment, and she began to pray for an end to the slaughter. For the first time she caught sight of Braddock shouting orders at his men to stand their ground. He yanked at his horse's reins and the horse reared, pawed the air, then screamed, blundered sideways, and fell. Felicity thought Braddock would be trampled to death, but in a minute he was up again calling for another mount. Men were running now as the battlefield flashed red and yellow with blood, smoke, and the glint of metal. Once again Felicity sought out Collier, but this time couldn't locate him. She didn't know whether he had been killed or wounded or had beaten his way back toward the river, but he was nowhere to be seen. She did see Halket and, a little later, Washington, gallop up to Braddock to present him with agitated argument, but whatever the issue of the dispute, Braddock angrily rejected the men's petitioning before they were swept apart by the tumult.

The initial confrontation between the armies had been carried out some distance from the spot where Felicity was hiding, but gradually, as the British lost ground, the fighting got closer. Felicity didn't realize how close until, some three or four hundred yards across the exposed battlefield, she saw the bushes shiver and a sleek naked body wriggle through. The Indian rose to one knee, took aim, and fired. Felicity screamed as a British soldier flipped backward, his lips parted in a ghoulish grimace, blood spurting from his face. She raised her own musket, but her body was shaking with terror, and her fingers were too weak to pull the trigger. She saw the Indian turn, drop to his knees, and crawl back into the bushes, but a moment later he rose again with his arms thrown skyward. He whirled in agony and fell. A momentary glimpse of dun leather and heavy boots behind him informed Felicity of the presence of one of the provincials, perhaps one of the Virginia rangers. Collier had obviously done what Braddock would not permit. He had ordered his men to scatter and fight from cover.

The nightmare was unbearable. Felicity sank to her knees and covered her head with her arms. Suddenly a slice of rock shattered inches above her head, pelting her with gravel and knocking off her hat. She leaped up again in panic. She was cut off from the river with the only escape being the woods behind her, and she turned in that direction, dashing out from behind the rocks to cut a circuitous route into the trees. She had only run a few yards when something smashed against the back of her neck. She thought she had been struck by a rock, but when she reached up to feel the spot, she touched raw flesh and her hand came away gloved in blood. She had been shot. At first she felt no pain. There was simply a throbbing in her ears and a pulsing warmth in the area of her neck and shoulder. She thought the wound must be superficial and continued to run, but then, quite unexpectedly, the ground tilted under her feet and she saw the bushes and trees swirl loose from their moorings. She reached out a hand to steady herself, but the tree trunk she reached for wasn't there, and she tumbled to the ground.

· · *40* · ·

She put a feeble hand to her chest and felt the drenched fabric of her shirt, then closed her eyes to fight off her nausea. There was a rainbow of colors behind her eyelids and in her ears sounds like someone pumping water from a well. Then, after a while, a voice spoke her name; not Lissy or Felicity but Miss Greenhill, over and over and with idiotic urgency. "What?" she mumbled irritably.

"Don't move," the voice commanded.

She opened her eyes to find herself looking up into the face of Captain Collier. She wanted to ask how he had found her, how he always managed to find her, but it required more effort than she could muster.

"Don't move," he repeated.

"How . . ." she managed to croak.

"I saw you running, the braids, I knew it was you."

"I—" She thought he would wish to know what she was doing there, but she couldn't seem to get the words out.

"Not now," Collier interrupted. "I'm going for help. Do as I tell you. Put your hand here, on the compress." He took her hand and pressed it against her neck. "Try not to move. Can you do that?"

She nodded. She was curious to know if she were going to die and thought she might try to ask, but then her eyes dropped to Collier's chest and she saw that he, too, was covered with blood. "You're shot," she croaked hoarsely.

He glanced down at his bloody jacket, then shook his head. "No. I carried you here. That's why I'm bloody. Don't talk. It's not wise for you to talk."

You shouldn't have, Felicity told him, surprised but relieved to find her voice restored to normal. *I could have died just as well where I fell.*

Collier made no comment, and Felicity realized that he hadn't heard her because she hadn't spoken the words aloud. How droll, she thought groggily as he got to his feet and strode off. I'm delirious. She closed her eyes and drifted away into a dream that plagued her with the image of a white-faced devil breathing fire down her neck, then drifted back to the brink of wakefulness. Holding on was an ordeal, especially with the chant of angels in her ears, but she knew if she were to let go, nothing would bring her back.

When, finally, she heard crashing through the bushes, she opened her eyes and cried out faintly, "Here. I'm over here." She heard gruff voices, then saw herself confronted with the devil of her nightmare in the guise of Ned Grubbe. Why, she wondered sleepily, had Collier sent Grubbe to rescue her?

But Grubbe hadn't been sent by Collier. He and Sessy Gray had stumbled on Felicity by mistake. The faces of both men were black with gunpowder and streaked with sweat. Grubbe's jacket was torn, and Gray had lost his musket. "I don't believe it," Gray muttered. "It's the captain's whore. What's she doing here?"

"Take her gun," Grubbe ordered.

Gray reached down and picked up her musket, then glanced around nervously. "Let's get going."

"Not so fast," Grubbe said roughly. "Collier may be around here somewhere. Is he?" he asked Felicity. "Is he someplace nearby?"

She nodded, hoping to frighten them away, but Grubbe said with satisfaction, "He is, is he? Fine. We'll wait for him."

"Wait for him?" Gray declared. "Are you crazy?"

"I want his gun, Sessy."

"We've got hers. That's enough."

"You think we're out of this so easy? We're in Indian territory. It'll take us time to get back down to the coast, and I mean to get there without losing my scalp. We'll wait for Collier."

"He'll try to stop us."

"We're two against one."

"What about the whore?"

"Look at her. She's dying. Anybody can see that. If she ain't dead by the time he gets back, I'll give her a helping hand."

Felicity tried to prop herself up into a sitting position, but barely had strength to raise her head. Grubbe put a boot against her shoulder and pushed her back down.

"Christ, Ned," Gray said unhappily, "get rid of her now. Suppose she gives warning?" He raised the musket to his shoulder and took aim.

Grubbe pushed the barrel aside. "You'll give warning by firing, you fool." He propped his own gun against a tree trunk and reached into his belt for his knife. "Leave it to me." He bent over Felicity. "It looks like I'll have my pleasure of you after all, girlie," he muttered, "maybe not the one I had in mind, but it'll give me pleasure just the same."

She wasn't frightened and thought perhaps it was just as

well that he put her out of her misery, except that she
wished she could tell someone he'd killed her just as he'd
killed Ridge Beckwith.

"What's that you're mumbling?" Grubbe demanded
roughly. "What's that about Ridge Beckwith?"

Felicity would have laughed if she'd had the strength.
She had spoken to Collier in her head when she'd meant to
speak aloud, and now she had spoken aloud what she
believed was only in her head.

"She said you shot Ridge," Gray declared. "Jesus, Ned,
you said it was redskins."

"What's the difference? He's dead either way, ain't he?"

"Why'd you do it?"

"I had my reasons."

Felicity didn't care very much what happend to Sessy
Gray, but she thought it probably true that Grubbe would
kill him, too, after he'd killed her, and she thought she
should, as a good Christian, warn him.

"Jesus, Ned! Jesus, Ned!" Gray's voice rose to an
hysterical pitch, his eyes suddenly wide with fright, leading
Felicity to believe that she must have already conveyed the
warning.

"What's wrong?" Grubbe cried out.

Gray began to answer but appeared to think better of it.
The gun slipped from his hand, and Felicity saw him fall to
his knees, then pitch forward onto his face. *He's fainted*, she
thought dully. *I frightened him more than I intended.*

Then suddenly Grubbe dropped his knife and darted for
his gun. Felicity heard a dull thud and saw him clutch at the
shaft of an arrow protruding from his chest, then crumple in
a heap onto the ground. She raised her eyes to the three
figures astride white horses: two braves and the medicine
woman, tall and still as the trees behind her. *Sarah*, Felicity
cried out, but the figure neither moved nor spoke. Felicity
made a futile attempt to sit up, but no longer felt any
sensation whatever in her limbs. It was as if she were water

evaporating to air. Soon she would be gone, no more part of the world than were Gray or Grubbe or Ridge Beckwith or Josiah.

A dark cloud obtruded between her and the world. When she blinked it away she saw the two Indian braves standing over her. They held bloody knives in their hands, causing her to reflect on the possibility that she was already dead, but then her eyes were drawn to the small bloody pelts slung at their hips, and she remembered why she'd lost consciousness. She shifted her gaze away from the savages and saw the hawk standing on the ground at her feet, its wings half-spread in the prediciton of flight, while behind it the woman stood, a stiff patch of dried blood on the fabric of her blouse and her face arranged into a fixed, fierce smile. The flesh of her face was leathery with wrinkles, her mouth shriveled and puckered inward, her cheeks and forehead blistered with sun scabs. But she was white. It was in her bones and in her half-hooded blue eyes. *Sarah*, Felicity said or tried to say, but the woman remained as motionless as the hawk at her feet.

She might have been carved from wood, Felicity thought wonderingly, except that her stillness had about it more an air of composure than lifelessness. She was neither young nor old, but had a majestic maturity like the forest or the mountains. At that moment Felicity accepted what Collier had told her, what she knew to be true. This was no white woman enslaved, but an elemental force with the power to command; a medicine woman, a white Iroquois. Was she Sarah? Felicity knew now that she was not, only that she might once have been.

One of the braves reached down to finger Felicity's braids, and she registered another shock. She hadn't realized that he was only a child, no more than ten or eleven, and that his eyes were also blue. It was like looking at a child wearing a mask to see those dark blue eyes framed by broad cheekbones, coppery skin, and coarse black hair.

A mask, she reflected dreamily, or a mirror, because his eyes were violet-blue like her own. Although she didn't know what he intended, she pleaded with Sarah to save her. *Tell him no, Saree. Tell him no.*

The Indian boy was fumbling with the strings of Felicity's shirt, and she saw him holding something under her chin. *Sarah*, she said, trying again to speak aloud, *I know it was my fault, but I never dreamed that any harm would come to you.*

You're dreaming now, she though she heard Sarah say.

Yes, I know I must be. Indians don't have blue eyes. I'm perfectly aware of that.

She could feel the blade of the boy's knife pressing against her throat. There was only an instant left in which to tell Saree that she was sorry, but when she tried to speak, she knew again that she hadn't made a sound. For want of a voice, she would die unforgiven. The cloud reappeared to blot out her consciousness, and this time the cloud didn't pass.

"Lucky she's still alive."

Felicity, hearing the words, struggled up out of her unconsciousness.

"It's about time," Meg's voice declared. Her rheumy eyes swam into view and Felicity, smelling her rancid breath, managed a faint smile. "How do you feel?" Meg asked. "No, never mind. You'd best not talk. Here, I brung you some soup."

"No," Felicity mùrmured. "Please, no."

"You should, yer know. Yer as weak as a babe."

Felicity did want something. "Collier," she asked. "Where . . .?"

"Never mind the captain. He's all right."

"Are you certain? Where is he?"

"Now lookee, you just take some of this soup."

Felicity couldn't have swallowed even if she'd wanted.

Instead she closed her eyes and slept again. When she woke a second time Meg was there with the cup, but Felicity pushed it away and said weakly, "Later, Meg. Not now."

One by one the other women stuck their faces close to hers to offer encouragement. "Another inch and the ball would of passed through your windpipe," Kate informed her cheerfully.

"You're lucky to have you hair still settin' on your head," Clara contributed. "We heard about Grubbe and Sessy. It was a fittin' end to them both."

"But it's a shame about the others," Gerda noted. "So many killed and wounded, and what for? To lay claim to this godforsaken wilderness."

"Like Braddock," Elga noted. "Captain Orme and Captain Stewart brung him over the river just a bit ago."

"And Collier?" Felicity whispered. "How is he?"

"Collier? He was with Orme and Stewart when they brung back Braddock more dead than alive."

"Might as well say dead," Meg commented. "A ball passed right through Braddock's arm and lodged in his lung."

"The battle's lost," Heavensent said bleakly. "We got beat bad. Half those who fought is dead, and there's scarce a man unwounded."

"What was you doing there, Lissy?" Nell inquired. "Did you go just to see? Did you not know you might get shot?"

Felicity's eyes filled with tears, and Meg said officiously, "Leave her be. She don't want to talk, dearies. You go on now and leave me to tend her."

The rest of that evening and most of the night as well were lost to Felicity, who was only vaguely aware of being bounced about on a litter and occasionally prodded into wakefulness to have water dabbed on her lips. Once or twice, however, she heard Collier's voice and was reassured that the women hadn't been lying to her. He was alive. The

Indians hadn't killed him as they had killed Ned Grubbe and Sessy Gray.

Then at first light Felicity opened her eyes to see Collier standing next to her. He wasn't wearing his jacket, and his open shirt revealed that his chest and shoulder were bandaged. "You were hurt after all," she said in an accusing whisper. "You said you were not."

"It's nothing," he told her, dismissing the wound lightly. "Just a crease in the flesh."

Felicity wanted to ask him what had happened and how she had been delivered, but she hadn't the strength. She closed her eyes again.

When she woke later that morning Meg told her that they had been traveling south all night in the direction of a plantation owned by Braddock's chief guide, Christopher Gist, where they would remain for a day or two before going on to the coast. The retreating army consisted of only the officers, the women, and about eighty men, all the rest having deserted. Washington had gone ahead to intercept Dunbar, who was in charge of the reserve troops and supplies, and Braddock, tended by an army physician, was still alive but growing weaker. According to Meg he had received his wound at a spot between two ravines at the northernmost point of the battle. By then men had been deserting in droves, and after he was shot no one would bear him from the field. Captain Orme had actually offered a purse of 60 guineas to whoever would carry him back to safety, but there had been no takers. "Braddock told Orme to leave him there and save hisself," Meg related, "but Orme wouldn't do it. Then Stewart and yer Captain Collier come along. That was after Collier brung you back here. It was him who helped load Braddock in the tumbrel and brung him back across the river, even though he'd been shot hisself. He's a bloody brave man, yer captain."

Felicity wondered if and when Collier would return to see her. By dusk she had begun to lose hope of a visit that day, but just as the sun disappeared behind the trees, Meg whispered in her ear that he was there. "Is she awake?" Collier asked as he leaned over the litter.

"She's been rollin' her eyes in yer direction all afternoon," Meg answered. "I'll just leave you two to visit whilst I get me some supper."

Collier crouched down next to her. "You're looking better, Miss Greenhill," he ventured.

"I have you to thank for my life, Captain Collier."

"After what happened to Grubbe and his companion," Collier said, "I was amazed to find you still alive."

Felicity said wearily, "No one was more surprised than I.

"I brought back a medical orderly and litter. You were unconscious when we returned. Have you any recollection of what happened?"

"Ned Grubbe and Sessy Gray were running away when they found me. They took my gun. They intended to wait for you and take your gun as well. Gray was afraid I'd call out to you, so Grubbe pulled his knife intending to kill me. Then the Indians came." Felicity faltered, embarrassed to find herself again on the verge of tears.

"Then they killed the two men?"

Felicity nodded. "The Indians who . . . did it, they were the Indians you and I saw, the braves and the white woman. Only this time I saw that the braves were children, not men at all, and that one of them had blue eyes."

Collier frowned. "And she? Were you able to recognize her?"

"No," Felicity admitted. "There was something about her like Sarah, but at the same time there was something not the same. Sarah was always . . . unhappy. But this woman, though not timid, was calm, almost tranquil."

"Tell me, Miss Greenhill, is it possible that *she* might have recognized *you*?"

"Look at me. I bear no more resemblance to the girl I was than does she to Saree."

Collier reached into his pocket and held something out for her inspection. "Look at this."

Felicity squinted at the contrivance he held in his hand, two splinters of wood bound by a piece of leather string. "What is it?"

"A clamp, rudimentary but efficient. The Indians pinched the edges of your wound with it. It worked like a compress to staunch the flow of blood. Without it you would have bled to death."

Felicity reached up to touch the bandage at her throat. "I don't understand why."

"Nor do I."

"What reason had they to help me?"

"That is something we shall probably never know. However, I thank God they spared you, for whatever reason."

It was still too soon for Felicity to feel any gratitude for life, and she murmured sadly, "I doubt that I shall ever thank God for anything again."

Collier said kindly, "You'll be more happily disposed once you're well again. We should reach Great Meadows in another two or three days. I'll send a runner ahead to let your family know that you're safe. I also intend to ask Colonel Halket's permission to assign two of my men to escort you back to Williamsburg."

"That's kind of you."

"Not at all. I consider it my responsibility. Good night, Miss Greenhill."

Meg bustled back with a steaming mug in her hand after Collier left. "I heard you saying good-bye," she bawled. "What's all this 'Miss Greenhill' and 'Captian Collier' nonsense? Is that how you generally address each other? Don't tell me he tips his hat before he climbs in bed with you."

Felicity smiled. "That's the way of gentlemen, Meg."

"Don't tell me about gentlemen. The way of gentlemen

is the same as the way of roughnecks when it comes to romance. Now, here, drink this."

"What is it?"

"Squirrel broth with a bit of marrow thrown in to give yer blood. Now, don't say no 'cause I'm bound you'll drink it. I should think you'd be hungry now you've had a good chat with yer lover."

"I am a little hungry," Felicity admitted, rather surprised that it should be true.

"Lord be praised," Meg declared. "The girl is gettin' better."

· · *41* · ·

For the next two days Meg administered to Felicity's every need from food to chamber pot, the latter a complicated procedure involving the rigging of a clothesline tent and a struggle to help Felicity balance on the tin pail without tipping it. Meg's stoicism in the face of such distasteful chores, as well as her distracting and well-informed gossip, was gratefully received by the incapacitated Felicity.

It was Meg who brought her the news that Colonel Dunbar, in a moment of panic, had destroyed the reserve of army supplies. "Burned one hundred and fifty wagons. Threw the powder casks and fifty thousand pounds of powder into the water, dumped most of the food and drink into the water too. There's barely enough to keep us going till we get back to civilization. So it turns out the rangers and some of the regulars are going to have to fend for themselves and ride on ahead. Halket's fit to be tied."

"The rangers?"

"That's right, dearie. The rangers were the only ones smart enough to fight like injuns, so they're the only ones still of a piece."

"Captian Collier?"

"He commands one of the ranger units, don't he? Anyway, yer in no shape to entertain him. Might as well let him go without a fuss."

Collier had put himself out to spend a few minutes with Felicity each day, and that morning he confirmed what Meg had told her. Dunbar had, indeed, wreaked havoc, rationalizing his decision to destroy the supplies as a precaution against the enemy getting their hands on then. It had been a reckless and pointless thing to do, Collier told her, since the French had pursued them no farther than the second crossing of the Monongahela. By his action Dunbar had blocked any possibility for regroupment for a second attack.

"A second attack?" Felicity commented. "Surely no one would consider such a thing anyway."

"It will have to come sooner or later," Collier said in reply. "But even discounting that possibility, Dunbar has also deprived the troops of the food and water they need to see them home."

"So you and your men will go ahead?"

"We leave for Alexandria today," Collier said. "I wanted to assure you before I left that I've made arrangements for your delivery home. You'll probably reach Great Meadows tomorrow, and as soon as you're fit to travel, Lieutenant Webster and one of his subordinates will take you by wagon back to Williamsburg."

"And you?" Felicity asked. "Will you also be going home?"

"No. As soon as I'm able I'll return to Great Meadows with relief supplies."

Looking at him, Felicity was struck by the realization that although they were both citizens of Williamsburg, they would soon again be strangers, on rare occasions offering a nod or a brief greeting on passing, but never again to meet as equals.

"What are you thinking, Miss Greenhill?"

"Nothing. I just wondered if you're not missing your plantation. I've heard how much it means to you."

Collier smiled. "How much is that?"

"I've heard it's the reason you've never found time to marry."

"I suppose, in part, it's true, although not entirely so. And what about you? Why do you remain a spinster?"

"I told you once that I work as a baker."

"There are bakers who are also wives. Don't tell me there's not a line of eager young men who wish to domesticate you, Miss Greenhill."

"The difficulty is in finding a man who does not wish to domesticate me, Captian Collier. I have no wish to brew tea or embroider doilies when there are so many more interesting ways to amuse myself."

"To my way of thinking there's no greater waste than a woman confining her energies to brewing tea or sewing doilies, but on the other hand, it's a pity for you to hoard your God-given assets."

"Surely I'm not a prize cow whose chief function is to breed calves and give milk?"

Collier chuckled. "Hardly. I was referring to your character, not to your physical attributes. Nonetheless, I think it possible to combine independence with the moderating influence of marriage and family, and in your particular case I think it would be wise to consider it."

Felicity replied with some asperity, "Such sage advice from the most confirmed of bachelors?"

"I take exception to 'confirmed' as being a trifle premature. However, I take the reproof in the spirit it was offered. Now it's time to say good-bye, Miss Greenhill. I wish you a safe journey home to Williamsburg."

"I wish you the same to Alexandria, Captain Collier."

Who was he to preach marriage and family, Felicity thought after he left. She chafed at his condescension, then scolded herself for being annoyed. What more than condescension had she expected from any man, especially one who was so prideful of his own ambition and accomplishments.

As Collier predicted, they reached Great Meadows the following day. There was no way to know for certain how many privates had died and how many had deserted, but a final tally ascertained that sixty-three out of the eighty-nine command officers had been killed or wounded. That evening, shortly after eight o'clock, Elga brought word that General Braddock had finally succumbed, with the parting words, "We shall better know how to deal with them another time."

"He might just as well of left off the 'we,'" Meg said stoically. "His dealin' days is over."

Felicity was considerably improved, able for the first time to stand with Meg's support and to take a few faltering steps. Early the following morning Lieutenant Webster visited her, and with her assurance that she felt well enough to travel, it was decided to start for home the following day.

That evening, Meg and the other women arranged a farewell supper for Felicity. Of necessity the supper was sparse on food, but compensated for by a convivial camaraderie that Felicity found touching and at the same time discomforting. She was, after all, a member of the group through false pretenses, their acceptance of her based on the premise that she shared their unfortunate life. To tell them otherwise was unthinkable. It would be an admission of such smug pretension that they would never forgive her. To perpetuate the deceit might be equally despicable, but in Felicity's estimation, the preferable alternative.

The festivities included singing, storytelling, and the recitation of Sir John Suckling's "Why so pale and wan, fond lover," by little Fern, who rendered the classic in a fervent singsong that owed more to effort than effect. Meg

rounded out the evening with a toast, "a long and loving life
to us all, especially to Lissy, who come so close to
croaking." And Felicity, called upon for a concluding
speech, could manage only, "My deepest hopes that you
will all be happy," knowing an attempt to say more would
have brought her to the point of tears. Later that night,
lying under the stars, she bid another farewell, one even
more melancholy and heartfelt. "Good-bye, Saree. Good-
bye, my lost sister."

*The men showed their respect with silent attendance to her arrival,
but she was welcomed back with cries of triumph from the women
and children, who clustered around her and shyly reached out to
touch her. Swift Deer and Forest Wolf were greeted with rejoicing,
too, and hands laid on to absorb their magic. It was as it should
be. The drums spoke of battle, of enemy lives lost, of the power of
Fire Hawk and her sons.*

*She dismounted from her pony, relinquished the hawk to a
servant, and permitted herself to be led to the chief, who waited
within the circle of elders. As befitted their equal station they met eye
to eye, but Swift Deer and Forest Wolf cast down their eyes in
deference as the chief, their father, spoke to her, then called for the
celebration to commence.*

*The feasting and dancing began and would continue long into
the night. Fire Hawk sat in the place of honor next to the chief and
listened to the singers relate the story of her coming. How, many
years before, she fell out of the fiery sky; how she was met by Racing
Bird, then only a boy but already destined to be chief; how she held
the hawk in her arms and would not speak until the evening of the
sixth day; and how, when she broke her silence to repeat back the
Indian word for spirit that she had heard spoken over and over,
the shadow of a hawk had been observed to fly across the face of the
moon.*

*It was her fellow tribesmen who had named her, and now it
seemed to her that she had never known any other name, though*

*sometimes the wind, in sibilant whispers, spoke "Saree" in her ear.
Now the tribesmen sang of her strength and of her magic, of her
love for Racing Bird and for her two sons. Then they sang of
battle. They told how the enemy, a thousand souls or more, rode
into the field with banners and drums to be met and slain. They
sang of vanity and courage, of bloodshed and victory.*

*Fire Hawk spoke next, reminding the assembly that she was
sister to the land and knew its secrets, knew how to carve, and in
carving set free the god spirits, and knew how to work her magic
against the enemy. She spoke of how she and her sons had crossed
the battlefield west to east and east to west, sprinkling the earth
with the ashes of sacred fires. She told them that Swift Deer had
heard an owl sing in midday, a song that carried the threat of
death to the listener, and that, in order to trick death, they had
lingered near the place where the owl had sung until the white men
came, and then killed them. Then she told how Swift Deer had seen
his image in the eyes of a bleeding woman, eyes that were mirrors of
his own eyes, and how he had saved himself by staunching her flow
of blood, which was, of course, not her blood but his.*

*The women and children shivered and cried to hear how close
Swift Deer had come to dying and chanted the praises of a
compassionate Great Spirit who had allowed him to cheat death.
Then at last Racing Bird spoke, telling them that immortality was
possible for all men of courage, that Swift Deer was an example to
them all, and that they must all aspire to such courage if the tribe
were to endure.*

*Fire Hawk nodded as he spoke. Had she not escaped the clutches
of the davey? Had she not confronted death and lived? Was she
not beloved of the tribe, wife to the chief, and mother of future
chiefs? Oh yes, she told herself, Racing Bird spoke the truth. He
spoke the truth.*

"An actor?" Nedda shrilled. Her curls bobbed with agitation as she set down her teacup and glowered at Providence. "From the sublime to the ridiculous. Letting that debauched Darby Littlefield make a fool of her, and then running from him straight into the arms of an actor."

"Don't speak ill of the dead, Nedda," Beriah cautioned.

"Littlefield's better off dead. Too bad the Indians didn't get him *before* he demeaned the name of Greenhill. Too bad the actor didn't go off to Ohio with him. Then they'd both be dead. I still can't believe it that Winnie and Robby Flower . . ."

"I can't believe it myself," Providence admitted. "Winnie has always been so ambitious when it comes to suitors. Not that I don't like Robby. He's a sensible young man despite his profession. I simply never expected him to win her."

"You mean you intend to give them your blessing?"

"I already have."

"Then I'm appalled."

"I rather thought you would be," Providence returned calmly. "However, I think it's about time we faced the truth about Winnie. She has a reckless and frivolous streak that frequently leads her to the brink of trouble. Sooner or later she was bound to become entangled with someone unsuitable, and it might just as easily have turned out to be a horse thief as an actor. At least Robby makes his living honestly and is genuine in his affection for her."

"Ma's right, Neddie," Beriah interjected. "Winnie's better off married."

"In which case," Nedda said hopelessly, "I might be better off dead. Wasn't it bad enough that Felicity left home to follow the army? Am I now expected to live down still another scandal?"

"Lissy did not follow the army, Nedda. She traveled under army protection."

"That isn't what people are saying. They're saying she ran off with one of the officers and that she came home again because he threw her over."

"Josiah Wrentham didn't throw her over," Beriah reminded her. "He was killed."

"And," his mother picked up, "Lissy told us why she went. It wasn't to be with Josiah. It was to look for Saree."

"Poppycock! How can you be so gullible? The very thought is idiotic. Trekking through hundreds of miles of wilderness looking for a long-lost sister whom she claims to be an Iroquois medicine woman? Who would ever believe such a thing? To say nothing of getting herself shot and riding into Williamsburg in the back of an army wagon like a common tart."

"That's enough," Beriah said sharply. "Not another word, Neddie."

"Don't tell me not to speak, Berry. Surely I have a right to criticize the family's lamentable loss of reputation. Lissy's been home almost two months and people are still talking. Tell the truth. Has anyone visited her since her return? I'm sure they have not. There's not a mother in town who would permit her daughter to socialize with Lissy. There's not a bachelor who would call on her anymore."

Providence couldn't deny it, and it was useless to point out that Felicity wasn't interested in being courted, since it didn't alter the essential truth of what Nedda was saying. She herself had heard the rumors and failed in her attempts to counteract them. People were still willing to patronize the bakery—indeed, business had nearly doubled since Felicity's much-gossiped-about return—but socially Felicity had become an outcast.

"All this notoriety is more than I can bear," Nedda concluded. "Sometimes I regret ever having married into the Greenhill family."

Providence, leaving the obvious unspoken, rose from her chair and began pulling on her gloves. "I'm going home. Berry, will you walk me to the door?"

In the hall, Beriah leaned down to whisper that Nedda would come round, and Providence gave him an affectionate pat on the shoulder. Poor Berry. It was he who bore the brunt of Nedda's chronic discontent, and she hadn't the heart to tell him that Nedda would never come round, that she would go on shrewishly finding fault with one thing and another until her dying day. "Of course she'll come round," Providence said soothingly. "I don't doubt it for a minute."

"Thankee, Miz Fettle. Enjoy them curly cakes. Don' forget tomoree's muffick day."

Pudding's booming voice carried back from the shop all the way into the backyard. It was unseasonably warm for early November, and Felicity had been gathering mums when Robby and Winsome joined her in the garden. "Pudding is so noisy," Winsome complained now. "I don't know how you can stand it all day long."

"She's cheerful and the customers like her. Besides, it allows Mama and me to alternate working days."

"She'd be good on the stage," Robby speculated. "She's got a voice would easily carry to the back row."

"Except she couldn't recite her name without prompting," Winsome pointed out.

Felicity laughed. "You're really too hard on poor Pudding. She does her job well, and I don't think she'd be in the least bit tempted to go on the stage. Now, tell me about you and Robby."

"You know that Robby stayed behind when the troupe left."

"I knew what I wanted, and I meant to stay till I got it," Robby interjected. "Winnie and I will join the company in New York in time for *Merry Wives*."

"Will they still want you?" Felicity asked.

"Want me? They can't do without me."

"The wedding will take place Sunday after next," Winsome announced.

"Sunday after next? Winnie, that's so soon."

"I'd make her Mistress Flower today if we could waive the banns," Robby said genially.

"There's more," Winsome added. "I'm going to join the troupe as an actress."

Felicity's mouth dropped open. "You, Winnie? You're going to act?"

Winsome looked exceedingly pleased with herself. "Mister Kean himself asked me before the company left Williamsburg. He said they could use some fresh talent."

"But how does he know you have talent?"

"I recited for him," Winsome returned complacently. She lifted her chin and declaimed the final lines from "A Lover's Complaint." "Oh, that sad breath his spongy lungs bestowed, / Oh, all that borrowed motion seeming owed, / Would yet again betray the fore-betrayed, / And new pervert a reconciled maid!"

Robby squeezed her hands in an admiring gush of affection.

Felicity, somewhat overcome, sat back and shook her head. "I can't take it all in. My little sister marrying, leaving for New York, and becoming an actress."

"Don't you approve?" Winsome challenged.

"Of course she approves," Robby declared. "How could she not approve? She knows you're getting the best of all husbands when you get Robby Flower. As for going on the boards, it's good, honest work, and no one approves more of good, honest work than Felicity."

"He's right on both counts," Felicity seconded.

"I don't think of acting as work," Winsome reflected, "not like being a baker. I should hate being a baker."

"Yes, we know."

"Almost as much as I should hate being an old maid."

Felicity flushed, and Robby leaped in to say hastily, "Who's to judge what it most pleases someone to do with his life? Anyway, Felicity's not old."

"She will be," Winsome insisted with her usual lack of tact. "She'll never get a husband now that she's ruined her reputation."

It was ironic, Felicity thought, how quickly Winsome had forgotten that she'd come close to ruining her own reputation. She hadn't spoken Darby Littlefield's name since the unfortunate incident of his party, not even to comment on news of his untimely death. Yet she was quick enough to note her sister's disgrace. Not that Felicity bore her any ill will for saying aloud what everyone else was whispering. *Felicity Greenhill is little better than a whore. Felicity Greenhill is socially unsuitable. Felicity Greenhill will never find herself a husband now.*

A few minutes later Robby bore Winsome off, leaving Felicity alone in the backyard. She looked at the still-flowering chrysanthemums and compared the tidy, attractive garden she'd cultivated to the barren patch it had been less than a year before. She loved the garden as she loved the bakery, with a fierce sence of proprietorship. She would, given another year, have sufficient money to buy the property, and since Mister Oatland had indicated his willingness to sell, her wish to make it hers would eventually be realized. So after all was said and done, she wasn't so badly off. True, she had endured more than her share of unhappiness, but she had also put her demons to rest, and now, even if she were to live the life of an old maid, she would do so comfortably and with dignity.

"Miz Greenhill," Pudding called out from within the shop, "there's a gentleman here to see ya."

Felicity thought it might be Silas Remington come to collect his pay for putting up fresh handbills. "Send him out here," she called back. "I'm in the garden."

She saw a chrysanthemum dangling from its stem and she

leaned down to break off the flower. When she straightened up and turned back toward the door, she saw Lawrence Collier standing in the doorway. She was so startled that she dropped the mums she was holding.

"Good day, Miss Greenhill."

"Captian Collier?"

"No longer captain. Having fulfilled a commitment made to Governor Dinwiddie, I've resigned my commission and come home to Green Meadows."

"In that case, welcome home, *Mister* Collier."

"Thank you."

Felicity was so flustered that when Collier walked toward her, she gave a startled little step backward. He bent down, retrieved the mums, and presented them to her. "You're looking very well, Miss Greenhill."

"However I look would be an improvement over how I looked when you saw me last."

"Are you completely recovered from your wound?"

Felicity put up a hand to touch the scar at her throat. "Yes. Completely. Although I'm afraid I shall always bear the reminder of it."

"So shall we all."

"Are you quite healed, Mister Collier?"

"Not totally."

"I'm sorry. Was the wound worse than you led me to believe?"

"Considerably so, I'm afraid."

Felicity regarded him with dismay. He certainly looked well enough, with his tanned complexion and vigorous demeanor, and he was impeccably dressed in riding clothes, which seemed to indicate that he was well enough to sit a horse. "Are you in the care of a physician?"

"Why should I be?"

"Surely a physician would be best able to treat you for a gunshot wound."

"*That* wound is completely healed. I wasn't referring to *that* wound."

"I don't understand. Did you suffer another accident?"

"An accident of the heart, Miss Greenhill."

Felicity found herself suddenly feeling rather weak. "I'm sure I have no idea what you're talking about."

"Then I shall explain. I have found myself distracted for the past two months by the constant vision of a certain woman, a spirited woman who is, incidentally, a baker by trade."

Felicity stared at him in disbelief.

"It's not her beauty that first captivated me, although I shall always remember her beauty as she rose out of a certain moonlit lake like some lovely and magical water nymph. Neither was it her stubbornness nor her strong will that first attracted me to her. Nor was it her courage in adversity. Do you know what it was, Miss Greenhill?"

"No," Felicity murmured. "I can't imagine."

"She snored, Miss Greenhill. On more than one occasion she slept within ten feet of me, and she snored; scratching at my consciousness with persistent snores until finally I was forced to take notice of her."

"Why do you mortify me?"

"How do you think I feel, Miss Greenhill, admitting that I'm desolate without those snores, that without those snores I'm bereft of joy and denied the will to live?"

"I hardly know what to say."

He was grinning at her. "Say something, Miss Greenhill."

"You should not have come."

Collier dropped his teasing manner and asked soberly, "Is there someone else?"

"I simply think it may not be fair to you to let you go on. You see, I've suffered some loss of reputation since my return to Williamsburg. It's generally thought that the circumstances of my journey were disreputable."

"I know all about it."

"You do?"

"Your stint with His Majesty's army is looked on as quite scandalous, Miss Greenhill, almost equal to the scandal surrounding General Braddock's miscalculated assault on Fort Duquesne. I've only been home three days and I've already heard your name mentioned at least a dozen times, and from the best of people."

"People," Felicity suggested bitterly, "whom I'm sure never knew I existed until now."

"No doubt."

"Then why would a man of your position choose to have his name linked with mine?"

"A man in my position can do anything he wishes without fear of censure—can, in fact, assure you welcome in any drawing room you choose to enter."

"I'm not certain I care for the pleasures of the drawing room. I'm a baker, most comfortable when I'm working."

"Then continue to bake, Miss Greenhill. I'm sure my reputation is such that it will suffer no setback because my wife manifests some rather eccentric leanings."

Felicity gazed at him with a mixture of astonishment and suspicion. "What did you say?"

"You heard what I said. And please don't tell me next that you don't enjoy brewing tea or embroidering doilies. If necessary, I brew tea quite efficiently, and although I can't embroider, it hardly matters since I tend to be indifferent to such niceties. In other words, neither of us need suffer any guilt for our lack of domesticity."

"Are you proposing marriage?"

"Am I wrong to think you might consider it?"

Felicity thought it over, then was forced to admit that he wasn't wrong. "But," she added carefully, "a marriage is a bargain, is it not? What do you offer?"

"Comfort, security, freedom, and adventure."

"What would you expect of me in return?"

"What do you think you can, in all good conscience, offer?"

Felicity paused, then said with spirit, "Constancy, of course, criticism if we disagree, encouragement in your endeavors, charity for your shortcomings, and companionship for your old age."

Collier asked softly, "Nothing more?"

Now it was Felicity's turn to smile mischievously. "Oh, and one other thing, Mister Collier." She reached up to put her arms around his neck, then whispered something in his ear.

"Ah," Collier murmured contentedly just before he kissed her. "My sentiments precisely, Miss Greenhill."

ABOUT THE AUTHOR

EDITH PIÑERO GREEN has written six successful mysteries—*The Mark of Lucifer*, *The Death Trap*, *A Woman's Honor*, and the three "Pinch" novels, *Rotten Apples* and *Sneaks*, and *Perfect Fools*. She is also the author of *Providence*, published by Bantam Books in 1982. She lives in New York City and Fire Island with her husband and two sons.

Magnolia Landing

By
Jessica Manning

In the ante-bellum South . . . life was passionate and uncertain. In Magnolia Landing, six families lived and loved as if there were no tomorrow.

Set among the panorama of opulent plantation life, MAGNOLIA LANDING tells the story of their passions and perversions, greed and lust, sins and secrets. From Royal Brannigan, a dashing professional gambler who wins the splendid Heritage Plantation through a lucky turn of the cards, to Lilliane, slave and voodoo queen who would do anything to protect herself from the lusts of her cruel master, share the adventures of the inhabitants of MAGNOLIA LANDING.

Wherever Bantam Books are sold, or use this handy coupon for ordering:

JEALOUSIES

By Justine Harlowe
bestselling author of MEMORY AND DESIRE

There is nothing as strong
as the love between two sisters ...

Nor anything so corrosive
as when that love turns to jealousy.

A glittering novel of the simmering antagonism between
two beautiful half-sisters, as different in nature as they are
in looks—both in love with the same man. From the
Outback of Australia to the couture salons of Paris, journey
with Shannon and Kerry Faloon as they sample all that
life has to offer and vie for the true love of one man.

JEALOUSIES

Coming in March '86 from Bantam Books.

Special Offer
Buy a Bantam Book
for only 50¢.

Now you can have an up-to-date listing of Bantam's hundreds of titles plus take advantage of our unique and exciting bonus book offer. A special offer which gives you the opportunity to purchase a Bantam book for only 50¢. Here's how!

By ordering any five books at the regular price per order, you can also choose any other single book listed (up to a $4.95 value) for just 50¢. Some restrictions do apply, but for further details why not send for Bantam's listing of titles today!

Just send us your name and address and we will send you a catalog!

THE LATEST BOOKS IN THE BANTAM BESTSELLING TRADITION